Imagi

by

Robert Beedham

Transcribed from the interview by Paige Wild

www.imaginebook.co.uk

Trailer: www.imaginebook.co.uk/trailer

Reality leaves a lot to the imagination.
John Lennon.

The story of the story.

Robert Beedham wrote his unique pop-culture book after discovering an incredible transcription of a film interview in a derelict New York lawyer's office made by a legal secretary.

It's about an intriguing young man discovering the truth about his astonishing identity. Readers climb on a roller-coaster from a secret island to New York, where the young man searches for clues to his past, hunted by a killer couple. Could the man's claims be true?

After being astonished by the transcription, Beedham spent years delving deep into pop-culture and discovered the cult phenomenon of 'The 27 Club': a long list of super-star celebrities that suddenly 'died' aged 27, including Jim Morrison, Jimi Hendrix, Kurt Cobain, Amy Winehouse and more. The discovery of 'The 27 Club' and the transcription, together with other allegedly dead celebrities, led Beedham to create the world's first 'found bookage.'

Imagine is a genuine page-turner that any everyone will be amazed by.

But, could it be true? 'Imagine' will make all readers wish it *is* true: a secret island refuge for some of history's most prominent 'dead' celebrities, and not just aged 27.

Imagine…

URGENT AUDIO TRANSCRIPTION FROM THE UPLOADED DIGITAL FILE TAKEN FROM THE INTERVIEW NOTES OF MS. PAIGE WILD, LEGAL SECRETARY AT WILD LAW OFFICES, 1994 BEACH FRONT ROAD, NEW YORK, NEW YORK U.S.A. 10004, THE INTERVIEWEE BEING JAMES (A.K.A. "JIMMY") BYRON, IN THE BOARDROOM OF WILD LAW OFFICES, DURATION OF INTERVIEW LASTING 4 HOURS 27 MINUTES, TOTAL PAGES NUMBERING 452, TRANSCRIPTION BY FREELANCE TRANSCRIPTIONIST NGUYEN MWANGI OF SPEEEDANDACCCURECY.COM TAKING APPROXIMATELY 27 HOURS 56 MINUTES, AFTER PLAYING THE AUDIO BACK, MANY MANY TIMES.

PAIGE: Testing, one, two, three… Is this thing working? This is Paige Wild, legal secretary, Wild Law Offices, filming an interview with Mr. James —

JIMMY: —Jimmy.

PAIGE: —Byron…

JIMMY: Excuse me.

4PAIGE: James Byron —

JIMMY: It's *Jimmy.*

PAIGE: This transcription is verbatim…

JIMMY: Excuse me?

PAIGE: The time here is…

JIMMY: Excuse me.

PAIGE: 2:32 P.M.…

JIMMY: Vurb, ate *Tim?*

PAIGE: Verbatim. It means I'll write down whatever you say, *exactly.*

JIMMY: But you're filming this.

PAIGE: So?

JIMMY: You're taping this. Why are you writing stuff down, if you've got a video record of this?

PAIGE: These are my notes.

JIMMY: Coolness.

PAIGE: Let me just check the sound. levels…Test…Test…Can you say something, please?

JIMMY: Nipple…Ass…Suck…F…

PAIGE: Fine! We'll forego the sound check, thanks. You're good for sound level.

JIMMY: Sound level?

PAIGE: Sound check?

JIMMY: Wow!

PAIGE: Can you please sit down?

JIMMY: Check out the *view!* Reminds me…

PAIGE: Is there…?

JIMMY: 'Scuse me, while I brush away a tear…Reminds me…*sniff!*… of…home.

PAIGE: The beach in the city. Rockaway Beach.

JIMMY: Awesomeness! The *Ramones*, 1977.

PAIGE: So, shall we start? Can we get started, Mr. Byron?

JIMMY: Jimmy.

PAIGE: Jimmy.

JIMMY: Sex and movies and rock and roll. And *murder*.

PAIGE: I was told…we'd discuss…

JIMMY: Yes?

PAIGE: …your *life* story?

JIMMY: That *is* my life story, Beige.

PAIGE: Paige.

JIMMY: Jimmy. Confused?

PAIGE: Only totally.

JIMMY: Shall I begin?

PAIGE: As you like it.

Square One.

JIMMY: So you're a what?

PAIGE: I'm a *what?*

JIMMY: You're a…a…

PAIGE: A secretary.

JIMMY: A *secretary?* Like the 2002 movie*?* With cool James *Blacklist* Spader? And will you be, like, on your knees? Taking things down, and, you know…

PAIGE: "You know…"?

JIMMY: You know…

PAIGE: Certainly not! I'll be *recording* your interview. *Nothing* else.

JIMMY: Beige…

PAIGE: Paige.

JIMMY: Izzit?

PAIGE: Yes.

JIMMY: Izzit like *Jimmy* Page?

PAIGE: I believe it's spelled differently.

JIMMY: Led Zeppelin II? Or IV?

PAIGE: What? Uh…*I?*

JIMMY: '69, good year, Woodstock, man on the moon, Mets win the World Series. Alright, Adele and Sam Smith's lovers. Kill, or kiss?

PAIGE: Excuse me…what?

JIMMY: Hmm, and…*hmm* again?

PAIGE: *"Hmmm"?*

JIMMY: I'm suspicious.

PAIGE: Of what?

JIMMY: Your hipness. And *taste.* In music, I mean.

PAIGE: O…K…when you're ready, sir. Let's —

JIMMY: I've never done this before.

PAIGE: Pardon?

JIMMY: Never done this before.

PAIGE: No.

JIMMY: And it's *Jimmy.*

8

PAIGE: *Jimmy.* Well, me neither, Jimmy. So let's just talk.

JIMMY: Talk.

PAIGE: In your own words.

JIMMY: Who else's words could they be?

PAIGE: Yes. Stupid Girl.

JIMMY: You're flirting with me, *again.*

PAIGE: *Again?*

JIMMY: James Spader...*Secretary*...

PAIGE: I certainly am *not,* sir. I...

JIMMY: You will.

PAIGE: It's just that, you remind me of...someone.

JIMMY: Someone, to use your word...*famous?*

PAIGE: Yes, famous.

JIMMY: Kinda like, um, Brad Pitt?

PAIGE: Shall we begin? Please?

JIMMY: Or Owen Wilson? Only, younger, cuter, sexier and um...*cooler-er?*

PAIGE: Yes...*no!*

JIMMY: No?

PAIGE: I...

JIMMY: Someone...*else?*

PAIGE: Yes. I mean, *no!* But, that's not possible. He's...

JIMMY: So they say.

PAIGE: I...please, Mr. Byron —

JIMMY: *Jimmy.*

PAIGE: Jimmy —

JIMMY: Beige?

PAIGE: Just look at the camera, and...

JIMMY: Gotcha. OK, here goes. Weeelll, when all *this* started, I didn't know much about...*here.* I'd never even heard *this* word, *your* word, crazy, stupid before...

Celebrity.
Known for...whatever.

JIMMY:…or *celeb, sleb, famous* or *famous for 15 minutes* or *star,* or *soap-star* or *Superstar DJs*…but I have heard of *rock-star,* and '72's "Starry Starry Night" — 'member that one, Beige? — and "Starman" and '73's "The Prettiest Star" by Bowie, and "Star Star" by The Stones. Ever hear o' them?

PAIGE: I —

JIMMY: Ooooh! And "Shining Star" by Earth, Wind & Fire!

PAIGE: I —

JIMMY: And 1980's "Video Killed the Radio Star" and Moby's 2002 hit "We're All Made of Stars" and 2013's "Counting Stars" and 2014's "A Sky Full of Stars and Stars" by Collabro, and then don't forget *The Fault In Our Stars, Star Trek, Star Wars* and 2015's *Maps to the Stars* movie film. And stars and stripes. I *have* heard of *movie-star* and *pop-star,* but not *starlet, child-star, radio-star, screen goddess, It Boy or Girl* or *bankability, body double* or even *quite well known* or *popular* or *wannabee* but of course I *have* heard of groupies and porn-stars and shooting stars and and and…

PAIGE: Mr. Byron? Excuse me, uhh—

JIMMY: …weirdness, right? I mean, *seriously,* Beige, how could anyone in your world not know the basics, like:

Populebrity.
How well you're known or liked.

PAIGE: Jimmy…

JIMMY: …*also* I've heard of Bowie's "Fame," '75, and 1980's movie *Fame… "Faaaaaame! I'm gonna live for-ev-aaaaaaa!"*

PAIGE: Was that…singing…?

JIMMY: … and some people who, like, actually *do* want to live forever, and…

PAIGE: Whoa.

JIMMY: Um, sorry, I don't really *do* singing.

PAIGE: Obviously. Now Mr. Bryon —

JIMMY: *Jimmy.*

PAIGE: Jimmy. I think...

JIMMY: ...*dirty* thoughts, Cage?

PAIGE: Paige.

JIMMY: Beige?

PAIGE: Certainly not! Dirty thoughts? Why I...I *think* you should tell people a little about yourself.

JIMMY: I...tell...*who, wha'*?

PAIGE: People who read, or will see this.

JIMMY: People will *see* this? How do I look?

PAIGE: Please. Sit down. You're fogging the lens. Don't...

JIMMY: Duuude. My hair...

PAIGE: Start with your age. Where you're from, likes, dislikes, things like that.

JIMMY: OK...please allow me to introduce myself... *Wait.* 'Nother Stones song.... I can't give my full, actual, my real true *real* name. It'll...give everything away.

PAIGE: It will?

JIMMY: And, um...where I'm from? I can't give that to you, either. 'Cuz...I don't *know.*

PAIGE: You don't? O...K, Jimmy. How *old* are you?

JIMMY: Old? I'm...*young.*

 PAIGE: I mean, what's your *age.*

 JIMMY: Age? Well...um...seventeen? Nineteen? Twenty? Whatever?

PAIGE: You don't know that either?

JIMMY: This is awkward.

PAIGE: Whoa.

JIMMY: It's like that scene in *Blade Runner* — you know, Beige —

PAIGE: Paige.

JIMMY: — when the Replicant like, *blasts* the interviewer, and —

11

PAIGE: I can come back. You know, I can come back, whenever you're ready to talk…

JIMMY: Like a date, Beige?

PAIGE: Just say whatever you like, then, Jimmy.

JIMMY: OK. Well, you know I'm Jimmy, around whateverage. The islanders say I'm a kinda air-head beach-bum freaky-deaky combo of *both* guys in 1989's *Bill and Ted's Excellent Adventure* sorta way. Or Owen Wilson. And they rib me a lot, for usually sometimes, quite a lot always asking too many dumb questions. And they sometimes call me "Your Hairness" 'cuz o' my "Werewolves Of London" perfect hairgasm. They tell other islanders to "lock up your lobsters" around me 'cuz…weeelll…ahem…

PAIGE: Your likes?

JIMMY: My likes?

PAIGE: What do you like?

JIMMY: Oh, my likes! My likes are like sex, music, movies, having sex while listening to music or a movie and even though, Pledge —

PAIGE: Paige —

JIMMY: — here's a bit *skinny...*

PAIGE: That's...probably enough, Jimmy.

JIMMY: Ya thunk? I was just warming up…sooo... Where was I?

PAIGE: You were —

JIMMY: I was…Oh, yeah. Likes! Like I never knew about *La La Land* or *Hollywood* or *Bollywood* or *Anyotherwood* or Hocus Pocus *focus groups, demographics, script doctors, wrap party gifts* or *premiering in Cannes, Sundance, Toronto or Berlin.* I knew zilch about *BAFTA* or *name-check* or *name-dropper, media-whore, red-top tabloids, media feeding-frenzy* or "*star in toilet scandal*" or "*Mitchellson in celebrity divorce settlements.*" *And I don't know who Oscar is.* Do *you* know? I didn't know the world, *your* world, was so:

Celebrity Obsessed.
WTF?

PAIGE: Wait. Press pause…

JIMMY: …La-la-la-la. I-know-what-you're-thinking. How could anyone, anywhere, anyhow, like, *possibly* not know that? I know, I know.

Well, at least, I know that *now*. But, how am I supposed to know about *ace reporter, newshound, press-baron, paparazzi punch-up, sleaze, phone-hacking, page three pin-ups, editors, anchormen, weathergirls, cover-ups* or *Lady Di?*

Or, *product placement or celebrity sponsorship* or *multi-million dollar endorsement deals* like Gillette or something Beckham?

And what's *celebrity TV formats,* with usually Z-list celebrities in them hoping to "re-launch careers" or "sell a book?"

I've never seen television.

PAIGE: You've never…?

JIMMY: Apart from in the movies. I knew zip, zed, zero, nada, nuttin' about *fanzines* or *real person fiction or star-struck* or *stalkers* or *autograph… hunters…*

PAIGE: Jimmy? Are you alright? You're a strange colour… Where are you going?

JIMMY: I need air. Need air. Going to open this window…

PAIGE: Man oh man, it's getting late… Please, Mr. Byron, can you bring your head back inside the window?

JIMMY: Hunters. A crazy couple. They…killed my friends. Tried to kill me and…Marsha, and little Andy.

PAIGE: Can I get you anything? Water, or…

JIMMY: "Uzi. 9mm."

PAIGE: Was that…umm, was that an Arnold Schwarzenneger accent? Seriously?

JIMMY: Alrighty… I'll have a seat, thank you.
(Slouches. Feet on table. Smiles.) I didn't know about
back-stage pass or *VIP Lounge.* But, I *do* know about
the green room and 2006's "Like a Star" by fine trio
Corinne Bailey Rae and "Je Suis un Rock Star" by Bill
Whyman.
PAIGE: "*Why*man"?
JIMMY: But, I never, ever seen *reality television
formats* like *Pap Idle* or *Fame Academic* or *The Ex
Factory* or *Simon.*
A better title is "I'm outta here. Get me a celebrity."
I-know-what-you're-thinking.
And, how the Hell am I supposed to know about *out-
takes, re-makes, re-runs, prequels, sequels, frequals* or
film franchises, either?
As you'll see, or *read,* there's just so much I had to
learn about your world.
'Cuz, I wasn't part of it.
We had this vote one day on the island.
"You guys want television, or radio?" *They* asked.
We all voted "The Hell no" —
PAIGE: Wait…that voice…?
JIMMY: Bad John Wayne impression. Sorry… in case
we learned stuff, only, what would we *do* with it? But,
we *do* have TV boxed sets.
Anyway, *they* didn't really want us getting stuff from
"the outside world"…
PAIGE: Um… hello?
JIMMY: Vincent Price. Sorry. More on they, later.
We don't need no education, so there's Just Enough
Education to Perform.

Arrested Development.
Not too smart, missed shit.

And there was sooo much performing.

Oh, I know about *film critics*, 'cuz the old man calls them *movie terrorists.*

Plenty islanders are awesome musicians, so it was live music, or we listened to millions of songs on the different formats we had.

PDubya, can I —

PAIGE: "PDubya"??

JIMMY: …ask you stuff, like what's a Blackberry? Or a MP3? And a.. *Podcaster???*

PAIGE: It's…Paige...my name is…

JIMMY: I'm such...a *Big Tease.* Anyways…everybody really loved listening to music, but a lot of the older ones would always quite often usually sometimes get all misty-eyed and stuff. They would talk about *vinyl* and *needles* and *fretwork* and *chord changes* and *the bridge* and *record sessions* and *record-players* but I never knew why.

More on that later.

They talked about *LPs* or *EPs* or *78s* or *45s* or *records* or *singles* or *albums.* Older people are sooo different.

Secretary, OK if I keep asking questions?

PAIGE: Only if you call me...

JIMMY: What's the king? Pop music? The King of Pop? The King of Poop? And listen to this one, a…blog? And…*twerking?!!* Anyway, Rumer went there was a few actual *books* on the island, but I wouldn't read any because what if they made it into a movie and then you've spoiled the movie? My 3DG…

PAIGE: Your *3…D…G?*

JIMMY: Um…Third Default Girlfriend?

 PAIGE: *Default…*girlfriend?

JIMMY: You know how sometimes you need someone more…fabooshka…then someone…*else?*

PAIGE: Must be some island.

JIMMY: Sooo…3DG knew someone who claimed she knew this guy who said his mother's father knew someone who read this list of books:

Douglas Coupland.
Bret Easton Ellis.
Alex Garland.
Damian Lanigan.
Jay McInerney.
Jennifer Egan.
Neil Gaiman.
And two called William, one a Golding and one a Boyd.
I like lists.
Lots of lists.
But I'm not sure that one person could read that many
books.
We've got mountains of movies and mega-movie-
multiplexes and most people had what you guys call
home cinema? So we watched movies a humungous
amount of the time and everybody really loved that. No,
I mean *really* loved that.
More on that later, too. Oh boy...
The old man, my great granddad, his favorite movies
are those Leo diCaprio ones, 'cuz he thinks I look kinda
like him, but younger at somethingteen years, 'cuz we
don't do age, but with less highness, more tan and hair
and looks but no acting talent. None whatsoever.
Plenty *others* on the island did.
You heard of Brad Pitt?
PAIGE: Brad...? Jimmy, he's...
JIMMY: By the way, *Paige.*
PAIGE: Finally!
JIMMY: Wild... *One.* What's straight to video? And
Videodrome? Pitt is a celebrity...I'm learning! And he's
supposed to be good-looking. Looks were
um...weirdness to me until I heard people talking about
it in the movies?
Pitt and Wentworth Miller are way cool enough to make
you want to be a woman.
And I hope you probably noticed that I'm trying to
broaden my:

16

Vocabulary.
Shit you say.

Four sy-lla-bles, right?
PAIGE: It's actually, uh...
JIMMY: I know a thing or two about famey celebrities now. Chris Martin of Coldplay is a very fine celebrity brand, yes, I know about brands, and I discovered that he married then divorced a celeb of similar quality. But, why don't they call music celebs A-listers too? Yes, I now know about A-listers. Wild thang… what's a MTV? Empty-V?
Another thing we don't do is marriage, but...yada yada movies movies. The old one's friend Shelley said "In Hollywood, all the marriages are happy. It's trying to live together afterwards that causes all the problems."
Another thing I definitely hadn't heard of was *celebrity magazines.* They're called ordinary words like *Okay* and *Hiya* and aren't about anything and a better name would be:
Why?

I knew nil about *boldface names,* either. *You* will all know all about all of *this,* of course. But I didn't, until recently.
You see, I am...*was*...am? One of the VSP's.Very…*Special*…People.
At least, that's what the old fella said. You'll find out all about that and him, later.
I didn't know I was part of that group.
But I do now.
I know what you're thinking.
Unbelievable.
I never knew about *opening week-end* or *Dakota Fanning's box-office tops $1 billion and Stones $100m world tour* either.
Oh, that's another thing.

Money's another weird thing to me, but *in the movies,* everyone always tries to steal it, aren't they? What for? Peach —

PAIGE: Paige.

JIMMY: —is a million a lot? What's a game-show? And, like, do they have *unreality* shows?

PAIGE: Try and get my name right, Jimmy.

JIMMY: Anyway, the old man said if I managed to escape...*impossible* he said...I was to visit his friend...something called an attorney...which is called Wild's...and sit and film my story, which I'm doing.

PAIGE: Mr. Byron —

JIMMY: It's *Jimmy.*

PAIGE: Jimmy, you know what?

JIMMY: Um...*probably?*

PAIGE: You know what you're doing here?

JIMMY: I just...like...*said?*

PAIGE: No, it's *how.*

JIMMY: Gotcha. Um...*WTF?*

PAIGE: It's like...*talk* writing.

JIMMY: Talk...*riding?*

PAIGE: Stream of consciousness? Like James Joyce?

JIMMY: Steam? *Unconsciousnessness...?*

PAIGE: James...Joyce?

JIMMY: James/Joyce? A man/woman? A Shemale?

PAIGE: The writer...

JIMMY: Coolness! A *composing* combo, wait... like...McCartney, and, gulp...*Lennon?*

PAIGE: Yes, Jimmy. And yet...no.

JIMMY: Huh?...sooo...the wrinkly one also said the *elevator pitch* is:

"A high concept, four quadrant celebration of pop culture."

Nevermind, I don't understand it either.

There's a lot I don't understand about most things.

After filming this, something called an *attorney* would give it to another something called *a publisher* if he hadn't heard from me after three months.

Only, how long is three months?

The old man also mentioned something called *publicity* and *book signings* and *Public Image,* confusing the crap out of me, but it's still one of the finest songs, opening chords and arrangement somebody ever wrote.

PAIGE: Help. Somebody…

JIMMY: — maybe this *publisher* thang is what you're reading now?

Maybe *you're* the publisher thang?

I find it mega-weird to think about filming this, or making something people read, when I've never even seen or read a one, so this is a…

Transcript.
Shit you say, typed.

And lovely *Pages* the transcribbler. Hey, cool movie title, starring Jason Statham…and I can promise right now, she *will* ask for sex with me, right?

PAIGE: *Help…*

JIMMY: I'm in some place she called a boredroom? I'm talking to a camera to try to make this as easy to read as watching a movie. Cage's face is maroon now.

PAIGE: *Heeeellllp…*

JIMMY: She said "Use a dictionary" and gave me hers which is a book without a glossy cover or even a story. But I know she *wants* me. They always do.

PAIGE: Sir, please, desist from…

JIMMY: This dictionary book is my first *ever* book and I would never usually use most or any of the words.

(Flips pages. Reads slowly)

"Great granddad said I should call my story:

Imagine…"

It meant nothing to me...*then.*
But now…you probably think I'm crazy, right?
Thing is? If you're reading this, or watching it…
I'm probably not alive...

The Great Escape.

(Jimmy's inaudible words. Laughter).
JIMMY: ...Norma's DFG1. But me 'n' Norma, we only had sex on the boat twice, even though we were on it a long time.
And Hey. 'Cuz of the choppy water, we didn't have to do much of the work. *(Nudge, nudge!)*
We were both kinda nervous because we were like, Hey ya...*escaping*...without ever saying the scary word aloud, and we knew that it was supposed to be *very* dangerous.
PAIGE: Jimmy, why that particular time?
JIMMY: A newcomer arrived, a beautiful, little song-bird from England, I heard. Security's eyes are on the prize, so...
Anyway, there was... or is it *were?*
PAIGE: "Was"?
JIMMY: "Were"?
PAIGE: I —
JIMMY: Anyway. All these rumours and stuff the old man said without trying to freak me out.
One rumour was —
No one's escaped.
Another was that some people did, and some people were never heard of again.
Anyway, this boat was huge, humungousoid, ginormously big, so we hid in the basement.
It was stuffed full with supplies and cigarettes and alcohol and stuff. I didn't do that on the island.
Oh...did you catch 2005's *The Island* movie with cool A-lister Ewan McGregor?
PAIGE: I —
JIMMY: And oh, again? I just remembered, there is one thing we read, apart from menus.
Screen credits.
Do you guys get them?

PAIGE: I —

JIMMY: Anyway, me and Norma had never tried cigarettes and alcohol and didn't on the journey either, because they might smell us, or we could get sick or drunk and they'd find us singing, sloppily slurring and getting the wrong words to Freddy's "I Want to Break Free."

Oh, and I did read part of a movie script once?

It's totally weird reading something that's not meant to be read. The old guy talked about *product placement* and *brand names* in movies.

They were new concepts to me, so I can't tell you what kind of brand name of boat we were on.

But, it had these big, massive, mammoth —

PAIGE: You're at the 'm' part of the dictionary —

JIMMY: — monumentally-powerful engines and smelt bad and was so big, we could hide without being found. It was painted black but not shiny and I think that's so you can't see it at night.

There was only two other people on the boat.

Or, so I thought.

More on…them…later. And it's kinda butt-nuggety.

PAIGE: Ugh.

JIMMY: I know.

Norma, she just wanted to be wonderful, and was.

She was way *fun-nee* too.

You would love her, everybody did.

Did…

Like…in the past.

And I can't believe I'm talking about my poor beautiful DFG1 Norma like that.

She looked like the illegitimate love-child of a lesbian miracle between Brittany Murphy and Grace Kelly…right guys? And curvy like movie stars from the old days, maybe Jayne Mansfield, and Marilyn Monroe and —

PAIGE: Uh, Jimmy, wait…

JIMMY: …a sexy dyed-blonde, with Pump It-Up bee-sting lips made for kissing and luckily, she was a big *Deep Throat* fan.
PAIGE: Uh, Jimmy…
JIMMY: They should totally remake that.
I haven't learned the word you would use for penising — *(Chuckles aloud.)* — yet, but I overheard a girl in New York saying it, so…
PAIGE: Jimmy…
JIMMY: Norma's body was a teenager's temple and she loved a lot of worship. I don't know your words for sex yet, apart from the words in blah blah…
Here's some space.
Just write *your* sex words here. In this space:

———————————————

I'll probably have a favourite sex words section anyway, some from the dictionary, and whatever I hear on the street.
You can add yours and compare with friends, even.
People said I was like the male version of Norma, DFG1 Norma, only mucho loco — *(affects atrocious Mexican accent, not exactly Robin Williams)* — only truly beautiful to behold and lots of people always wanted sex with me.
Because that was pretty much all there was to do, or what we *wanted* to do on the island.
I've had sex with almost everyone that I want to, apart from Marsha, who could be *actual* girl-friend?
PAIGE: Marsha?
JIMMY: Mmmm?
PAIGE: Is Marsha —
JIMMY: We would make such a pretty pair.
On the island, everybody always wore nothing, or perfume or light beach clothes as it was always hot, really hot, or storms.

23

But in New York, me and Norma —
PAIGE: DFG1 Norma —
JIMMY: — started to feel cold as we got close to the pretty city lights.
That was when we had sex the second time, to keep warm and in case we got lost or murdered or slipped through a time-traveling wormhole and would never do it again and we would miss it and so that's why I thought of Marsha and '89s *When Harry Met Sally* but without all the noise and sex faces, and...
PAIGE: Hold on.
JIMMY: Hold on?
PAIGE: We have a problem.
JIMMY: Hey, *Apollo 13!* 1995. Coolness.
PAIGE: Not that, Jimmy, it's...
JIMMY: Space. The final frontier...sooo...
PAIGE: Nooo...It's —
JIMMY: ...the boat sailed closer to the city and all we could see through our tiny window was all these, like, big gigantic buildings, height-wise.
We knew they were for living in, or having office affairs, as we had seen stuff like that *you know where*.
As we got closer, we could see lights travelling really fast along the ground.
We knew they were cars, like in *Bullit* 'cuz the stooped man told me about the 1968 movie, but I've never seen it. We weren't allowed to even *know* about it.
We didn't need cars, but great granddad *loved* talking about them.
Remember that, and *Bullit* 'cuz they're *really* like, important?
There was also this really high statue of a tall woman holding a torch in the air. I think it was the lovely Daryll Hannah in *Splash?*
PAIGE: We have a problem. I —
JIMMY: She rocked in 2003's *Kill Bill,* which one of the founders said sounded like a:

"Counter-terrorism political manifesto."

It's alright. I don't understand it either.

What's happening, Temporary Secretary? *(Gargling sounds, which are actually just more of his terrible 'singing.')*

PAIGE: I'm phoning. *(Dialing the landline. Tapping a finger nervously and waiting for a reply.)* …Sally? I'm filming this interview with Jimmy? Can you help? I need the skinny on naming celebrities, pop groups, producers, brand names, song, movie and TV show titles, author names, quotes from books, lyrics and movie dialogue.

JIMMY: You forgot advert tag-lines.

PAIGE: *(Into phone.)* And advert tag-lines. Thanks. *(Click!)*

JIMMY: Um…the…*skinny?*

PAIGE: We need to be careful.

JIMMY: Um…I *could* use a rubber, extra-large?

PAIGE: Not *that,* Jimmy. I…Extra…?

JIMMY: You prefer…bare-back?

PAIGE: You could get sued.

JIMMY: Sue? Is she *sexy* Sue, just like you? Hey, I made a rhyme!

PAIGE: No, Sued.

JIMMY: Suuue?

PAIGE: *Sued!* Legal deep shit, dip-sh…

JIMMY: Like *The People vs. Larry Flynt*?

PAIGE: So…

JIMMY: And the answer is yes, dummy, to the Daryll question? Anyway, her stone statue looked as welcoming as her in all her utter gloriousness, and we took that as a good sign.

The boat slipped smoothly along the water and cozied up next to a big, greasy dirty dark pier. Norma and me rubbed against each other like Pussycat Dolls to see outside, but the place was mostly in blackness with a few really pale as piss lamps that made it really shadowy and spooky. That would never work on the island, where night was almost like day, mostly.

There was these steel girder things, kinda 1954 *On The Waterfront* which I only got to see about ten years ago and the place looked deserted and mega-not-new, paved with disgusting, oily cobbles.

Filth like this just never happened on the island. Everything was always new.

You got up the next afternoon and hey, look, *new!*

Crawford and Hutchence, islanders from the not popular group, at least we thought it was them, tied up the boat and we could glimpse a few other boats tied up, but none were as big or sleek as this one.

They also had girly names, like Natalie and Kirsty and Geraldine and Shannon and Robin and Gretchen and Hortense and Penelope and Prudence. Or men's names like Maxwell which reminded me of a silver hammer, but ours didn't have a name.

It could have just been called Black or Black Pearl or Black Beauty or Black Licorice or Paint It Black or Back to Black or maybe Jack Black.

Maybe that was already painted on the side, in black.

After a few minutes, they walked down a long, wooden plank to step onto dry land. In the blackness, it was hard to see it was them, but it couldn't possibly be anyone else, 'cuz that's who's been driving the boat.

It was just that we were used to seeing them naked or nude or in swimwear or beachwear. But now, they looked like the beeyootiful, cutiful people I seen in the thing called a Zagat's.

More on *that* later, too.

PAIGE: Okaaay.

JIMMY: Anyway, they wore black to be maybe not be seen like the boat and they looked totally different to any other people I had ever seen in real life and they both dressed the same.

They wore dazzling white shirts under black coats that you probably call expensive, or ritzy, or ritzy-titzy, but we wouldn't because we don't do money.

The Woman in Black is tall, slim and deliciously curvy, with shiny black hair like it's been yacht-varnished and has a cute oval face like Vivien Leigh, quite frankly.

And she had Bette Davis eyes.

I've not had sex with Crawford yet.

Joan, not Broderick. *(Shivers.)*

Though some of the guys called her a dickfridge.

Hutchence was tall and slim too, muscly like Zak Efron. He had a *Blackhat* over his expensive hair, and tried really hard to look like he hadn't tried really hard to look like Jim Morrison...hear o' him?

PAIGE: The Doors...

JIMMY: But like a more modern version.

Maybe like fine screen actor Colin Farrell?

They were not part of the coolness gang because to be honest, they were both a little grouchy.

I heard they did *training* something on the beach a lot.

But, they did look gorgeous.

Next, for some reason, Norma DFG1 sang to me in her pretty, pouty, breathy voice...

NORMA
Happy birthday to you,
Happy birthday to you,
Happy birthday Mr. President...

Although we don't do birthdays and I'm not El Presidente, the next thing she says is...

NORMA
Ever thought of a threesome
with them?

27

That's how screenwriters write words in a film script. It's called dialogue.

PAIGE: Thanks.

JIMMY: Norma didn't expect a reply, knowing I probably *have* thought about that, or done it, or would plant the thought in my peanut brain for the future anyway.

Another fine mess I'd get myself into.

So, they walked away hand in hand and their shoes clicked really loudly.

Click-click! Click-click!

PAIGE: I get the idea.

JIMMY: *Click-click!* I know it will seem funny to you, but I had only ever heard SFX-oh, that's sound effects-like that in a movie, or in Roxy Music's excellent "Love is the Drug."

Crawford and Hutchence disappeared round a corner and I ran outside to make sure they had gone...wherever.

Hey, I just remembered another reason why a lot of islanders don't like them.

Remember that amazing '95 movie called *Seven*?

I hadn't seen any of the first six, but this one was all about the seven deadly sins, many of which get this guy's tick at the ballet box.

Anyway, we had rules on the island.

A *really* important rule was:

NEVER GIVE AWAY THE ENDING OF A MOVIE.

You're soooo right. Total *Shatner.*

Anyway, Crawford and Hutchence were always together and up to stuff. And listen to this!

They gave away the endings to *Seven, Sixth Sense* and *The Fifth Element!*

I counted on it being *The Fourth Protocol* next.

Another thing, people who pretend they know the endings to movies, like...don't.

Anyway...

PAIGE: Anywaaay...

JIMMY: "It's OK Norma, they've gone" I said a little too loudly, by mistake, and hoped they didn't hear.

I was cold and rubbed my bare arms and tucked my Ralph Lauren brand very sticky polo shirt into my washed out, cool, barely hanging together Levi 501 brand cut-offs, scruffy Converse Chuck Taylor brand sneakers below.

Norma appeared right next to me, looking swagalicious but stunningly nervous and freakazoided and hugging herself and, thank-you cold, perma nipple-erection.

"Let's escape to a warmer climate" she said. A sense of humour in a beautiful, curvy woman is my ideal package.

PAIGE: Hmmm.

JIMMY: Well, that and...

She stretched like a blonde, Bond-movie human cat.

"I need that Hershey bar now."

"What is it with women and chocolate?" I said and she had rehearsed and knew her lines.

"What it's *not* with men and sex."

Love her. And she means *other* men, obviously.

PAIGE: Obviously.

JIMMY: So, she produces this misshapen, deformed, d-for dessicated, denuded, warm, half-melted Hershey bar from the back pocket of her deliciously pear-shaped Gucci brand ultra-short-shorts and flops it in two and peels off — *Whiiip! Whaap!* — the gloopy silver paper.

Then she guzzles both halves — *Gnaw! Gnaw!* — giving me a wet, gooey, slimy chocolatey kiss.

Then, she licks her Sticky Fingers.

I plan to explore the dark promise of chocolate further.

PAIGE: Please.

JIMMY: "What are we doing here, Jimmy?" said she.

"Searching for secrets" I said, keeping dialogue short and kinda curt and mysterious, screenwriter style, like Night.

PAIGE: M.

JIMMY: She gave a big, breathless, soulful sexy sigh and slumped against me.

We both looked warily along the dark, deserted street and she looked even more nervous, like Fay Wray, *King Kong's* cock dribbling above.

I took her hand in mine.

"Let's go, Norma."

DFG1 wiped some chocolate smears from my face.

"Crawford and Hutchence looked so...different. I can hardly believe it was them."

"Wonder why they're dressed so fabmazing" not really a question.

"To look cool and *hot?*"

"Um...we'll be fine...ish."

We stepped along the plank, which swayed a little and made our legs and our balance wobble.

Then, we just said goodbye to the boat, looked at the long walk and began.

"Escape to New York" she said with a cute wink and grabbed my hand again and we strolled like we do on the sand back home.

It felt strange to say *home.*

I've never had a reason to think of it that way before.

We kept the walk slow and careful, not knowing where the next step would lead.

It would lead to the end, which was so totally sweargasm nigh.

Norma stopped dead.

"You forgot our bags!"

She grabbed me by both arms and half turned.

"Me? But...*gulp?*"

I looked back where a boat called Twenty Seven bobbed.

And the walk looked even longer from this side and to be honest, scary 1973 *Exorcisty*, 'cuz we never had pitch black to think about or stagger-stumble through, even for sandy, after curfew sex on the beach or in the water or in Mrs. Robinson's big fancy bed, pretending you know *who's* not watching and...

"Uh...you thinking what I'm thinking?" she said.

"I doubt *that*. But, hey, who needs clothes."

We looked into each other's baby-blues and I smiled.

"I'll keep you warm," I said and pushed her against the wall.

It seemed like a plan and we kissed.

Smooch!

But, the place smelled bad and barfy and looked way worse, the walls covered in blood-red *American Graffiti,* like...

"I-wreck. I-raq. I-ran. I-merica."

Later, This Charming Man told me that was something called political.

I didn't understand at first, then thought of the founders and then I did.

We had some political, but nothing like 1976's *All the President's Men* or '74's *Parallax View* or *Nixon* more like, um...

"Let's maybe leave it until we're more escaped," Norma breathed, waving her hand over her nose.

It was too cold, anyway.

And small, like a little pig's pink tail.

But hey, not usually!

I pecked her on the cheek.

Peck!

Took her hand and we walked.

And walked and walked and walked, suck's fake!

At least there's more people now and I reached a corner first and walked around it and

"Sweargasm!" But, it came out in a kinda cool Tintin Quarantino meets *Zoolander* goo-looking way.

31

Norma stopped and looked really frightened.

"Whoa" I said and stopped dead.

"What is it?"

"It's, *gulp*...I'm *Clueless.*"

I could only stare ahead with my stupid head on.

"There's all kinds of colours on your face," she said

"Like...psychedelic zits."

Great name for a boy band, right?

PAIGE: I —

JIMMY: Norma began to peek around the corner.

Suddenly, a hand clamped her shoulder from behind!

Norma's scream hurt my ears and she spun around in

panic, scaring the bejesus butt-nuggets out of me.

I couldn't believe what I was seeing!

How could this *be?*

Ladies and gentlemen!

Meet another of the characters.

Island girl.

It was Grace, DFG2 —

PAIGE: DFG2?

JIMMY: — from the island.

And yes, of *course* I have.

Her and Norma launched excitedly at each other like

girls do, all giggles and shrieks and smiles and hugs

and kisses and smoochies and, and, and *always* deep

joy to watch, much breast-squashing.

I might ask them to re-enact that, only naked, with

melted marshmallows, me in the middle, then...

It was like they'd never seen each other before and

never will again.

How true *that* turned out to be.

Anyway, let me introduce Grace.

PAIGE: DFG2.

JIMMY: From the island.

PAIGE: Gotcha.

JIMMY: There's this movie called *Hot chicks.*

If Grace was in it, try *white-hot* chicks.

PAIGE: Eeek.

JIMMY: I think she's maybe, what eighteen? years smart, but nobody really knows or cares or talks about age on the island.

Even at home, it's no biggie, unless your family makes it, but they keep that quiet from everybody else.

'Cuz the founders are *very* particular about anything that reminds people of the past and they try the hardest to help people forget.

Grace had the longest legs, covered with tight, skin-tight actually, dark brown leather jeans, perfect with her big, bouncy auburn hair. And she had a matching sweater on. Clever girl and sexy sassness in a dark, kinda sultry, sorta almost dangerous femme fatale kinda way and she had used cigarettes and alcohol and other drugs. So she was a known druggy.

She was also known as a dickbasket and stuff that I mean to get into sometime.

Personality wise, she is...*was*...

PAIGE: *Was...*?

JIMMY:...sex goddess.

"Grace! What bus did you get here?"

Norma —

PAIGE: DFG1 —

JIMMY: — giggled which I thought was kinda strange because...we don't do buses.

Grace looked a little uncomfortable and looked between us both.

"I...was up late and saw you two. I...*followed* you."

"That's...stalkery," I said, maybe just a little suspicious snarky snarl in my usually friendly, especially to girls, voice.

Don't think I'm obsessed with girls, it's just that I like them more than Boys II Men.

Not in this dictionary storybook?

Kissogynist.

Steal it and I think something called an attorney goes after your money then steal it for themselves.

Norma kicked my shin with her little clean white Nike brand name and it hurt.

"Well, it wasn't to watch you two meat puppets, Jimmy, if that's what you think."

Norma kicked me in the other shin and that hurt, too.

"It was way past curfew."

I looked at her stupidly, of course.

PAIGE: Of course.

JIMMY: "You were carrying bags, pea-brain."

"*Runaway?* Remember?"

"Right. *Prison Break!*" was all I could come up with.

I wasn't good when girls outnumbered me, except...

"I hid on the boat too?"

It was then that I slumped against the wall, shaking my empty-headed head and cool hair.

"What's the matter, Jimmy?" she said. "You usually look happy to see me. *Very* happy."

"Um, sorry, Gracie."

"Wait. You don't think..." she said.

She trailed off, too scared to finish the sentence.

"No, no. I'm sorry, really, really sorry, I'm pleased you're here, Grace."

"The more, the merrier, right?"

"We're safe here, aren't we, Jimmy?" Norma said, her voice shaking and quaking.

I couldn't think of what to say, but Grace did.

"I just wanted out, same as you two."

Grace was close to tears and I felt bad, but spoke my mind.

"If you must."

Neither of the girls seemed impressed by that.

PAIGE: Imagine that.

JIMMY: "Listen, if you don't want me here, I can just go."

I wondered vaguely where exactly Grace would go and how or when, but thought better of saying it aloud.

Norma took her by both shoulders.

"Grace. Don't worry. It's just another rumour that *they* put out to spook us."

Norma made a scaredy-cat fright-face and Grace faked a little laugh. More a giggle, actually.

"Do you want us to try harder at, like, reassuring you?"

I go and Grace nearly smiled.

Then her face twisted into frightened, then something close to ugly.

"You think I could have led them to us!?"

She looked so sexily sad that I knew I had to come up with something, um...reassuring?

"Gracie. Kiss me like you do when Norma's not there," I said, and I was plenty impressed by that.

Norma's face looked tighter than a hen's ass.

PAIGE: Nice image.

JIMMY: Grace made a smile, leaned close and breathed into my mouth. *Whooosh.*

I thought that was fucool.

Then, she grabbed my face and kissed me really really super-hard on the lips, her arms wrapping me up.

I never closed my eyes and that's when I seen Norma shake her head and look at the Iron Sky.

Grace finished with me and I winked at her because it was a really great boy-gets-what-he-wants-from-the-girl-movie-standard classic kiss.

Norma stood, faking i-for — *(Jimmy stops. Refers to my pocket dictionary.)*

Indifference.
No, no, don't care.

I just smiled like I'd been at one of Bob's parties and grabbed both of their hands.

Then, I led them both around the corner, into...

Street Life.

JIMMY: I didn't even look round the corner.
PAIGE: Why not?
JIMMY: I just watched the girls' faces.
They were priceless and had moving colours on them.
The colours came from huge signs on millions of high
buildings that were full of *Viva Las Vegas* light and
brand names that wouldn't stay still, so they made my
eyes bug out and hurt to look at.
Some I even recognised because I had the names
back home *somehow* and they were Sony, Kodak,
Virgin and Pepsi. KFC and AT&T and IBM and Taco
Bell.
Then, I just absolutely had to turn to the street.
It was jumping with the strangest roomful of people I
had ever seen in my ageless life and let me say, I've
seen plenty on the island.
But this, all the walks, talks, shapes, sizes, types,
attitudes, colours and clothes, was incredible.
I know what a lot of these people are called now and I'll
try and make 'a people' list:
Goths.
Punks.
Pimps.
Hookers (Jane Fonda in *Klute*. Right guys?).
Heavy Metallers.
Bikers.
Skaters.
Haters.
Hobos.
Hippies?
Winos.
Junkies.
Cons.
Ex-Cons.
Cops with *The Usual Suspects.*

Ordinary People.
Homeless.
Jobless.
Penniless.
Toothless.
Ruthless.
Nurses, in *white uniform.*

Transvestites.
The really cutiful ones are men.

And I wondered, would I…?
PAIGE: Would you…?
JIMMY: Hip-hop porn-princesses.
Street-vendors.
Mind-benders.
Modelicious.
World's Gym jocks.
Pagester?
PAIGE: Yes?
JIMMY: What's anabollock steroids?
PAIGE: I —
JIMMY: I probably left some out, but it was a lot to take in.
The hip-hop girls dripped dirty sex and the drag-queens looked they would have the most fun and I liked looking at them.
I was reminded of, was it Lady Boys of Bangkok?
PAIGE: I don't —
JIMMY: And of course, Paolo Nutini's excellent "These Streets."
Naturally, I wanted to remember where this place was so I could find it again and looked around to get my bearings.
High on a lamp-post, something read Times Square.
"Venus In Furs" by the Velvets unsurprisingly popped into my prune-for-a-brain head because it felt so right.

I wanted to wear those shiny boots of leather at that moment and dress up as Wayne County.

But somebody was shaking my arm — *Shake! Shake!* — and snapped me out of it.

"So, is this New York city?" Norma goes.

"How should I know?" But Lou Reed and Nico and our *friend* lived here, so it would be so fucool.

Grace had been gawping at this ancient grizzled guy forever.

"I was really hungry, but now..."

We've got guys and *women* like that on the island and this one was serving steaming food-like gloop from a street-trolley and *The Hunger Games* began.

Speaking of which, I know I'm a total hair-head, but to prove the importance of hair, check that movie. Right? *Thank* you.

So, this foodish stuff? Even though it looked kinda revolting and we didn't recognise it as something you would eat and live through, or escape a long night of butt-gravy.

Mostly droopy-eyed people were munching and dropping most of it onto their shoes, luckily.

We decided to walk a little to find somewhere where we could maybe keep the food down.

Somehow strangely sexy in overalls girl with heavy toolbox suggested Fedora in West Village, but, how do we get there?

Along from the Times Square, we stopped outside something called 'All you can eat. $10.' The stuff absolutely looked like it could be food maybe.

We watched people eat all they could for $10 and it was important to us that they enjoyed it, 'cuz eating was another island pleasure.

But, we had a problem.

People would finish eating, wave the waitress over and hand her a small plastic card with printed stuff on it.

One was even black.

There seems to be black everywhere here.

The waitress took the cards away, did something we never saw and came back with it on a tray.

People wrote something down and the waitress smiled, tore something and, like, gave it to them?

That was truly weirdness.

"Want to see something else crazy?" I said.

Norma said "What are you going to do to me?"

I laughed, then got to thinking, but, nah, still too cold.

Grace looked kinda envious, yet peckish.

Then, a group of kidiots did the waving thing, only this time, they gave the waitress a lot of green paper.

(Pauses. Deep in thought.) Transcriber?

PAIGE: Yes?

JIMMY: What's a ATM?

PAIGE: ATM?

JIMMY: IRS and WMD? WTF??

PAIGE: You should, uh…take your feet off the table.

JIMMY: I copied that move from *Casino.*

"What are they doing?" Grace said.

"It's, um…*Dead Presidents,"* like the movie, only not?

The girls looked at me like I was Norma Bates.

PAIGE: *Norman. Norman* Bates.

JIMMY: "They call it cash money?" I tried.

"I don't remember that movie," goes Norma.

"From '95? Vietnam vet struggles back in the Bronx? Made by the mighty Hughes Brothers?"

"You know *everything* about movies and music Jimmy, but actual real life? Nada. Zip. Zed. Zilch."

"Coming from you, that means a lot, Grace."

"So *that's* what it looks like in the flesh!" Norma said, her face more confused looking than usual.

"It's what we need, if we want to eat all we want for $10" I said.

Then, I pointed to a bunch of cool funsters at a table, one modelicious in a Melvins t-shirt.

We all smiled at each other, but them even *knowing* about The Melvins confused the Hell out of me.

The waitress was fairly attractive but Olive Oyle thin, so not for me.

She was older though, usually a tried-and-true turn-on as they're more grateful and have more tricks.

And she did have lovely dark skin, another turn-on when you look up at the ceiling mirrors and glimpse pink between tasty dark spider's legs.

PAIGE: Ugh.

JIMMY: She smiled a big toothy smile and I smiled back.

The girls both nudged me at the same time.

Nudge! Nudge!

I knew what that meant.

"OK, here goes. Full frontal flirt!" I said before marching toward the waitress.

She gave me another big toothy smile and tried to look kinda angelic? But her voice reminded me of "The Sound of Breaking Glass." *Screeech!*

I was too hungry to care about that, even though I don't listen to women with high voices because it hurts my little earses.

I turned on my studio central casting hyperhero look and I worked her for about a minute.

From the side of my eye, I was aware of the girls' hunger and you could see them dropping dress sizes by the second, Perez catwalk careers beckoning.

The waitress's smile fell a notch and her jaw dropped and then she grimaced then she nodded and I waved the girls over.

The waitress led us to a table and we all sat, snatching at menus.

"So, you guys don't have any *money,* right?"

"Right, no...uh...money..." Norma said.

"Always before my coffee break," the waitress griped and her voice had become a tad more nasal, probably jealousy because of the gorgeousness of the girls.
"How do you get this um...money?" I asked.
"Honey, you could get it anytime, anywhere."
There was a kinda weirdness in her voice and a kinda leery look.
"I...could? How?"
I just stared back at her and she just looked at me and shook her head.
"Always on my damn shift," she muttered.
"Damn shift?" I said and she just shuffled away, hopefully to get some fully loaded coffee.
We all watched her go with the same hungry, but for food, look.
The girls turned their attention to the menus.
I looked for American Pie, then got scared thinking about the day I die.
"They kill some strange animals here," Grace said, but that didn't bother me or Norma.
Norma bit her lovely lip and said "Cheeseburger," then said "Wow, they do Coke here," and then added "And fries" helpfully.
The waitress arrived with a tray of steaming mugs of coffee and we happily took them and wrapped our little cold hands around them.
The waitress ruffled my hair like you would do with a pet-thing and produced a greasy notebook.
I instantly checked my hair for grease.
"Um...can we just order three cheeseburgers, fries and Cokes?" I said and the waitress nodded.
"Coming right up, guys," she said, already on the move.
"Hey, gang. This is kinda like *Fast Food,* the '89 comedy with the juicy sex-star Traci Lords and..."
Nobody listened, just all looking round the fast-food joint.

41

I looked around myself and it was deserted apart from us and that was another new experience.

We were to have a lot of new experiences in this city.

"How do you sit with all the chairs on top of the tables?" I said, half to myself.

The girls had already started chattering in no males, only Girls Aloud talk, so I checked out.

I looked in the direction of the kitchen and the waitress was doing cooking under the window.

She was reading at the same time and would look between the cooking, me and the book.

The book was called "William Burroughs" and the next time she looked at me, I pointed to the book, then her, then me.

She got my point because it said *Naked Lunch* on the book jacket and I think her face turned red, even though she had that funny leery look again.

She looked like she could be touching herself.

And that wasn't just wishful thinking.

She eventually turned up with the food and it looked and smelled nice enough to eat.

I hoped she washed her hands first.

Or, maybe not.

"Finish this, then go back to Akron or wherever you come from. This city will eat you up and spit out the pips," she said and looked serious as a gun.

I chomped on a huge mouthful of fries and my smile must have looked like Jim Carrey.

"And you, stay away from the gay bars," she said, smiling at me like my mother.

My mother...

Sigh.

I swallowed the food too quickly so I could answer fast.

"Will they *serve* me?" I asked hopefully.

"Boy *will* they serve you," she sniffed, but I didn't understand and must have shown it on my face.

"Listen, you want money, take some of that jewelry to a pawn shop," pointing to stuff hanging on Marsha's kissy neck and fingers.

"A...*porn* shop?" Norma said.

The waitress groaned again but I don't know why.

PAIGE: Of course you don't...

JIMMY: I'm sorry?

PAIGE: Nevermind.

JIMMY: She shook her head again and walked away.

"Like *Pawn Shop Chronicles* from 2013, starring Paul Walker, Matt Dillon, Brendan Fraser and Vincent D'Onofrio?"

Nobody listened, and Grace's chomping face was smeared with tomato ketchup.

Some ran down her face, onto her hair, all oozy and drippy and bright ruby red, like...

... a sign of what was coming.

I'll be watching you.

There must have been somebody following us and watching us and spying on us and stuff and I can only really *guess* what happened, so I can only try and tell it that way.

We were all still just sitting eating.

Me and Norma were really hungry, pigging out, wolfing down, hardly talking.

I had just taken the biggest chomp at my burger that I could and chewed away — *Chew, chomp, chew!* — stroking my cutesy lower jaw where it hinges because something toothy was wrong.

Grace maybe wasn't hungry anymore or ate chocolate on the boat or didn't like it, I don't know. She just kinda moved things around the plate and to be honest, I was eyeing it up for myself.

We had no idea at all that there was any risk or danger or worse...

Whoever was watching us probably looked at our clothes and thought 'dumb tourists' and that would be right.

PAIGE: A-men.

JIMMY: But they didn't mean they had to do what they did.

The person, or maybe more than one, male or female, young, old, thin, fat, tall, short, I didn't know...

...must have darted between all the parked cars and then sneaked up quite close to us.

That's a butt-nuggety thought.

All the while, we ate and I couldn't stand it any longer and grabbed for Grace's half chewed burger.

Swipe!

I smiled at her and she didn't say anything.

I thought at the time that maybe she was thinking about what we said when she arrived.

PAIGE: Which was?

44

JIMMY: Which was "Our waitress for the evening" was what she said and I called her that too, must have been washing dishes below the window. She would work, look up, watch us eat, work, look up and smile, like the routine of a bored person...

PAIGE: *Yawn...*

JIMMY: ...or lonely maybe.

A big yellow taxi — I know that *now*...chugged by and I watched it to try and read writing on its side.

Solo slutty Soho girl inside contorted to get a better look at me and I smiled at her, because I hardly ever get that on the island anymore.

And there's no taxis, of any colour.

Over my shoulder, I could hear the girls getting back into chick-speak, but quieter this time.

That meant they were talking about you, or girl-plumbing, or someone you know that they don't want you to hear them talking about.

I've got a headache just thinking about it.

That was when I think I definitely might have seen someone across the street, or maybe not, because it was so dark and I'm not used to staring into invisible blackness.

I thought I seen shadows...one, two? Between parked cars, head across the street towards our way, pretty fast and low.

But that didn't mean anything to me.

Why would it?

I munched on Grace's burger and turned to where our waitress for the evening was still busy. I waved and smiled, pointing at the burger with a satisfied face.

She gave me a big smile back with her sex-face on, then started to wave.

But...

PAIGE: ...But?

JIMMY: ...she stopped her scrawny arm midway and her face changed.

She looked, um...
PAIGE: ...Uh?
JIMMY: Um...
PAIGE: Uh-huh?
JIMMY: I think... that she saw something behind us
that she didn't like.
Our waitress kept looking between the street and us.
And she was drying her hands over and over.
I was looking at her and I thought she must have been
really scared.
And, have really dry hands.
I turned from her to scope the street, but I couldn't see
anything.
When I turned back, she started to back into the
shadows of the kitchen, then stopped, so I could still
see her.
Meantime, the girls are totally not aware to whatever
this was or wasn't or might be, maybe.
Norma actually had her arm around Grace's shoulder
because Grace looked kinda glum 'n' gloomy.
"You OK, Grace?" I asked.
She shook her head and Norma made a face at me.
She said "Maybe if you stop staring around and over-
petrifying her...us..." and I thought they hadn't noticed.
But, you know girls.
I stood up and went to them and put my arms around
them both.
Grace was crying very softly and I felt bad.
But then I thought I heard another cry.
PAIGE: Where?
JIMMY: From the kitchen.
When I looked over, our waitress for the evening, kinda
wasn't.
I stood up again and didn't mean to startle the girls but
did, so figured:
"I'm just going to have sex with our waitress for the
evening" was worth a shot.

PAIGE: Wonderful.

JIMMY: Creamy.

PAIGE: Ugh indeed.

JIMMY: Both girls make the same kinda twisty, jealousy only not face, so I walked toward the kitchen. To be honest, I had a very not good feeling.

I didn't want to hesitate in case I spooked the girls more, or myself.

So I got halfway there, when our waitress appeared. Her face was really terrified, like the rest of her.

She started to say something, then it was like she was yanked backwards from behind, like in *The Forgotten?* I thought I heard a soft hiss, then that was it.

Our waitress for the evening.

Took the evening off.

I thought we should all do the same.

But, although I'm not Bruce Willis, I'm not Pee Wee Herman either, so...

It was no use.

I just had to look at the girls, then the kitchen and then girl radar because Grace knew and kinda whispered: "It's them, isn't it?"

And all I could say in reply was: "Our waitress...isn't for the evening" in a lost, but still cool way.

Norma went for a light, rom-com tone and managed: "No underwear? MV?"

PAIGE: "MV"?

JIMMY: MV is island-talk for moist vagina.

PAIGE: How...delightful.

JIMMY: I think you probably have a lot of great words because vagina isn't and I'd like to hear them, but I do know you still use vagina because I once overheard Crawford and Hutchence talk about something they'd seen.

Vagina Monolgues.
Now you're talking.

By the way, it's mostly sorta movie-English we speak on the island, though there's lots of people from places like China and India and America and Latin America and they sometimes talk in their own languages too and they must be smart or not want you to understand. Norma's laughy attempt only made things worse.
Grace started to really look toiletty.
"It *is* them, isn't it?"
I definitely maybe thought there was a half-chance it might not be.
"I don't know. But at least one of us should be Paranoid."
I was in the 'f' section of the dictionary book and had accidentally tried f-for flippant, then thought of the timeless Sabbath anthem.
If only I could see her, our waitress for the evening, would be lying in her own kitchen, in a pool of her own blood with a hole in her own forehead.
In the shadows of the diner, Grace's face looked all twisted and a little freaked and scared.
Norma was on her feet, hugging herself tight in that 'Please mister, don't hurt me' body language kinda-sorta way.
I upped the action-hero act and stepped to the kitchen window, looked through but not for long, then hurried back to 'protect' the girls.
I know now that *they* had night vision goggles, so this scene all happened like Green Day.

GREEN:
Grace slowly reaches a hand out to Jimmy, and Norma frowns because it looks like a flirt, then Grace strokes Jimmy's face.
Grace's hair flutters a little.

Ricochet.
A bullet whines, not you.

I remember the sound of a bullet somewhere hitting something metal.

Pa-taaang!

I was used to that sound from movies, so it was nothing new, or nothing to do with me.

Or so I thought.

But, even though I had never heard it in real life, that *Pa-taaang!* meant nothing, absolutely nothing, so we didn't duck or anything.

Norma and Grace never even noticed it, because Grace was reaching out to touch my face again and Norma was so pissed.

She, and me, didn't see that there was...

A red dot.

Crawling across this very nearly not poster boy, stunningly, shamelessly, flawlessly handsome anymore face.

I know *now* that it was a laser-dot from a gun.

I just looked at Grace like an icehole, with my raisin brain.

But then, she jerked, only just a little.

Her eyes fixed on mine.

Next thing...the next thing...

PAIGE: ...Yes?

JIMMY:...blood...

PAIGE: Oh God.

JIMMY: ...oozes from her lovely red lips, then more, then more and now...

It's pouring and gushing and...

I'm sorry...*Sniff!*...I never cry, it's just...*Sniff!*

Grace collapsed against me...and she was...her weight was...really saggy and not thin and diety and...I could only...only lower her down carefully.

There was blood everywhere, like a Pekinpah movie.

But no *Bang Bang*, like *Assault on Precinct 13* and I so don't mean the 2005 remake.

49

Then, through all her nice hair and blood, I noticed a horrible, gaping, gushing and pumping hole in Grace's forehead.

Norma stood mute, hands over her face, eyes popping.

I was wiped out at seeing that.

I tried to make the blood stop...

Make it stop...

I tried to make it *stop!!!*

And I put my hands over the wound, but it *wouldn't* —

PAIGE: — wouldn't?

JIMMY: — stop —

PAIGE: Oh no!

JIMMY: — and blood seeped between my fingers and then Grace had a strange kinda glazed look and she gasped and then she just...

Died, right there.

It took seconds.

I can't even *begin* to tell you what it feels like to have a person you grew up with...

...someone you...you *loved!*

Shot, and actually die.

Anything like that ever happen to you?

PAIGE: I —

JIMMY: Pagester?

PAIGE: I —

JIMMY: Hey?

PAIGE: I —

JIMMY: You don't look well.

PAIGE: I —

JIMMY: I really hope not.

I didn't know how to behave.

I mean, I've been to island funerals and stuff, but this was real life and made me realise how like, totally *unreal* the island is.

I felt grief, horror, rage and...stupidity.

And it was Norma who snapped me out of it.

"They just *killed* her!"

I leaped to my feet and I looked around, because now I knew exactly what was going on.

I grabbed Norma and shoved her hard between two big trees because it gave us a little cover.

"Are you OK, Norma? Are you hit?"

To be honest, I really wanted to rant myself, plenty, but kept a lid on it, only with real difficulty.

"Hit? With…*what?*"

You have to realise, all of this kinda, bullety stuff was, is, totally beyond our thinking.

This only ever happened in the movies and you knew it wasn't real.

Because you watched the same actors in their next film and there was no bullet-holes on their magnificent *Lara Croft* bodies and at the end of the movie, a make-up artist got a screen credit, which I would think would include bullet-holes, right?

Norma's voice came out all strangled and broken.

"What's happening, Jimmy?!"

"We've got to get out of this place!" I said, only vaguely thinking about the '65 Animals classic and grabbed her hand in a hurty way by mistake.

"Oh, my God!"

Then, she screamed and it hurt my ears and I had to put my hand over her mouth because I knew what was coming next.

I dragged her along, keeping my eyes glued to where I thought he or she or they or them or it was, or were or could or might be.

"Norma, we have to leave her."

"We can't just leave her lying there!" she shouted in my face and I knew she didn't realise yet.

And it broke my heart to have to say "It's the only thing we can do."

"NO!" she screamed into my face, trying really hard to get out of my grip and boy, she was strong.

I heard a car drawing up and my stomach flipped because I figured it was them and it was our turn for the silent, violent bullet.

All I could do was push Norma deeper among the trees and maybe they'd not see us or miss.

I think it must've been panic that made me forget about green night-goggles at that time.

'Cuz this next scene is in...

ELECTRIC BLUE:
A strong beam of light sweeps over the 'All you can eat $10' sign and Jimmy holds Norma very close and tight.

"What is *that?*" she whispered and I hoped she would begin to understand the danger we were in, soon.

A black and white vehicle drove slowly along, its big blue light fanning the street.

"A police car" which I knew about from massive re-watchings of *Police Academy 4*.

"It's not just a rumour, Jimmy, is it?" she said and I felt terrible because of how her face looked.

I just shook my head, whispered, "No" and tried not to look too, um, overly-butt-nuggetty.

The cop car continued along the street really slowly and that's when I figured it out.

PAIGE: What?

JIMMY: Who?

PAIGE: *You!* What did you figure out?

JIMMY: I grabbed Norma's hand and we ran up behind the car and kept close to it, trying not to die from exhaustion, because I didn't think *they* would shoot up a cop car.

If the cops stopped the car and came out and asked us what the Hell we were doing, well at least we could ask them to 'Protect and serve' us.

But for reasons you'll understand later, I couldn't tell the cops about Grace and that hurt, badly.

Kinda strange they didn't seem too interested in two terrified faces on people dressed for Echo Beach, but then I'm not a cop and I only know what they look out for on-screen.

Plus they were overweight and eating police jelly donuts.

That was when I...said a silent goodbye to Grace's beautiful body.

The car sped up a little and we had to hurry to keep up and the smoky fumes were killing us, making us cough and choke, like being at one of Bob's parties.

It turned a corner and we were right behind and then it happened.

PAIGE: "It"?

JIMMY: We collided with two heavy shadows!

Slaaam!

And then my heart stopped because everything went black.

I knew that we were dead.

And, I had these new sensations, feelings.

A stomach pain like I swallowed razorfish.

Or a squirrel.

Legs like my bones had been taken out.

And guilt, big as The Berlin Wall.

Because, it was all my fault we were here.

Everybody knew there was a secret world off-island!

But I just *had* to be the one who just had to know.

Every time a newcomer arrived, it just made me think all the more. It wasn't just the usual 'kids grow up and leave home' or Rebel Yell.

It wasn't even to work my way through the hopefully billions of girls on the planet.

I wondered if I'd live long enough?

No. It was to discover more about...just one person.

The old man.

Great, really great granddad.

Him and...and all his talk about his *mysterious past.*

I had to.

I'm sorry.

PAIGE: Sorry?

JIMMY: That's how it happened.

PAIGE: That...?

JIMMY: That I dragged my close friends, lovers, into their deaths.

And that's what I thought.

Poor Gracie.

The First of the Gang to Die.

The Darkness.

Everything went black because something was pulled over my head and my hair and the shock made my heart pound like, I don't know...a scene from *Hairspray?*
I yanked at it, but something was strong and it wasn't me.
The scream was deafening, it was a roar, it was an ocean, and I think that might have been me, too.
Just as suddenly, whatever was pulled over my hair, wasn't, and then I heard it.
PAIGE: "It"?
JIMMY: Laughter.
The shadow peeled away and stood under the extremely pathetic and pissy street-lamp.
It was Mac and I just cannot believe this!
Mac!
Is that an abbreviation or a nickname?
"Jeezuz!"
"Nah, it's only me" he says.
Soon the whole island will be here, I thought.
"Fix your freakin hair, Pixie."
I fixied it.
Mac was the kinda tough guy in the gang, the main man, the top jockey, the big cheese, the real deal, the head honcho, the flip-flop, the whole enchilada, the Mac in machismo, *hombre. El Duderino.*
Um...sorry...um...
He always had all the answers and told you that and bossed you and loved his own voice and loved women who loved him back, big time. And although he's not either that big or small, he *is* a strong wiry guy, like his granddaddy. Things were never dull around Mac.
He always wore his trademark blue jeans and white tee-shirt. And if it was true he was around n-n-n-

nineteen, then he was the oldest in the group, but not the most mature.

That would probably be Marsha, can you believe?

And he was always challenging me to this or that.

But, even though he is angry young man with his Badfinger jabbing in your face, he really was cool and his dirt-bike seemed part of him, like *Robocop*.

He looked at me and laughed, chuckle-wuckling right in my face, but not taking the rise.

He stared at the cop car picking up speed and it really is dark round this corner.

"Don't tell me. You hid on the boat?"

He scowled, then "Whatafreakinboutitshitface?" with his multiple sweargasms.

"Nice to see you too, Mac" and he snorted.

So I'm shaking my head in that 'we're all going to not live' way when it happens.

PAIGE: "It" again?

JIMMY: The second shadow, in the…um…

But this one is more welcome than any other welcome shadow I know.

I'd like to introduce to you, the one and only:

Mouth, and other body-parts watering, *Marsha*.

She's a dangel, sashaying into the light like she was walking onto a yacht and she Takes my Breath Away.

Marsha is *Crazy/Beautiful,* the most tasty, sassy, sultry, exciting woman I've ever seen in real life or in any movie, apart from maybe Rihanna, *Frida* or Beyoncé, or any of the Playboy sex magazines you have…you *do* have those, don't you?…or any dream. Her skin is the colour of hot chocolate or Brown Sugar which I could lick forever ever.

See those hips sway.

Oh, and that neck, and those little ears.

And The Flaming Lips? They were made for me.

Her hair is big, it's piled high, it's reaching for the stars, and she carries curves like you design in your head when you're having sex, alone.

PAIGE: Alone?

JIMMY: With your...you know...

PAIGE: Oh.

JIMMY: She loves lots of jewelry, and it loves her right back.

She's kinda poetic and musical and also plays guitar in that sexy way that women do.

Think Robert Palmer's "Addicted To Love" and you're a hundredth of the way there.

Marsha gets called a dippy-hippy on the island, and *profuckative* which is so fucool.

Her voice purrs and you could listen forever to her whisper in your ear, something like

Her fashion sense is funky and crazy and wild and Va Va Voom and you maybe guessed that I really quite kinda maybe thought about more than eye-smooching her.

Not just in that thrashing in the water kinda way, even.

And, she's as beautiful inside, too.

Norma is first to speak but in a spluttery "Marsha! It's really you!" kinda way.

They fall into each other's hugs with fits of the crazy giggling and shrieking that girls do.

But, crying big crocodile tears, too.

They part and Marsha opens welcoming arms out to me.

Now, as much as I've tried over the years-*boy* have I tried-and as good-looking and full of the Wonderstuff that girls want as I am, I have been trying for years to get Marsha to open up those...arms to me.

Maybe it's because we're on V-a-c-a-t-i-o-n?

I gave her a big Chiclet smile and we hugged.

She smelled like...nothing I could find in this dictionary.

I didn't want to break the spell, but she did.

And, though it was tough, I had to tell her.

"Marsha…they…they…killed Grace."

Her face went all twisty and Norma took her hand.

"What?! *Who?! Whoa!!* Oh, no…" she just trailed off and even Mac looked the tiniest bit spooked, no Little Feat.

We all kinda exchanged the same sickly look at the same sickly time.

It went all quiet, then…

All the girls totally went *fffrrreeeaaakkk!*

I've never seen that in real life and didn't know how to deal with it.

Even action-man Mac was useless.

Somehow, I managed to calm them down after what seemed like a long minute.

"Guys, we don't have much time. The bad people are somewhere around here."

"Where is she?" Marsha looked totally horrified but not ready to believe it yet. She was staring all around and crying, but wanted to, had to know.

"We…I had to leave her, Marsha," and she looked like she could stab me in the face with a stiletto-heel.

She stared at blood spots on my polo shirt.

"We've got to get out of here," I said as if no one else thought of that and I was the boss of the bleedin' obvious, like the English guys on the island say.

Now, we all knew a terrible truth.

The rumour was no *rumour.*

And nobody wanted to say it aloud, but I think everybody felt vomity and toiletty at the same time.

Then, I heard a quiet scuffle right behind me!

I whirled around, expecting?

PAIGE: What?

JIMMY: I don't know.

Another something over the head.

Cops.

The killers.

Random-man.
Our waitress for the evening?
But not another islander!
Andy's just a kid, what, thirteen of your years, maybe?
But there's a kinda wiseness in his baby blues.
Describe wise, he's got a Thin White Duke face, spotty
like it's been splattered by pizza. His longish,
stragglish, blondish hair always needs a shower, his
strangely scary dark baggy clothes ditto. Probably his
scrawny bones too. He also has a strange mysterious
quality like he knows something you don't.
Damned if all of that, those eyes and shyness and
thinness and lack of laundryness and laid-backness
aren't a total magnet for girls?
He'll never want for action.
And he's one of my favourite people on the island.
He just kinda stands there, more like hangs, in a kinda
'I don't do gravity' way and smiles goofily but with 'star
quality' then for some reason, I suddenly desperately
want to be a casting director or a producer and call up
The Gersh Agency or Lynn Stalmaster and arm-wrestle
about cast, availability, rates and up-and-comers and
auditions because that's their job but insist on certain
people 'cuz —
Everybody works for *The Producers*! Seen that movie?
We should maybe run part of the opening credits here:

MURDER CITY
A major emotion picture.

STARRING
(in order of appearance)

Jimmy as reluctant hero, searching...
Norma as funny, blonde babe
Crawford as man Hunter
Hutchence as woman Hunter

Grace as the sultry one
Mac as angry would-be leader
Marsha as hippy-musical-love-interest-sex-bomb-sex-bomb
Andy as acne'd-shy-quirky-but-chicks-love-that.

And I would maybe cast Rita Ora as Marsha and DJ Squalls' kid brother if he had one as Andy.
Norma, with more than a hint of understatementness says:
"Andy! I don't *believe* it!!!"
Then launches her body at his, gives him a hug and not in a big-sisterly way either that to me, promised many years of future fun.
Has anyone ever come up with a cool new word for *virgin* in cool New York?
Andy's beetroot face squeaks and gasps and gurgles and burbles and I swear I heard something go —
Snaaap!
Even if he wanted to speak, I don't think he could, so he attempts a smile at me.
"Andy..." Norma started to speak about Grace I guessed, but I put a finger to my lips.
I grabbed Andy and gave him a bear-hug and said:
"Kid!" like The Pretenders song, like a big bro.
And he says "Hey man" and I thought of "Suffragette City," Ziggy '72.
Everybody just watched me and I thought it was because they knew they should not all be here, and that's what I would think.
Which was true, but, I was also thinking, a list.
One, we don't have time for this.
Two, mega-über-urgent, priority-wise? Who gets the blame?
So I shouted...
"We gotta get out of this place!"
PAIGE: Again?

JIMMY: Only in a more Mac kinda loudy, brassy, bossy, actually very nearly leadery way.

Mac is right on cue.

"Do I have to keep telling you?" and the first thing I noticed was that he didn't...

"Don't tell me what to freakin do!"

And he has his Badfinger out, but you still love when he swears to the rhythm.

But, bullet in the head-wise, I decide we're in the wrong place at the wrong time.

"You're not wrong, you're right."

But still, the girls and Andy were staring at me in that 'Take charge, guy' kinda way and that was so not *me,* no siree, oh no, not at all.

I must have showed it, 'cuz the girls produced floods of tears and both blurt out what sounded like:

"You think we *led* them here?!!!"

Yes, I did. But my big guilt trip was, who led *you* here?

And with just that, I said...

"Let's go" and started to run to where I hoped was the place where the watchmen and murdererists were not.

I didn't know how to be a leader, so I just wished that they would see the sense of what I was doing and follow, and fast.

I was building up a little breathless speed and kinda half-turned, half-whirled.

The girls had Mac by his elbows, kinda draggy with him, girl-style and he lapped it up but pretended he didn't, Mac-style.

Norma has an arm around Andy's waist and he just shrugged and tagged along in a clunky loping motion, Andy-style.

I was trying to learn how to maybe, *lead?* Jimmy-style.

So, off I galloped, in my head kinda Harry Styles, but truly?

Gangnam style.

Breathe.

This bit is partly what Oh Ancient One told me, partly what I figured out, partly what I seen for myself, partly guess-work, partly theory, partly a shot-in-the-dark, partly c-for conjecture, partly Mystery And Imagination, partly what I didn't want to believe and partly what my heart wouldn't accept and partly from seeing too many movies, good, bad and David Lynch, Jimmy Stewart from Mars.

Here it was.

We know the rumour is no lie.

Grace's killers were the hunters.

But before I get into that, I need to get into this.

You see, no one was ever known to have wanted to leave the island over all its years.

I don't know how many years either, but a lot, maybe sixty, seventy?

Anyway, no one ever left.

PAIGE: Ever?

JIMMY: Never.

Why would anyone?

It was everything, *had* everything.

Anyway, where would you go?

How would you get there?

And what would you do when you got wherever?

And how would you get back?

All these questions and more.

PAIGE: Amazing.

JIMMY: Astounding.

PAIGE: Makes my head spin.

JIMMY: One very important topic though, was that...
You would have to get a...*gulp*...j-o-b!

What's a job? What do you do? For how long? What for?

PAIGE: Who for?

JIMMY: It's just that I have...WAS.

PAIGE: "WAS"?

JIMMY: Work Aversion Syndrome.

I knew nothing about:

Hard work, employees, a *factory, no vacancies,*
day shift, night shift, swing shift, doubletime, overtime,
undertime? Deadlines, customer service, the customer
is king, or *the boss* or *sexual harassment* or *business,*
but I have heard of *are you looking for business?* Or a
businessman, business card, business class or
merchant bankers, false expense claim, insider trading,
the financial district, fat cats or *I overslept* or *drinking*
with the boss or *shove your job up your ass* or *I quit,*
debit or *credit* or *maxed out Mastercard* or
redundancies or *promotion* or *strikes and unions* or *bad*
debt or *the repo man.*

But I knew about *working Nine to Five.*

Which leads me to the 'Why?' and just *listen* to the
answer.

It *earns you wages* which you use to buy *nice stuff,*
then marry *a nice girl* and have *nice kids.*

You're kidding, right?

That whole thing was like, way too...*nice.*

Truth be told, I must say, all this niceness and working
for a livingness sounded more than a little scary —

PAIGE: No kiddin'.

JIMMY: — so no wonder no one wanted to leave,
right?

The subject just did not take much of anyone's time up
and never became party material.

We had plenty other stuff to gossip about.

But, it was an island rule.

No one leaves.

And another more scary rumour was that if you did
The hunters come after you.

No one had ever seen them, so we were like, well, I
don't want to go anywhere, do you?

Nope.

Exactly.

Hey, have you heard X and Y or…

Did you watch the new…

Or, did you catch Mackenzie the other night?

Anyway, back to the hunters, I'm afraid. They sit in probably an evil, dark vehicle with dark privacy glass to plan your dark fate in, like, the dark, privately?

And if *rarity* was their thing, then maybe one of only 95, the 1985 model AC 3000 ME?

Or if was a *muscle car,* perhaps the 1963 Corvette Stingray, or the '69 Camaro, '71 Roadrunner, '72 Firebird, or for raw *speed*, the Ferrari 328 GTS 1987 model?

For *style*, there's the 1947 Bentley Mk VI 2-door Convertible coupe, sir?

But, let it not be a freakin jeep machine, which are just so genuinely funcool and…

Just how does car crazy great granddad *know* these things?

Another rumour was that the founders had television and newspapery stuff and the old man was allowed to see them if he wanted.

The hunters car would of course really be all of the above and be dangerous and black and shiny-winey, outside and inside, with maybe touchy-feely suede seats.

PAIGE: Oooooooooh…mmm…

JIMMY: The hunters would use gadgets like 'computerers' to find out about information. The oldie called it 'satnaff' or something? And other stuff, but mostly to find anyone who escaped.

Like *us.*

And on those probably black suede seats would sit the hunters asses, plotting what to do to you when they got you.

Not *if* they got you.

They would be like the car, sleek, fast, cool, fly, bold, dress in dark clothes, be full of gadgets and deadly when they hit you.
Maybe they would talk in movie murmurs and dialogue. Another rumour was they were supposed to even be a couple and maybe the guy might sound and look kinda grim raperish and be big and...

Michael Madsen.
Don't cut my ear off! How will I wear Ray-Bans?

...but maybe feel bad when he put that silent bullet through an innocent young woman's lovely head.
And maybe the woman would look and sound like her in *Twin Peaks,* the sexy brunette, something Finn? Fenn? Never seen her in anything again. Hey, I'm a poet and I know it, hope I...and have manicured nails and a shiny new expensive haircut and a hand-tailored suit and designer jewelry.
Only, be ruthless and heartless and pitiless and countless other words ending in 'less', more than the man. The Female Of The Species Thing old guy said. They would obviously both have hyper-thin black probably German guns with maybe long silencers to totally blank sound out, so a bullet seemed to hit from nowhere when it was them all the time.
And maybe they would have the latest cellphone which would be tiny but bigger than in *Zoolander* and one of them would say into the latest Sony brand cellphone in that movie murmur:

ONE OF THEM
(murmuring)
She breathed in, then didn't
breathe out.

Which I admit is cool dialogue, but they would be
talking about someone I cared about, so it is funcool.
I'm so scared about the future.
PAIGE: Whew. Gotcha.
JIMMY: 10-4, good buddy.
PAIGE: I know what you mean...
JIMMY: Anyway, the woman would be classy and have
a fetish...lurve that word...for say, shoes...OK, it's
maybe my fetish, because I seen a lot of shoes
pictured in Zagat's.
I've got it with me.
It's a crumpled mess and there's blood on it.
It's...it's poor Grace's blood and here's 'the hard for me
to do shoes' list:
Jimmy Choos.
Prada.
Louboutin.
Louis Vuitton.
Manolo Blahnik.
Gucci.
And something unpron...unannouncable?
And have them lying in the back seat so she can
admire them and herself in them, but not wear them
outside.
Because she would need to be able to *hunt.*
But, and this is the hugest but...
Just who would one of them be calling on the island?

SOMEONE ON THE ISLAND
(like a founder?)
And?

In a sinister, but not movie nasty voice.
Because he or she is real.
Try asking Grace.
(Turns to transcriber.) Excuse me Peach, can I have
some Evian brand water?'

(Jimmy stifles a cry. Handed a bottled water. Drinks.)
JIMMY: Thanks... *Glub!*...It just... *Glub, glub!*...hurts.
Next, one of them would say:

ONE OF THEM
Just her. Cops arrived.

What he would mean by that is, he only managed to kill
one of us to death.
Someone on the island would think, and maybe we:

CUT TO:
INT. SOMEONE ON THE ISLAND'S OFFICE - NIGHT

The room is expensive and e-for expansive and big.
The décor will be breathtaking and m-for minimalistic at
the same time, with brand new shiny stuff and really
old antique stuff like sculptures and painter brands like
Gustav Klit dotted just so, to convey understated
tasteness.
There will be a boardroom table where all the founders
would have um...bored meetings? to discuss brands of
stuff they wanted, or
It will have huge picture windows, floor-to-ceiling.
Does that make it a window, or a wall?
PAIGE: It —
JIMMY: Who cares?
Brilliant sunshine would stream in, not yellow but white,
like high-grade cocaine. Ever see *Blow*?
If you could stand that brightness, you could go to that
window and take it in.
Magnificent views of crystal-clear water like the Perrier
ocean, gently lapping like it was on a giant timer onto
dazzling, unmarked sand.
The sand is also cocaine-white, looks just out the
wrapper, or imported from *The Beach* then bleached.
Beached n' bleached.

Naked people stroll, getting themselves wet, then cooling down from the heat.

And past that, there's another sea. This one has u-for undulating lush mounds, like women in green string bikinis.

The green is grass, trimmed like lady's fingernails, little sand-pits sprinkled here and there.

They have a name, or is it a phrase, for this.

It doesn't do justice to this design of sportiness.

It's called...a *golf* of course.

Back in the room, gadget-wise, yes, there will be, but what?

I don't know.

You got any ideas?

PAIGE: I —

JIMMY: I suppose stuff to get news back from the hunters.

Seatnav?

Big screens and little cellphones?

Maybe like the lawyer's office that Al Pacino had in...I forget. *And Justice For All*?

I've also heard that there's a head of security up there, but nobody knows his name or what he looks like, but the rumour is he keeps us on:

'The protected' list.

But, protected from what?

Or who?

And, quite frankly, protect us how?

Are we in danger?

What kind?

Why?

When?

And now that I know it's true about escaping then the hunters coming to kill you.

Why?

Who are they?

Where do they come from?

Why not let us live?
Is that protecting us?
And I'm starting to really wonder why I've never really
thought about all this before and my chipmunk brain
hurts and thinks Ty-one-on Extra Knock-out-ol.
Anyway, someone on the island would wear quality
brands of beach wear and formal wear for meetings
and big glasses maybe by Ralph Lauren and would talk
to the hunters in a powerful, intense, important way,
but not brash or badwordy because he's so important
and say:

SOMEONE ON THE ISLAND
There will be no slip-ons.

Short, kinda bullying, without seeming like that and...

ONE OF THEM
There won't be.

Knowing they're being chewed out really ssshhh *quietly*
but having to take it, then...

SOMEONE ON THE ISLAND
You've no idea what's at stake.

Then just looks out the big windows at the water
lapping onto the sand like soap powder.
Maybe even wonders about playing around at golf and
doesn't even need to hang up because one of them will
and that's kinda cool.
But me, I get to wondering...who is *this?*
And...they don't know what a *steak* is?
I think I might start smoking to calm my nerves, maybe
Marlboro, man.

Jimmy Jimmy.

Now the gang are all staring at me and I know what they've gone and went and done.
Unspokenly Alice Coopered me, Elected *me* to tell Andy about Grace.
I do not want to be The One, like *The Matrix*. The Chosen. Who chose? Why me?
We've run and walked quite a ways from where *it* happened.
And now that we're maybe safe, or at least safer than before, we are exhausted out and still really Purple Hazed.
So when I said "We should lose ourselves in a crowd" Mac says "Who made you *The Big Boss?*" and I waited for the sweargasm, only nope.
We turned from this quite busy, dark street into a really, really busy less dark street.
And there's tidal waves of people rolling and surging everywhere and it makes me queasy and makes us even more nervy because we don't like so many people around, bumping into you on purpose and not saying sorry, or giving you leery or strange or queer or odd looks, or you trip over some or they stink or ask for money and make threats or idle warnings or are vomity drunk or miles high or taking a leak in the glittery gutter and have glassy eyes or make funny noises and jerky twitches…

Care in the community.
Look after them. We can't.

And I remember the old guy saying New York is the city that never sleeps. Just like rust.
I thought that must be why everybody looks so tired and kinda annoyed.

Mac was walking and nudging me in the ribs while his head nodded in Andy's direction where right in front of us, Norma and Marsha had Andy in either arm.

Andy in a girlwich.

Lucky man.

I just mock glared at Mac because this was not the time or the place to be telling a kid like Andy that his close friend was shot to death and gunned down in the street.

Oh, and hey Andy, guess what? I nearly forgot?

We're probably next.

So, I caught up a little with Andy and the girls and just said "Hey, people" in a kinda so *movie-speak* way and I knew that girl radar would pick up on my r-for reluctance to let Andy in on Grace's murder.

Sure enough, Marsha smiled at me more than Norma did, so I tried my line again.

"We can lose ourselves in this crowd" and Mac was instantly behind.

"The take charge guy" and quicker than *Flash,* Norma's usual sense of funness kicks right in.

"You know Mac, I like you better as designated scapegoat."

Must be some kind of zoo pet animal.

PAIGE: Ha-ha.

JIMMY: The girls laughed but Andy, never offensive to anyone, barely half-smiled.

Mac spit on the ground as he does when he's in one of his *Raging Bull* moods and I only fake laugh, 'cuz I didn't really get those long words, even though I at least know it was a joke, maybe.

Mac snorted like Mr. Ed and gave a big horse laugh and I blanked him, focussing all my efforts on avoiding people who all should be in *A Day at the Races.*

They should visit the island for lessons in what speed to walk at.

And politeness.

I wasn't just doing that, really, I was watching the reaction the girls were getting from mostly, but not always, men.

But truthfully, my eyes fixed on Marsha's so fucool walk.

You can tell the way she used it…That strut…

But, I'm in denial.

I was giving all my attention to her, so I didn't have to think about taking Andy aside.

But suddenly, he turned right around and stared at me, in a 'You are the boss of me' way and I started to panic until he says:

"Jimmy, I'm hangry, Jimmy" and then…

PAIGE: These odd words. *Hangry?*

JIMMY: Pissed coz you…um…need snacked?

So, Mac noticed how Andy does this and he is not pleased.

"He speaks!" Mac says and his face got even more twisty when I went:

"Some people only speak when they've got something worth saying."

Profound.
Smarter than I really am.

And that impressed mostly me and maybe the girls and they sang.

PAIGE: Please don't.

JIMMY: "Us too, Jimmy. And thirsty."

"Me too, Jimmy." *(Sarcastic voice.)* Mac says with a face to match and he goes

"Oooh. It's truuuue, all truuuue. You escape and Scary Monsters come and get you and kill yooooo dead" like Vincent Price and looks at Andy who looks at me, confused.

Of all people, it's Marsha who turns on Mac and she doesn't miss.

"Listen, turd-brain! You followed us, the hunters followed you. Then they...they killed poor Grace. It's our fault, it's *all* our fault."

And I felt terrible because I couldn't look at Andy and escaping was all *my* idea and I wondered if Marsha meant that, instead of blaming us all.

Mac clutches his heart and in that Mac way

"You really got me" and mock dies, but I can only think of The Kinks '64 hit. Not the VH remake. Eddie Van shredding.

Not Mac's best move because the girls rounded on him together and I knew they were thinking about poor Grace and that's why Norma said:

"You...*Shatner*...Grace died! They *killed* her!"

I reckon she could have slapped his face.

Nobody had paid Andy any attention until I looked over my shoulder, like t-for tentatively.

He was standing statue-still, staring at the ground, people just barging past like he's not there.

Barge!

His face looked like stone and even less milky than usual, like a gloopy sloppy breakfast cereal.

I went to him and took him by both shoulders, really bony shoulders like he never *did* really eat.

"Andy, I'm so sorry. I was supposed to tell you. I...didn't know how. I'm so sorry" I tried.

He looked at me with his chocolate-drop, puppy-dog eyes and I really felt for him. He was hurting badly. He...cried.

I took him in my arms and hugged him tight and that made us both cry.

Sniff!

"It's OK, Jimmy. It's a hard thing to tell," he said in a choky yet really kinda clever Andy way.

Mac looked away, found guilty, and the girls came over and we all hugged Andy, long and hard.

All you need is love.

I was racking part of my sprout brain about what to do, how to move on.

I led us away and I thought that Mac looked like he might disappear and be on his own.

"Mac, let's go and eat something."

Luckily, we came to a square where there was a store, but even more people and they poured in and out of the store like aimless ants.

I wondered who all these people were and where they were all going and why.

They're going to, like...jobs?

"Our waitress for the evening said pawn some jewelry, right?" I said and I had to look away from Marsha because that put a bright white spotlight on her face.

"Jimmy, what are you asking?" she said and I said.

"We need money, Marsha. Money, money, money —"

(Jimmy attempts Abba in his terrible 'singing' voice.)

PAIGE: Ugh.

JIMMY: — trying to kinda lighten up because she and her jewelry were very much in love with each other.

I imagined being her necklace, just above her perky breasts and able to see and appreciate.

Or her belly piercing.

Or...no. Too ooow, painful.

We close in on the store which says Seven Eleven and I thought of about at least three movies.

Marsha meantime isn't looking her best, all sad and angry and glarey, but she knows she's all we've got, so "Let's find a pawn shop, then" and that was brave, what she said.

I realise we're going to need to ask one of the bleary-eyed irritated people with bags the size of Samsonite suitcases under their eyes and arms.

I try several "Can you please tell us where a pawn shop is pleases?" politely, and with a toothy grin.

I tried a lot of people, but they were all full of speed, and that was that.

Mac was sniggering a lot at me, but Andy looked like a shell-shocked soldier in *Saving Private Ryan* slouching against the wall of Seven Eleven, or a Gap poster-boy. The girls were attracting plenty of attention as per and I wondered if we'd be better getting one of *them* to stop a passer-by from passing-by.

But just as I thought that and moved over to them to run it past them...

"Unfriendly place, huh?" says this guy behind my ear and way too close for my liking, invading my personal space and air like he knew me.

I turn around and there stands this little guy who reminded me of Dustin Hoffman's Ratso Rizzo —

PAIGE: — *Midnight Cowboy?*

JIMMY: Jon Voight was very movie Cary Grant and I thought, if he ever has kids...

Anyway, this little guy is the total opposite of Mr. Voight. He gives this big, yellow-tooth smile and he needs dental floss and mouthwash and oral hygiene wash and every other kind of wash.

Marsha and Norma are curious as we've never met anyone like him.

Mac spits and slouches and glares as he always does when he first meets anyone, male or female or not.

The little guy held his little ratty hand out and I shook it, even though I knew it would be filthy disgusting.

I even managed a smile because we were getting nowhere with all the other people.

A quiet voice in my head was asking 'How come he's the only person not in a hurry?' but I ignored it.

I would come to listen to that voice later.

"Hey, mister. Can you help us, please?" I suggested.

He smiled and nodded, then eyed up the girls and mostly Marsha's jewelry and perky breasts.

It was a really strange kinda sideways nod.

"How can Mr. Wendal help you pretty things?"

None of us had ever been called that, like the English band from the 60s, and I thought of *Arrested Development* too. The show, not the hip-hoppers.

"Well, we um…need to find a pawn shop?" I said and looked into his little ratty eyes.

He clasped his hands together like he was in church. Nope, we don't do churches, or God…our Gods are guitar gods…rock gods…and he turned really pleased.

"You got lucky babe" he says and I thought about Tom Petty, my heart breaking, then he took me by the elbow.

"Step into my orifice, Jimmy," he says.

And he knows my name? Whoa.

PAIGE: Huh.

JIMMY: And kinda starts to lead me away, then winks at the girls to follow, but not Mac or Andy.

I wondered what his orifice looked like.

"We could do with some luck," I said, then "Everybody just doesn't even look at us."

He smiled and nodded and "Welcome to *Sin City*" was what he said and that really mind-melted me.

I don't remember seeing him in it.

Was he hiding under Mickey Rourke's make-up?

"We're not used to being ignored," I said and he said "You're *not?*" he says and he really does look amazed.

Marsha says "Jimmy, I'm not sure…" and trails off not wanting to be too tough on the little guy.

"Where you guys from?" he asked.

That, friendsters, is one very tough question.

I just kinda looked at him, then not.

He looked around all of us one by one and everybody shuffled about kinda sorta.

"I know where you're coming from," he said and I was amazed and about to ask how he knew, then remembered I've heard that line before.

He gave that nod again like he was a good character actor in a bad movie, Bob Hoskins-style.

"Understood. Mr. Wendal is very discreet," was what I think he said.

I looked up the word.

And he's kinda sorta leading me by the arm which I don't like and so I untangle from him and d-for disengage and he does the nod.

Nod!

"Mr. Wendal can help Jimmy and the beautiful princess," he says to me and Marsha.

"I...um...are *you* Mr. Wendal?" I say because his way of talking was peculiar and weirdness.

"I am the one and only —" *(Jimmy 'sings' yet again.)*

PAIGE: God no...Please...stop...

JIMMY: So I have a short think and consider our options.

Re-like-phrase.

Our *only* option.

"Let's just go, gang," and give a kinda beggy pleady look and...

Without waiting for a reply...

"Walk this way," says little Mr. Wendal like the so fucool RUN-DMC-slash-Aerosmith song and shuffles along, leading us all away into...

The Money Fingers.

It's like he's taking us to the *Edge of Tomorrow.*
It's as black and scary as the pier and just as deserted, but more stinky.
Mac doesn't like Mr. Wendal I can tell, and neither does Marsha.
Because he'll be the one that takes her precious.
Andy just keeps up that half-smile, without talking.
Norma can't make her mind up about Mr. Wendal and keeps catching me watching Marsha.
Like she knows that my thoughts are.
Mr. Wendal keeps trying to talk to us about random stuff, but none of us feel like talking and, manners and R-e-s-p-e-c-t aside, not to him.
He doesn't ask again where we're coming from because he knows.
We turn a corner, whip around it, then another —
Whiiip! — and you know, I'm getting more than a little nervy and lost with each whip-around.
The street lights that actually give out street light are pale yellow, like thin custard. Like lemon Jell-o.
The streets themselves were…crunchy under my feet…interesting.
There was Garbage everywhere and broken windows and stuff painted on walls like Fannypack, Balkan Beat Box, Uptown Funk, Girl and *The Magnificent Seven* which Mac pointed out to me, was it the Steve McQueen flick or The Clash song?…confusing us both.
Chasing Cars seemed to be the thing around here, because some kids sprinted after a rusty car down the street and it would probably join the long line of wrecks, soon.
A few red-eyed drinkers stood around a bucket of fire and Marsha pointed that out 'cuz she was really cold.
The drinkers never even said hello or howdy or how-are-ya or a thing.

I guess we all would have been more than spooked if the street wasn't so familiar from, you know that movie...um?

Oh yeah, I know.

Every movie.

And after a while, Mr. Wendal pointed out this tiny light in the distance.

"That's it. My pal's shop."

He did the nod — *Nod!* — and a wink and smiled at Marsha and she looked really sad and I felt so sorry for her.

As we got closer, we could see a smashed sign that used to say 'Pawn shop' and now said 'Pawn sh...'

It looked ancient and there was a dog barking inside and chains and locks and bars and sounds like we were actually starring in *It Follows.*

We don't have pets on the island because it's supposed to be risky to bring them in and they make too much noise and mess and need to be walked and groomed and petted and then get sick and die.

Hutchence had a pet rat for a while, but that was just to scare Crawford because rats terrified her in a *1984* with rats eating your up your face kinda Richard Burtony-John Hurt way.

Lurv the Sex Crime soundtrack.

Inside, the light was so small, it was like it was a candle and we could just make out two people? through the dirtiest windows I had ever not seen through in real life.

Marsha was getting more kinda Zombie twitchy the closer we got, so I put my arm around her and she liked that but Norma didn't.

We stood outside the place while Mr.Wendal hammered on the door with his little scratchy claw.

Bang! Bang!

"Hey, Joe!" he croaks, in a Hendrixy cough-cough groan.

I smiled and looked over at Marsha to check her reaction to *that,* but she's too strung out.

Then Mr. Wendal screams like a stomped-on kitty and keeps battering and slapping this filthy door.

Bang! Bang! Bang!

We could hear a man's voice inside sounding mad.

"Don't let them give you anything more than a hundred," Mr. Wendal said to me and Marsha.

"That's a lot of money?" Marsha asked.

"Heaps" he goes and I remembered from movies that it's usually millions that they wanted.

It took a while and a lot of noise with all the locks being opened inside but eventually, a guy opened the door.

"Whadyawan?" and sounded gruff and angry but funny, like John Goodman after four hours singing like AC/DC.

"I got some good customers for ya, Joe."

And Mr. Joe opens the door a little wider to give the good customers a look.

He was like *Bigfoot*, high, round and fat, wearing a filthy-wilthy vest that was only ever white once and maybe just for 5 minutes and a big leather coat and a silver cow-horn buckle was holding up faded and holed jeans. You call it d-for distressed I think, but these weren't just distressed, they should have been in an institution and pumped with drugs, like in *One Flew Over the Cuckoo's Nest*.

Mr. Joe needed an extreme makeover. A tailor, a shave, shower, mouthwash, dental work, skin treatments, a haircut, a head transplant and a new body.

He looked over our shoulders first, at Mr. Wendal, then the drinkers.

Then, us.

He wore an eye-glass and when his other eye was finished checking out us, his eye-glass settled on Marsha.

He smiled and I really wished he hadn't.
Then, he opened the door wide to let us in first, like a
person with manners.
Mr. Wendal was last in and I glanced behind to see him
rub his finger and thumb at Joe.
Money fingers, I heard someone call them, but I didn't
understand.
But I really think that's a great name for a band.
PAIGE: Not bad. I —
JIMMY: There was a rustling sound and it got just a
little lighter.
A woman, I think, a bit like *Swampthing*, stood up.
She was lighting a candle…never seen a real
one before, we use electric ones…and appeared by
Mr. Joe's side.
She was like, really old, maybe forty something, but
dressed like a cartoon witch from *Scooby-Doo* and just
as bent over and horrible and stanky and smelly
clothes as well.
I hoped that she wouldn't speak.
"Out of towners" she said…was she asking or telling
us? And her voice would turn milk sour and her smile
was worse than his.
"*Way* out of towners."
She tried a smile again but I could see she was overly
puzzled and she went back behind the counter to
stroke a mangy mutt.
Marsha sat on a grubby little low stool and handed Mr.
Joe a watch and even though we never use them,
Marsha looked really upset.
He had Stiff Little Fingers and took the watch which he
called a timepiece in a greedy, graspy, gropey way and
looked on the back with his eyeglass-spyglass.
He let out a little harrumph.
"Harrumph."
Then, he handed it to the woman to look at.

She used an eyeglass, looked on the back and nodded to herself.

She passed it back to him.

He looked at the back again and we all wondered why.

Then, he weighed it in his hand, then on little scales.

Then, he looked at the back again and said:

"Inscription legit?" and Marsha and me looked at each other, mixed up.

"Um, li...jet?" I managed and he kept his eyes on the watch and said:

"Lee-git-i-mate. Not ree-po. Gen-yoo-wine. Ko-sher."

"Of course. I think." Marsha said and she was pissed.

"Stolen's OK," he mumbled to his, what, wife-thing?

Mr. Joe nodded and said "I'll give you a hundred" and that sounded a good deal.

The woman produced some banknotes and they were disgustingly filthy crumply, then counted them out on the dirty glass counter.

I could tell Marsha didn't want to touch them, so I grabbed them and stuffed them in my pocket.

"That a lot of money?" Marsha said.

"Loads," Mr. Joe said with his smile.

"How long will it last?" I asked and woman-thing spoke.

"Forever, you don't spend any," and I nodded.

"And we can buy the watch back?" Marsha said.

"Long's you got money," Mr. Joe said.

The woman was eyeing Marsha's bangles and chains and stuff.

"Could always pawn more stuff," and Marsha looked totally horrified at the idea.

Mr. Joe ugly smiled at Marsha.

"Or sell something else."

We all kinda looked at each other and I'm thinking 'What, my Levi's? Hair? My kidneys?'

OK, not my hair, but I've seen those movies.

And Mr.Joe fixes this leery look on Marsha.

"Lady there's sitting on a fortune," and he stares at her and so does woman-thing and Mr. Wendell and we don't understand what happened or changed, but we know something just did.

I vaguely remember some movie with that kinda dialogue and guess it's something kinda sorta smutty, so I smile feebly and and nobly and lead Marsha out by the hand which Norma doesn't like.

Mr. Wendal is right behind.

Clomp! Clomp!

"Where can we buy some clothes, Mr. Wendal?" and he looks pleased to be able to help again.

"Top a the road, hang a left, stores are right there, kid."

"We can't thank you enough," Marsha says.

"I think you can," and gives her a leery lusty look, but she is mystified, puzzled, waiting for more and sure enough…

"I've got overheads, expenses," he says and we all look at each other, puzzling our puzzlers.

Must be for his orifice.

But Marsha has figured that he maybe wants or needs or deserves something.

"Of course!" and that makes him reach up to one of her necklaces and pulls it over her head not too gently.

"Thanks. I'll take this."

Marsha is surprised and shocked and petrified and horrified.

But then he says "And…this" and steals a kiss from Marsha's mouth, making sure to brush his ratty hand over her perky right breast.

It's more than I've ever done.

Me, Mac and Marsha collide as we all go to slap him at the same time —

Slap slap slap!

— but Norma and Andy get in the way on purpose.

"I'll break your little weasely face!" Mac snaps and I have to struggle to hold him back.

"Don't Mac. He helped us!" Marsha says and you have to admit that took something special.

Love her.

Mr. Wendal just smiles, turns and scurries away somewhere really fast, stuffing the necklace into his old coat pocket.

You would call him a scam artist I think.

"I'm sorry, Marsha. I know how much your jewelry means to you" because all of it came from her father and they were really close.

Marsha wipes her mouth, disgusted at his slobbery mouth and he probably tried a tongue down her throat too, if he had any sense.

I remember standing rubbing my jaw at that point and there was a really funny sensation in my mouth, one I never had before.

And I still wondered if I had to take Andy aside and tell him more about Grace's murder, or has the moment gone, or am I The King of Wishful Thinking?

Television.

We were following the scam-artist's directions and ahead we could see a steady stream of mostly skinny-jeans guys that I think must have been doing jobs of working, heavy-hauling racks of clothes around between brick buildings.
But better still, there was actual genuine New York movie-steam coming from the ground! And we all ran up to it like little excited kids, like Andy kinda.
You could get a heat and then we all tried to remember our favourite movie where they used steam as a prop.
I tried to remember who old guy said is in charge of the steam in the credits. Was it the art director?
Then we asked one of the workerers pushing his rack of dresses around where we could buy stuff.
"Um, clothes that will be cool only not, because they'll need to warm us up, JC," and I used his name 'cuz it was on his sweater and his second name was Penney.
He laughed, started to explain something, then changed his mind after scoping my dumb as a donkey face.
"Well, you're in the right part of town," he said with a big smile, only I thought this was a city?
"This is the garment district," he said but I must have still had that dumb expression on, so he just gave me directions then went away, and I think he thought I was maybe:

Retarded.
See 'Arrested Development'.

After a quite long, quite serious and quite frank discussion with creative input and spurting from the team, we all agreed that we liked the steam best of all in some slasher movie that nobody could remember the title of.

85

It would annoy me all day.

But, hey. Eat first, or buy clothes and warm up?

The boys wanted to eat first, the girls buy clothes, so obviously we followed JC's directions and pretty soon we were among storefronts and some them were seriously long and high.

Meantime, the sky was lightening up a little, if you can call that colour of grey lighter.

But I did have a Michael Kors brand t-shirt that colour back home.

We passed a little television store and that was really exciting as none of us had seen one in real life!

We were all amazed at how tiny they were and how hard they must be to look at, because we only have really big gigantor screens.

The store had them all on and they were all showing different pictures.

Brand names kept coming on like

Hilton. Coolness, Paris in *Bottoms Up!*

Max Factor.

Coca Cola.

Ford. Tom, like, makes... *cars?*

Chanel.

Importantly, Budweiser alcohol brand.

And Bloomingdales.

Right in front of our eyes! On the televisions!

We could hardly believe it.

Maybe we *should* get TV back home?

'Cuz weirdly, we had some of these brands on the island.

Then on top of that, it got even *more* strangerer.

Quite a lot of the televisions kept showing, but wait, this was seriously crazy to us...the *weather?*

We *never* waste time thinking about or talking about weather and so this is the longest conversation I've ever had about it and I'm quite bored now.

We only ever get little fluffy clouds, sometimes a Hard Rain's Gonna Fall and *Hurricane.*

The one good thing at least was that the televisions had good-looking talking hairdos called...weathergirls. How about that?

The girls were drifting away toward a store that said 'Discounted designer labels.'

What's discounted? And designer?

PAIGE: It's —

JIMMY: It's *crazy.* Because a sign on the door said 'Closed.'

This was becoming a very weirded out day.

A store...*closed?*

What for? What happens if you wanted, like, stuff?

We just all looked at each other and fell about laughing. Giggling. Guffawing.

Har-har-harrrrrrrr!

"The city that never sleeps, um...*does"* I said, then told the gang that the old guy called New York that.

We peered inside and I see someone inside, mooching about grumpily, like a midgetty old Daniel Radcliffe.

And I was not wrong.

A round, saggy, ancient face appeared and jabbed really bony-maroney fingers with a bandage on two of them at a sign where there was face of a clock.

He was trying to tell us something, I think.

And as I already said, we don't do watches and we don't do clocks or time, either.

I mean, what for?

Madge, what's a Rolex, FedEx, LAX and Lax-ative?

PAIGE: It's *Paige.* Jimmy, for the last time...

JIMMY: I must have been using my dumber than a puppy-dog expression yet again, because he opened the door a tiny crack.

Craaack!

"Tourists, huh? Foreigner, huh? 'Cold As Ice,' Huh? Not from here, huh? Yeah," in a squeaky whiny squealy sorta voice like a tough street- fighting cat. "Damn tourists. No English, huh? No English?"

"Um, no. We're not English" 'cuz I heard of English and London from the British guys back home.

Now it was his turn to have the dumb expression and he did it really well.

He muttered something that Mac laughed at, probably swearyiness, then said:

"Come at eight. Got that? Eight!"

Slam!

— in our faces without telling us the most important thing.

How were we going to find out when eight is?

'We could have used Dad's watch' was what I thought that Marsha might say, only she didn't.

'But none of us know how to tell the time' I would've replied.

Instead, I thought I better come up with a plan.

The old man was starting to put lights on and so I said the plan aloud.

"Let's watch television!"

And we got excited so we ran back to the television store and watched awhile and somebody passing by called what we were watching commercials and we laughed at that and then a cool fashion commercial came on and the girl was gaunt and a skeleton and a *Walking Dead* deathless clone and would maybe have been a model slash actress.

But The Betsey Johnson commercial was great.

Then, the sports came on!

Me and Mac got really excited so we went into the shop and gave Norma the j-o-b of flirting with the owner to let us watch in the warm for a minute.

Because a football game had come on!

The rules? Please explain?

PAIGE: Well —
JIMMY: And the players had cool, weirdy names.
Mipcom.
Prozac.
Artichoke.
Katchagoogoo.
Ringo.
Pomegranate.
But, the...*rules?*
We watched for a minute and wondered if the owner
was at *a job,* then left and wondered about sportswear
and me and Mac discussed the joys of girls in beach
volleyball bikinis and wondered what the World Cup is
and are you blind, referee?

Dress to the left. Dress to the right.

Fashion.

I said to Marsha in the old man's 'Discount designer labels' store and she giggled, like this word:

Coquettishly.
I want you, now, shyly.

I found it in the dictionary book when I was looking to see if cock was there.
We use cock on the island.
Power to the, um…peenis.
(Sniggers at that word. Stops. Quiets self.)
It was really good to see the girls and Andy and even Mac try to forget to remember about Grace and the hunters.
I couldn't think about anything else, but I was at least good at something…hiding it.
The old man looked near to death when we first looked at him in the grey store under the grey sky but in the bright lights of his store, he looked a lot less like Gary Oldman in that vampire movie than I thought.
Of course, the girls trying clothes on and preening themselves and prancing and giggling sometimes half-naked in front of his tall mirror would waken the dead.
Pagie surely, serious fashion gaffes?
PAIGE: I —
JIMMY: Whale-tail and muffin-top?
PAIGE: I —
JIMMY: And don't get me started on hair.
Oh, and on the subject of mirrors, usually my closest friends, I haven't been able to look at my stupid face since…after Grace.

Anyway, the old man even smiled and then he would cackle and those teeth were too perfect so must be fake and the girls played him like...girls do.

They took him aside and give him some Girls Talk.

They even got his name.

Charlie Feathers.

They said they loved him and his name and Mr. Feathers' old creased face lit up.

And something weird happened.

Passers by, *didn't.*

Men walking past the shop, didn't.

The place started filling up.

People were trying on stuff, buying it and catching big baggy buggy eyefuls of the girls.

Me and Mac were trying stuff on too and some of the men also gave the coquettish look at especially Mac, and his face made me laugh and chortle and I only gave him really tight clothes to try on.

But I could see another big problem coming up.

If we were all going to buy clothes, would we have enough money?

I thought the best plan would be to try and have a whisper in each of the girls' ears and so I did that without even been tempted to nibble or work or slip a tongue on in there.

PAIGE: Ugh.

JIMMY: Man smart, woman smarter.

'Cuz...the girls figured the money thing all along and mentioned phrases like 'cash-flow'?

I could have kicked myself, because the words they used were 'buttering him up' and I smiled and thought of *Last Tango in Paris* and wondered about Marlon Brando buttersex.

Well, at least one good thing would come out of this.

I would get to see two slick female butterer-upperers spreading it on thick.

How many times will that happen in your life?

They fussed around Mr. Feathers, sat him down, sat on his lap causing a crunching sound, a loud hacking cough and almost a toilet accident, spoon fed him coffee, fixed his hair into a new style…which he suited…made him wear some of his own list of fashions:
Nike.
Burberry.
Hugo Boss.
Alexander McQueen.
Lyle & Scott.
Ozwald Boateng.
And he looked much better and he thought so too.
"Call me Charlie," he said but we don't do phones and Charlie don't surf and he proudly stood to his full probably Wee Man height.
We had all picked out our winter wardrobe stuff and had it piled on the chair next to Mr. Feathers.
And when they both kissed him, I thought 'That's it. Heart attack, dies happy.'
I was *Thinking out Loud* and said to the girls "Hurry up" with the buttering and I think they thought the same because they circled then moved in like two sharks in *Jaws* in bloody pursuit slicing through the water only smiling and waving and looking so fine.
"Chaaarlie…" Norma said, then "I've been a bad girl. You'll need to spank me!" and she toyed with a long shoe-horn.
I seriously thought the old man was about to not be around any longer.
I nodded to Mac and Andy, then the door.
They got my drift.
We kinda wandered away and pointed out stuff in the window then went outside to look at it.
After about five minutes, he opened the door for the girls like a person with manners.

And he had the hugest most humungousest biggest friendly perma-smile on his face, like an orange George Hamilton perma-tan, man.

He nodded at us happily and sorta hornily and let the girls out with their bags of clothes.

They looked happy and not guilty and I was confused.

"Girls, that was the best fun I've had with actually my clothes on. When will I see you again?"

The girls kissed each cheek, and he shook.

"And if you ever need a job..." then drifted off and the thought of the girls needing or even doing a job was a laugh riot.

"Bye, Charlie!" they said like two-part harmony and I thought of *Charlie's Angels,* 'cuz they were.

"Most people go to TJ Maxx," he said, confusing us and gave Marsha the hundred dollars, a lot of money, back again.

"Bye, girls and boys!" he said and cheerfully and kinda blearily waved us off, so off we went.

"He was nice." Norma said, swinging bags as we headed towards, as Mac, and Clint Eastwood would say:

A.

Total.

ClusterFuck.

Slaughter on 10th Avenue.

PAIGE: You mean…?
JIMMY: We all had our un-cool sweaters on and they
were called different brand names not like Kenzo or
Marc Jacobs, but hard to say foreign maybe Italian
names?
There was, or is it were? some O'Neill hats that were
cool, though I never put any on at that point as they
would mess up my hairgasm.
And it looked like Mr. Joe was right.
This money would last forever, or longer.
By now, we were really hungry and maybe lost and the
only place we could find to eat quick and easy enough
was something we overheard called 'a greasy spoon'
but we checked the spoons and they looked ungreasy.
Which was disappointing. It was a kinda van type thing
and the side door opened up to let the chef feed people
from there from big vats of steaming gloop…what *was*
that?
Was it…*food-based?*
Norma had meantime re-discovered my waist and
clung hard to it with a lot of fingernails and sideward
looks in either Marsha's direction, or at Marsha herself.
Jealousy was not something that any of us were clear
about and it was weird to be stuck in the middle of it,
like that Stealers Wheel tune.
Marsha herself was looking up at a blackboard where,
um, a-for alleged *eating* choices were to be made.
We were all trying to recall if anyone had actually ever
seen Andy eat or munch or chow down and he said he
did, but not according to us and he didn't try too hard to
change our minds.
Mac was talking to random dickwaffler girl who was
flirting with him while her boyfriend ordered hot-dogs.
We all agreed that we knew what hot and dogs were,
so we'd risk it and I ordered the same all round.

It did cost us money though and when it came, it came fast like the other fast-food joint and we stuffed them into our over-hungry faces at un-cool speed.

The crowd was mostly bleary-eyed people and they said they just left a cool No Ordinary Monkeys party 'cuz something called 'substance-abuse' ran out.

A lot of them tried staggering and falling over, but all of them were enjoying themselves, so good for them.

They were laughing at jolly jokemeister, and it made them spill hot coffee on each other but they were invulnerable until tomorrow morning.

We didn't get even *one* of his jokes.

And I don't remember one either, to tell you here.

What none of us noticed until it was too late, was these *3 Idiots* who dressed like the *Three Amigos*, older than us by a lot, who were kinda peeking and peering from behind the van and eyeing us up.

One of us, specifically.

They reminded me of Vinnie Jones looky-likey-lo-to-no-budget-movie-bad-guy-extras.

I should have noticed that they were suspicious-looking because not one of them was eating or drinking anything.

Maybe they knew something we didn't.

And so when dickwaffler's boyfriend returns, the shape of a bluebottle, he is not impressed that his parking space has been taken by Mac.

He tries to kinda bundle Mac out of the way and I would sooo not recommend that.

But Mac just flashed the girl a smile —
Flash!
— and she leaned close and said something which would contain scenes of a sexual nature.

Because that happened a lot to king-cock.

Her boyfriend was unhappy and went to grab her by the hand or maybe by the throat to drag her away to

God knows where and he spilled and splashed coffee on Mac, but, that wasn't what triggered the mayhem. Mac grabbed her boyfriend, almost gently tripped him and laid him on the garbage on the ground. He was really too gone with whatever and wasn't clear what just happened.

"Please don't get up, man," Mac said and added a gentle foot on the chest to e-for emphasise.

She was drunk too, but recognised his kindness and sexily mouthed "Thank you" to Mac, still looking very interested in having Sex on the Beach with him.

He winked and tittered and I could tell this girl was in at least two minds whether to go with Mac, or now lying on the ground boyfriend.

She whispered into Mac's ear.

"Gimme your phone number," and that made me laugh. On the ground, her boyfriend was struggling to stand and the girl's, um…conscious? maybe got the better of her and she helped him up. Before they staggered off someplace, the guy bumped into Mac and…

Then it happened.

The three amigos approached and they were really slick and the following happened.

You have to read this really fast because it happened at Bruce fight-scene speed:

First man raced up, then barged into Marsha, spilling coffee on her hand and she said "Ow" to him.

"Hey, you!" I said and moved to him, angrily and not just always trying to impress Marsha.

Second man walks up even faster than first man, and he's big as a Ewok. He shoves me and Mac hard out the way and we stumble. Then, he grabs for the chains around Marsha's neck and yanks some off.

Then, he passes them to the third man who sprints up the street like *Forrest Gump.*

The other two follow and not even that fast, more kinda lumbering, just a glance over the shoulder now and then.

Me, Andy and the girls are all dazed and confused, like that Matthew McConaughey flick or the Led Zep riff-ripper.

But Mac is multiple sweargasming.

"Fuckin fuckers stole your fuckin chains!" he spits out and I know he's going to go after them.

All I can do is block his path and Norma helps and the men just disappear around a corner.

Marsha is statue-still, shocked and frazzled and frightened.

"They..." she starts to say fighting tears and she's taking off the rest of her chains, The Bangles, rings and ear-rings.

"...were my favourite things" she says and she angrily grabs my shaking hands.

Norma shakes her head and I think I hear her say "Then, go home" but I can't be sure.

But Marsha just pries open my fingers and drops her precious jewelry in them.

She's tugging to get rings off, but they're Stuck on You. *(Trying an Elvis The King hip-swivel in his chair. And failing. Sighs.)*

The partygoers around us are all making "Aw, shame" and "Thieves!" and "Let's go get them!" squeals, but I try to calm things down.

That wasn't the nightmare part.

PAIGE: No?

JIMMY: Trust me. Squint-eyed college kid kinda grunts and his eye condition must be that substance abuse stuff and he wants to go after the muggers, so I explain.

"You want to, like, stagger after those three huge, strong, sober, desperate to score drugs professional, ex-con thieves, probably escaped from Alcatraz, who will be armed and muscular and extremely dangerous?"

He is nodding all the time at me, until his eyes come into focus, then he hesitates, has a good think and says in a slur:

"The voice of reason, kind sir. I thank you," he says and salutes, then gives me a slobbery kiss near the mouth.

Slurp!

The crowd applaud and I have the strong and silent urge to take a bow, like some West End stage actor.

The kiss was nightmarish, but not the actual nightmare part.

PAIGE: No?

JIMMY: Not.

And once yet again, my jaw is really sore, so I'm stroking it to soothe it.

"Poor baby got a widdle toofache," Mac says in a kinda creepy grating Elmer Fudd sorta way.

"Not just a little toothache," I answered because it was getting more worser by the second.

But, I stuff Marsha's jewelry deep into my pockets, scoping the place for any more would-be ex-con thieves.

"And that's the second time tonight," I said.

"I see teeth here," says Norma.

"And some of them are real?" I ask.

"So, that means there's dentists, right?" and I manage a smile at her.

Just because I crave for Marsha doesn't mean I don't love Norma still.

Or moving.

Squint-eyed college kid is in hysterics at his own jokes and I tune in, wishing I could understand them.

But I zone out just as fast, none the funnier.

One was 'Some people shouldn't drink on an empty head.'

People, like, um…talked totally weirdy around here.
I stroked my jaw again and said:
"First time was..."
Then, squint-eyed college kid starts horsing about,
bumping into other partygoers and friends and
companions and best buds and there's some shouts.
I turn around and there he is, reeling and staggering
and falling and crumbling to the ground in a heap.
I didn't like the way college kid dropped.
Now comes the nightmare part.

Killing Joke.

That little voice in my head became a terrible scream, drowning out the partygoers, cracking jokes and laughing.
Or, the scream might have been the college kid's girlfriend, kneeling on the ground with him.
Then, I knew.
Sucksfake!
I took one very fast look at college kid and there was blood on the girlfriend's hands.
She screamed at exactly the same time as the voice in my head.
"AAAAAAAAAAAAAAAAAHHHHHH!!!"
I span around as fast as I could and scoped the streets.
Everywhere was in darkness because most of the streetlights had been punched out and I wondered how in Hell people ever got around, but only for a heartbeat.
'Cuz I was really looking for *them* and I totally knew the *American Sniper* just shot the poor college kid.
But they missed *us!*
I ran over and bent over him, now a corpse with a bullet hole perfectly between his eyes, blood splashed and spattered and splattered everywhere.
His friends were starting to wonder whether this really was the college kid funster, or a Kodak moment.
I crouched and ran to the van for cover, not searching hungrily for hot-dogs, but the dark streets.
Then, sweargasm!
Under one of the few working streetlights, the dull, long gun silencer spewed a little wispy smoke, if your eyesight was really good, not like mine.
I got a fright and nearly jumped out my skin a second later when Marsha spat in my ear.
"Jimmy?" was all she said and we both knew that was enough.

But, because of my weak eyes, I pointed.

"Is that them, under that streetlight?"

But the gun withdrew into the shadows and the moment was gone.

I was still certain and made this hasty plan.

It was the 'toss banknotes in the air and shout hey, free money plan' and the crowd would go wild for the free money plan and that's exactly what I did, and so did they.

The crowd went nuts as I danced about tossing specially-selected, not high-value dollars in the sky and then I rounded up my friends at the same time in a, I thought, non butt-nuggetty way.

"It's them, isn't it?" Norma said in a harsh whisper and she was freaked.

The crowd were laughing and tripping over each other and grabbing at thin-air and i-for intercepting dollar bills and stealing off each other.

Things were heating up because cups of piping hot coffee and hot-dogs were thrown into faces and in the confusion, here's what I did.

I grabbed Marsha and Norma and said not quietly at Mac and Andy:

"It's them, fer suck's fake!!!"

The girls screamed into my face and that frightened me more than the killers to be honest, because it made it more real and dangerous, plus it *really* hurt my ears.

Mac stared at me blankly and was surprisingly the only one you could describe as actually rooted to the proverbial headlights.

The crowd were like Tumbling Dice and I wondered if any of that was because of the silent bullets, substance-abuseness, drunkenness, or greed-ness?

"This way!" I shouted and hared off in the opposite direction of where I thought the hunters were and the girls were on my heels, Andy on theirs, Mac taking up point.

As we sprinted I could see a spooky sleazy dark alley right ahead and thought we could make it.

I am not the fastest runner, even while waiting for the sound of various ricochets and shattered car windscreens and car alarms and innocent bystanders taking bullets meant for us.

The girls Kardashed past me at Taylor Swift speed and I hurried Andy and Mac along as fast as I could.

At that second, I dared a peek to where I seen them.

They, were gone.

I figured that as a very bad sign because next thing, in every movie, they, are right in front of you.

How do they do that?

PAIGE: I —

JIMMY: But for now, they weren't.

It was just my bad eyes, because I could def see two figures in the shadows with two very long dark guns in the distance.

Our big problem was that in the distance was getting um…not.

I turned to look at the people at the van and one guy turned college kid over, then looked at his blood-soaked hands, cried out and then others joined him and there was screams and screams and running away.

The alley looked very scary as Hell out here, but we all launched ourselves into it.

We could hear the screams getting more frantic and that made me run faster miles an hour.

The alley was gloomy, filthy and stinking, and I couldn't believe the garbage, or rats the size of cats.

Every surface of every wall was drenched in slogans like Advertising Space and Bowery Ballroom and Bad Blood.

I slowed, then stopped.

"You're fucking nuts!" Mac, of course.

He was so puffed out, he could hardly speak.

"My…nuts?"

I was so puffed out, I could hardly speak.

"They…can find us whenever they want, people."

Sucking air, the gang all fearfully looked at the entrance to the alley.

Deserted.

"Not if I was in charge." Mac again.

"Please. Take charge. Here, I don't want it."

Everybody was heaving for air and watching the entrance to our *Blank Space.*

I seen a pale light ahead and started to make my way there, dog-tired and dog-eared.

"Jimmy's got us this far," said Marsha to the rescue.

"Where is that, exactly?" Mac said and I thought…and you have to admit…is a good question.

PAIGE: Hmmm.

JIMMY: But I just said "I never felt the need to prove myself" and kinda wondered where that came from because it didn't really sound like me.

And to be quite honest, I felt I was becoming less of me, not like hairless mini-me but more like *another* me because I was having to deal with things I never had to before and like, survive.

I fixed my eyes on the entrance to the alley, more than half-expecting those big, long, high, gargantuan and Gothic shadows you get to scare you, and then the bad guys appear.

A little over-used that device, I thought, then said to myself quietly…*device?*

But no, they wouldn't use that scene, 'cuz at that moment, the scene I figured the hunters would be re-enacting was:

Hunter man would hold a tracking-device in a hand that wears expensive gloves, black of course and definitely illegal, from a rare animal at risk from extinction…oops, too late! Or, is really well manicured and skin-lotioned, tanned, smooth, not hairy. His other hand might slowly

103

turn a dial here and there and that hand might have an unusual ring or maybe an interesting tattoo in an interesting place to suggest coolness and help you know the bad guy is in the story when the camera cuts to the unusual ring or skin mutilation.

I don't know anyone with a mutilation and no, they are so funcool, unless on Samuel L Jackson, or a movie with Samuel L Jackson in it.

Worse still would be other skin mutilations, like pierced tongues.

PAIGE: Yiiikes.

JIMMY: Yeech.

That's the sound of a person with a tongue-piercing trying to say yes.

And me using the dictionary and being r-for repulsed. Although, a tongue-piercing and BJ's...

We wouldn't see much more of the man, maybe just a glimpse of a steely eye, or a Steely Dan, or a cool cuff-link, a hint of square jaw-line, a silhouette, stuff like that.

You can make up your own.

These get storyboarded like comic books into the script so the director knows his shots, great granddad said.

But he never did tell me the difference between
a director of photography and a cinematographer.

And there would be music, sweet music, which in certain scenes would heighten emotion...

Appropriately.
Jeez, that was scary!!!

Oh and:

Manipulative.
Made you jump!

Carrie did that best.

And the music would be written and composed by
Trevor 'soundtrack of the 80s' Horn or Hans Zimmer.
And the script would be written by Alan Smithee or it
may as well have been since no one ever cares about
writers.
Name a screenwriter, never mind a *famey* one?
I won't bother leaving any blank space.
And the man would let us see, probably in close-up,
that the device he holds has a blinking red dot that
should be moving when tracking persons on the move,
but is in fact, i-for immobile.
The device even shows street and store names,
making it easier for them to find you, then the silent
treatment.
Fantastic gadget, I figure.
Hunter woman we only get the very slightest glimpse of
at this point, because she is deep in the shadows,
statue still, as she ponders what old guy called
'character wounds' the story gave her — Rattus
Norvegica-fear of Norwegian rats and The Stranglers
— and she is scared.
But not as much as me.
My jaw hurts even more and cupping it in my hand to
warm and heal it doesn't help much, not even the
affectionate hand of Marsha or the jealous hand of
Norma.
"Want me to knock your bad tooth out?" from Mac.
I hold a finger to my mouth and make a sshh and Mac
says "You sound like a girl doing the toilet."
The girls glare at him, unimpressed.
Either way, there's five pairs of fearful Bright Eyes fixed
to the entrance to the alley, not counting The Stray
Cats and all the fat rats and that's a lot of eyes.
It's like we're all holding our breath, waiting.
Norma takes me in her arms and cups my aching jaw
and whispers "Poor you" and I nod, very slowly.

Because I know what the toothache means and how they can find us whenever they want.

I must have given it away in my face because Mac is right there with "Aw swearfuck, Jimmy! When did you realise?"

"Back at the greasy spoon. The college kid."

The girls and Andy are trying really hard to keep up or are in denial, especially Norma.

"Wait. Jimmy...you don't think...?"

Not usually, no. And I didn't want to be the one who breaks it to them and so, I kinda let the question hang.

PAIGE: Only making things worse.

JIMMY: It wasn't.

PAIGE: It isn't?

JIMMY: Don't you see why?

PAIGE: The whole thing is making me dizzy.

JIMMY: Mac rubs one eye. "And here's me thinking the chip thing was just another cheap rumour," Mac says and Norma snaps.

"Another cheap rumour?! Our friend is dead!"

Andy and Marsha swap looks that say 'We're so very dead' and I wish I could console, I admit, mostly Marsha.

I think Norma sees that and cosies up to me in a 'Please save me' kinda way and I held her close.

"The, um…chip..." I start to say.

"Must affect your tooth when they lock onto you," Mac says but, the s-for significance of it, the fact that it's *my* tooth in my fine head it's implanted in, o-for overwhelms me and my head drops.

"Or, when they get, *gulp*…closer" I say.

It's ironic.

I will be the one that leads the hunters to all of us.

And there, in the long shadows.

I could…

Cry.

But, I do the second thing I can think of.
PAIGE: What's the first?
JIMMY: The second thing —
PAIGE: Yes?
JIMMY: — and that's shove everybody in front of me and herd them deeper into the alley.
Even Mac seems OK about that.
It occurs to me that we're running for our lives.
You ever have to really run, for your *life?*
But, Marsha is a big surprise.
She's actually more angry then she is scared, and she's scared plenty.
On the move, she kinda snarls.
"I didn't escape to die here!"
"Where else do you want to die, then?" Norma r-for retorts bravely and briefly resuming a Barbra Streisand *Funny Girl* role.
"I need a dentist!" I said.
"Or a big knife," Norma says and somehow finds a smile inside her head.
"Or a sock on the jaw," says Mac.
I was learning new things not only about myself, but my friends too.
We were flying and I overtook, my sights peering toward only one place.
The dim light up ahead.
But suck's fake, it was narrowing and I speeded up, to my massive, monumental, unfit surprise.
I see it's the back door to a kitchen, some sign suggesting we're some kinda club or whatever.
A fat rat is chewing on something red and glistening on the ground and doesn't even flinch when we tear up.
City rats are different.
Pager?
PAIGE: Hmmm?

JIMMY: What's the rat race, a Boomtown Rat and Environmental Health?

PAIGE: Please Jimmy, continue.

JIMMY: I thought about rats and then, just briefly, wondered about rats and other entertainment-based business references.

Oh yeah, *Ben* the movie, starring...rats. Sequel to 1971's hit *Willard.*

And that song.

PAIGE: Please...don't...

JIMMY: And the old one who used to say "You dirty broad, you killed my rat," and only the ancientest people laughed.

From inside the club, music plays and the bass is thumping too hard and I just so cannot believe it.

I...know this song...it's def not Lulu's, but...*his* version of "The Man Who Sold The World"?

But we've no time to ponder the imponderness of that. The dull light gets thinner because a fat, hairy *Popeye* arm with probably scratchy jailbird tats and a tacky yellow metal bracelet is closing the door.

I guess it's a man and gesture for Norma to do the Norma stuff she normally does.

She nods instantly and we're a pretty good duo, like *Starsky and Hutch* but who do sex together.

Me and Marsha and Mac dart eyes back and forward between the alley and this door.

Norma launches her body through the door and we hear a man's voice go "Sheeit!" but in an impressed way, so I was actually right, for once.

"We need to get in there!" I hear myself say on autopilot.

"Like in a movie?" Mac asks.

"We might have a chance," I reply.

"Like what movie?" he says again.

"And should we start talking movie-dialogue?"

He won't let go.

"Something by oooh, David Mamet, perhaps?" he p-for persists.

That's the name of a great screenwriter, by the way.

Mac says "Here's the thing," very Mamet-like.

I ignore it and inside the kitchen, I hear Norma murmur Sweet Nothings.

"The *thing* is..."

Along the lane, the shadows arrive, slow, no rush. No *2112.*

No "Spirit Of The Radio."

No need.

"We could split up," Mac says, looking between Andy and Marsha.

"You do that," Marsha says and doesn't even look at him. She suddenly barges past Mac and me to hurry into the place.

I'm right behind her beautiful butt...hey. I'm only petrified, I didn't go blind...and Andy follows me and I just know that Mac, however r-for reluctant? is just behind Andy.

Where else to can he go?

Because, there's murderers behind him.

The kitchen is pretty grubby and things used to be white or stainless steel, which they almost nearly managed to clean.

There he is, greasy old worn looking chef-man leaning on a worktop, l-for languidly...the 'L' section in the dictionary has some great words and not just lesbian or labia and lips...smoking and talking to Norma and I see he does *hard work* 'cuz I see it all over his kind face which could be *1,000,000 years BC.*

On that face, is a look of only the vaguest surprise at us, and you just know those eyes have seen it all.

And I try not to think of the one thing he's maybe not seen coming down the alley, or that that we're putting his hard-working life at risk and does he have a well-

109

fed loving *Shrek* wife called Marge and three chunky children who'll grieve?

And his hands and arms are all covered in cuts, blisters, callouses, scratches, scars and burns, old and new, just like torture or a self-harmer. Or maybe it's pizza?

"Stavros" Norma says, "These are my friends" and he smiles and beams back.

"Hey, Starvos. I'm Jimmy, this is Mac, Andy there." And Marsha just sashayes right up to the man.

"I'm Marsha," and just kisses him on his chubby, amazed face.

"Pretty please we can come in?" and the way she says it would melt an iceberg's heart.

Stavros's face creaks and he breaks into a huge and strangely enough, lovely smile.

"For yoo, I keell a thousint bools" in a bad movie-foreign accent and you know he means it because he goes to the door, shuts it and locks it.

Clank!

"Geev yoo chust a leedle more tam" he says with a wink and the wisdom of the old and the city.

He rattles the door really hard to make sure it's locked tight and jams a broom handle against it.

Jam!

He walks past us with a strange kinda rolling walk and I think 'East European ex-mercenary self-treated war wound.'

"Yoo keedz thees way" he says "Dey maybes bust de doors" and leads us away without a backward glance.

"No cops, huh? We talk de boss" he says and I wonder who boss is, then the girls catch him up either side to spread some buttering up, but it's really narrow to walk through the passage-ways and it's gloomy with pipes everywhere scarily hissing and leaking and dripping stuff I hope is only water.

Strangely, that makes me thirsty. You?

PAIGE: Not one tiny bit.

JIMMY: The floor could do with a serious scrub, but no one says anything like that because we're just so grateful that someone was helping or even nice to us. As we got closer to the door leading upstairs, a rock music track just ended and I so totally *swear* it was Jim's song.

But, that would be impossible, wouldn't it?

You'll understand…later.

Another track started playing and I didn't recognise it, so I wondered if it was maybe just my imagination. The Temptations original, not the Stones' cover.

It had been a very long and strange day.

Nobody Told Me there'd be days like these.

Chef-man collided against a door with a steel bar across it —

Bang!

— and the screechy noise —

Screeeeeeeech!

— gave us a big scare, but it said Exit and it opened.

We all followed him and I let everyone go in front of me so I could take a look at the back door.

No sign of the hunters.

I breathed a massive sigh.

SIGH.

The steps upstairs were steep and narrow and the bass thumped through the walls.

Lousy soundproofing, I thought.

Never get that on the island.

Sound was massively important to us, and we loved B&O brand.

Here we go up into what chef-man says is a hip club and I vaguely wonder if it's some kinda medical facility, then remember…stufus…hip also means cool.

He opens another door and although it's marked 'Private' we go in anyway.

Norma bundles past Marsha to catch up with me.

111

"I want to hold your hand" and she does.

I can hear Mac behind me sweargasming about something he's stood on, but not too loud.

I can't hear Andy at all which means he's there.

Music plays and I like the sound up here much better, thankfully, though it's much louder that we have on the island 'cuz we *talk* when we're in a club and in this place, you couldn't hear "Your place?" or "*How* big?"

I start scoping the place and it's kinda neat.

It's really dark, much darker than we have 'cuz we like to look at the people we're talking to, or thinking about talking to, or having sex with.

The décor is dark too, looks like more just black to me, but it's hard to really tell as the light, isn't.

Light does come from above the bar, with, wait, is that a neon lights saying Heroes?

Like the song! Fucool!

Paygee?

PAIGE: "Paygee"?

JIMMY: Can you give me a few secs…Hey, that sounds like sex…while I ponder:

People as cool as David Bowie?

Lana del Ray.

And other signs go Budweiser and Schweppes and Moet & Chandon I think it was.

There's a huge mirror-ball on the ceiling, which sprays little, gulp, bullets of light everywhere.

Chef-man walks to a door-man at the front door and he's massive and he blocks the way if he needed to, and reminds me of Dolph Lundgren.

Ouch! Poor Sly!

There's another two door-men, less huge, just large and the threesome are dressed the same, like the Motown music format cover.

They made me wonder what kind of evil goes on here.

Later, I discovered that all over the walls and around the place was:

112

Memorabilia.
Collectable Shit.

That was very *very interesting.*
They also had a giant cinema screen over the back
wall and an old black and white movie was on and
though I didn't instantly recognise it, I thought, hey.
awesomeness!
Dolph-man was looking, no glaring into me, but that
chef-man was in his ear, so he might help.
There's only a few people in, some at the bar, some in
booths making out, and some dancing and they were
'this list of people:'
Grungey.
Punky.
Preppy.
Metalheady.
Slutty.
Nutty.
I like this hip club.
And one of the slutty girls kept giving me that leery look
I thankfully keep getting and she was beach-dressed
and so was her skin.
Payjay?
PAIGE: Hmmm?
JIMMY: What's a tanning bed, a flower bed, a water
bed and good in bed?
PAIGE: Have you seen a sex-addiction specialist?
JIIMMY: Whoa! They hook you-up? This *city?!* Anyway,
I was interested in asking slutty girl to dance, natch,
and exploring one of the things I knew a lot about, tan-
lines, but then something *very* strange happened.
The track finished, and someone playing the
music...he is a DJ...played another one.
We all just open-mouth *stared* at each other!!!

And Marsha is the first to speak and she sounds totally, like, freaked.

"Listen to the music!"

We're *all* freaked and Doobie Brother'd-out and statue still and amazed.

'No way! Ride a White *Swan?!"*

"How the swearfuck?!" Mac says.

But suddenly, it's like the bag is pulled over my hair again.

Things went black.

And next thing, Dolph-man has me in a choke-hold and is dragging me to the front door.

I vaguely make out Marsha and Andy being hauled after me and I think I hear Mac saying something like "Hey! Cool your freakin jets!!!" to the various door-men.

I'm thinking of death, Born to Die and especially Lana del-icious Ray, when I hear this female voice, shouting.

"You were never a kid, were you, Marvin?" and Dolph-man stops and turns, loosening his grip on my throat.

My eyes manage to travel up from the ground to high spiked heels, curvy legs, stockings, tight is that pedal-pushers? wide black belt, polka-dot top over more but bigger curves, then I'm allowed to stand.

"Pay to Play, Jayne," Doplh-man says.

I see a woman, tallish, shapelyish, biggish make-up, bigger eye-lashes, the biggest hair, not young but not old, dressed kinda like a Doris Dayish movie.

She has a lovely face, but not right now.

"It's nearly 'king closing time, Marvin," she says and Marvin must be his name and she looks at me while I rub my neck which is probably purple.

That will leave a mark.

Wish I went to those JKD lessons.

The other door-men let the others go and look at the Jayne person chick. The girls look seriously annoyed, I think Mac will punch someone and this grungy girl lurks by Andy.

114

Marvin looks at me like he could eat my ear.

Jayne is shaking her head at the three door-men in, like, a trilemma.

"They're Stavros's guests" she says.

"A Croatian Chilean cook...with a goddam *guest-list?*" Marvin says and I recognise sarcasm.

"I'm sorry, folks. Please, have a drink on the house," she says and I'm wondering what that meant.

But suddenly, the front doors rattle hard and Marvin's head, big and shaped like a badly carved totem pole, darts there.

The doors are pounded hard and he hurries over, the other door-men right behind.

Jayne gives me a lovely smile, pats my hand, smiles at the others and gestures to the bar and I get to thinking she meant free *alcohol!*

We all nod our thanks and head for the bar where cool bar-man stands watching this Dancing Queen and bikini-face waitress turns on her charms for me, which saves me work.

"ID," she goes.

"Hi Dee. I...Jimmy."

"Uh, for alcohol, kissy-face."

"Um...sorry, no ID. But, about the kissy-face..."

She looks with pity at me and I turn to look at the front doors and Marvin shakes his head 'No' to two people through the glass, then stands back.

I see them peering in.

And I just can't believe it!

Is there some mass immigration programme on the island?

Will everyone I know, eventually turn up here?

Is everyone all escaping at the same time to the same place?

Is this some kinda Islanders Reunited thing?

I just cannot believe it!

It's only Crawford and Hutchence!!!

Obviously we know they travel back and forward from the island to here for supplies and stuff, but now they're *here*.

Were they *escaping* too?

OK, they're wearing these black mask things, kinda like that film, oh what's the title? with Tom Cruise and Nicole…yes a little thin but I absolutely would…and these masks somehow manage to look cool.

Maybe more like *American Sicko?*

PAIGE: *Psycho?*

JIMMY: Right-o!

Marsha sees my incredulous incredible face and turns to the doors.

"My god…?" she beams.

"The gang's all here!" she says, totally not unhappy.

"Hey! Come on down guys!" Mac says, amazed and Andy says…nothing.

Norma's hands are clamped together like she's praying, like she seen the future.

Her future.

"Can they come in? They're our friends!" she asks Jayne and waves frantically at Crawford.

The door-men have confused door-men looks on their faces and look to Jayne for 'executive mask-related decisions.'

Jayne looks at Marvin and he shakes his head giving a Mr. Grumpy negative.

Hutchence looks pissed and tries his toothpaste-commercial ultra-bright smile, which I admit looks ultra-cool with the mask.

He's quite old, maybe thirty, but his tallness, skinness, smooth dark hair, modeliciousness, clothes and general altitude look so fucool, he could be me.

Crawford tries to smooth-talk Marvin to let her in, teasing with her mask, revealing little glimpses of that beautiful Goss Mag model face, moist porn-actress tongue, glossy pout and writhing promises.

Marvin is having fun…but not enough to let them in.
Maybe they've got a mask code?
We boo and hiss and pout and Jayne goes to step up.
But then, Hutchence points at Marvin and…*Shatner*.
Hutchence makes a gun with his fingers.
And my flesh crawls.
I must've gasped or something because Jayne stops
dead and looks at me and so do the others.
I take a good, long hard look at Crawford and
Hutchence.
Then, at the little guy with the little voice on my little
shoulder.
What do *you* have to say?
Ya thunk?
I think you're right, Wee Man.
I instantly start herding everyone into a booth out of the
view of the door.
"What's going on?" Marsha says.
"Something not right" and ain't that *always* the truth.
"With those two?" says Mac.
Marsha says "I don't know...Crawford and
Hutchence..." and I think she has the same *Basic
Instinct* that I have.
Suddenly, there's the sound of breaking glass, then
two black things appear, only really long and thin, and
it's like they're smoking.
Marvin and the door-men back off.
'Cuz they're guns, and belong to Crawfraud and
Hotsheeit.
They, are the *they*…the *hunters!*
And I just notice that my tooth really ow, hurts.
The hunters point the guns right at *us*.
"EVERYBODY GET DOWN!!!" I shout, like that song,
and shove everyone to the floor, under the booth.
The customers have already emptied themselves from
the dance-floor and bar, scrambling to the toilets and
other hidey-holes.

Marsha and me cling deliciously together, and I grab Norma close too, and she has an arm around Andy, but Mac boils with rage, glaring at the murderisers.

"Not them! It *can't* be. They..." Norma gasps.

The doors get battered over, and over and over, then again, like that horror movie, oh yeah...

Every horror movie.

"There must be some way out of here!" Marsha says, then stops and shakes her head at me.

Her dialogue was important.

I'm scoping the place for maybe the back door, expecting a hail of bullets and blood and pain, or at least doors blasted open, but...none of that happens.

After a minute, I risk a crawl out and take a peek at the door where Marvin approaches carefully, cautiously, watching for the violent fallout, the other door-men on either side.

Marvin scopes outside, then gives the thumbs up to Jayne.

"They've gone!" he shouts.

Jayne slithers out and we follow.

The place empties of customers, fast.

"So, what the 'king Hell are you guys mixed up in?!" she says and she must say 'king instead of f-bomb.

We all stand and dust ourselves down and my eyes are fixed on the door.

Marvin's eyes are fixed on me, hate-bombing.

"I'm calling the 'king cops."

And we all shout "NOOO!!!" at the same time.

Jayne gives us all a good look over.

"Want to tell me your story?" she says and we all kinda just look uselessly at each other.

"You'd never believe it," I say.

PAIGE: So true.

JIMMY: Jayne gave me a wise look and even a teeny smile.

"Try me," she says and the first thought that occurs is well, maybe thirty pounds ago but off-island, it seems better to not say these kinda things aloud.

"Alright, I'll try you," and she licks her lips.

A club always looks weirded when it's emptied and Heroes is no different.

At a low-lit booth, Marvin, chef-man and waif-waitress slouch, smoking and drinking a clear liquid in a bottle called a Smirnoff. There's a Bushmills and a Canadian Club on the table too, and I've never heard of them. They must be brands you get here.

I vaguely think about our alcohol drink brands because they're called things like 1964 Chateau la Tour or Dom Perignon or Cristalle or Krug.

Marvin doesn't drink and sits facing the doors, which I recognise as good security practice from *The Bodyguard* but it's scaring the crap out of me and I don't want to look in case the others cotton on.

The door-men keep giving us glances that turn to sneers. We know the other two are called Hopper and Rock…coolness, like the movie stars…but which one's which? And when they give us those looks, Mac sticks two fingers up at them, but they're not bothered.

We're sitting at the bar with just bottles of Coke, Gatorade and new golden stuff I love called Irn-Bru.

I love its colour and taste and sweetness and that combo makes me think about Marsha's thighs— love that word — again, then Norma squeezes my hand, her girl radar fully functional and turned up full.

We've already had food-like gloop, something called a microwave pizza which looked, tasted, smelled and felt like it had been eaten already.

PAIGE: Word.

JIMMY: Jayne is behind the bar and clears our politely nibbled-at pizza-like thing plates away, all the while swigging from something called a root beard whatever that is.

And she doesn't take her really heavily made-up, beady eyes off me for a sec, which is kinda serial-killery.

I believe her look is best described as retro but she manages to look kinda cool.

Norma takes my hand on top of the table with a sideward sneer at Marsha, who has my other hand under the table. Stairway to Heaven.

And I know who's hand to let go when I want to drink. Andy has gone to check out the memorabilia.

"I can't 'king take it in" Norma says and she's hard to hear.

"I just can't believe they are the, um...*they*" I go and Mac shakes his head.

"How can you be so sure? You never usually are."

And he would be right about that, back home at least, only now, I'm maybe getting more...*something*.

"It was my tooth...it just didn't feel right," I say at the same second Andy walks past and talks.

"Crawf used to baby-sit me," then wanders off again.

"Is somebody going to 'king say something?" says Jayne.

"Like what?" Mac snarls and Marvin leans back to see who was snarling at his boss.

Mac gives him two fingers and Marvin blanks him.

"It's...hard for us to tell you," I say to Jayne.

I'm vaguely interested in Andy, who seems to be paying a lot of attention to posters on the wall over there and he looks over to see who's watching.

He waves me over excitedly, but...

"Just start at the beginning" Jayne asks anyone.

"Why would they want to *do* that to us?" Norma says —

PAIGE: Seriously.

JIMMY: — and in the same second, Marsha speaks.

"What could *make* them?"

We're all exchanging glances and looks of guilt and Ball of Confusion and I can tell Jayne is getting tired of all this vaguenessness.

"Enough already! What's the 'king goddam big secret?" she spits out.

I take her a very good place to start advice.

"They're…the hunters!" when suddenly, Marvin jumps to his feet and spooks me.

The front doors d-for disintegrate and *Shatner!*

And it's deafening really loudly and then there's lots of ricochet which I always thought was a cool Irish rocker's name and its surreal, because the blast of bullets is, like…not.

The mirror ball explodes and it's a stunningly cinematic, stylistic scene.

I can vaguely hear Marvin shouting or screaming or shrieking or maybe that's me again?

Bottles behind the bar shatter like a shooting gallery — *Smaaash!*

— but I somehow find myself launching at the girls, then we're on the ground, crawling and scrambling like human crabs behind the bar.

Mac covers Andy with his body and I can see two opposite emotions.

Mac is cursing under his breath and you know it's "When I get outta here, you guys are so bad word bad word" and I pity them.

While poor Andy looks totally petrified.

"Who are these 'king hunters??!" Jayne screams into my face, somehow making me think of the hunters starring in a remake of *The Hills Have Eyes*. The Coolness Version.

My arms cover what I can of the girls and so you get the full picture, here's what I think Crawford and Hutchence's POV…um, that's point of view, would be.

THEIR POV:

121

SLITS IN COOL MASKY THINGYS:

Crawford and Hutchence stand on the steps to the club like royalty.
They look gorgeous, guns blasting, spraying bullets everywhere, glass flying but all in wide-angled slo-mo, teeth gritted, eyes squinted, *Bonnie and Clyde* get QT'd.
They probably think the door-men have guns, so don't come in, hoping their bullets are like movie-bullets where everybody always gets hit.
The production design is Sam Peckinpah meets *Kill Bill* Volume 15 but with silent-movie bullets instead of huge sharp swords.
The bar is almost totally trashed, then the Dolby sound soundtrack available from your retailer kicks in, starting with "Small Town Boy" by Bronski Beat.
The hunters must've heard Marvin shouting into what must be his latest cellphone.
Alcohol brands called Benedictine and Grand Marnier and Remy Martin and Hey! Laphroaig, Scottish whisky the old one loves, spill onto us and in my mouth. Yum.
When splinters tear up the bar top and rip right through the bar front, we realise, this, is it.
PAIGE: "It"?
JIMMY: *Showtime!*
PAIGE: Oh.
JIMMY: I look around at my friends and lovers and think:
This could be The Last Time.
Another Stones ref?
I don't know.
And I realise you won't have that many friends in a lifetime. Then we hear what must be police sirens and I'm kinda impressed that they got here movie-fast.
I hear curses and guess that must be Crawford and Hutchence, not Mac, because he's vaporised.The

hunters let go a few more noiseless shots. I hear noises and dare to peek out.

Oh no, funcool. Funcool.

"Don't do it, Mac!" I'm telling him.

But Mac doesn't want to hear and crawls and creeps along, close to the wall, making the shadows work for him.

It would maybe have worked if he turned the volume on his seething, snarling swearfuck down, even a little.

He holds a bar stool, ready to go.

Against guns? Is what I think.

Marvin is under a booth, his big arm protecting the waitress and he calls her Janis but there's blood coming from her shoulder and I feel very not good.

And chef-man's there beside them and when he winks at me, I feel even worse.

I look back at Mac and just as he gets close to the doors…oh Foxtrot Uniform Charlie Kilo.

The hunters choose that moment to come in, guns sweeping the place.

My peanut-brain is racing and I can only think of one thing and that's shouting.

"Over here!" to Crawford and Hutchence and stand up in the hope these deadly, professionally-trained assassins don't ha! see or hear Mac.

Or me.

But Crawford at least half-spins around to me and in that instant, Mac has multiple sweargasms at full volume and crashes the bar stool onto Hutchence's gun-hand. He squeals like a big Jesse J and drops the gun and clutches his hand in pain, bent over like that old rickety Chinese man in *Big Boss*.

In a blur, Crawford whirls and crunches her gun onto Mac's head.

Clunk!

The sound is sickening, because that's my friend's own personal skull.

123

But Mac's a tough guy and he yells just a little, even though the blow was much harder than Hutchence took.

He doesn't even stagger, just stands holding his head with both hands and blood seeps between his fingers.

Hutchence recovers some and moves toward him.

But Crawford holds him back.

She reaches out a hand to Mac and I stufusly figured that she was about to apologise.

Because, she smiles.

And next she would say "I'm so sorry, Mac! All of you! We all grew up together and this has all been some terrible mistake."

I expected that, only...

PAIGE: Yes?

JIMMY: ...not really.

Because I remembered how they killed Grace without a thought and probably had that same little smile.

Crawford just raises her gun and totally *mashes* Mac's fingers and he howls like *The Jackal.*

Then, she...she...I'm sorry for crying, Paygee. *Sniff.*

PAIGE: It's OK... *Sniff*...

JIMMY: She...stood over him and...she's calm so I *still* think *maybe*...

But now, she points the gun close to Mac's head.

And he looks at her and I've never seen him plead.

Poor Mac.

And she just...did it.

She smiled and fired.

Point Blank.

Booom!

At his little fingers covering his head.

Those silent bullets.

Mac spins with the force and hits the floor.

There's Mac's blood on her stupid mask, suck's fake! It's no use.

I can't stop myself from running toward them.

But Crawford has grabbed Hutchence and they start running toward the fire exit doors.
Because the police have just screeched up to the front doors and I was oblivious to them.
I kneel next to Mac and I know I'm...totally *useless*.
"Have they gone?" someone says, I don't know who, maybe one of the girls, 'cuz they appear.
"I scared them off," I try for a light touch.
The girls and Andy look shocked and terrified and tremble like little fragile babies standing in cots, frightened in the night.
Marvin helps Janis stand and she's very white and scraggy, but in a quite attractive way.
Jayne is by my side, shaking her head, spitting nails and shocked and sad at the same time.
"Where's Mac?" Marsha says, her voice small and weak and shaky.
Then, her and Norma and Andy see me on the floor, with so much blood pouring from Mac's head...
And the girls scream and scream and don't stop.
Or is it me?
I have to confess.
PAIGE: Yes?
JIMMY: It *was* me.
Crying...Over You.
Another of my friends just died in my arms tonight.

Do You Want to Know a Secret.

Other stuff I didn't know much about were hurt, pain
terror, grief, tragedy, worry, horror, Rick Nielsen riffs,
and loss.
I discovered them in your world, off-island.
I don't know how I found myself in Jayne's office, but
there I was.
Dazed and Confused.
And I now understood why people had pharmaceutical
fun, and relationships with The Chemical Brothers.
It was for *escape.*
It was escape that got us in this mess and now, I
wanted to escape *it.*
I remember Jayne's office was tiny, teeny, weensy,
cramped with heaps of different music formats and
over-filled, dusty cartons and crates of alcohol, stuff
called Rolling Rock and Coors and cartons belonging
to two people called Stella Artois and Jim Beam.
We all got *totally* distracted by the posters covering her
walls.
Not the cool stuff, like The Pixies, Flipper, Jesus Lizard
or even Bikini Kill but, *so fucool* Buddy Holly, The Big
Bopper, T Rex and The Who?
PAIGE: Who?
JIMMY: Exactly. All *ultra* fucool, but raised the hugest
question yet *again.*
Just how did this stuff *get* here, fer sucksfake?
Harsh language made me think of Mac and I zoned
back into the conversation.
Marsha was red-eyed like Norma and Andy is
comforting the girls for a change, sitting cramped
together on a sagging, over-stuffed old, stained...with
what? couch.
Jayne's expression is somewhere between sadness
and "Oh no, my bar has 'king gone and it's your fault,
you 'king..."

I couldn't have felt more sad and guilty, and one thought flashed through my head.
It was like some movie poster, with a neat slugline.

Murder City.
And then, there was four.

I wished someone would break an island rule and tell me the ending.
And that made me think of Crawford and Hutchence.
It's like living in a disaster movie.
"I told you, Marvin handles cops," Jayne said in a snippy — snappy, actually — well really kinda time of the month way, but who could blame her?
I feigned interest in her ancient computer, maybe six months of oldness.
I had never seen one up close and personal, but was mostly looking to distract myself.
As I was doing this, blue light from the cop cars flickered between the blinds creatively interestingly.
"Jayne, we're so sorry. Your lovely place..." Marsha said again for the zillionth time.
In Jayne's angry hands, she was playing with what you call a CD.
It said Our Secrets Are The Same and I thought that was cool and right-on at the same time.
But, there's much weirdness going on here, in the whole off-island, but...what?
I feel Jayne's eyes boring into me and turn to look at her so she can talk at us, like 'the kids awkward conversation about sex'.
"Lemme see if I got this right" she says and boy, is almost every word a sarcastic inflection. Hey, cool phrase!
"Those...'king...*people*...are your 'king *friends*?!"

We nod, like a row of those plastic dogs in the back of Mustangs with two bumper stickers, one a fish, the other something like 'Seriously...I hate you guys.'
"You're sure?"
"I...we think maybe..." I try.
"And, they killed your *other* friends?"
Or it might be a red Cadillac Coupe Deville car sticker that tells you to Spanish Stroll.
"But, you didn't *know* they were killers."
Or a speeding 1939 Buick Convertible, with 'Coke. It's the thing, really.'
"I know it sounds absurd," and I agree with her, we all do.
You should have seen the look she gave me.
And the Buick would stop and I would moon Jayne and she'd go:
"'king absurd?" She looks like she's drinking vinegar.
PAIGE: Yuck.
JIMMY: "You don't even know what *cops* are, or what *city* this was!" And she is getting angrier by the second.
Or a Little Red Corvette by Prince back when he was Prince and not a squiggle and the bumper sticker says Blood Fire Posse.
She lets out a huge, chesty, smokers' sigh that, sadly? is kinda erotic.
"I'm real sorry about your...*friends*."
And she stands like at the end of a business meeting.
"But, oh, what was I going to say...?"
Can't wait.
"Oh, yeah, I know, 'king go! And when you're finished doing that..."
But I expected that and had been working on my lines while Jayne was doing hers.
"OK, Jayne. I 'king do that. But, it's *my* fault, not theirs" and the girls and Andy start to i-for interject on my behalf.
"Please Jayne, let them stay."

Jayne looks at me as if I have two brain-cells.

PAIGE: Hmmm.

JIMMY: Yes?

PAIGE: No comment.

JIMMY: "You think I'm 'king crazy?" Jayne says, and yes, I do, 'cuz she *totally* looks crazy right now.

"Stay? Where?" she says and actually laughs.

"Crazy!" she says, stands and looks out the window.

It's like something kinda happened between me, the girls and Andy at that very second.

We all suddenly want to talk, tell her.

"Crazy? You want to hear crazy?" I say to Jayne's back, eyeing her padded but not totally unattractive ass.

PAIGE: Hmmm.

JIMMY: "We were all born on the island...but we don't know where it is, we don't know you to get back...home," Marsha says.

"The founders run things, but who *are* they?" I go.

"We don't know how our parents or grandparents or great grandparents got there," Norma adds.

"Or when they went," I say.

"Or why," Andy adds.

"And the founders are like...*caretakers,*" Marsha says and I look at her, surprised at her i-for insight which she had just vomited up.

We just all look at each other after our quasi-religious —that right, Plage?

PAIGE: *Paige.* I —

JIMMY: — experience and stand to leave.

"Anyway, thanks Jayne, for everything you've done," both of the girls say and we head straightaway for the door.

"You know what's worst of all?" I say to her hopefully-will-soften-any-minute face.

"We don't even know who we are."

And I think that thought, that whole notion, the reason I escaped, the reason they followed, the reason for all of our existences, hits everyone in the room at the same time.

Boom!

I feel all their eyes on me and I turn the door handle.

Then, a surprising thing from a surprising person.

"No one should have to live like that."

Young Andy, old mind.

And I suddenly realise that this is *their* journey too, the reason for their Blind Faith, minus the Clapton and Stevie Winwood stuff, or the Stevie Wonder bio.

I smile and want to kiss them, but turn to go.

"I must be 'king crazy," Jayne says and I think of King Crimson and King James and Royal Blood and wince at the thought and now Jayne's teary when she turns and gives me a lovely, real adoring smile. She comes and embraces us all, and it's a good, warm, fuzzy feeling...

Identity.

…apart from the fact that Mac keeps worming into my head and strangely, his Badfinger's in my face.

Jayne brings us big steaming hot — ouch! — mugs of coffee she said was made with java beans, which I thought would be a great name for The Strokes next music format.

Oh, and we're back down sitting at the bar again, and it's a lot less messy and much more tidy because Marvin hired some local street kids to do a job of sweeping up.

Some other guys in white bib overalls had a job and were plasterers? and were filling holes now that the police had finished bagging bullets, like in buddy cop detective movies, like, um…or serial killer movies like, like…

Sorry, but my head's not on entertainment industry mode right now, somehow.

Apart from I would swear on a stack of Eric Clapton CD formats that, somehow, Popatop is playing in the b/g, that's background, but I'm kinda distracted because Marvin is sweeping up too, and keeps glaring at any one of us stupid enough to catch his eye.

The door-man Hopper comes back from a store with a treat for us that Jayne made him get and he's pissed he had to get stuff for "The sock-cuckers that got your place all shot up," he snarled.

He slammed ice-cream cartons down on the bar-top — *Slaaam!*

— and the girls "Whoopee'd" and he said:

"Yeah. Whoopfuckinee…" and swaggered toward Marvin so they could talk about us.

I thought of Mac sweargasming, then poor Gracie. She adored ice cream and the tricks you could do with it. (Nudge, nudge.)

131

PAIGE: Oh, Christ.

JIMMY: I had the pecan-nut with toffee in her honor and it was better than sex with DFG4 and 7.

PAIGE: How many DFGs do you have?!

JIMMY: Jayne is ready to lap up more of our story and she's behind the bar again and my eyes drift to the doors, 'cuz the last time we sat like this...

The girls are stroking the coffee mugs like...

A...ahem...and they wait for me to be the one to start and I look outside to see it's almost New York's version of daylight.

"Here comes the sun," I say and Jayne smiles.

"Maybe it escaped from the island too," she says and bores her eyes into mine and I know when I'm beat.

I clear my throat.

"Ahrrrrgggggh."

This is not an easy story to tell, or start.

Or begin to understand.

I can tell they're all absolutely *desperate* to hear it, and Marsha jump-starts it.

"Jimmy overheard his great granddad talking one night."

Norma looks at her, thinking: 'You told *her* and not *me?*'

"He lived in New York..." I start.

"Yeah? Where?" Jayne asks me.

"Um...New...*York?*"

"State or city?" she goes and everyone gawps and gapes at her.

"Nobody ever tells. Island rule," Marsha says.

"He...raised me up," I go.

Jayne settles comfortably, like she's about to watch her favourite movie with her favourite man, and buttery pop-corn.

"My parents and grandparents were killed in a car accident. So, Pops came to live on the island."

Everybody sorta leans forward to hear better.

132

"This night, him and *The Rat Pack* were celebrating something they called a a milestone birthday? They didn't usually drink much..."
The gang looked at me like students about to dissect the frog. Because, I haven't told them this story either.
"...but *that* night..."
PAIGE:. ...Yes?
JIMMY: "...they forgot to stop."
And they're all staring at me like I was *The Theory of Everything* man.
"I hid behind Otis Redding."
Jayne gasps, but I don't know why.
"A statue halfway up the marble steps."
Jayne looks disappointed for some reason.
"They didn't say that much," I said to foreshadow — oh, in movies, they drop little clue-bombs and that's called foreshadowing — 'cuz I didn't really have too much to say.
"They talked about the past. It was...*Unbelievable.*"
I looked around at the faces.
"The things they *did!*"
"Who was there?" Jayne kinda gasps.
"It was just golden oldies," I say and she leans closer.
"What were their *names,* Jimmy?"
"Um...lemme see, Steve, Norma, Martin...I forget who else..."
And Jayne is staring at me really weirdly.
"Anyway, I thought that if I discover who the old guy really is...I would find out...who *I* am."
And now that I say it *aloud,* it sounds...kinda *cheap* and I'm waiting for one of them to say something like:
What? You...!
But they all look like they totally understand.
That took me by surprise.
I guess a lot of people need to know that about themselves.
Whatever, because it reached them.

"And I thought it was just youthful rebellion," Marsha says with the loveliest of smiles which Norma sees and takes my hand again.

A song starts playing and I must be *hearing* things! That...can't be...*can* it?

PAIGE: What?

JIMMY: I gape at the gang...

PAIGE: Yes?

JIMMY: ...and Marsha is now looking at me in a completely different, more gooder-er way.

Which Norma brings back to planet Earth.

"Poor Grace...and Mac," she sighs.

Marsha comes to my Emotional Rescue.

"Will these...police...uh...keep the hunters away?" she asks and I think that's in innocence.

"Oh, poor Grace and Mac?!" Norma says.

And I can see things between these two may never be the same again and that saddens me big time.

"Uh...uh..." and that's the most Andy's said in a long while, then:

"Waitress alright?" he manages.

Jayne kinda grimaces and slugs on a drink she called a cock-tail and it looked a laugh-riot with brightly coloured things sticking in and out of it.

It was her third and her eyes were starting to meet in the middle.

Try the cock-tail, was my first thought.

No, you know what it was.

"I can't think of anything else to tell you" I say.

"No," Jayne says and I just know she'll be...

"Apart from the 'king hunters" and I was right.

Sarcastic.

"Life goes on," Jayne says and pats my arm like it's a cat on her lap.

Pat, pat, pat!

We all go silent, thinking our sad thoughts.

Without thinking, I rub my jaw and...*Shatner!*

The girls and Andy leap to their feet and start to scramble behind the bar.

Jayne is confused as Hell and so am I.

"No. It's not them!" at least I think, but I still take a good look over my shoulder.

Phew.

"It's just that, I need a dentist," I say.

Andy is first to laugh and the girls do too and we can be back to being Shiny Happy People.

"You...know about dentists?" Jayne asks.

"Some people have real teeth on the island," I say.

Jayne actually laughs out loud — "Ha-ha-haaaaa!" — and it was good to hear human female laughter.

"Just like my man. Funny, a little, uh...and way too beautiful," she says.

I heard that people use compliments like that off-island.

"Does he live with you?" Marsha asks in the way that woman do that can mean something else altogether.

Jayne lets out a big sigh.

"Tucson, Arizona, last I heard," and she looks distant, then slugs at her cock-tail.

"I live alone, above the bar," Jayne says.

"Single room, unfurnished."

And the girls give girl radar nods and one day, I'd like to know what it feels like to be a woman.

PAIGE: I'm terribly sorry.

JIMMY: You can guess one of the reasons.

PAIGE: Must I?

JIMMY: Jayne finishes her drink in one, licks her not un-kissy lips, checks a fat wristwatch she called bling? Then grabs what I know is a real, not movie-phone.

"You run a bar in this town, you need to know a guy that fixes teeth," she says, then flips what she calls a 'Role-o'dex' thing and removes a card.

"Can I see that?" I say excitedly and she slides the Role-o'dex over to me.

"Thanks," I say with a happy face and flip the cards.
"Who haven't I called lately?" I say and Jayne smiles.
There's numbers for interesting sounding places, like Shake Shack and Sugar Shack and Otto's Shrunken Head.
She goes to pick up what she calls the handset.
"Um, how does it work?" I say and she shakes her head.
"Pick this up, listen for a dial-tone," and I stare at her, so she knows I'm thinking *die tone?*
She lets me listen.
"Then punch in your numbers," and while I make a fist then she does that. "Wait for a reply, then say politely…" and doesn't give me the handset back.
"…hello. Mr Fripp please," and I nod. Fripp? Hmm.
"Then you wait till the person you want gets to the phone, then…"
Sounds come from the handset and Jayne hangs up.
"Answering machine," she grumbles, "They're not open yet."
Answering machine?
I hadn't noticed that Norma was getting more and more nervous.
"What are we going to do, Jimmy?" she says, staring right into my eyes.
"Um...root canal?" I try out on her.
Marsha again comes to my rescue.
"I'm feeling a little better now," she says, sounding like she might even have meant it, it wasn't just for Norma's sake.
"I'm not as...*petrified,*" she goes on.
"We'll *all*...learn things, won't we, Jimmy?" she says, then…
"But, I just can't stop feeling guilty" and puts a forgiving arm around Norma's shoulder and she's grateful for that.
I was too.

"It's my fault, Marsha. I was the one who wanted to come here," I say and I feel terrible all over again.

"You're so right, Jimmy," she says and it's all falling apart like that Michael Douglas movie again, but...

"But we didn't have to follow you" she says, her eyes fixing into mine.

I put my arm around her shoulder.

"You kids must be exhausted," and she is right, not wrong. Right, Plage?

PAIGE: I —

JIMMY: "How 'bout The Chelsea Hotel" and we all give her this curious, strange Norman Bates hotel *High Anxiety* look.

"Course. No hotels," she says, shaking her head again and she will do that an awful lot over the next while.

"I'll get you lovers some blankets," she says, looking at me and Marsha.

Hurry.

Get the blankets.

I laugh, Marsha sniggers, Andy smiles and Norma glowers and Jayne looks between me and the girls.

She stands and heads for the door.

"Um, Jayne..." I say and she stops.

"Can I...um...use the phone?" and she laughs again.

"Sure, why not?" she says and reaches the door.

"And Jayne?" I say and she mock-sighs and turns.

"What's an answering machine?" and she laughs so loud it hurts my ears and I still hear her laughing all the way down the hall.

I pick up the phone and play with it uselessly.

Because I don't know how to use it, or who to phone or what to say and who to.

And as for sleep, I had been trying to avoid it, like mirrors, because I knew Mr. Sandman would hurt me.

Jayne came back pretty fast and gave us all itchy and scratchy woolly blankets she said were made of tartan wool from some store called Scotland and they were really warm and made you sneezy and snoozy.

We just all kinda snuggled up on her big fat sofa and I thought Marsha's thighs made an effort to get next to mine because there she was and with Norma on the other side I thought hey, but, no real three-in-a-bed action was attempted.

PAIGE: Thank God.

JIMMY: At least for now.

PAIGE: Ugh.

JIMMY: We were all beat and although we talked for a while, nobody could keep their eyes open for long. We could hear the work going on downstairs but...it...was...getting...quieter...and...quieter...by...the...

I actually did manage to drift into a tartan sleep, like having warm Scotch alcohol for blood and was…

In Dreams.

Great granddad and me were out walking on the beaches, just me and him.
I always loved doing that.
Not in a running toward each other in slo-mo along the sand kinda Bo Derrick and Dudley Moore *10* way, though.
It was a lovely day, so, hey, surprise!
Old islanders called him 'a wonderful, striking man with charismatic, cinematic presence and ultra-über-talented.'
He passed on all his genes to me, no, not his *denims,* his g-e-n-e-s, though those vintage 501s…
Not too small or high, in good health, strong and fit, not even carrying only a few extra pounds, thick blondish, mop-toppish hair and bad eyesight. He wore these strong, thick, Coke-bottle-bottomed horn-rimmed glasses, funcool on anyone except him.
His age was meaningless and he was considered wise.
He wasn't one of the founders, but was an 'early adopter' to the island whatever that means and was influential and did admit they kept asking him to be a Founder, but he would never point to someone in the street like Donald Sutherland in *Invasion of the Bodysnatchers* and squeal he is one of them.
The old guy was always cool whatever he said and wore and did at all times.
I wanted to be like him if I ever grow up.
I always joked with him every time a Martin Sheen movie came on because he was kinda like him.
But that day, he was in the weirdest mood, I thought, because he was saying things, telling me things that in terms of making sense, like, didn't?

139

"How many movie stars does it take to change a light bulb?" he said in his slightly raspy voice and I looked blankly at him. No change there.

"Light bulb? What's a light bulb?" he said and cracked himself up with laughter.

Then, he stopped like it was never funny to begin with, which I would go along with.

"Jimmy, ask me a question" he said.

"A...question?" I said, surprised.

"Any question. I think you have a lot," he said and I wondered how he could know that.

"Um...can you play *dental* records?" I said and he gave me the most *knowing* look I've ever seen him give. Keep that important thought in your head for later.

"No, Jimmy. I meant...something...*serious.*"

"Gotcha. Most funcoolest? Ava in *Ex Machina* or The robot in *Spare Parts* or Ahab in *Moby Dickless* or ZFI in *The Fifth Element* or the Dodge Challenger in *Vanishing Point* or The Magler in *Minority Report* or..." And I see he's searching for something else.

"A hole..." I let it hang for added comic, smutty effect, then "...in the ozone layer?" I said.

"You're smarter than you think, Jimmy," he retorted and I had never thought that and you won't either, but he did, for some reason.

I start to skim stones and I can make them go really far over the clear, flat water.

"Ever wanted to follow the stones?" he says.

Weirdness. He knows...I'm a fan. I've got all their records. I lurve Keef.

"Imagine the world outside?"

I nod yes.

"The truth is out there" he says.

"I...*think* about it."

"Looks, talent, choices, can mean a glamorous life, Jimmy. Then it's hey, I just became famous."

He stopped beside me and skimmed some stones into the horizon.

"Next thing, it's the money, girls, cars...whatever you *think* you want."

"Um, about the *girls*..."

"Everywhere, your flawless, air-brushed face on magazine covers..."

Hair...brushed?

"...winning the glittering prize..."

Hey, Simple Minds. Coolness.

"...voted Xth most talented and handsome man in the world and..."

And a funny tone has started to creep into his voice.

"...on the studio lot with your agent and manager and dialogue coach and there's distribution deals and a few points off the gross and all the best meetings are taken."

Is he losing it?

"...and every script becomes the girl or the drugs or the money or Space Ninja Gangsta Cowpoke."

I'd...like to see that.

"But where is *originality?*"

"Well, there's Space Ninja..."

"Huge explosions, piles of dead extras, the car chase, the shoot-out, the big kiss..."

I briefly think about him kissing, then don't.

"Life is written for you. And it's a good part..."

I finally understand.

He's *reminiscing.*

"...and the dialogue's snappy."

And I grab his head in both hands and kiss him on the mouth and say "You broke my heart, Frodo," because to be honest?

I'm getting scared he's maybe having an old guy stroke, or something.

He laughed at that.

"A wide emotional well to mine, method style, thanks to Konstantin Stanislavsky and Lee Strasberg."

Are they *football* players?

"And you ask...what would Geilgud do?"

I thought of Dr. Feelgood.

"I'm your biggest fan, she sexily lisps. But, then, they *all* are."

I'm about to suggest a visit to the doc, but...

"But who do they love? Me? Why do they stare? What are they looking for? Stardust?"

Alvin...?!!

"And they all *know* you, all got a claim on you, all want a piece of you."

"Ooookaaayyy," I say nervously, then...

"Movie sets you could live in? *Blade Runner* or *A Royal Night Out* or..."

"Working the room, pressing the flesh, shmoozing the money people, then vogueing in the 54 with Madonna and supermodels," he says, skimming more stones.

"The power and the money, a...men."

His stones went further than mine, like they had disappeared across oceans.

"Then...they own you."

"Who does?" but I didn't really think he was talking to me.

He looked really weird, so...

"OK. Di Caprio, de Niro, or di Depp?" and he smiles and I go:

"A...ow...*Brazilian?*"

He laughs.

"A false passport?"

"Lynyrd Skynyrd's finest hour?"

"Chatlines?"

"Graceland, Timberland, Timbaland, Neverland, Wonderland, Iceland, Scot-land...?"

But he had stopped laughing.

I desperately want to rescue him.

"Movies that shocked the world and don't cop out with *The Exorcist, Clockwork Orange, Fahrenheit 9/11, Women in Love, The Antichrist...*"

"The Imitation Game," he says, to himself, and I think about what I know.

"Their expectations..." he goes, but the movies I had obviously been thinking were *9 1/2 Weeks* and *Boogie Nights* but...

"...were so different to mine."

I don't think I like the way his head is heading, one bit, or mine.

"Idolised worldwide, but marooned in your own manufactured myth..."

Macarooned?

"I...started despising mirrors and various exciting projects at different stages of development."

"Old guy..." I said, getting more and more anxious.

"The praise business," and I look around for someone to help me get him back, but our desert island was, um...

PAIGE: Yes? Yes?

JIMMY: ...deserted.

PAIGE: Oh.

JIMMY: "Then self-love becomes insecurity and insomnia and self-pity and panaceas, pills, bottles, struggles with inner demons, battles with outer limits..." he says.

I'm thinking 'Somebody Help me.'

"By the time you realise, it's all...it's...too late."

"I'm not keeping up here...dude."

"But, one day, Jimmy. One day..."

"Um, one day one day what???"

"One day, you get a moment of...clarity."

Is that not...*wine?*

But I do know that I'll try a different approach.

"OK, Pops, movies about...*identity?"*

That got his attention, and he stares at me.

"There's obviously *Identity* and *Volver* and the so fucool *Bourne Identity* franchise and *Secret Window* and…"

"*Shutter Island?*" he says and we just stare at each other now.

"So…how d'you think da Giants'll do this season?" I ask 'cuz they're his team and it's a standard line in every buddy movie.

Then I punch him lightly on his little shoulder and say, "Bud?"

And that shakes him from his mood and he laughs aloud.

"Like I said, you're a smart boy," and he looks at me, really super-intensely.

"Sorry, Jimmy," he says and ruffles my hair, then laughs as I straighten it instantly.

"I can't believe it was…fifty years ago."

And his mind goes way back, lemme guess, fifty years? for a sec.

"Right" I say, but "What was, old man?"

"When I did something…out of character."

"I can see clearly now."

He smiles at me.

"You're scaring the Hell outta at least one of us," I say.

Then, he starts to walk and we're on our way home.

"See the whole of the moon, Jimmy."

"You mean…like The Waterboys?" but I don't think that's what he means, so I kick sand.

"What about that quarterback, Courgette?" and laughs and steps back into character as my super-great granddad.

…Patch —

PAIGE: Paige —

JIMMY: I would have only one other conversation like that with him before…I escaped.

PAIGE: You must miss him.

JIMMY: Saw him yesterday.

PAIGE: You did? Wow. What did he say?

JIMMY: Told me about the cool '27 Club' and…

PAIGE: The 27 Club?

JIMMY: About rock-stars dying at 27? Yeah? Anyway, I couldn't shake the thought in my head that things had changed between old guy and me, but to who knows what or where, so after our talk, I lay on the sand and shifted the set to another dream.

To be honest, I try to guide my thoughts to the perfected fantasy dream.

Involving Marsha, the balmy outdoors at night, a hot-tub of Champagne, moonlight, chilled Muscat de Baume de Venise, dripping smearing marshmallows and over-ripe papaya, whipped cream, melted chocolate, melted butter, hot baby-oil, overhead mirrors, Magnetic Fields and Dobet Gnahore as the soundtrack, handcuffs, stuff with batteries.

But you can't do that with dreams.

They lead you.

You don't lead them.

So, I find myself in the company of Grace.

And, it's not a dream, but a terrible, terrible *nightmare.*

Grace is smiling and waving and flirting and talking and joking with me.

She wears the same dress, her hair fixed the same way...

And I want out.

It's a Shatner part.

There's no dialogue.

The cinematography looks all nada budget Euro-trash, sub-titled, cut 'em upper.

Then, an ECU, that means extreme close up, of an actor, playing me.

And another playing Grace.

I don't know if they're A-Listers.

And my character has a red dot crawling onto his face.

And Grace's character strokes his face, maybe tries to rub the red speck off, but it won't come off, like a spot or a scab or a tattoo, or cancer.

Then, for some reason, the Grace character shoves the Jimmy character and in ultra slo-mo, a spinning black bullet, the latest CGI, that means computer graphic imagery, heads, well...for her head.

And she lets out the tiniest gasp...

...gaaasp.

I remember other times, other gasps...then gives a simple smile and the bullet explodes into her lovely head, bright red blood spouting and spraying also in slo-mo then...

I wake and I'm a total wreck.

Everyone else is asleep, even though it's light outside.

But what woke me was this.

Grace has *seen* all those movies!

The ones with the red specks, what they're for, what they cause.

And I realised something...sad and incredible.

PAIGE: Yes?

JIMMY: Gracie...

PAIGE: Yes?

JIMMY: Sacrificed herself for *me.*

Exit Music.

I feel like a sex-worker.

Because I just want this thing out of my mouth.

If I didn't, I'd lead the hunters to us and we'd all be dead, or worse.

But wait, duh, of *course*, everyone else would have them too, wouldn't they? Maybe they don't hurt them, or whatever.

I had to tell Jayne it wasn't just me that needed a dentist, but all of us, as a p-for precaution.

We all musta looked really Wide Eyed and Legless and filthy dirty.

Might be fun.

But priority wise, breakfast was first.

Jayne had found something called a McDonalds and I snacked on yummy eggs.

Jayne had burned her lip on her breakfast, an apple cake, and even though there was a 'Warning! Warning! Hot!' notice on the box, she ignored it and so held a nice pack to her lip.

"Tell me more, tell me more" — *(Cue bad singing.)* — so we did.

"They find you through...your 'king *teeth?"* she said, just a little sarcasm creeping in there.

I nodded, mouth full of scrumminess.

"And they can do this among all these dazzlingly expensive molars?"

I was beginning to suspect that I don't think she really kinda sorta half-believed me.

"You sure about that, Jimmy?"

"Well, when they're near, something must happen with the thing..."

"Your 'king...*thing?"*Jayne says in a mocking tone.

"I don't know, whatever, but my jaw hurts when they're near us."

"Any of you kids get a sore *thing*?" Jayne says, but I don't think they do.

"Maybe they're just after *you,* Jimmy" Marsha says, *totally* terrifying the butt-nuggets out of me.

"Suck's fake! Thanks, Marsha."

"Do you remember getting it put into your tooth?" she asks.

"Nah, but it could have been put in anytime I was at the dentist?"

"Point conceded," she said.

"Jayne, I *know* it sounds like *Marathon Man 2* featuring Colin Firth's bad guy debut and Liv Tyler as Dixie Chicks with a cool soundtrack by Avril Lavigne starring Justin Timberlake as our handsome hero, pursued through the streets with the *thing* in his kissy mouth and..."

And everyone stares at me like I was a fish-pet in a bowl.

*"Everything...everything is...*movie-and music-referenced," Jayne said.

"Welcome to me."

But I don't think she totally gets it.

But she did promise to take us to the movies and music venues called The Living Room and McCann Park.

She'd drive us to the dentist first, but first, I was going to have a huge treat and an even huger surprise.

It helped take my mind off the nightmares which had become day-and-night-mares.

About Mac and the hunters, yet strangely warm thoughts, guilty thoughts, about Grace and now Norma.

Did she love me too?

Should I be not lusting after Marsha?

Could I make that happen?

Did it matter because we're all going to die?

The big surprise was:

Jayne's car.

Only a beautiful, classic 1955 Porsche Spyder!

Motor-heaven.

Wait till I tell the old crazy about cars man!

I'll phone.

A letter, maybe?

To: Great granddad, The Island, Wherever.

RSVP: Jimmy, New York. Wherever.

But I wasn't going to let that spoil the experience.

Jayne didn't realise I was a petrol-head, she said.

A...wha?

"What car do you drive?" she queried.

I gave her the look.

"Maybe I could pimp your ride for you?" she said.

I looked at her in my usual totally expressionless empty blank way, though what she just said did sound kinda slutty.

"Never mind," Jayne said.

I walked around the Porsche slowly, like a panther examining and appreciating its glistening lunch.

She was a beauty, and I stroked her and purred.

Purrrrrrrrrrr.

Then, I kissed her.

I instantly need to wear a wet, white, cap-sleeve t-shirt revealing my really buff muscles and slowly wash her with sex-starved female jail-birds like in that Paul Newman movie watching and groaning with frustration, especially the female wardens and particularly the lesbians and some of them would slide a hand between their legs then...

I entered her.

She smelt of leather and perfume and gasoline and alcohol inside, all the smells a man could want and I stroked the seat, resisted the temptation to sniff it, then checked the roof for footprints or stiletto holes.

"Jimmy!" Marsha said, shaking me out of it, then she said the three most important words in the world.

"Want. To. Drive?"

"Well, gosh and gulp, I'd love to. Only, we don't do cars, and pollution and car crashes and road-rage and..."

I'm looking for *The Others* in a big yellow Joni Mitchell sorta taxi behind us but I want to keep looking at Jayne's car until I die and that reminds me to force myself to keep making sure *The Kids are Alright* behind, and they are.

We're driving along the road at faster miles an hour and there's cars all over us, but this is "Before nine in the morning," Jayne says.

Nine in the morning. So...what?

And Jayne calls it something I recognise.

Rush Hour.

And "This traffic 'king sucks" she says and I think that means that the cars and motorcycles and massive gas-guzzling trucks like in *Mad Max Fury Road,* all choke up the air.

That's probably why I don't see any spiders and snakes or animals or parrots or plants or trees or too many primates walking, like back home.

The ones who are, I notice, are not like the night-time people but are very different.

These ones are dressed in suits mostly and have, kinda strangely, Reeboks, Nikes and Adidas sneakers on their feet. And Pumas.

That looked i-for incongrous to me, that dictionary said. I wondered how many of them actually *were* the *Nightcrawler* people.

But there's lots of very attractive Zagat's type women and the 'they wear the same uniform as the men' list:

Suit.

White shirt.

Glasses.

In a hurry.

Bored shitless expressions.

Fat briefcases.

"With uh...laptops?" Jayne explained, and they manage to look very sexy and I think of *Wall Street* and when Jayne tells me that's where we are, I love it and ask: "This is...*Manhattan?*"
But, instead of thinking about Woody Allen or Rachel Brosnahan, I say:
"Can you take me to where Patrick Bateman works? Or, *The Wolf of Wall Street?*"
"Who are they?" she says and I suddenly remember another island rule:
IT'S NOT JUST A MOVIE.
"Oh, nothing," I shrug and say back to her.
We're not really moving much and a heavy donutty cop ...watch *him* catch a thief...directs traffic and I'm not really thinking about anything, until suddenly:
"STOP!"
I say, and Jayne gets such a fright she slams the brakes on —
SLAAAM!!
— and we get *Whiplash* and red screamy faces and some cool new bad words.
"What 'king now?" she says, eyes boring into me.
"Um...sorry, Jayne. It's not *them*, it's...there?" and I point like *ET* to a building ahead.
She cusses under her breath, starts the engine and puts the pedal to the metal and away we go, this way, that way, onto the path of the single biggest, meanest, dirtiest truck with the craziest driver I've ever seen, like maybe from *Jeepers Creepers* who looks like he wants do the same to our eyes and other body parts.
Jayne's car fish-tails, pulls a 360, but she manages to right it, and we get sound-polluted by red faces screaming who look like they will have very limited life spans.
"You want me to stop at a *building?* " she squeals.
"Oh yes, please. Sorry, I didn't mean to *Casper* you."
She gives out this huge sigh, then laughs, def big relief.

151

"In *this* 'king traffic?" and she laughs, her do wobbling. "It's really important," so then she looks at her mirror. She signals and tries to stop and we get another blast of shouts and curses and horns and honking and stuff. I look out the window and I can see Marsha, Norma and Andy in the big yellow taxi and the windows are open so I hear them shouting and waving like Ten Thousand Maniacs and I know they've seen IT too. Jayne manages to stop the car and wedge it carefully between boring cars with no style and you'd think the classic elegance of the car would be, like, appreciated by other motorists, wouldn't you? But nooo.

Honking, shouting, screaming, fist-shaking and some fucool fingering gestures I'll use, and swearing that makes me remember Mac.

Anyway, maybe the driver of the yellow taxi can't speak English or watch any movies and doesn't understand the concept of 'follow that car' and shoots past us, the girls and Andy shouting and waving at me like a fart movie, I think they're called.

I vaguely wonder and hope the girls would moon, like fart movies always do.

I jump out the car and see them up ahead, the taxi allowed to stop with the help of another yellow taxi, and the gang jump out.

But I can't wait and run along the bustling and busy street and then, there it is, right there —

PAIGE: What? Where?

JIMMY — right in front of me!

PAIGE: But, what?

JIMMY: I had never seen one in real life and then the others are standing next to me and we are all in awed silence.

I think they feel the same as me and want to do a 'we're not worthy' routine.

It was a freakin' Warner Bros movie theatre!

"I'm thinking Frankie goes to Hollywood and Welcome to the Pleasuredome, kids. And listen to this, the Escape Act Video Mix" but they don't hear, just staring all excited at the different movie posters and Jayne arrives out of breath.

"Look...at who's in *this* one," I say, marvel in my marvellous voice and face.

"What the 'king Hell is it with you guys?" she says.

But we're all gaping in amazement at the theatre like kids seeing *Avatar* or *Bombay Velvet* for the very first time and she understands, a big grinny smile on her face.

"It's called a multiplex." she says and the gang all go "Wow" at the same time.

"No, it's not" I say and Jayne looks um... multi-perplexed.

"It's called, a *shrine,*" and she giggles like she's a teenage girl in the back row of the movies.

"Your innocence...delights me," she says and yep, I don't get it either.

We touch the stone that the shrine is made from, the glass or plastic covering the movie posters, the ground it's built on and the general impression anyone passing by or going into the cinema would be of four escapees from a school for people who are wired very differently, perhaps aliens, or the marrying cousins from *Deliverance* or that other one, um...

People, lucky movie-goers, simply just walk in and we are so envious of their coming soon popcorn pleasure. We study them, full of wonder, seeing how they are, how they act and walk and put money down at the box office for something called a ticket and we're m-for mesmerized.

We immediately launch into a discussion about the long list of movies made *in* New York or *about* New York or *coming from* New York and then watched by New Yorkers and everyone has their favourite movies

153

with a New York connection but not in alphabetical order list:

Ghostbusters.
The Godfather.
King Kong.
Last Exit to Brooklyn.
Mean Streets.
Miracle on 34th Street.
West Side Story.
On the Waterfront… which we're not supposed to have seen, 'cuz well…
PAIGE: *Sophie's Choice.*
JIMMY: And *The Bone Collector.*
Splash.
New York, New York, 'course!
The French Connection.

Which was my input of course and there's a lot more, but…

Most importantly of all…

How will they talk *after* the movie?

Do they re-enact scenes?

Do they say things like "You talkin' to me?" or "It's been emotional' or "I'll be back" or "Is it safe?" Or…

We desperately want to go in, until I remember that avoiding death is more pressing.

Johhny Rotten.

In movies, they're always called Dennis.
Ever noticed that?
"Tooth hurty. Need dennis." Right?
PAIGE: Uh, I think —
JIMMY: So I have that chowder-for-brains thought in
my p-for perspiring head and smirk as we go up the
not-that-nice stairs to the dennis and the girls are brain-
farting because they're wary of how probably *ancient*
the surgery will be, and how the pain factor will set at
the highest decibel level imaginable.
We do decibels because it's to do with music.
A young, kinda grungy, thinorexic, quite spotty, spooky-
pale with penetrating troubled eyes but kinda cool
janitor slops out the hall floor with a bucket and floppy
mop and the girls like him because he kinda looks like
an older Andy and they do a triple take.
Whip — whip — whip!
He doesn't even do a single take, shy or something.
Then I see he's got ear-plugs in, listening to music and
I thought 'Interpol?' 'cuz they're New Yorkers but
mostly, would I *know* it, 'cuz this city was a puzzling
gig.
I know gig, of course.
Jayne leads the way to the door where it's painted on
glass 'Mr. R. Fripp. Dental Surgeon' and the girls are
maybe right, but once we get inside, Everything's
Alright.
The um...décor? is the colour of the pale grey sky
inside, including the furniture and a carpet.
The shiny, sharp, painful, cutting, gouging, digging and
bleeding tools of the trade are the same as back on the
island, but bigger, and somehow manage to look like
Edward Scissorhand's scary-sharp stuff if he took up
dentistry.
Will they hurt more? I wondered.

I thought I might cry for my mother.

And that made me think of her then, but I forced the nice thoughts away.

Andy looks outside between the blinds.

"Ever get weather here?" which is a fair question.

I've never seen any weather here.

We all think it's hysterical that there's *news*papers and magazines on something called a *coffee* table?

Then we get all excited to see The New York Times and check for stories by Robert Redford and Dustin Hoffman like *All the President's Men* then look at Forbes, but they're hard work, with not enough pictures.

It was kinda sweet as the girls might say, that we all lost our 'news virginity' at the same time, like some information orgy we'd never experience again.

We def would.

Mr. Dennis himself seems ancient to me and really red-faced, with *Nutty Professor* hair, bad skin and a big round "This cost a fortune" he said, belly.

He was perfectly colour-coordinated to the same colours as the sky and I could tell that he had a soft spot for Jayne that probably got hard a lot.

For some reason, I found myself in the part as casting director in a scary office with a camera pointed accusingly at people in auditions.

I would be saying stuff like "So, Mr...um...Brooks. Tell me about your body of work?" And because the studio exec character is cast too young to remotely have a body of work, the guy, who I would cast as Mike Myers, says snarkily and sarcastically, "You first."

The creaking bones man told me about something called casting couches they used to have and the dual purpose they had and I miss hearing particularly those stories from him.

Or the time Missy Diva threw a hissy-fit and a cell-phone and it hit her help, then the press but she tried denying it but an aide? sold the story to the press for money.

You can do that? What for? Then what?

Anyway, it seems I'm first and Mr.Fripp dennis-man leads me to this chair so I lie there, waiting.

The others crowd around, all intrigued and curious and curious-er and Mr.Fripp has to bundle them out the way.

He has this eye-glass thing on like the pawn-man and also has a light on, staring into my mouth and poking about with something.

Then, he says to me:

"Aha."

I naturally thought of the timeless classic "Take On Me."

 PAIGE: ...Don't sing!

JIMMY: We need you, guys.

And Never Gonna Give You Up guy.

"I see it" and I see him frown.

"What *is* that thing?" he says and looks at Jayne.

"You don't want to know, Robert," she says and he says

"Yes, I do," and it see-saws like that until women always win.

Then, it hits me. No, not a silent bullet, or a drill.

Robert. Robert *Fripp?* Who guitared on *Heroes?!*

"Mr. Robert Fripp, did you..."

"I'll just Novocalne you a little," and he has this funcool massive terrifying, javelin-sized *needle* in his hand.

"Um...let me think...um...oh yeah, I know. Nah. You won't," and he seems kinda disappointed, and the others laugh.

"Got any spray?" I ask and he's surprised at this, but that's what he uses.

The high-pitch drilling was ear-rape-ish sound-abuse in my ear, a shock as I had never seen or heard one, except for Steve Martin.

But, if pain had a sound, this was it.

We don't have equipment or sounds like that, even with all the wierdness the musicians are always trying out. Mogwai or AC/DC probably made the closest sounds, or maybe that time...

"Alright, but this will hurt" the Frippster says "Say aaahhh" so I did and boy, was he was right, so it should really have been "Say aaarrrggghhhh!" I think.

To distract myself and knowing the others were next, I watched their reactions.

They all looked kinda green with faces that visitors to hospital death-wards have when they look at what's left of bloody, rich road-kill relatives, hey, cool zombie-movie title, without a last will and testament.

That scared me so I stopped that fast, but not before Marsha could make a cry-baby face at me.

I won't let them hurt you, the hunters, I thought.

But Mr. Fripp worked fast and gently and after not long, he produced a tiny little silvery and bloody gadgetty thing and held it to the light to study close.

"What the Hell is this?" he says and he washes a tiny little bit of my personal blood off, but Jayne already has one of those little clear plastic baggies you get in every serial-killer movie in her hand and tells him to drop it inside and she is the boss of him.

He spends a little more time in my mouth with some kinda gloopy paste stuff and words like "Don't eat or drink for an hour," but, what if I'm hungry?

I stood up and although my jaw hurt, it was a mighty relief that it wasn't from you know *what*.

"Who's Next?" he says and I think of The Who's '71 record while everyone backs off, all toiletty.

"Go on, cry-baby!" I say to Marsha and she sits down pretending to be brave.

She was too.

She tried to smile at me, but just looked crazy.

"Women have higher pain thresholds in preparation for the intensity of childbirth," I say and where *that* came from?! The old guy?

Marsha looks impressed, winks and I love her.

I pretend not to notice Norma's little jealous look.

Marsha tries to mumble as Mr. Fripp works on her.

"She loves to talk when her mouth's full," and I'm pretty sure I saw Jayne blush.

I wonder why she did that?

Norma doesn't seem too delighted either.

"Don't like doing this to healthy teeth," Mr. Fripp says, turning to Jayne.

"These teeth are 'king rotten, Bob. Believe me," Jayne says.

He holds up a second gadgetty thing to the light.

The thought of this thing, and what it does freaked me, and I almost butt-nuggetted and lemonated my pants.

"Want this one too?" he says to Jayne.

"*You* don't, Bert," she said and I'm confused.

I thought his name was Robert or Bob or Dennis or Mr. Fripp?

Anyway, she bags that one too and whatshisname asks Norma to sit.

She looks nervous but does what she's told.

And so, we all get these...what *tracker?* things drilled from our mouths and I hope it makes the others all feel a little safer.

As for me, I'm not sure.

I had a very not-good feeling.

I had this thought that if the hunters were as smart as I'm not, they would have another way to find us.

To...kill us.

PAIGE: Yipe.

JIMMY: They would have another way.

"I'm scared to ask what you're going to do with them," Whatshisname says to Jayne.

Me too.

The Police.

The problem was that although we all had these things
in our mouths taken *out,* we still had them *with* us!
Or at least, Jayne had them in something she called a
handbag which sat by her side.
I hoped she knew what she was doing what she knew.
We kinda felt we had to go along with the whatever
plan Jayne had as we were all grateful that she was so
kind and helpful.
And had a great car.
And also 'cuz she had piles of money to pay Dennis.
I'll never get over this place.
I didn't want to let anyone else sit in Jayne's car 'cuz I
loved it so much and so here I was again, just fondling
and caressing her carogenous zones.
Every now and again, I would look over my shoulder to
check that Marsha, Norma and Andy were in the big
yellow taxi behind and sometimes they weren't and I
got antsy but Jayne said it was just rush hour but not
Jackie Chan and they wouldn't be far behind but when
I asked her how long it usually lasted, she couldn't give
me a straight answer.
It wasn't just an hour, was it?
To be honest, all the sights we were passing were
incredible and so every minute I was asking stuff.
"What's *that?"*
All the time and getting weird answers.
"Gun-store."
"Fishion Herb Center."
"A tattoo parlour."
"A hole in the wall?" like The Hole in the Wall Gang.
"Hangwai, Korean vegan food."
"A *gas* station?"
Or "Banks" who steal your money.
And *Mad Hot Ballroom.*
Then, more questions, like:

"Who's that?"

All the time and getting wacky answers.

"FedEx guy."

"Twitch the DJ."

"Bieber."

"Nils Bernstein from Matador Records."

"*Pet Detective.*"

"Mark Wahlberg" and I go "So fucool."

"Matis Yahu, Hassidic Rapper."

"*Birdman.*"

"A Futures Broker."

"Quinn the Eskimo."

"You haven't asked if we're nearly there yet."

I thought about that for a few secs.

"You're trying out sarcasm" I said and she squeezed my knee making me think that wasn't all she was trying out and the startling thought in my head was:

I have never had sex in a *car.*

That made me take a good look outside at how many people would see, then the size of the car and Jayne. Would having sex in a classic car like this break some petrol-head taboo? And so I came up with my own answer of 'No' to the sex, at least at this point, in this back-breaking car.

But, what about a big yellow taxi?

About ten minutes later, Jayne pulled over in the street and I checked that the yellow taxi was close by and had a better driver this time.

But it was OK, there they were.

Jayne unclipped her seatbelt, grabbed her handbag thing and opened the door.

She scoped the street like some kinda surveillance expert in a conspiracy movie starring Gene Hackman, but still felt very butt-twitchy.

'Cuz, if the hunters were going to be anywhere, this was, *gulp,* a great ambush spot.

Jayne didn't get out and that started to make me antsy.

161

But then, two police cops walked up these steps in front of us and Jayne relaxed.

Before we got here, she had emptied all her personal stuff out of her handbag and I was interested to see the contents of a woman's handbag because I probably never would again.

Crazy chick, like *Girl Interrupted.*

The crud women keep in their bags?

PAIGE: Sheeesh.

JIMMY: Don't get me started.

PAIGE: Exactly my point.

JIMMY: Shall I continue?

PAIGE: Please do.

JIMMY: Anyway, out she gets and the view of her from here is actually kinda cool and I manage a smile.

She goes up the steps and I am scoping the streets nervously in case they are lurking.

I manage to frighten the crap out of myself when I start checking my face in the mirror for little red specks!

And suddenly, the door gets yanked open!

Sweargasm!

I was about to be so outta there and so was my food.

But, it was Jayne.

In she gets and that's another interesting view with the car being so low slung and her skirt only just covering things and I swear I maybe managed to get a sneaky-peeky glimpse and see some dark spider's legs, different to her head hair colour.

"They won't go 'king looking for you in *there,*" she says with a fabooshka face.

She gets herself comfortable and watch *these* girl antics.

Skirt riding at the most impactful position?

Check.

Tug it down about half a millimetre which I've always thought a killer move?

Check.

162

Glance to her audience of me?
Check.
Lipstick on, just so?
Check.
Hair, make up and teeth perfect in the mirror?
Check.
Seat in correct position?
Check.
Switch engine on and rev it high?
Check.
Seatbelt on?
Check.
Handbrake pulled, um...suggestively off?
Check.
Adjust buttock cheeks in creaky, probably moist leather seat?
Check.
Look in rear view mirror?
Check.
Fingers stroking the gear-stick?
OK. I made that bit up.
PAIGE: Check.
JIMMY: Where was I?
PAIGE: Indicator.
JIMMY: Indicator on, look over well-fed shoulder, smile f-for flirtatiously at a cab-driver, lick lips e-for evocatively, smile and we're away.
PAIGE: Wheeeee!
JIMMY: It was quite a performance and watching her drive, I begin to understand the whole 'women driving sports cars' thang that he who is about a hundred mentioned, particularly in supercalifornia, where girl drivers love to put one leg up for air to cool...things.
I loved Jayne's well rehearsed-performance and she knows that I did, so I just looked at her, then made sure she saw me looking at her skirt and thighs.
Then I smiled and slowly applauded her.

She liked that.

And I wasn't even faking it.

I had a question for her.

"How do you feel about...*riding*...in cars with boys?"

She got it immediately, laughed and punched my shoulder and it hurt and I said "Ouch."

"So, why won't they look for us in there?" I say.

"Look behind you," she answers.

I do what I'm told.

The building she went into is called a '134th precinct' and police officer cops stream in an out.

"Told them I found this bag and wanted a reward if anyone claimed it," she made a big deal of licking her teeth where some lipstick had smeared.

"Smarts," I say and mean it and I can tell she liked that. I looked behind to check on the gang and there they were, so I wave and Norma makes a gesture, a hand mopping sweat from a brow meaning sweargasm that's done, and she got that in one.

Jayne fidgets with the dial on what looked like a really ancient some kind of music system? and a rock song comes on but I don't know it, so I start fidgeting with the dial too, getting what Jayne calls mostly static.

"Hurt my car and I 'king kill you," she says and I get that.

"Jayne, um...Marsha said you played T Rex at the club last night..."

"She did? Amazing," and I recognise sarcasm again, but I *so* want to know the answer.

She checks her wrist where a beautiful, glittery old watch is strapped.

"Let's get some food" and I'm interested but curious.

"What is that?" I ask.

"Well, when you're hungry and..."

"No. That," I say and point to her wristwatch.

"A classic Patek Phillipe, wait, you...don't know...?"

"Well, Marsha's Dad gave her a Ro-lex? Which I know is a watch but..."

I didn't know what you're meant to say.

"We do island time" I say proudly.

"Island time?" she asks.

"Right. Day time, night time" and she lets out this big smoker's laugh and punches me on the shoulder and to this day, I don't know why.

Is it New York flirting?

Because, like…ooowww?

Paradise.

Jayne drove us deeper and down into a dark place which really Caspered me and I could see the others in the taxi behind were rattled too.

Norma was banging on the glass and shouting soundlessly, like she was trapped and being taken to a gruesome death, like the babe in *The Long Good Friday*.

"That handsome guy Pierce Something will go places," the old man always said, but...*where?*

Jayne called the dark place a car-park, only under the ground, and I tried not to think about *Saw*.

She saw my head had moved on to *Hostel* and said: "It's alright. You're safe," then licked her teeth, like she meant, "But not from *me*."

City girls. I was liking them.

She pulled the car into a space and a sign said 'valley parking' and the foreign language of this place was totally turning my brain to guac...gwak...gorka...gwaka...mush.

I watched the taxi stop behind us and suddenly...

Screech!

The door is yanked open! Again! Sweargasm!

And this huge big guy with teeth like Donkey in *Shrek* is smiling at me really weirdly.

"Relax. He's going to park our car," and I nodded like I understood.

The others climbed out the taxi and I was impressed as Hell watching Marsha pass over some banknotes like an expert to the valley parker man, including what I discovered later was something called a grachewity.

The language here is explodifying my head!

Norma was glaring at me, again, and Andy was looking at me like I was a fool, again.

There was a sign with a big arrow that said Hard Rock Café that went up to a diner and with such a great name, I was loving it already.

We went up something called an escaliser, kinda like stairs only lazier which opened up to this huge whopper of a place with totally excellent rock music stuff all over the place.

There was quite a lot of cool people at wooden tables and some at the bar.

And to be honest, at this moment, the realisation that maybe we could make it through this, was helping give me an almighty appetite.

Andy went to stare at posters on the walls, while a really gorgeous but fatorexic waitress with a name badge that had Billie on it showed up and said:

"Hi! My name is Billie and I'm your waitress today," sounding like she could be a relative of our waitress for the evening.

I felt sad at that thought.

This one also had forehead complex with a funny fringe, but her zits weren't as bad as she thought.

Jayne also confusingly whispered:

"Look at all her bling," and we looked at her all over but…um…is bling a *disease?*

Anyway, Billie sashayed us to a table like we couldn't find one ourselves.

In the booth, there was these big menus and the colourful pictures of the food made it really easy to help to decide which picture you wanted to eat.

She asked what drinks we wanted, then I watched her sashay away, semi-interested, if you get my meaning.

But then, me and the gang had a laugh, pointing at the menus like the first place we went.

We looked at each other, then over-acted much shrugging of shoulders, face-making, grimaces, groans, stuff like that, all for Jayne.

Jayne took one look at all of us and she laughed aloud.

"Wait, you're 'king kidding?" and we giggled like kids.
"Prices?" she said.
Then Andy actually *sprinted* back and gave:
THE LONGEST SPEECH OF HIS LIFE.
"They...they've got these *really cool* posters
everywhere and I don't mean the Skid Row, Bliss, Pen
Cap, Mentors, Stiff Woodies, Devo, REM, Big Cheese,
Angelique Kidjo, Celtic Woman, Calvin Harris and
Paolo Nutini posters. It's...there's...*Janis Joplin*
and...*John Denver* and...*others!*"
"WTF..." I managed to gasp out because I was...I just
couldn't take this in, this place, these posters.
How did they get here?!!
The girls mouths flapped open without a noise for a
change, but Marsha managed an eensy mousey
squeak because she noticed something.
You great big, beautiful doll.
Gleaming against a wall, only...a Wurlitzer!
This place, this day, this city, was turning out to be one
very weird yet wonderful journey.
We looked away from Andy and the menus to look at
the Wurlitzer in a totally amazed, 'praise you like I
should' way.
We all wanted to go and touch the Wurlitzer and
maybe wetly kiss it, then slide a fondling hand down to
see what pleasure it had to offer, but our waitress for
today arrived back and everyone asked for fajitas or
burgers or salad or whatever.
But the way this day was going, I thought:
"A fried peanut butter and banana sandwich, please,"
thinking that they just might, just maybe.
"Huh. Die young, stay pretty," she said, kinda snooty.
Her tone, glare and stance said, "Sir, I have daddy's
monster trust Trust Fund and I do this uh, 'job' only *not,*
to escape *The Bodyguard* and the penthouse, then I
give my Ha! *Salary* 'pittance' to homeless people when

168

I serve them sloppy soup from our own silver platters..."

But then she beams a big, gap-toothed smile like Madonna in that film on top of the car when William Defoe might just have his tongue right up...

"Oh, it's off today?" I say and Jayne watches me work, a master-class in flirtology, then I order *Tortilla Soup.*

I can tell Jayne wants to *be* that waitress, or even just younger, but she shouldn't worry about that because I definitely would.

Billie gives that big smile that says with her, I would have a lot on my plate.

"How could you not know what prices on a menu are?" Jayne asks me.

"Well, that's a good question. Marsha?"

Marsha smiles un-competitively unlike Norma and looks at Jayne with eye-daggers.

"Well, we don't do money..." and trails off.

"We...don't do...the cost of *any*thing," I say, then...

"Excellent answer, Marsha."

Jayne has a completely flumboozled —

PAIGE: "Flumboozled"...?

JIMMY: — expression on her face which is kinda cute.

"How did you expect to survive in this 'king city?" she said, another fine question.

"We didn't know what to expect" I say and the others nod in agreement.

"All we knew about New York was...Zagat's!" Norma pipes up.

"So, we thought, at least, we'll eat quite well," I said.

"If you can get the right table at the right restaurant, like maybe The Frying Pan at Pier 64," I also added.

For some u-for unexplained reason, Jayne is shaking her head and it makes her beehive wobble and I s-for surpress the urge to chortle.

"Without *money?*" she asks.

The others just stare at Jayne blankly.

169

"You must have money on the island?"

More blank stares, and butts shuffling in seats.

"But, how do you *pay* for stuff?"

"We…don't. Everything's paid for already," I tell her.

She looks weird, flustered, confused, bewildered, then comes to some sort of decision.

"We need to talk..." she says then "...my little puppies," and I love what she says and the way she says that.

The food was great, though I don't remember what I had, not because of what we talked to Jayne about, but her reaction.

She *freaked.*

The service was great too.

And yes, my portions were massive.

And yes, probably.

I'm finishing off a huge slab of delicious New York cheesecake and glancing at Billie.

She keeps looking at me from different parts of the restaurant and waving a big coffee pot at us which we always nod 'Yes' to and Andy totally loves it.

"Caffeine's *cool* and hot," and he's probably out of his head with it 'cuz he doesn't get it back home.

Home again, home again.

PAIGE: Jiggedy-jog.

JIMMY: I've been talking between mouthfuls which my mother would be not impressed by and I must confess I haven't thought of her much and I wish I could call her and the others chipped in with other stuff when I silently chew and Jayne is desperate to talk more.

I don't think I've seen a more *totally astonished* face the whole length of my life.

She sat quietly, curious as a cat but, with every sentence, her face grew more, well…

When we finish, she shuts her eyes and takes the biggest gulp of air and looks a bit like Stan Laurel.

"Lemme see if I got this right, my babies," she says and her expression is ecstatic.

I should know.

CUT TO:
EXT. THE ISLAND, BEACH - DAY

Crystal clear water like San Pellegrino brand, softly
lapping onto the most dazzling pearl-white sand, like
Persil brand washing powder, little shells rolling back
and forth with the ebb and flow.
A brilliant bright golden sun hangs in the clear blue sky,
not a cloud to be seen.
People frolic in the shallow water, playing with a big,
colourful whatever brand of beach-ball, tiny fish
dodging between legs, eating foot skin.
The young people are all naked or topless, whatever,
and have trim, tanned bodies, mostly.
Momma turtle breast-strokes along with her brood of
turtlettes in tow, then claws onto the wet sand, making
its slow path along to wherever turtles play.
A long row of palm trees sway in a little breeze, some
reaching to the water where some more people flop
lazily, trailing hands in the water, tiny little glinting fish
nibbling perfectly manicured fingers playfully.
It's A Beautiful Day.
I know exactly Jayne's thinking.
'Cuz it's what we told her.
"The island is lush and tropical, in some ocean,
somewhere...far, far away," Jayne sighs.
She briefly opens those thick huge Dusty Springfield
eyelashes that must be really heavy.
She doesn't wait for a reply, doesn't want one, doesn't
need one, eyes clamped tight once more.
She's wearing a wacky Hawaiian shirt, skin-tight now
she's slimmer, cool white capri-pants, big white framed
sunglasses and a lazy smile as she strolls at the exact
right island vacation speed down a sandy island road.

It's lined with tall, thin palms and big planters of lush, beautiful, colourful flowers which wave at her, and gently waft a thousand of only *her* favourite, musky scents.

Big, old trees sway like hula dancers and she can see rich rolling, green hills and mountains in the distance, a heat haze dancing dreamily.

"The population isn't big, mostly English speaking." Everybody is really friendly and smile and say "Jayne, awesome look," or "Cocktails tonight?" and Jayne returns their million-watt smiles, dazzling people.

But not as much as the stunning *famous* couple who walk past her and she stops dead in her path and turns, to see…is it really *them?*…and if anyone else has noticed them, but they haven't and the ice-cream vendor gives her a tall, ice frosted glass of multi-coloured and flavoured delights, topped with nuts and roasted, ground coconut with a dash of syrup and she saunters, licking, sashaying, smiling and flirting.

Through the thick planters and trees, she can see some shops and makes her way through strands of hanging ivy which tease her hair and tickle, or was it, ooh...young man.

"There's so many 'king shops," she says and that's just the way she and everyone else likes it. One is called Floyd's and though it's not pink it's a kinda cool café with antiques and candles and Tiffany-twisted paintings, an old bald guy singing a ballad and a small crowd applauding, deservedly so, because very few can pick at that guitar and write and sing those haunting songs so perfectly.

"You...you never have to pay for *any*thing?" and she is surprised at that, but not at Winona with a clutch of bags and stuff in her small hands, smiling and nodding at her, good naturedly.

Jayne sits at a table, orders some food and recalls a visit to a cool night-club, the music so wonderfully 1970s Club Tropicana.

"The island gave me a special *Boyhood*. School sometimes, if I wanted. I didn't."

She shakes her hairdo for some reason.

"Or, if there was someone in class maybe even sharing your interest in Quantum Leap or whatever, you *might* attend school.

A teacher sits on the floor in a grass hut with no walls, a few students there, or milling about, but all having fun, interested, interesting.

"And he would talk of the rights and mostly wrongs of that off-island world beyond, The Outer Limits, and no one wanted to hear that much more about that, only "Lissen guys, the new Editors format, Ed Sheeran, George Ezra or Elbow?" 'Cuz we're doing letter 'E'.

Through the walls of the hut in shimmering heat, rake-thin, braided rasta mon dances dementedly, hair like an Octopus's Garden.

Jayne says "There's music, sweet music," and a gorgeous threesome fidget with an old LP record until it's placed on top of an old gramophone, plays and off they Shut up and Dance, fun and laughter echoing.

"But, what did you do for *fun?"* Jayne says, playfully.

"Fishing" I go, and the gang shake their heads.

"It's, totally all about that bass," and Jayne punches my shoulder and I tell her "Ow."

I rub my shoulder and stare at Norma, recollecting a fabulous night, alone and wet in the warm water, the moon shining off her shoulders like she's a screen goddess.

And then we're panting like tigers and then we stand and tumble onto the sand and it's hot.

"You always know when someone new's arriving," Jayne goes on, reminding me of watching So Solid

Crew build this awesome house, while a second crew work on this swimming pool for Syd.

"They just turn up one day by boat? Funny no one's ever seen a boat," Jayne says and she looks suspicious.

And of course, I have seen that boat, at least now, *Black Beauty*, ripping through water, fast, scary, hurrying two killers who right this very minute…

"Though, someone's supposed to have seen a plane. Once," Jayne says, probably not really believing that either.

But, where did it come from?

Jayne is unstoppable.

"Beach Boys tidy things, just before it gets dark," and I know she imagines these muscled six-packed big-bicep'd young guys with blonde hair and a tan who will smile at her as she makes her way back to a promise that later tonight…

But then she says simply:

"I don't believe it."

I didn't think she'd believe such an out-there story. Would you?

PAIGE: I —

JIMMY: But I was wrong.

Again.

Because then, she caught me and I think the others totally unawares too, with

PAIGE: Wait. Pause. Time-out. How, could you…*anyone*…run away from…*THAT?*

Something in the way…

"They gave us *everything,* Jayne…" Marsha said.
"Except…*freedom"* I finish for her.
I can't help notice a finely-boned raven-browed
Chinese girl with amazing eyes, hair and skin carrying
a book I have actually, no *seriously,* at least maybe
heard of, and it's name is *Perfume* but I can't
remember how I know it?
Jayne's face has shifted gears from various *Altered
States*, including, but not limited to:
Disbelieving.
Incredulous.
Bewildered.
Curiousity Killed The Cat.
Dree-ee-ee-eams.
Envious.
Could it…
Accepting.
Nah.
Just in case…
Is there a brochure?
Book me a ticket.
July too hot?
But all she says to us, who all stare at this
transfornication like we're watching *Jekyll and Hyde*
or *The Seven Faces of Eve* and I want to get her a
mirror from the make-up girl and show her 'cuz I get
the impression she will never have gone through so
many faces, like a female *Mr. Bean.*
But again, she surprises us.
"But home was a strange unknown Hell," then she
nods to herself.
"Yeah, yeah, yeah," in that sarcastic Beatle-y way she
has.
"Jaynie, I don't think you understand," I say "You can
never leave."

"But, why would you? Who would anyone want to *ever* 'king leave *that*?"

"It was like...quarantine," I say, a new word I found in the dictionary, convinced the 'Q' section would be a word desert.

"Quarantine? I don't...get it."

'Well, it's kinda like being *grounded,* only on an island." She shakes her head at me, for whatever reason.

"Join the gang, Jayne," Norma agrees with…what?

"It was to stop us escaping," I say, but I'm thinking u-for uneccessarily.

"And, to stop others from discovering the island," Marsha piped in.

"But, surely..." she said trying to find the right words.

"Surely *someone* must have..." she trailed off again, then put a hand up to her gloss lipstick, shocked.

"Someone *would* have..."

CUT TO:
EXT. THE ISLAND – DAY
HELICOPTER POV:

The drone-camera sweeps and swoops *Into the Woods* then zooms along the magnificent beach, above swaying palm trees, over lush, rich green, rolling hills where it pans over a crash.

Wreckage.

Of a Cessna brand of plane, rusty, crumpled, burnt-out and torn, bullet-riddled, the pilot on the latest crazed diet fad, wearing a threadbare skeleton body, dead and broken.

Jayne mouthed a vaguely slutty: "My Gawwwd."

"Someone...*did,"* she said, maybe more to herself, because we had never seen or heard of anyone ever finding it.

But, Jayne's right.

Someone would have, must have, surely?

176

And that's what I thought, but never said aloud as it might frighten the girls and Andy and if I said it aloud and if we discussed it forever ever it would do the same to me.

Jayne looked really horrified, because she was thinking about people finding the island...and the hunters.

"What kind of 'king place *is* that?" she eventually says, c-for contradicting herself.

"Maybe now you're starting to understand," I say and the others all nod and even Jayne does, at last.

"Where...could it be?" she asks desperate to know.

"We...um...don't know," I tell her.

"We...um...had no reason to need to know," I say logically, like Mr. Spock.

Jayne nods again and sucks on her empty coffee cup.

I scope the place for the waitress and she appears by my side as if she's on roller-blades.

Play a little hard to get, Miss over-available, I'm thinking.

"It must be...*some*where," Andy says and doncha just love the kid?

PAIGE: Who doesn't?

JIMMY: "Andy's right," Jayne agrees "But, *where?*"

Everybody does a whole routine of 'I don't know' or 'Who me?' or 'Don't look at me' gestures from every film we've ever seen and I'm thinking the French films are the best at mime and meaningful stares stuff.

Marsha bites her lip and stares out the window.

I want to bite her lip and not stare out the window.

"And these...hunters..." Jayne goes on like she's complained to a waiter in a restaurant about the food and when he brings it back and she tastes it, he's dipped his...

"Why do they have to...*kill?*" she says. And why all this secrecy?" she keeps at it.

"It's like they're...protecting something," I add and the whole table stares at me hard.

"But *what?"* Jayne asks, nuttily.

"Well, one thing we *do* know" I say.

They all stare at me like, *en masse?*

Wait, did I just use um…French letters?

"They're not protecting *us."*

"But, what *are* they protecting?"

"You'd have to ask the founders that," Marsha says, intelligently.

"I'll call them," Jayne jests, then: "They in the book?" And from our dumb expressions, particularly mine, she realises we don't know what the book is and she says it's for phone numbers.

"No one would know who to put you through to," I say.

"Who *are* these founders?"

"The people who run things," Marsha says.

"Only, no one admits to being a founder," I say.

"You must have some 'king idea, people talk, gossip, guess, eavesdrop, speculate?!"

I looked up the last two.

"They are very, very secretive," I tell her.

"Like Masons?" she says and we all exchange looks that question her sanitary.

PAIGE: "Sanitary"?

JIMMY: "More like…um…*The Duh Vinci Code?"* I venture.

She laughs — "Hardy-har-harrr!" — and shakes her head again, the hair like a wobbly Marge Simpson.

"Don't mess with the 'do," she says, so we won't and don't.

"Won't they be worried about you?" Jayne asks.

"Our parents will," Norma says, until I say:

"Unless…some of them…are founders."

Oops. The wrong thing to say out loud, because the very thought, the slightest suggestion, sets Norma off on a fraught journey of nail-chewing, rag-nailing, navel-staring, brooding and ruminating and ponderingness.

"The founders *will* be worried," I say and can't stop my mouth from running away.

"Worried we're not dead."

The line drops like *Black Hawk Down* into the room and it's too late to take back.

Marsha, Norma and Andy gape open-mouthed at me and I suddenly want Miss overly-available waitress to re-appear with more caffeine. Or maybe a spade and I dig a hole I can climb into, or even her bed.

Then I figured, well, I've started, so I might as well.

"Thing is, if any of them admits to being a founder, *then* they have to admit that…they *sanction* the hunters."

I know the word sanction from I think a hot or Cold War movie or maybe it was Clint Eastwood, or both?

Andy and the girls just slumped like their strings were suddenly cut.

And that's just how I feel, now I've spoken my innermost thoughts aloud.

Jayne looks between us, unsure of how to emotionally rescue us.

"My God...no wonder you wanted to escape!" she goes. I lift up my head and eye-smooch her.

"No. That was something completely different" I say.

Kid.

"Back into holiday-of-a-lifetime mode," I say to Jayne
and her face presses close to mine like she's against
glass, with my face pressed on the other side.
"It was a glorious day, with a production designer's and
cinematographer's perfect heat-haze shimmering and it
made everything kinda druggy and dreamlike."
A little like some of the scenes in *Trainspotting* or Fear
of living in Las Vegas, maybe.
The whole table was looking at me now and I felt like a
diamond with all the pressure.
To get this part of the story right 'cuz…
It was how this whole mess got started.
"Norma and me had to um…cool down," I said and
thought of that day and how when she wrapped her
legs around me…
I must have drifted off because all I heard was:
"Uh, lover-boy?" and I recognised Marsha's voice with
an unimpressed tone.
"Oh, sorry. I um…I can't remember if we were naked or
maybe not naked," and I said this for Jayne's
expression and to test Marsha, but she had on her
Mona Lisa Smile.
"I had chased her along the beach."
I didn't really but thought of some movies.
"Kinda like watching *Ten* only it's *Ocean's Eleven,"* and
I squinted at Norma's face all puffed and pretend-
pouty-like with the compliment, then Marsha's and I
definitely see more than a hint of the green one.
"After she let herself get caught, we went into the
water. There was no one about, so Norma said "Let's
Get Physical" and so that's what we did."
"Wow" I said and that's all.
I could feel all eyes on me just like Tupac.

180

"After...hiding the salami, we ran into the water again and then started to play 'the splashing to wash sand off delicate little pink and furry places' game."

Females shifted on seats around me and I don't just mean our gang or the waitress.

"We cleaned ourselves, then flopped onto some palm leaves and waited till the sun did its job."

Jayne must have a good imagination, I could tell from her face and I briefly wondered where her other hand was.

"We didn't notice the kid, because we were talking about The Manic Street Preachers again."

I was watching the looks on Norma, Marsha and Jayne's faces and they were a riot.

Anyways...

"He was a great kid, maybe something around like, six? He had that coffee-coloured skin that never seems to burn and was very handsome good looking, kinda like actor Salman Khan, only aged six? We called him the kid, but his name wasn't that. I...don't want to give his name, because of who his mother is.

You'll...*know* her.

PAIGE: I shudder to think.

JIMMY: He was all alone and I could see him splashing around the water's edge and he was having a great old time.

He had built some cool sand-castles and started kicking them apart, laughing his little head off.

That must have been when he noticed us.

He couldn't have seen us having sex, but anyway..."

I glanced at the girls again and could see that the body language had changed.

Norma all open to me, Marsha not, Jayne thinking about it, the audience all the way.

OK, I messed up with Marsha again.

Anyway, back to the story.

PAIGE: Please, quick.

181

JIMMY: "Me and Norma started kissing again," and I'm thinking, 'Stop saying stuff like this around Marsha, stufus.'

"But by this time, I'm too kinda aware of the kid. And now, he stands looking into the water and I'm thinking that's to pretend he hadn't seen us."

It's so weird thinking back on this now.

"Maybe he'll wander off," Norma says again and now she's panting like a bloodhound and Norma nearly chokes on her drink and I can tell Marsha wishes she would, or me, maybe.

"I was, um...occupied...so I didn't see him, but he musta seen *it,* in the water."

Jayne is wondering what the Hell is it I'm talking about, I'm thinking.

"And I can only guess that he picked it up, but it didn't interest him, so —

Then, a shadow covers us and I drag my wet face off Norma's.

She shields her eyes from the sun.

And it's the kid, staring at us.

Next thing, he's giggling away and I wonder what's on his tiny little whatever year-old mind.

Suddenly, there's something soaking wet and slippery and slobbery on Norma's face, then his giggly face and little legs are outta there faster than I thought a kid ever could.

Norma lets out a girly squeal and the...thing...it...slips slowly down her face, onto her neck, then her shoulders, over those breasts, onto her stomach, between her moist thighs and..."

I look up at everyone and become aware that most of the people in the diner are staring at me with that kinda leery look.

"Jimmy, what the 'king Hell was it?" asks Jayne, the first to break The Sound of Silence.

"Um...well...Norma made a big mock squeal like she was Sigourney Weaver in *Alien* after Face-Hugger um…hugged her face and she tossed the thing off her onto the palm leaves."

"Jimmy!" squawks Jayne, impatiently.

"Well, I um...didn't know, at least at that time," I said to Jayne and she coulda maybe shoulda probably slapped me.

"But, when I had stopped laughing, I looked at the soaking wet thing," and I nodded my head at Jayne. Her eyes look up to *Heaven.*

"And when we had...finished...and it had dried a little in the sun..."

"JIMMY!!!" Jayne shouted at me.

"I picked it up and we had a look at it, and..."

"AAARRRGGGHHHH!!!"

Jayne starts to pound her head off the edge of the table and that was funny.

Marsha's not laughing, though.

"Jimmy," she says and I like to hear her use my name, but would prefer to hear it when she says faster or Love Me Harder or you're the only one, or come on, big-ish boy.

PAIGE: If that is appropriate.

JIMMY: Believe me, it is.

"Well, I think it was..."

Now a lot of them look skyward.

"You call it, um...a book?"

They all start to stand at the same time as if to leave.

"But, it wasn't a book, at least, I don't think."

They're all starting to leave now.

"It was..." and I'm laughing now.

"It was...Zagat's" I say and Jayne stops dead in her tracks.

"What!!! Zagat's...made you want to leave *Paradise?!!*"

"Um...like…kind of," I said.

"Jimmy. Do you always talk in riddles?" she says.

183

"Well, it wasn't Zagat's. It was...what was *in* it."
And I remember I'm back on the island, peeling damp
pages of Zagat's apart carefully, tearing pages.
"But...places to eat and clubs and…?"
"No, not *just"* I answered back.
Now it's her turn to say "Uh..." totally brain-fried.
"It was about..." and everyone's waiting for me.
"It was about *New York."*
"AND???" she says on behalf of everyone.
"Well, that was it" I reply.
"WHAT WAS IT???!!!"
"Well, it was full of places to eat with five stars from
critics and probably you can only get the toilet table
and some sniffy maitre...um...'d *pretends* you can't..."
"It made you want to see..." Jayne guesses,
"the...outside world."
I give her my practised nobody-home look.
"I've had enough," she says, then, "Let's go," to the
others."
"It made me want to see...*New York!"* I say to her back.
But, she just can't resist, and I just *know* she'll say it.
"Why, Jimmy?"
"Well..." and I give her my million-watt, way more like
lightning than Tom Cruise's smile.
Works every time.

Hey little rich girl.

"It was because...I had to find all I could about *him,*" I told all these attentive ears.

I half expected them all to get really impatient with me now, but —

PAIGE: Yes?

JIMMY: — wrong.

They looked *interested.*

"The man who started me on my journey."

They just all stared at me, like watching a movie where a man peers into a pet shop window and all the pets have begging Pixar eyes that plead 'pick me.'

"The old man," I say, but Jayne's not joining the dots right.

"My great grandfather?" I tell her.

She asks: "Right, but how the Hell did you make it outta there?"

Norma squints at me, kinda sorta pretty embarrassed.

"Well, there was a curfew...that's when you're not supposed to go out after..." I start to tell Jayne.

"I know what a 'king curfew is, Jimmy" she says, sarcastic again.

"Right. Well, we were out late. Up...late," and I glance at Norma and then at Marsha who shakes her head, really pissed.

I'm going to take that as a sign that she's interested.

"*Very* late. Very...*up,*" I go on.

Then, I'm thinking about that night.

Big stars twinkled in the deep blue sky and the temperature was perfect for...

The water was warm like a bath and welcoming and moonlight would have shone on our naked bodies in our favourite little bay.

Palm trees drooped across the water and sometimes we had sex on them, lying or standing, or up a tree.

But that night, we were on the sandy beach, waves lapping with Norma on top 'cuz she only comes when she's on top, so it's her personally preferred poke position which is:

Illiteration.
Words that start with the same letter, smarty pants.

PAIGE: Jimmy, that's *a*-lliteration.
JIMMY: I can feel all their eyes on me, except maybe Norma who is maybe getting bored with all the sex-talk with her as the only girl involved.
And I think that's Marsha clearing her throat to bring me back to earth.
"Oh...sorry. It's just that, it all seems like...like another lifetime ago," and I know that connects with them because I feel waves of sadness and maybe regret.
"Anyway, I thought I heard a noise," I continue.
"A peeper?" Jayne asks.
"A...pooper?"
"A peeper. A peeping Tom? A perv? You know, someone spying on you, watching you having...you know...peeking at you...in the water...dogging?"
And I'm staring at her like she's has totally lost it and the others look between themselves.
"...and one hand can't be seen, because..."
Suddenly, she looks mortalfied.
"You don't have...you don't do…you don't…" and Jayne looks really uncomfortable.
"No, of course..." and she wriggles a little in her chair, so I take advantage of her, obviously.
"Would *you* have, Jayne?" in a starey, challengingy, slightly I-was-a-teen-male-slut *American Gigolo* way. She looks shocked so natch, I keep going.
"Would you...*like* to?" and it's torture to keep myself from laughing, but the girls come to her rescue.
"Stop that, Jimmy!" Marsha says, keeping a snigger in.

"He does that to us all the time, Jayne," Norma says and Jayne realises she's been had.

In her dreams…

"I'll spank you," she says to me.

"With a wide leather belt? Or a whip? Then after, pour Grand Marnier onto the welts and lick it off slowly? Then, the cream...which seeps…"

And it's no use, I explode into laughter.

I just notice that the waitress was within spying distance and she looks all dewy-eyed and hurries off to the toilet for some reason.

Jayne shakes her head at me.

"You are a naughty boy," she says and in that moment, know that she is a *very* naughty girl and more than my interest perks.

I can tell she picked up on that.

"But, the...noise?" she asks, changing the subject.

"Yeah, a kinda weird noise."

"I thought it was Norma at first," and she digs me hard in the ribs. Between that, and my shoulder…

"It came closer and louder," Norma pipes up.

"A kinda scary, chugging sound, big and powerful," I tell her.

"Like I said, I thought it was her."

"We had never seen one before," Norma interrupts.

"It was really hard to see, because it was painted all in black," I say.

"The only way we could make out it was because we seen someone's pale skin on deck."

"It was a boat or whatever, big and fast, then slow as it got closer to shore," I told them.

"Then, the engines were purring like a big pussy and I thought..."

Norma mock glared at me again.

"...I heard voices, a man and a woman and I thought I recognised them, but couldn't quite place them."

"I heard them talking about bringing in supplies," Norma said.

"And…a visitor," I said, then "Rumour is they let certain people take a look before living on the island."

Jayne looks hyper-ventilated-interested.

"Next thing, the boat's at the water's edge and ties up at a little jetty that we never even knew was there. There was trees and palms covering it. They lifted off. Musta been electric."

I nodded at Norma.

"We decided to get up closer," she went on.

"They never heard us coming," I said and no really, I totally promise it wasn't a sexual reference, but, once you get a rep…

Anyway, Jayne mock punched me on the shoulder a little too hard and I kinda liked it and the air suddenly changed between Marsha and Norma.

They realised my trilemma, they had…a *competitor.* At least, I thought that would be what they would be thinking.

"After a minute, a little dinghy chugged through the water with a third shadow on board, a tiny little thin woman."

And my mind went back to that, just when they helped the tiny little thin woman climb onto the jetty.

Onshore, someone shone a flashlight at her and we could see she was bird-like and over-dieted looking and was dressed like, what, a hippie? And had bigger hair than you, Jayne.

And the woman waved and went toward the light.

I heard the two voices say something about the visitor, something about her being an amazing talent, but not what for.

The old fella told me some people changed their names when they came to the island, or used their real names, not their showbiz names.

At the time, I remember thinking, why would anyone want to do that?"

Not any more.

"Anyway, I didn't catch the whole story. Next thing, they're back on the dinghy and load stuff onto it. I heard the woman say how much they loved Madras Mahal Indian Restaurant in New York.

I have several thoughts at the same time. What's an Indian Restaurant? What's this amazing talent do? And, most importantly of all, these guys went back and forward to...*New York.*"

"We thought those voices belonged to Crawford and Hutchence but in the dark, we couldn't be sure," Norma said.

"That was it for me. I made up my mind."

"We knew security would be all about *her*, the visitor, so perfect chance," Norma said and *this* time, it was Marsha who frowned at Norma.

Interesting air.

"We didn't think too long about it. We just grabbed some stuff from home..."

The waitress arrived yet again, looking a little flushed, and I am getting a little bored by all the attention and wired with all the strong-as-rocket-fuel caffeine.

I can see who the waitress thinks is *her* competitor among all the others because her eyes settle on surprise surprise...

PAIGE: Who? Who?

JIMMY: Marsha.

PAIGE: Ooooh.

JIMMY: City girls seem to find out early.

"I was Down In The Park...with Mac," Marsha says and we all kinda go quiet, thinking about him and Grace shot to death by people we thought were friends.

That is a hard thought to bear.

How would you feel if it was you?

Marsha fidgets with her coffee cup, happy thoughts of Mac in her gorgeous head, probably.

"We saw them with bags, running. We knew it could only mean one thing — escaping. That was scary, but Mac, he's...he *was*...headstrong. We grabbed some stuff and followed them."

"Norma and me hid in the boat, once they dropped supplies off," I said.

"Me and Mac waited for our moment and sneaked on."

"We thought the noises were Crawford and Hutchence," I go.

"What about you, Andy?" Jayne asked.

Andy has been his usual deep-because-I'm-interesting-because-I'm-deep printed on a t-shirt self and seems to jerk awake.

"What? What was that?"

"Escape. How did you do it?"

"Me? I just...tagged along," he said and went back to wherever he was in his head.

Jayne just shrugged, maybe finally getting used to Andy's silences.

But it has made a big hole in our conversation and we're all kinda thinking stuff, mainly around the theme of 'what do we do next?'

"I think...we owe it to Grace and Mac and *ourselves* even, to kinda find out more. Find...what we came for. Is what I think."

And I feel all the eyes on me.

Accusing?

Hating?

Wanting?

Waiting?

For me...to justify my...

They all seem to have this silent-movie like *The Artist* conversation with their eyes...which is a gurl thang as everybody knows...and they come to some sorta girl decision and I feel like the accused in *Runaway Jury* or every other courtroom drama.

"Ok, Jimmy," Marsha says, the 'designated spokesperson' she said and I wonder why I feel like I've been found guilty.

And I find myself briefly daydreaming about the possibility of years of back-breaking work...in a women's prison.

If you could see it, then you'd understand.

"But..." Marsha says, breaking my dream up at the part involving steamy showers, prison soap, foam, a bull dyke, a blonde, a brunette and a redhead, each from a different and mixed race, cornering me and...

"*How*, Jimmy?" Marsha asks and my daydream is ruined, until another day, or maybe night would be better.

I am thinking of an answer, any answer, but Jayne says

"Another thing I just don't get."

And I wonder how many things that *I* don't get?

At least, I did *then*.

"Security must be *seriously* heavy there. How the 'king Hell did you get past it?" Jayne says, a good question.

Right.

How did we?

I'm thinking about h-for hypothesising and also c-for conjecture.

And...

PAIGE: ...And?

JIMMY: *True Lies.*

Always Wanted to go into Space, Man.

But remember, this is straight from a guy who's trying really hard to see too many movies and is a huge fan of science fiction.

Alien, Blade Runner, Avatar and *Gravity* are obviously the best sci-fi films ever made and I totally love *Pitch Black* and a lot more, but these are the best of the best, even though the sex is sparse or not even there in fact, apart from the fakery in the *Emmanuelle* ones. Wait.

PAIGE: What?

JIMMY: Is it alright if think I maybe just accidentally invented a new movie genre?

Science *friction?*

The first movie is maybe called *Alien Sex* and the 'premise' is 'relationships between various alien species.'

Creatures like in *Men in Black* would feature alongside actors like Billy Bob Thornton, with the sound-track by Bjork and instead of this.

CHILD STAR
I'm feeling more gooder now.

It could be:

FACEHUGGER
I'm feeling that I'd like to
stick this down your throat now.

Which I think people would pay to see. Insert…

YOU
Your own dialogue.

Anyway, we open to a colossal X infinity black sky and the stars are out tonight, and spinning planets.
And maybe some cool CGI of space debris, but no coffin clichés.
OK, maybe the odd floating coffin.
OK, maybe the floating astronaut cliché, *Lost In Space*.
Could there maybe even be a shot through the Ha!
cock-pit window of a threesome in a clinch? A man, an alien and a woman?
A black hole?
And right there, hanging in the sky, is what I believe old guy called a six finger satellite.
This, my friends, is *The Spy Game*.
It will observify whatever it is programmed to watch, then report back to...where?
I wish I knew the answer to that biggie.
Anyway, its fingers are cracked.
It manages to hang in the sky alright, but what twinkled before, twinkles no more.
It is useless.
Like in a wilting condom moment.

SMASH CUT:
EXT. SPACE - NIGHT

The camera sprints through space, down to earth, across green and blue to fix on...
Where!!!!???

ECU:

That's extra close-up, film-fans and this man, say, a head of security person, at a computer desk, scratching his balding, clichéd, square-jawed, grizzled ex-military head.

And maybe someone by his side, say a founder, but in the shadows, maybe raging mad at the head of security about the faulty fingered satellite.
Me, my fingers *always* work their magic.

The Web.

Jayne said she'd "Take me to a strange and wonderful new world you've never been before."
You know what I'm thinking, right?
Older woman vibe, cougar-bait, *Barbarella,* but just with women. *(Winks.)*
PAIGE: Chauvinist.
JIMMY: Until she goes and spoils it all with "Where we can find every answer to every *thing."*
Like Who-i-am?
I clambered into her car again all excited, like I was a little kid going to something called Disneyland, Jayne said.
I wondered if we were going to the airport to wow! *Fly* to this new world or NASA, to take like, a Virgin space-taxi or something.
I was asking lots of dumb questions.
PAIGE: No comment.
JIMMY: "We there yet?"
"How much longer?"
"We there yet?"
"Can you stop at the toilet?"
"Got any snack?"
"What kinda music do they play?"
"Um...about the girls there..."
Jayne was having fun with this stuff, too.
"Passport please."
"Did you pack your own bags and could anyone have interfered with you?"
"Please bend over for your body cavity search."
"Have you heard of the seven mile high club?"
And as I'm sure you'll realise, only the club was of any interest to me.
Before I left the Hard Rock Café, the waitress, ignoring the girls shamelessly, said "Can I add you to my fuck-fone?"

"Sure. But…um…your *what* phone?"

"Uh…*fuck*-fone? Friends…who fuck?"

We all just smirked at each other, thought of home and smiled at the waitress.

"Cell, home or office?"

She moistens and I looked around and invented stuff like Kayser Soze in *The Usual Suspects,* gave her a number and she frowned, but I kissed her on the mouth anyway.

She had a beautiful, luscious and willing mouth and smelled truly L'Orgiastic.

The gang took a taxi behind us and we drove toward this brave new world and I found myself getting excited and stoked and hyped and psyched about what it would look like and how it could help us.

We stopped after about how long is half an hour?

Jayne seemed amazed that she found what she called a parking-place and fed tin money into another thing called a parking-meter in case Lovely Rita Meter Maid gave her something called a parking-ticket?

Next thing, Jayne locks her car door in case of thieves? And I'm thinking, this is one ultra-weirded place.

She hurries us along the street, then stops outside this place and with this huge smile, directs us toward it.

It was called 'Café Internet.'

We went in and there was all these people at desks playing at desk stuff.

I didn't see too much Café-ing.

Jayne said "It's full of gechno-teeks," I think.

After I asked her a few more times, she tried to explain in an accent I knew was English.

"There ain't 'alf been some clever bastards," she went. Hey, coolness! Ian Dury!

It had chrome for décor but isn't chrome something you just get on all the old cars, but you don't get now, so they look like shit modern cars?

Jayne gave me her version of Norma's *Mona Lisa Smile* which I understand is her being spyish.

"This is it," she smirks.

"Michael Jackson?" I ask.

"The Brave New World," she says "Of computers."

"Cum...pewters?" I say, confused, yet strangely aroused.

I take a look around at some of the computeters.

"All the knowledge the world knows is in here. Somewhere," Jayne says and I'm thinking she's *Gone Girl.*

She gives the guy behind the desk some money, then leads us to a chair that becomes empty and sits, and so we all crowd around her, like a football huddle.

She starts tapping at what she calls 'a keyboard' that doesn't have any keys, telling us about her impressive WPM, words per minute, and wha'?

"It's called the Internet" she says.

"I...um...know. I, like...read the sign," I say.

"No, no. Not the café. This," she says, talking about something she called 'signing-on.'

"It's also called the world wide web," she explains helpfully and not one of us understands.

"That's why websites start with www."

"We'll try a travel search engine."

"Is this...I mean...are you talking, like...*English* only...not?" I ask.

"The information super-highway. You can access all kinds of data from anywhere in the whole world, just sitting here," she says, looking pleased, then says:

"Like...Sandra Bullock in *The Net?*"

"Why didn't you say that?" I go and we all get it now.

"We could Google you," she says to me, which sounds like a laugh-riot.

I look at the girls and Andy and we all fake enthuse.

She buys it, starts tapping in stuff and I go for some café.

And start thinking about the hunters, where they are.
But, could maybe even *thinking* about them act like
some kinda beacon?
I don't panic.
But my stomach does.

Let's dance.

I imagine what it would be like to be Kevin Bacon in
The Invisible Man.
And so, my imagination takes me on a journey.
No, not in the girls toilets, or Marsha's bedroom!
I'm outside the hunters vee-hicle and I see it's not
shiny, but painted Matt le Black, like the boat.
It's menacing, the blacked-out windows like the closed
eyes of a black panther, the engine running, purring so
you can barely hear it, ready to pounce on its unwitting
and probably quite *stufus* prey.
And there they are, inside.
It makes me think of Pitt in *Troy,* the Brad part where
soldiers sneak out from the horse's ass to strike terror
and death, so beautifully.
A hand flexes, tendons tense and taut like piano wire
and then I see it belongs to Hutchence who then holds
up cool Zeiss brand binoculars to his *Quantum of
Solace* eyes to look closer, but at what?
Sitting right next to him is Cruella de Ville aka Trap
Queen aka Crawford, her *Bewitched* nose stuck cutely
into Zagat's, studying well-thumbed pages really
closely.
Then, after flipping another page or two, but not many
because this is a woman who knows her mind and his
too, tosses the book over her shoulder where it will
land — plop! — perfectly on top of heaps of boxes of
shoes and close neatly, movie style.
Both will wear their trademark black, but you can bet it
will not be the same clothes, but whole new ones from
a wardrobe where everything is different, always
different, always matches.
Hutchence might now whine a line like:
"Try not to lose that one" sarcastically to Crawford.
She is most likely fixing her already flawless face on
with a not big but *compact* mirror and jars of Bobbi

Brown brand and the reddest, glossiest lipstick that I seen here on a poster with fabulous actress S...

SUE: S-stop!

PAIGE: Oh...uh...*(Paralegal assistant Sue Baker enters the room, law-books in a trolley, one open in her hand, lusting at Jimmy.)*

SUE: The...uh...information you wanted, Paige. Uh.

JIMMY*: (Holds hand out.)* I'm Jimmy. You must be Law Sue?

SUE: So could you be, if you mention *that* particular name. *(Sue walks to Jimmy. Lays the book down. Points out a name. Lusts at Jimmy. Then doesn't leave).*

PAIGE: OK, Jimmy. This lady...I'm showing him the entry in The Law Gazeteer...won her court case against an author for defamation of character. *(Long silence. Blank stare).*

PAIGE: Once I *write* the transcript, *you* could be in trouble.

JIMMY: *(Reading.)* Inflammation...of character?

PAIGE: That's *defamation,* Jimmy.

JIMMY: I don't want to, like...unfame anyone.

PAIGE: Will I delete any reference to her?

JIMMY: Would she...like...attend court?

PAIGE: Highly unlikely, Jimmy.

JIMMY: Oh well. Catch *you* later, Suzie!

SUE: Bye! *(She leaves, reluctantly).*

JIMMY: Anyways...

PAIGE: Where were we?

JIMMY: — adding to Crawford's sex-appeal will be the shortest skirt, little more than a yummy suspender-belt in thickness. She will probably mock yawn, turning her face this way and that in the mirror, pretending she's really alone, then, and say:

"Fuck off, cunty."

I have heard her say that to him on the island.

I never thought anything of that before, but now I realise it's a little thing between them, between lovers. Between killers.

And then with Hutchence's throwaway remark, I realise it was maybe her Zagat's the kid found on the beach.

She must have dropped it in the water.

If only she hadn't.

Friends of mine would still be alive.

Crawford still doesn't look at Hutchence.

"Shoe-shopping at Ash then Dolce Vita..." and I see she's not asking him, but telling him what his life is.

"...then, mmm, Lamb Balti at The Madras Mahal," and bleats like a little lamb dying.

"Baaaaaaaaaaa..."

He makes a sound like he has a choice.

But can only sound pussy-whipped.

"I wanted to go to The Indian Palace," he whines like a drunk desperate to get just one more drink, please?

I have heard him snivel like that on the island.

And I think that these two islanders are spending too much time off-island, picking up bad habits.

She looks at him for the first time, a glutton about to eat him.

"And I like how you taste after The Madras Mahal," she says and doesn't mean from a kiss.

He lets out a moan as she very slowly leans to his lap, playing him like a musical instrument, a mouth organ maybe.

It's something she can get her teeth into and she's perfected the technique, where her clever mouth gets his zipper between her even white, perfect dentistry and lowers it.

"Ooooh..." she lies easily.

"Is that a .40 ESP European self-loading pistol in your pocket..."

And the poor boy can't even speak.

"Or..." she mumbles "...are you just pleased to see me?"

And his eyes will roll in their sockets at her exquisite Chinese courtesan standard expertise.

Which she can control like a tap.

She zips him back up in a blur...hey, *careful* there...then climbs like a *Mulan* catwalk model out of the car.

He almost cries from what *Clockwork Orange* called lover's balls.

He checks his weapon...ahem...then fixing himself into a more comfortable position, follows her.

Outside, Crawford is fixing her stockings, teasing the Hell out of him and anyone else watching.

We probably hear cars crash.

We would get a glimpse of her gun, a part of her outfit.

She looks off into the distance.

"Let's dance," she says.

I've heard her say that on the island.

I know what she means now.

I used to think she was talking about sex.

PAIGE: She wasn't?

JIMMY: She wasn't.

She meant killing.

Chapter 27.

PAIGE: You really just want to say *Chapter 27* Jimmy?
(No reply.)
Seems weird, even for you. *(Awkward silence.)*
Why do you want this part in? *(Shifts in his seat.)*
JIMMY: It's…a *movie.*
JIMMY: What about?.
JIMMY: About…90 minutes.
PAIGE: Jimmy!
JIMMY: Jared Leto plays…Mark Chapman.
PAIGE: Who plays who? *(Annoyed silence.)*
What is this, Jimmy?
JIMMY: I said I'd mention it…if I made it.
PAIGE: What do you mean, Jimmy?
JIMMY: He's interested in numbers. Number nine especially.
PAIGE: Jared, or Chapman?
JIMMY: He's interested in doppelgangers, too.
PAIGE: You, know what that *means?*
JIMMY: We're on the same page, Paige.
(Jimmy gets up. Leaves the room.)

Computer Love.

Jayne is totally absorbed by computer love, which I wouldn't know how to even turn on…is there even a switch on anyway?

I'm scoping the place, running hot girl count, but there's nothing on my Radar Love.

Jayne calls a lot of the people here 'anoraks' and 'nerds' for some reason, and although I keep asking over and over, she can't really explain what she means.

Earlier, she told me she 'logged off.'

Sounds like a butt-nugget poking its nose out.

And I'm increasingly wondering and puzzling about how crazy this new world is.

And how the old man would take it now.

The computer machine made some noises that I think would make great SFX in a horror movie, maybe by John Carpenter or Danny Boyle, reminding me of *White Noise.*

"It's a virtual library.," Jayne says, and I look around, but hardly see any books.

"*Virtually* a library?" And as I scratch my head she shakes her hair-do and me and the gang start off what will turn out to be many long exchanges of totally confused glances, stares, frowns, much shoulder-shrugging, surprised looks and nodding in chimp tea-party understandingness.

I vaguely wonder what aliens would make of this.

Then I realise we *are* aliens.

Jayne informs us about:

"Damn pop-ups," she says to the computer like she expects a reply.

We exchange one of those looks I mentioned.

But we ask if it will talk and answer whatever questions she asks it.

She says, "Well not exactly, but yes, too."

"So fucool," I reply.

Then, one of those looks to the confused gang.

"Well..." she catches my stupid face.

"...it can, but I don't know how. But it can *tell,*" she says, thinking that would be helpful.

"Can it *tell* where the island is?" I go.

"Alright. We'll Google," she says and we all laugh aloud.

Google???

Like hip movie *The Intern?*

"Maybe you're on social media, Jimmy."

WTF? Who makes stuff like this up?

The anoraks and greeks?

I ask Jayne and she says people like Bill Gates and Steve Jobs.

People who make up computery stuff need to have weird and unusual names, I think.

"OK, look at the screen. This, is a map of the world."

None of us has ever seen a map of the *anywhere.*

So, this is incredible to us.

So is thinking about the man who sold it.

Did he really own it?

Why did he sell it?

Why didn't he just rent it out for the summer?

And how do you, like, *decorate* a place that big?

Jayne says she's some sort of über-typist.

"Um...Jaaayne?" I start.

"Can you, like, leave that for a minute?"

We are all crowding her, nudging her, peering close, pointing this way and that, talking about countries where we've heard rumours that maybe islanders came from originally.

We're excited.

We're breathless.

This brave new world fills our little heads with amazeness, and we're all frantically racking our brains, trying to remember places and movies.

205

MacFarland USA.
One upon a time in America.
Viva Cuba.
Bombay Velvet.
Lost in Thailand.
Escape to LA.
Sunset Boulevard which, even though it's in black and white, is one of the best movies ever.
Gangs of Wasseypur.
American Beauty.
Then ooh, surprise-surprise, our heads tuned into songs and songsters.
Angel of Harlem.
One Republic.
Midnight train to Georgia.
24 Hours to Tulsa.
The Detroit Spinners.
By the time we get to Phoenix, realizing we do not know the way to San Jose, we even tried to sing parts of some songs.
Shanghai...Nights.
Dum de dum...Rio...
Where do you hm hm my lovely...
Dee dee dee...San Francisco...
Hm hm...Philadelphia...
Hm hm Japanese I really think so, which is, sadly, one of the few songs about masturbation.
Then…
Hong Kong Garden.
The Madras Song.
Out of Africa.
Greece.
PAIGE: "Grease"?
JIMMY: Lawrence of Arabia.
Brazil.
Our Man in Havana.
Te dejo Madrid by boomshakalaka Shakira.

Then Trench Town and Barcelona, much coolness.
Wait till you see what I mean by *that.*
Then, we started trying to make random connections,
like songs and musicians and movies and actors all
together.
Boston and then *The Boston Strangler.*
Micha Paris and *Paris, Texas.*
Then just…
The Texas Chain Saw Massacre, the original version,
of course.
Then back to…
Gino Washington and Denzel Washington.
Japan and Big in Japan.
Dresden and The Dresden Dolls.
The banks of the Ohio which makes me think of *Wolf of
Wall Street.*
Whitney and Houston.
And Jayne is getting pissed and she says:
"What on 'king earth…"
And we interrupt because the word earth has sparked
off stuff.
Planet Earth by Duran Duran.
The awesomeness of Another girl, Another Planet.
Moonage Daydream.
Olly and of course Bruno Mars.
And Venus and Mars Are Alright Tonight.
Here comes the sun…and I look round at the gang, but
their excited faces are stuck to the screen.
I can't think of any involving Uranus —
PAIGE: Thank you, God.
JIMMY: — so I say:
"Life on Mars by David Bowie," and we stop for breath.
Clever Jayne next.
"Look. All these little specks are called *islands,*" and
she points to an ocean, somewhere.

"Island Girl," I say to her and we all applaud and try to sing, fail, try again, fail worser, then try to think of others.

"Which leads us to..."

"The island."

That was cutesy and I give her a solo applause.

She nods, pleased that her work has been credited.

"America. Horse with no Name" is the only thing Andy has said since we got here.

"New York Dolls," Marsha adds weakly.

"Tinseltown...in the Rain?" I ask, trying to restart our fun using musical wonderfulness, but it's gone.

Jayne let us play with the machine and we searched long and hard for the way to Amarillo.

We couldn't find Suffragette City.

The Blue Nile.

Nut Bush City Limits.

Route 66.

Streets of Baltimore.

Stairway to Cleveland.

Or Club Country.

We found Las Vegas but no *Fear and Loathing* or Johnny.

"I'm going to grab us all some coffee. You guys can finish this...this…'king *conversation*," Jayne says and off she goes.

I start looking at the map pointlessly, because I don't have a clue where to start.

"Any...um...of you guys hear any stuff from, like family, about...?"

A row of blank stares.

"Maybe a newcomer let something slip? A sex partner?"

Andy looks at me like he's got something.

"Andy? You got something?"

"Uh. I...uh..." thinking seriously hard.

"I...oh, yeah. No."

I give back an Andy kinda look.

"That's...great, Andy," I say and he's pleased to help.

Jayne arrives with a tray of steaming piping hot over-caffeinated coffee that looks like it would scald your liver off and sits at her spot.

She goes straight to it.

"OK. Anyone have any idea how long you were on the boat?"

"Long? How...um...long is *long,* Jayne?" I say.

"What time did you leave? What time did you arrive? You know?"

Her voice trails off.

She shakes her head.

"Is it, like, important that you know that?" I ask.

'Oooh, just a little."

'Um...right, only…"

"Because I would be able to at least guess how far you travelled to arrive here," she tries.

We all look at her, not really understanding her point.

"Right, my puppies," she says with a big sigh and taps some keys.

"You've no 'king idea how long you were on the boat" she says, e-for exasperated.

The computer screen jumps at her command and something called The Itlantic Ocean pops in front of us.

"But, you landed in New York, so..."

And there on the screen, is the coastline of New York! Awesomeness!

We all exchange impressed-as-Hell looks for the first time since we got here.

"...that suggests New York is the nearest big city."

"For supplies," she adds, clearing it up for us, then:

"But near to *where?"*

"The world is…*humongous,"* I go.

But, supplies remind me of the hunters.

Jayne taps more keys.

Tap, tap, tap!

209

"Jeez. We don't even know where we come from," I say, not believing it myself, and the gang agree.

Jayne suddenly looks closer at the screen.

It doesn't mean a single thing to me, whatever's there.

The Caribbean? I think she said.

Or something.

Did I say that right, PayPal?

PAIGE: *Paige.* It's P —

JIMMY: I started thinking again about pirates and Johnny Depp, then Keith Richards, and...

But Jayne looks like she's maybe been struck by lightning, or spent too long in the sun, or the bar.

She is shaking her hair in what I would call...shock.

She turns to look at us, then her expression changes.

"MY GOD!!!"

She kinda chokes on it and leaps to her feet.

Marsha lets out a scream that almost deafens me.

I don't need to follow her terrified stare.

Time to get back on the set of *Groundhog Day.*

John Woo boo hoo.

"MY GOD!!!" Marsha screams over and over and over again.

Jayne is on her feet, staring in total terrified terror at something, outside.

And that's where Marsha is looking.

I stood up and turned around.

So did Norma and Andy.

We all knew what it was anyway.

It wasn't a what.

It wasn't a who either.

It was a *them*, you probably guessed.

Like in a John Woo movie, only real.

So I imagine I'm sitting in my chair stencilled *Director* and the director's assistant fawns over me with coffee and cigarettes and drugs and money and girls or whatever.

Or maybe you only get that in the green room?

The old timer told me about the green room.

That's where the cast and director and *The Producers* go for drugs or alcohol or a steroid abusing, six-feet-six Thai transvestite with a blonde beard and red wig, a chihuahua under one unshaven armpit and tattoos and huge...well, you get the picture.

PAIGE: I wish I didn't.

JIMMY: But he didn't tell me why it's called the green room.

Anyway, cut to:

EXT. NY, STREET - DAY

THE HUNTERS stroll, slo-mo, across the street without needing to dodge traffic.

Because that's what's done in movies if that's the director's...um...directions?

There might be light rain for cool stylistic reasons, for example, the director might like rain on the camera lens, or water trickling down sleek car windows, or down Wayfarers, say.

Or the window of a Café Internet.

Or, onto a dead, bloody face.

And the music, which will appear in the soundtrack available from your retailer, will be hot and *appropriate,* maybe like Ultraviolence by Lana del Ray.

The characters will look super-cool, like in a remake of *Shaft* but with a white couple.

Shag could be good for a title and box-office sales.

They smile and talk, relaxed and casual with each other.

And with what they are about to do.

And this will need to be in the dialogue, so the audience knows that this is a mega-moment.

HUTCHENCE
'There are things known...'

CRAWFORD, oh, the screenwriter capitalises a character when they first appear, but not after that, will not even give a smile or sideward glance to maintain the coolness.

HUTCHENCE
'...and things unknown.'

HUTCHENCE stops, with probably a half-sneer, a superior, complex and in-character expression that suggests he's profound and intellectual. We care about him, even though he's a nemesis or antagonist character.You'll know them better as baddies.

I know them as the killers of my friends.

Crawford will maybe catch her reflection in a glass window and fix her hair to let the audience into her character.

That will tell us that she's cold as ice-cream, calculating, ruthless and she's so vain.

And well dressed.

We already know her *outer* motive which is:

WHAT DOES SHE *WANT?*

She wants to kill us.

BUT...

We don't know her *inner* motive which is:

WHY…

Does she want to kill us?

Stuff like that goes on in a movie-script without you even knowing.

Whatever, this dialogue is some sort of 'narrative thread' which is a storyline through the story structure, say, a game they always play for *Killing Time* before killing people, but most probably to maintain cool and that Hutchence expects an answer.

Crawford, see what I mean? will half-turn to Hutchence and half-pout to say in her semi-breathless whisper.

CRAWFORD
Give me just a little more time.

But there's maybe back story to that line.

Back story is the other story, that is, the story behind the main plot and sometimes it's more important than the main plot in movies, which makes it odd that it's in the back.

The old man told me all this shit. Oh boy, is it a brainf**k.

As to the back story to this story, *my* story, well, you'll have to wait.

And yes, it *is* more important than the story you *think* you're reading, or watching.

213

HUTCHENCE
That's what you always say.

Which gives us the clue that yes, indeed, this is their game, their fun.
But never mind all or any of that.
PAIGE: Okaaay.
JIMMY: Crawford will produce her gun, super-slo-mo, brimming with sexual tension, innuendo and, like…noise-free death.
She might even stroke the gun, just to reinforce the point that she's Fanatica Sensual and ruthless.
She'll check how that looks in that glass window, too.
I have to admit that she does look hyper-cool.
Like she needs me to tell her that.
The old guy used to always say that movie stars were all about two things.
You wanted to *be* them, or *f**k* them.
That would be her, alright.
So, she raises her gun very f**kably.
Hutchence watches her.
He loves to watch her, at work or play, or any other time.
And, they love to tease each other, physically as well as verbally.

HUTCHENCE
Jim Morrison.

Is all he says, with a small, sly smile.

CRAWFORD
I knew that.

She should have, she *so* very did, but she didn't.
I can explain later.

They both know that and exchange an appropriate glance.

Walking is another thing characters use.

For example, check the walks in QT's *Reservoir Dogs,* particularly the awesomely badass Michael Madsen.

And now, our baddies are stepping toward the window and we catch their evil reflections in the glass.

Me, I *still* can't look at my face looking back at me.

You know, I always wondered how that was done without the audience seeing the cameras reflected?

Anyway, that was why Marsha was screaming.

Windows.

I know that word means something computery to you guys, but not this time.

Marsha suddenly goes totally silent, in shock maybe, understandably.

She starts to back away from the window, and her mouth forms a perfect letter 'o' like a gorgeous inflatable-doll.

I think of lip-gloss brands, then hair roots showing, which is kinda hot, then Debbie Harry.

Norma backs away too, knocking tables over —
Boom! Boom!
— and people in the place look at them like they're worse than junkies.

Andy and Jayne are totally rooted to the spot, which I don't think they wanted to be.

Me?

Well, I was mad at Crawford and Hutchence, too mad and stupid to even *think* about the danger.

All I could do was clench-fist glare at Crawford.

She was advancing, still in super-slo-mo, a light breeze perfectly catching her glossy hair and coat, like a wildlife documentary about big, hungry cats.

She smiled at me.

I smiled back, then waved.

And wondered and hoped, that maybe over a nice Zagat five-star four-course dinner we'd discuss things.

"Could all of this be, like, some terrible mistake? Maybe you just want to say sorry, or, is this part of something delicious and excellent and mysterioso, like *The Game?*"

That writer is one smart person.

But, Crawford pointed her gun right at my face.

That did it for me.

Wrong yet again.

Will I ever get less shit at judging people and situations?

I snatched Marsha and Andy and Jayne and hauled them to the back of the café.

Now, the whole place was looking at us, when maybe they should have been looking where we were looking.

Some kind maybe manager-guy started walking toward us, and I thought he had a good walk.

We all tore for the back.

One well-fed kid looked outside and then it was his turn to scream.

I heard a quiet hiss, then the big window shattered into a zillion pieces.

Smaaaaaaaaaash!!!

Jayne screams at the top of her ample lungs.

"AAAHHH!!!!!"

I see a computer has a big hole in the screen and there's smoke coming from it.

Customers Twist and Shout and bawl and scream and swear and dive for cover and it's raining glass and madness and blood and software.

A lot of poor innocents got cut up, pretty badly.

I feel very bad about that, because it's our fault.

My fault.

Obviously I'm desperately looking around for a way out and there, behind some coffee cartons marked 'Coffee Coloured People' I see a fire exit door.

"THIS WAY!" I shout to the gang and I herd everyone toward the door.

I glance over my shoulder and I can see Crawford and Hutchence outside, just talking, cool and relaxed, in no particular hurry, guns at the ready.

A kinda Marlboro man makes a movie moment. Cool! More illiteration!

But, I'm panicking now big-time, so I toss all the boxes of coffee aside and I see a bar on the door which I slam, hurting my hand.

217

"YEEEOOOWWW!"

The doors don't open all the way because I can see all this crud piled on the other side.

I'm shoving frantically, pushing and thrusting and shoving, looking behind all the time.

After what seemed like forever, there's enough space for us to squeeze through into, and aren't they always, a dark alley.

It's like a scaredy-cat version of *What we do in the Shadows,* but not as scary as what was behind us.

There was filthy rotten garbage all over the place, and we are not used to seeing this, so we're all disgusted.

"Icky," Marsha says as she tumbles into the alley and slips on something and nearly falls on that perfect face.

I wanted to say something important.

"Run for your fucking lives!!!"

And that annoyed me because Crawford and Hutchence were making me mad.

Norma pushes past Marsha quite roughly, dragging Andy by the hand and I yank Jayne out and we climb over slime and goo and crap and gloop and probably dead things and living creatures and maybe some poor homeless guy's cardboard crib.

I scope both directions for the best way out and at the other end, I see a street and people walking past and even though I'm tired of saying it, I still say it.

"We need to get among a crowd..." so shout to everyone.

"Come on!" as if they needed to be told.

We're all trying to run down the alley, but it's really r-for repulsive with slippery gloop everywhere and we're skidding and sliding and sprawling and it seemed like every inch of wall was covered in graffiti.

Some of it was kinda cool.

The ones I remembered were Who Are You? and *Daredevil* and Ashkay Kumar and especially, Queen.

218

I take a peek over my manly shoulder, but there's no sign of the hunters.

"Anyone hear the cop siren?!" but no one answered. I had to keep reminding myself that this was not some movie where the cops magically appeared right in the nick of time. And, I didn't want to think what the terrible twins were doing?

OK Computer.

Here's where I think they are, and what they are doing, and what they will go on to do.

They step through the new entrance they personally created at Café Internet.

And they swagger casually through the place and the manager-guy clings to the wall in terror and customers hug the glassy, bloody floor, not wanting to look but finding it impossible not to, in that horrific, always fatal eventually, *Final Destination* kinda way.

Some moan in pain, some groan in fear, holding bleeding heads and hands and *mouse* mats?

The computer is now on fire, black smoke spewing.

I like that word.

Spew.

I immediately think baked apple because the computer machine has a brand name called a Apple.

And because it's cold outside and there's no window, it blows freezing cold inside.

So, in the spirit of coolness, Crawford and Hutchence warm their hands at the flaming computer.

They talk quietly, maybe about the latest Vivian Westwood Collection, drinks at 7B, the merits of their weapon of choice versus the snipers choice, the Remington 700PSS in *Behind Enemy Lines*, or which of us they would prefer to shoot first, and when.

They scope the place, hoping for target practice on have-a-go heroes.

Or at the very least, someone who just looks their way.

There's one in every movie and 'cuz movies are based on life imitating art imitating life…

Sure enough, someone obliges.

That must have been when I heard a young girl's agonised scream.

I imagine some cutesy girl, probably wearing not Ray-Ban glasses, I'm Not a Girl, Not Yet a Woman, taking a geeky peek between long, thin, maybe piano-playing with actual musicality fingers to see what's happening. And of course, it would be Crawford who notices, smiles, takes aim and fires into the cute girl's lovely not anymore face.

Because that's where she liked to shoot, destroying how you looked and your personality and the part that looked back at the freakin' bitch in judgement.

The cutesy girl would fall onto her back, blood gushing from her open eye, glasses on lop-sided, pierced by a silent bullet. Another life gone...because of me.

The coffee machine would be undamaged, because I know how much these two love quality coffee.

"Coffee smells drinkable," Hutchence would say and then step toward the machine, over broken glass and cowering, bleeding, petrified targets.

Hutchence, comfortable in his professionalism, would take time to carefully pour steaming coffee into two tall glass mugs, not adding anything, carefully sipping, nodding as he's fairly impressed, passing one to Crawford.

The 'why aren't they chasing us' list:

Have they given up?

Do they have new orders?

Is the coffee that *good?*

Or, do they have another way to locate us?

They warm their hands and sip coffee —

Sluuuurp!

Then Hutchence walks to the fire exit.

He climbs over stuff and peeks out, way far.

I had slipped and fell and hurt my knee, so the gang were helping me up, when I look over my shoulder.

And that's when I see him, even with my bad eyes, and He sees me.

He smiles, then makes a gun with his hand, shoots me, and blows his finger.

We all take off again, over-petrified.

221

Hutchence steps out into the alley and his probably hand-made or Gucci loafers maybe stood on something yukky and he lifts his leg for a look.

It's sticky and white from nothing recognisable, a melted condom, maybe.

Now, that's what I *call* friction.

Crawford comes out after him, takes one look at the place and makes a revolted face.

"Ugh," she says.

"Crawford..." Hutchence is teasing.

"...it's alright. They won't eat you," he laughs and at first, she thinks he means us.

Until she steps out, her elegant elongated foot just narrowly missing standing on a filthy fat rat.

There's a squeal, and it's not the rat.

Remember that deadly, ruthless assassin Crawford's just one little pedicured, smooth-shaved, lightly-tanned, slender Achilles heel?

Rats.

I kinda see her point, actually.

She points her gun, not at the rat, but at Hutchence and he puts up his hands in mock surrender.

Crawford looks down at the end of the alley and just catches me about to herd the gang around the corner.

Suddenly, Crawford takes off like someone out of *Chariots of Fire* fast-mo and the boy can run some.

He takes aim and fires.

KA-BOOOOOOOOOM!

There's an almighty ricochet as the bullet rips into a dumpster with graffiti that coolly, says Hole.

The bullet missed me by a hair's breadth and I have to fix my hair.

"Suck's fake! My...hair," I say.

"Hurry up. Hurry up!" I tell the gang, a little r-for redundantly?

Silent-movie bullets spit and whine and tear into the walls, brick dust and parts of doors and garbage flying. I take another look over my shoulder.

A kitchen-porter appears down the alley, needful cigarette in his greasy, pudgy hand. Eyes shut in full appreciation of his break and its reward, he sucks gratefully, oblivious to the hunters. Hutchence is suddenly on him and thumps into him so hard that the man, even though he's a big, lardy guy, bounces off the door and slides to the ground in a crumpled, doughy heap.

Before I turn the corner, I take a half-look and then I see Hutchence bearing full-tilt-boogie down on us like an *Unstoppable* train.

"They're coming!" I shout and push and shove and force them along, even harder, taking the corner fast. We're making for Jayne's car, close by.

She's last around the corner.

I listen for sirens, but nothing.

What I *do* hear though, is a gasp of pain and Jayne falls against me and I try to support her, then we round the corner.

And I'm drenched in her blood.

Sweet Jayne.

Jayne has been hit somewhere in her meaty but lovely
shoulder, at least as far as I can tell.
It looks bad and I think how big the bullets must be.
Yet another innocent victim.
Good work, Jimmy.
She's fading fast and I'm struggling to keep her on her
not particularly light feet.
She's muttering something to me, but I can't hear
exactly what it is, but it's something like:
"If you leave me..."
I'm wondering, could she bleed to death?
And I wish we were in a movie like *The Truman Show*
and remember that movie shots to the shoulder are to
slow people down, not kill them.
Marsha helps me, but Norma is having a shell-shocked
white-out moment, so Andy supports her.
He looks determined and keeps surprising me.
I expect people to stop and offer help, but of course, no
one does.
All people do is make a wide berth around us and
avoid getting blood on their designer clothes or
attouché cases.
Jayne is getting weaker by the second, making it even
harder for us to kinda half-drag half-slide her along.
Marsha doesn't look at me once and I'm thinking that's
'cuz I've got us into another fine mess.
I am also expecting the welcoming sound of just-in-
time police sirens.
I keep looking over my shoulder, terrified that the
hunters would appear.
But thankfully, and *weirdly,* there's no sign of them.
Trying to orient yourself in a strange, unwelcoming city
while pumped full of adrenalin and guilt when you're
carrying a possibly dying and really should be dieting

woman when your hair's probably a mess is no mean feat.

So all I can do is my best.

I see the car.

"Look. The car!"

But dammit, it's across the street and the street is jammed full of rush hour.

But, hey!

Struggling to race in the street is a beautiful pencil-coloured Sledbed, a '69 Chevy and a yellow Mustang! Wow.

I have no alternative but to try to get over the street.

"Follow me!" I shout, wondering if they will, like waiting to pass some kinda leader test.

It's a good thing the rest of the cars are nose to tail, because that gives us a chance to thread our way through.

Even though nothing is moving, we still have to endure a Phil Spector or Glasvegas wall of sound from drivers and horns.

Jayne is semi-conscious now and me and Marsha have real trouble trying to get her between cars.

And when I check on Norma, she doesn't look much better.

Andy is calm as can be.

Don't ask me how, but somehow, even though we struggle and slip and trip on Jayne's blood and stagger and nearly fall, we're at the Porsche.

And I see there's at *least* three reasons why the hunters were so relaxed.

First, all four tyres have been slashed to ribbons.

I dread to think of what razor sharp lethal weapon probably Crawford used there.

Secondly, this is a Porsche Roadster, right?

Two seats in front, two seats in back.

For *Hobbits!*

Three, where would we rush to?

"Sweargasm!!!' is the only answer I can think of.
We're so screwed.
I think I hear police sirens, or maybe A Rush of Blood
to the Head, but then, no, I really do think it is.
But just as I'm thinking 'We're saved' I see them.
The hunters.
There they are, appearing around the corner, all
perfect looking and cool as a water-fall.
But *I'm* not, and I tell you, that makes me sooo angry.
They look over at me looking over at them and then
they do it.
PAIGE: Whaaat???
JIMMY: They wave at me, then blow kisses.
"Suck's fake!" I say like the last words of a dying man.
I look around frantically for another escape plan.

Massive Attack.

It's something called a Tower Records.
A huge, glass-fronted building thing, where I guess
they have, like, towers of records?
Maybe available on vinyl, too? But, different *colours?*
It reminds me of the old folks back home like in *Cocoon*
discussing the merits of various formats like 45s, 78s,
EPs and LPs as I round up the gang.
"Marsha, Andy, help me with Jayne."
Norma looks at me sideways, all terrified and even
though I can't blame her for thinking, 'It's every woman
for herself,' I stare at her.
"Norma, get over yourself!" and she snaps at me.
"Like you're not overly in love with yourself."
"Agreed, but, um…this way!" I tell them first, before
smiling at Norma.
I actually, like, really do *lead* everyone toward Tower
Records as fast as I can go, the three of us struggling
to carry Jayne who could drop several dress sizes, or
give birth to triplet rhinos, maybe.
Now I definitely hear what is music to my ears.
Cop sirens getting a little louder.
"Listen, gang. The cops are on their way!" I tell them.
"If they can hurry past the rush hour."
I take a look toward where the hunters were and there
they are *again,* like *Edge of Tomorrow,* casually talking
as they head our way.
Hutchence hears the sirens, checks what is most likely
probably a fine Frank Muller timepiece and might say
to Crawford:
"We've got about a minute," 'cuz of the cops' i-for
imminent arrival, please.
At Tower Records door, there's a young, obesely
overweight round guy with a bull neck and shaved
skull, dressed all in more black with what looks like
headphones stuck in an ear, and I assume he's

listening to some cool sounds, but he takes one look at us and says something like:

"Shir, yoo cain't..."

But ah cain, and I ignore his amusingly squeaky voice and barge past, Marsha right alongside me, Andy taking Jayne by the legs, Norma kinda wandering in by herself.

The young guy, is he some kinda guard? tries to stop us, but we lower Jayne to a chair before she collapses. Her head lolls, all blood soaked, and her shoulder looks real bad.

"Can you get help?" I shout at the guard.

This doesn't work.

"Whatchacallit? An ambulance?" Which I think is a perfectly sensible question, but he looks at me like I have two heads, *both* stupid.

"You know, the guys that fix people when they're broken? A swearfuck ambulance!!!"

Nothing, not even, "Yoo cain't be in heah."

I grab a cool, white XXXL sized t-shirt-*wait!*

*…it's **Tupac?!** And totally **freaks** me out but I'll have to tell you later.*

I ball it, then press it against Jayne's shoulder.

She moans but in a good way, because that means she's alive, anyway.

And I'm thinking, this t-shirt is freakin' massive.

The guard or whatever is pestering me to leave after I pay for the t-shirt but all I'm in shock.

Tupac. Hunters. Tower Records. Survive, suck's fake!

Then, the guard's joined by another guard who's barking guard-talk into his pudgy, sweaty guard-shoulder and they look across the street to Café Internet.

None of the two of them look helpful, or even nice and friendly and glare at us like we're bank robbers.

Norma finds another chair and flops into it, her eyes all glazed and druggy and not focussed.

Andy watches the door carefully.

There's no sign of the hunters, but they will check in any second, don't worry.

I'm frantically scoping the place for a way out or an exit or something and see for the first time that:

Tower Records is a truly **AWESOMELY** cool place.

There's music formats on CD, DVD and vinyl, and books and life-sized cut-outs, and even cooler mannequins of musicians and they amaze me.

I...KNOW some of these people...personally.

And reason they amaze me is...

THEY SHOULDN'T BE HERE!!!

At that time, I had no c-for context for why they are here.

I find myself stunned and stupefied into more stupid silence than usual.

Then, I see huge posters on the walls and all around me.

And, endless racks of music formats?!

The Arctic Monkeys, Michael Buble, Cheryl, Daniel Ho, Drake, Dresden Dolls, Elbow, Embrace, Eminem, Flaming Lips, gorgeous Ellie Goulding, Flaming Lips, Gorillaz, Gaga, Hozier, Paloma Faith, John Legend, My Chemical Romance, and I know it was totally the wrong time to do it, but I had a good look to see if they had KD Lang, The Kooks and LL Cool J.

And you know what? I get a little...*scared.*

And a big bit wierded out.

What kind of place is this?

This city?

WTF, what, where, whoa, wow have I got us into?

But I'm fascinated by this Tower Records place, so I keep looking around.

There's Miley, Nina Simone, Pharrell, Pearl Jam, Sam Smith, Ed Sheeran and I suddenly realise why you guys do *alphabetical order.* It's to find stuff easy.

Everyone's here and I think I can remember some more in the right order.

Beyonce who somehow, does singing AND movies!!!
Swearfuck!

And there's Cream and Darius and The Eurthymics right all the way through to like, Lynyrd Skynrd, Nicki Minaj, Pink, The Proclaimers, The Streets, Taylor Swift, Ten Years After and Wishbone Ash and X-Ray Spex and Hey! I totally *luuurve* this place!

A kid stands in a booth, Danny Trejo at whateverteen, wearing massive, probably ancient, deafening, heavy on the bass headphones, listening to what I think is I Could Fall in Love in aural aurgsm I totally relate to and he stares at a book called Twenty Seven.

He's oblivious to what's happening around him.

And all around Tower Records, interesting people are flipping through the music from different artists and decades excitedly and this is all happening at The Speed of Sound and natty what, sales assistants? Glance at us and wearing, wait for it:

MICK RONSON TEE-SHIRTS?!!

And they're serving a long queue and I realise.

All of these people are indeed, very, very special.

These people are actually...*fans*.

And for what seems like forever, I am touched by their presence, dear.

The thought that they really are actually music and movie fans makes me stare at them, looking for, I don't know?

But it fills me with wonder, and I immediately think of the old guy.

He spoke about the fans a lot of the time.

Which reminds me why I'm here!

Which makes me think about our situation!

Swearfuck!

I look up to see Andy has left his spot at the door.

230

In fact, he's right beside me, but he's shaking and knee-knocking like a little new toiletty puppy dog probably would, if you were allowed one.

I look from him to the guard guy shouting at his shoulder and I don't know where the other one has gone.

Suddenly, Andy whimpers.

I tell the guard.

"The ambulance on its swearfuckin way?" but when he turns and stares at me, there's nobody home and blood runs down his face which is 'cuz o' the hole in his head from another whispery silent bullet.

And that was why Andy whimpered, I guess.

The guard guy seems to slide to the floor like a sheet of paper in the old toons, dead like all the others.

The thought of all the people dead because of me, was making me feel spewy.

But I have to try and get us out of this.

Norma and Andy are rooted to the spot.

They haven't seen the hunters and neither have I, but who else could it be?

I grab a bunch of t-shirts and lower Jayne to the floor with what I see is a cushion of Liam Gallagher's cool, sneering, printed faces for her pillow, many a girl's dream.

Jayne's drifting in and out of consciousness but manages to smile and gasp a weak thanks, obviously an Oasis and Beatles fan.

I talk to myself.

"You're just as bad as the hunters, Jimmy." I'm not actually shooting them, but I may as well be.

A few customers become aware of what's just happened and dive for cover in Hey! McBusted! shelves and exit doors.

That makes the other customers take notice and soon the place is a sea of people panicking and shrieking and running around and bumping into each other and skidding and slamming heads and hitting the deck.

I don't know, I can't tell if the ones that hit the floor have been shot in the face or head, or not.

Marsha grabs Andy and they hide behind some long racks of formats.

One, gulp, is A Teardrop Explodes.

Then, I grab Norma and we hunker down beside Andy and Marsha who actually manages a smile, but a *strange* one.

All this smiling from people is making me feel more and more sick and guilty as Hell.

I see the natty sales assistants have ducked down behind their desk where Blink 182, We are Scientists and Wheatus posters are stuck and one keeps peeking out for a look because we *still* haven't seen the hunters.

And I see a hand as natty sales guy reaches toward a big red Bond-movie button under the desk.

Suddenly, he hesitates.

I follow his frightened gaze.

No, not The Spice Girls poster showing actual *reunion* tour dates?

Crawford.

She looks wonderful tonight.

She even flicks at what must be an imaginary speck of lint on her coat, then smiles for her terrified audience. All eyes fix on her.

And for some insane reason I'll never know, *Marsha* has stood up to stare at Crawford!

Call me shit-brain, and lots of people do, but I can't help thinking that facing down a deadly armed assassin Hell-bent on your death while un-armed, is not one of your better ideas, Marsha.

I'm going to get her.

"Crawford, we can talk about this," Marsha says, all shaky.

Crawford smiles engagingly at Marsha and for the tiniest of moments, I'm talking to myself again.

"Hey, maybe Marsha's called it right," and so I decide to give it just a sec.

But Crawford produces her gun in one slick, stylishly-smooth motion and points it at Marsha.

I see from the side of my eye that a young girl is gesturing madly to the Mexican-looking kid wearing the headphones who is still oblivious to what's going on, even the Marvin Gaye song probably, calmly and contentedly reading a format box with The Feeling on it, which I totally relate to.

Crawford speaks softly and quietly, without malice in her voice.

"Alone and Easy Target."

Hutchence walks in handsomely, scopes Tower Records expertly, and naturally lingers on the shapely Lady Gaga inflatable-doll, which I'd like to take home.

Hutchence takes us and Crawford in, and smiles.

Crawford cocks her gun and the horrible, pre-death sound echoes in the silence.

Marsha does not flinch!

Man, she is one brave girl.

If that had been me...

It *should* have been me.

Finding new levels of stupidity and some small measure or maybe DNA material of *Gattaca* bravery or it might have been the lust at work to impress Marsha, I launch myself at her.

I crunch not unhappily into her and we roll to cover beneath the racks of music which I notice is the 'K' section and for the briefest sec, wonder if Wiz Khalifa have anything new.

Greatest hits, *live*, would work great, right?

Hard as it is, I decide that it's the wrong time to check the nearby 'B' section for what Bowie's up to.

Andy and Norma are on their bellies, snaking across the floor to hide deeper into Tower Records.

Then I *Definitely Maybe* hear police sirens blare and cars screech up and shouting and loud cries, mayhem.

I wonder if the cops are outside, or coffeeing at what's left of Café internet?

Either way, they'll be here soon, I hope, and think about trying prayer, then Jesus and Mary Chain.

Which seems to be some sort of cue, because then, all kindsa Hell breaks loose.

Crawford and Hutchence start firing wildly all around Tower Records.

There's terrified screams and shouts and cries of agony and yelps of "Yipe!" and twinges of torment and I force myself to take a look.

They are shooting up the place like we're on the set of, and are actually *appearing* in a *Die Hard* movie killing the musicians cardboard cut-outs and mannequins, sending fragments flying of assorted fluff, cool posters and CDs in alphabetical order.

First to go are Aerosmith and Al Green all the way through to Galantis, Maroon 5, Rihanna and Tove Lo, not forgetting Zappa and Zutons, of course.

Then, something else totally insane happens.

Jayne is crawling toward the front door!

She leaves a trail of blood, kinda like a poor, wounded, walrus-sized, but in a nice way, snail.

My heart aches for her.

I go to help her, suddenly noticing that the place has just gone quiet.

I look at Crawford.

She looks back at me.

Then, she takes aim.

Suddenly, Marsha dives at me, knocking me to safety below some upturned racks of the lovely Dolly Parton that look really cool.

But, Crawford had been toying with me.

234

I peek out and see her game.

She slowly swivels to point her gun at Jayne, now close to the door.

Where are the cops?!! I'm thinking desperately.

Crawford follows Jayne's slow and painful progress and cruelly, lets her reach the door.

I try to stand, but Marsha grabs me and I knock my head hard off David Guetta and I'm dizzy.

Then, with a big smile, Crawford fires...into Jayne.

PAIGE: No.

JIMMY: All I hear is a tiny, soft whimper and I try to focus on poor Jayne's body.

I am close to tears and full of rage.

I jump to my feet —

PAIGE: Yes?

JIMMY: — and charge toward Crawford.

And right at that second, a bundle of cops appear at the doors in a crouch, guns drawn, carefully scoping the place.

One cop fixes on Jayne's unmoving body, the others on the hunters.

Crawford and Hutchence whirl to them at the same instant and Marsha hauls me to the floor.

We all crouch behind Daft Punks and Clean Bandits which look sturdy and maybe bullet and hopefully Crawford and Hutchence-proof.

Crawford fires at us —

BLAM! BLAM!

— but the rack does the job, though sacrificed in our place, is Jamie Foxx!!!

But, he's an...***ACTOR!***

He was in *Ray?!*

Him...Beyonce...

What...the *SWEARFUCK?* is happening?!!

"Put your weapons down! NOW!" a bossy cop commands and sho nuff, the hunters ignore him.

Crawford spins and fires at him.

235

He gets nicked in the ear and he curses, not realising he's an Emerson, Lake & Palmer lucky man.

Then the cops dive for cover behind some Mumford & Sons racks, one with his gun at the ready.

Bossy wounded one is mad and blood seeps between his fingers.

He gets on his radio or talkie-walkie and talkie-talks and the other one shouts.

"We WILL fire! Put down the guns!" but the hunters rain bullets on them, us and all around the place.

It's filling with gun-smoke and dust and fragments of various formats, and Pablo Honey, Vanilla Ice and Hot Chocolate pour down my face so I can't Jay Z a thing.

Then Brian Eno and Morissey land on top of us, and where's Kelly Brook?

I wish me and Marsha and Norma and Andy and Jayne were likenesses in cardboard.

I hear even more sirens, more screeching tyres, doors slamming and scurrying feet.

Scurry, scurry!

Dozens of cops appear at the sides of the door, darting heads in and out cautiously, guns high.

They look kinda scared and that makes me even scareder.

And I think we're really not in some shoot-em-up made for television MOTM.

But The Real Thing.

Crawford and Hutchence fire at the cops while they run to the back of Tower Records.

There always seems to be doors painted 'fire exit' in New York and that's where they head.

The cops peek out and try to get a bead on the hunters with their weapons but they Zig and Zag like crazy experts and anyway, there's too many people about who might get hit in an 'innocents caught in cop crossfire' newspaper headline I seen kinda way.

At the fire exit, Crawford kneels and fires over and over at the cops, who stay put behind the walls.

Hutchence gives an impressive side-kick and the doors crash open against walls —

CRAAAAAAAAAASH!!!

— really loudly.

Then, they both fire again and I think.

Where are all the bullets coming from?

But before we realised, they were gone and some cops followed, while bossy wounded one still barks whatever cops do into his radio.

Norma is already kneeling beside Lunchmoney Lewis CDs and Jayne on the floor and she's shell-shocked.

I run over and I see a big pool of blood on the floor and Jayne looks...she looks...dead to me.

Marsha steps up and looks down, horrified, silent.

Andy is by her side and just takes one look and has to turn away.

Sobbing and cries for help start to come and I think that maybe other people have been hit, so I take a look around.

Sure enough, there's a few casualties, but considering the amount of bullets flying, we got lucky, babe.

I look back at Jayne just as two angry cops come up to us, guns at the ready.

They look like they would kill, hopefully not us.

Lots of other cops pour past and head out in pursuit of the hunters and they better be New York's finest.

Scraggy cop kneels to Jayne and checks her vitals.

The big cop barks at me.

"Do you know this woman?" and that makes me think.

If I say yes, or no, what will happen?

You have to remember that this kind of thing never *ever* happens to islanders and I only know about it from etc. etc.

The scraggy one checking Jayne looks up at his partner and I can't tell what that look means in *Cop Land*.

"Um..." I say, buying time.

The cops give me a dead-eyed stare.

Then, they look at Marsha, Norma and Andy.

"Um...we just met, so no...I...um...don't."

"*Any* of you know her?" he says but gets our blank, scared witless stares.

"You should see the medic," he says and both storm out the fire exit.

I look at my friends.

They look awful, skin like The Zombies, mouths open in shock and fear and dread and horror, tears in all their eyes.

I look behind where there's cops and medics and wounded and nice people, music and movie fans, blankly staring at nothing, one at a PDiddy CD and girls staring at DVD formats with Gerard Butler, Shan Rukh Khan, and Tyler Posey, boys at Eva Longoria and Selma Hayek.

Me, I'm staring in shock. 'Cuz, on the floor —

PAIGE: Yes?

JIMMY: — is a CD —

PAIGE: Yes, yes??

JIMMY: — that has Otis Redding on...the...cover... WTF...

Then a beautiful girl screams loud as a train in Harry Potter.

I caused all of that.

Me.

I am...

The Idiot.

Somehow, even though I was in a bloody, foggy, dizzy daze like *Virus* and people I think are called 'sensationalist reporters' and maybe detectives and definitely medics kept trying to I think *help* us, I need to get us outside.

But there's a massive crowd of people blocking the door and noise and cameras flash like a Cannes movie premier, old fella would say.

Just plain curious and the blood-thirsty and those I believe get called rubber-neckers which is truly awesome and a-for axiomatic which means it does what it says on the tin, right?

But, I want to ask them.

What *exactly* do you get from staring at dead and dying people, and photographing them?

And there's dozens and dozens of police cops swarming around asking people stuff and writing it down.

Outside, the road is crazy with blocked traffic because it's crime-scene-taped like CSI and cops and cop cars and ambulances and the big red monster machines like *Transformers* are called fire-engines.

A lot of names are written on the side of the vehicles for some reason and a lot of women flock to the guys in uniform with offers of sex.

I figured that Crawford and Hutchence will have been in shoot-em ups like this before and will be long gone 'cuz they were so good at their chosen professions.

My mind drifted to that excellent Charles Bronson and *The Mechanic* where for a change, the remake was good.

Maybe the hunters would kill each other?

Yeah, right.

Important-looking but harassed guy in a nice blue suit arrives and the reporters and cameras all swivel onto him, so he must be the Chief of Police, aka designated shouty Irish fall guy.

I think there will be big pressure to find the shooters and maybe they will get caught and we'll be safe.

I'm learning stuff about myself.

Naïve.
You figured wha'?!!

Seems like maybe we could get outside now.

We are family.

I lead...no...that's what a *leader*, an example to people, a brave and decisive not crackhead man without a plan would do.

I am planless, rotten *pomegranate* and fruit-flies for brains.

The results are all around me.

I just try to get through without looking too much at the people on the floor, wounded or...worse.

Medics kneel and poke and dab at wounds and it looks to me like it's mainly, hopefully s-for superficial cuts.

Tower Records is mayhem, people lying everywhere, apart from the deserted Brittney Spears section.

The loneliness must be killing her.

I head out the door first and because there's nothing else anyone can do, the gang just follow.

We fight our way through the heart of a crowd of cops and detectives and probably pick-pockets and cops try to stop us, but the crime-scene is just too crimey for them to manage, so we get past them.

We have to, 'cuz of what they would ask.

"What's your address?" What would we say?

Or even a lot worse, what if they asked the $64 million question?

"Next of kin?"

That really is something worth waiting to hear, reader, or um…watcher.

PAIGE: Both, Jimmy.

JIMMY: Heavens.

Gulp.

A medic lopes up.

"You guys alright? You need some medical attention?" and I think, 'frontal lobotomy?' And stare, so he runs to a wounded girl on the floor.

There's rubber-neckers peering in from outside and cops try to hold them back, but most take photos and use ancient video-cameras and some hold bulky cell-phones and sweep the room and call the press.

I see TV vehicles and cameras outside and there's all these perfect suits with talking hairdos and unnaturally white teeth and tan that all look the same, reporting the same news.

What will they report?

Will we appear on actual *television?*

But, my...hair.

People are blocked off up across the street too at Café Internet and I think of the two things I have shown genius for.

Murder and mayhem.

Cop cars and ambulances are parked all around.

Some smart hot-dogger has materialised selling stuff at what I overheard someone say 'obscenely inflated' prices but they buy anyway.

I see some bench seats further down the street and so I tell everybody:

"I see some bench-seats further down the street," and that's where I head, not wanting to like, even remotely, *lead.*

And so we all waddle and trudge there, feet all tired and lead heavy.

But, at least it means that we can actually find seats that are not occupied by old ladies, hobos, weeping winos, jobless or skate-boarders.

I get the sensation that this is a film set, say on Universal's lot next to *The Fast and the Furious 50: The Space Generation* or something.

Above us, smokers sit on windows with cats and talk and point at who knows what?

Norma collapses into the seat and just stares and Andy sits right by her, his spaghetti arm around her shoulder.

Marsha stands next to me as I look back on all that damage to places and people.

And at that point, I really...*hated* myself.

I wondered if any of the gang hated me too.

I say "I keep trying to protect us and keep messing up."

I'll probably never look at a mirror ever again.

Marsha puts a hand on my shoulder and it feels really nice.

"That's what the police are for, Jimmy. To protect and serve people."

And she looks at me, I guess kinda knowing how I feel and feeling sorry for me.

"Let's go to them, Jimmy," she says.

I wish we could.

"What would we tell them, Marsha?"

"We could tell them that the hunters are trying to kill us and...and...killed our friends, and..."

She sort of trailed off.

"We can't even answer *one* of their questions," I tell her.

"What questions?"

"You know, the who, what, where, when, why and how stuff?"

And they all look at me for solutions.

Again.

Norma pipes up.

"Maybe...maybe we could give ourselves up to Crawford and Hutchence?"

And Marsha looks at her like she should be in *Gothika*.

"We grew *up* with them. Maybe..."

"Norma?! They killed Grace and Mac and Jayne and...and they're trying to kill *us!!!*" Marsha snipes.

We all watch Doctor and the Medics in the distance, loading what could be poor Jayne's blood-soaked body into an ambulance.

"We're never gonna survive," Norma says in a whisper.

"It's not anyone's fault," says Andy out of nowhere and we all turn to him.

He's having the hardest time with this and I'm thinking that we probably *all* look as bad as the kid.

"The founders *caused* this, the hunters *did* this," Andy says.

That kinda stops us.

I really hadn't given much thought to the founders and if you think about it, it's not the hunters acting alone. They are working on the orders of the founders.

People we will have *spoken* to, been to *parties* with, visited their *homes,* made *friends* with, had not *too* boring sex with their sons and daughters in *their* beds and even sometimes probably one of *them.*

"If only we could call them, explain it was all a terrible mistake," Norma says.

"Even if we could, it's way too late for that, Norma," Marsha says.

I'm thinking that too and also something different. Very different.

PAIGE: What, Jimmy?

JIMMY: I'm thinking about my dirty guilty secret.

I...won't tell anyone, at least not yet.

"There's no one here for us, Jimmy," Norma blurts out.

Andy consoles her with a hug, mussing her hair.

"We're all alone," she cries.

"In New York New York," Marsha moans.

The soundtrack should maybe now kick-in with The Doors, This is The End.

My beautiful friend Norma says:

"I...want my...mother," and it's one of the saddest things I think I've ever heard anyone say, even in a movie.

Apart from maybe something from, like maybe *Love Story* or *Kramer versus Kramer* and *Titanic* and *PS I Love You,* all fine quality near-tear-jerkers.

The others look at me in that we've lost our mommas kinda way and truth be told, we all sorta *have.*

"We can't even tell our families where we are," Marsha says.

I need to think of something...uplifting.

Team morale is plum...plumit...not good.

"We're our family now," I tell them and I must admit, that impressed the Hell out of not only me, but especially Marsha and thank goodness, Norma and Andy.

We group hug, like before the big game.

Whoever we are...

And I finish on that mystery, because my whole thing about coming here was to...*find that out.*

Not the "Who am I, why am I here?" man's hugest 'quasi-philosophical' question.

Wait, who said that? Was that...*me?*

It was! And listen the Hell to this:

Serious sentence construction, right?!

Hey, did I just say that too?

Never mind that.

Just wait till you hear the rest...

Nightswimming.

Andy's got me floundering about the founders now.
He's right about what he says, but that's not what I'm
really thinking.
I'm thinking about what they might, could, *would* be
doing right now, and it goes something like this:
It's dark and at the picture window or wall, you would
have a fantastic night view of what Jayne described as
paradise and then *The Garden of Eden* then she
mentioned The Shangri Las which makes me think of a
60s girl-group and *She*, both the song and the movie.
And staring out at the brilliantly-illuminated golf course,
probably with his back to us to add mystique, might,
could, *would,* be his Maj, the founder!
We used to swim around at night to see if we could see
anyone in there, because for a time, we were totally
curious.
What does this Mistry person look like?
The day we realised that we wouldn't know who he
was even if we *did* see someone vaguely founderish
looking, we gave up that game.
But I do know he wasn't the first.
That's one of the most important things I have to tell
you.
There was this rumour one time, from a long while
back.
One really ancient man's name kept surfacing as the
original founder...I think it was Trent or something...and
he was the talk of the town. Only, ours isn't really a
town, more a big village, but no sign on the highway
reading The Island. Population...um...'cuz no one
knows how many people live here. Or cares, apart from
maybe the founders.
But, as a guess, I'd have to say, roughly...*exactly* the
right amount.

Anyway, what happened was that yet another rumour started, like we don't have enough.

'Founder found floating' it illiterated.

He drownded and got replaced-ed.

He was invited to so many dinner parties where he played the character of mystery man that he got Robbie Coltraine giant-size.

But, he never was the founder.

And to this day, we still don't know who is.

And, we stopped caring.

Until now.

So I have formed an image in my tiny mind about what the founder might look like.

First up, I think it's a man.

Really ancient in your years, maybe much more than fifty. Or seventy or eighty something? Good head of hair, which would be thick and brushed back with lots of grey showing, so he looks like maybe George Clooney or Hamilton, but not so Jason orange.

I think he would wear glasses which would be heavy and horn rimmed and strong for weak old eyes that have a brand name like, maybe Dolce & Gabbana? But, we wouldn't get to see his face, because that, is The Big Secret.

He would often wear a suit, superbly cut, probably dark, made to measure in Ha! *Virgin* wool! from his own personal tailor who would know his every measurement and there would be light linen suits too for summer days and beachwear, all made just for him.

He would look fit and healthy with a good, even tan on his back and on his legs.

He would probably have a personal trainer too, so that he was in the best personally trained shape.

Maybe even what you guys call a life coach? To advise on every aspect of living including time management?

And there would be someone else to help keep his head in shape along with his body due to the rigours of the Presidential-ish job.

A keen observer might recognise someone like maybe Aristotle Onassis?

But it's not him because I seen his picture in one of great grandad's secret stash of magazines and though he does look kinda the founderish, it's not him.

But mostly, I liked Arisotle's taste in women, standard movie-star white draped over him in yachts.

Today, it's hot, so the founder would maybe wear a fancy Versace Polo shirt with Hugo Boss khaki shorts and cool Paul Smith leather sandals but not socks as he is sartorially elegant?

PAIGE: *Sartorially?*

I don't understand that either.

Right now, he's amusing himself by watching two men in smart Scottish golf wear because that's the best, in a gleaming golf cart, gliding across the perfectly manicured like a billiard table golf course, shiny golf clubs in the back, waving up at him.

He smiles, an orthodentist's most successful client and gives a little wave, thinking he's *King Arthur.*

The two golfers?

Well, I know their names and I now *know* their names would mean something to you.

Because they are what you, but not me, would call that word *famous.*

What even is that anyway?

PAIGE: Well, it's —

JIMMY: The famous come to a stop, climb out, grab their golf bags and make putting, 'come play' gestures to the founder.

He waves them on and they bow, over-the-topness giving them a good laugh-riot.

248

The founder would pour a good measure of probably a good whisky like the old one has, say, a Chivas Regal, into a chunky glass without ice or anything else.
Why?
PAIGE: Why?
JIMMY: Well, because oldie used to go nuts when folks added anything at all to any drink when its inventors put so much time and love into making it pure for your pleasure, he would say.
He would also mention things like product and brand development too?
I think of him, wondering if I'll ever see him again.
Anyway, I think the founder would be the same, as they are both about the same age, old man said.
He would toast the famous golfers who would smile and give two thumbs in agreement to his drinking.
He might then half-turn to his speakerphone thingy to take a call without wanting to stop taking in such a magnificent serene, Japanese, Zen-like garden, poor Jayne said.
He would listen for a while, saying nothing.
And the voice he would be listening to, would be?
Crawford.
"Mac won't be tearing up beaches with his dirt bike again," is roughly what Crawford would say with a sneer and superior snigger in that silky, sultry, snaky kinda voice.
The founder would just sip his whisky, saying not a word, just thinking, rolling ideas 'round in his ancient skull, maybe planning, probably scheming, definitely plotting. And Crawford might tell the founder her big surprise. "But Jimmy is...surprisingly *resourceful*," as she is more educated, most people, than me.
But, hey, surprise, *surprise.*
Resourceful? Me?
PAIGE: You?
JIMMY: Twist my major limbs if I'm not.

PAIGE: No thank you.

JIMMY: Resourceful. Check *that* out in your dictionary book! The founder would turn quietly angry at that point, because that's not the news he wants to hear. But, he would say nothing.

And down the telephone line, that angry saying of nothing would speak volumes to Crawford who would think 'Oh fuck,' but not actually say that to him.

To try to recover some ground and calm him, Crawford would say something like "There's only one place left they can go now."

He would ponder that, maybe agreeing, maybe not, but certainly hoping that was the case.

And as a distraction from the weight of office, he would maybe wipe his already spotless eyewear clean and I think that would also be to make people sweat, waiting for an answer or not.

Crawford can't stand when this happens.

Things like that never ever happened in her life, where she was totally in control of everything all of the time.

She would maybe even need a sip of water to wet her dry, anxious, delicious mouth, before saying something that the founder really wanted, needed to hear.

"Tonight's the night," not the Rod Stewart tune, but to the point and kinda final.

What would the founder say to that?

PAIGE: I dunno. What?

JIMMY: Nothing.

PAIGE: Oh.

JIMMY: He's the founder.

Has people to do all kinds of stuff for him.

Even kill.

And I wonder, is he brave or cowardly or just smart?

And for some reason, I remember one day, the old man called the founder *Macbeth*.

"No blood on his hands," old guy said.

Is Macbeth his real name?

Anyhow.

Crawford would be the one that hangs up.

She loves power and powerful people and demonstrations of power.

This demonstration of the founder's power strangely, makes her feel powerful.

And horny.

Now, even though Hutchence is more scared of the founder and really looks it, Crawford doesn't care about his quaking fears, or his shaky-voiced question.

"What did he say?" and then gulp.

She would just toss her cell-phone away, then those red lips would launch at Hutchence's face and eat. She'd smear lipstick on his mouth, her other hand groping at his crotch, her fingers lightly then not at his zipper, lowering it, getting him more turned on and stroking it over and over, then in the back seat of the car she unzips herself, raises her hips, doesn't need to peel her panties off 'cuz they're crotchless...

OK, OK! So it's *my* fantasy.

These Streets.

Whether Crawford and Hutchence and the founder had that conversation or not, there is still this truth.

There really *is* only one place we can go.

But, there's just one problem.

How do we get there?

Same as it ever was.

We've driven here and walked there and ran around and we are totally disorientated.

Who…wha…where…when…why…how…wow…whoa …and WTF?

PAIGE: WTF??

JIMMY: My fault, again.

I don't really know what to do next, but decide it's best all round if I at least pretend that I do.

In that leader of the gang, but not Glittery way.

So, we head down the street, leaving all the madness and mayhem and bedlam behind.

I confess, I think I'll always be naïve.

Leave it all behind?

It's only just *started!*

But, the gang at least *think* I have a plan, so that's enough for me at this point, considering that just a while back, we were almost all murderised to death.

I see yet *another* very weirdy thing ahead and hurry up to get a better look at a sign that says:

Subway.

Isn't that…a *sandwich?*

I get closer and see all these people tearing down this big, what-*hole?*-in the ground that, when you get closer, has stairs and nasty smells and tiles on the wall all painted with foreign languages like:

'DEST

ROYR

OCKN

ROLL.'

And 'Aw3som3.'

There's hundreds of ant-people listening to Ant Music streaming up and down, bumping into other people like they don't exist and hobos begging with shivering midget dogs begging for change, and I agree.

We must change, all of us.

Then, I suddenly get it. The subway must be a portal, like *Alice in Wonderland,* to a *j-o-b* maybe?

And I'm thinking, there must be an awful lot of jobs in New York.

Could this subway take us to where we want, need, to go? I wonder.

The gang are by my side looking like little cute curious kids into the subway, then at me, as if to say "Weeell?"

I lead them on down into what can only be described as insane.

But, I do hear an echoey lonely acoustic guitar, which sounds like it's playing...

Nah, that can't be right.

Can it?

And I scope the place for the musician to pay seriously big respec' but there's just too many bad mannered people and we're all getting thumped and bumped and there's a risk that:

"We'll get split up."

"He *groped* me!"

"Help."

"Stay with me, baby."

And that's what happens.

"What's that smell?" Marsha asks, pinching her nose.

"Not guilty," I say.

People stand in long lines with money for, how should I know? Then feed tin money into what I think I heard a lovely maybe African voice say "A hungry, snappy machine," then barge through barriers, never in anything other than a massive hurry without a shard or a shred of politeness.

A bunch of maybe could-be Oriental Chinese people stand peering at a wall which has a curious puzzle on it.

I'm curious too and walk up, firstly to see what the China Girl is looking at, then to see if it could be of any use to us.

It's got things like Queens, Harlem, Brooklyn, Central Park and Staten Island and stuff all over it, in different colours.

"Statue of Liberty?" one little guy says to me, at least I think that was it, and I smile good-naturedly.

He frowns at me, then asks, "Ireland? Ireland?"

And I instantly jolt.

He's not saying Ireland. He's saying *island?!*

The little guy is jabbing his finger at this puzzle, and so I peer closer with my bad eyes and then it hits me.

This, my friends, is not our island map, but...

The subway map!

Demme.

I look around for someone, anyone to ask how to read a map like this, but to be honest, I'm too scared of the size of this angry crowd.

Then, Marsha has a finger on the map and it lands on an island called Coney Island and she's excited.

"It's too close, I think," I tell her.

"That would take no time, in even a slow boat," Norma says with a superior snigger at Marsha.

"Unless they went round the long way to fool us," I say, then instantly feel like changing into my Stupid-man cape.

"You know what?" I try diverting.

"Maybe if we had, like, a *list* of the names of the actual streets here, that might help?"

Everyone looks from the puzzle to me and we just kinda drift away.

Somehow, against the cruel flood of people hurrying and scurrying toward us, we make it back up the stairs like a salmon leap and stand outside.

I look up and down the street which leads to another street and another street and another street and they have a lot of streets in New York, don't they?

I'm not going to ask anyone if they have a list of streets, but up ahead, I see Andy talking to two young prostitots, Kylie look-alikes, in their *dreams!* Who show him some folded, coloured pages and he's looking at them, then the prostitots, and they give big, I think sweet Serbian smiles.

They point down the street and Andy looks at us, gives a big wave and surprised, I head toward him.

"We can buy one of these down there!" and he points at this massive entrance to *something.*

"It's called a map, is that right?" he asks and the prostitots giggle at him.

I lead on down and the girls look very disappointed, but it's time to make progress to get a map and when we get there…

Station to Station.

This station is the biggest station I have ever been stationed in, in my whole life!

How the Hell can I describe it?

PAIGE: Try.

JIMMY: Well, it's airplane-hangar size, like in *The Aviator* and though there's swarms of people hurrying 'n' scurrying as usual, it's so goddam hugely *gigantic!* you hardly notice them.

It's got lots of glass and there's pigeons swooping and diving and toileting and eating crumbs off the floor.

It's shiny marble everywhere and a lot of people have a big job of keeping it that way.

There's places to buy clothes and stuff, all open, even.

There's a lot places to have coffee and cake and food and stuff and sit and talk and chat and gossip.

I see the place where we can buy a map thing and so I point it out to the gang.

I go over to this guy with his face buried in a Playboy magazine with air-brushed curvy naked girl on the cover.

"Could I buy one of those map things, please?"

And he reaches behind without straying from his reading.

"Three bucks," and I think *Uncle Buck* then nearly laugh, until I remember that bucks is another name for dollar money and give him the three bucks.

"What is this place?"

And he gives me the look that I have grown used to here, snorts, hands me the map and reads Playboy which I look at closely and consider buying, but he stares me down, so I don't instead.

And if I hadn't been so quite rightly interested in Playboy I might have noticed the newspaper headline that said something like 'Killings connected?' and had pictures of Grace, our waitress for the evening, college kid, the Tower Records guard and insulting, bad-hair artist impression mug-shots of Crawford, Hutchence, and, gulp, Badly Drawn Boy — *me.*

We all find a seat at a café place where we can't resist ordering coffees with the most wacky names and I think mine was mocha-choca-locha-lotta-latte-happy-frappy-crappy-skanky and what's *not* in it?

I take the map thing and look for the names of streets. Staring at the small print nips my eyes.

"The Streets of New York," Marsha says, thinking about Martin Scorsese and Leo, like me.

I can't read the thing with my crap eyes and that's why she shakes her head and takes the map off me, not impressing Norma who was about to.

I'm gaping at Marsha, frankly surprised at her map-readingness.

She turns to the back of it, runs her finger along, finds the name of the street, flips to the map, mutters about something called *co-ordinates* then finds the street!

I'm trying hard to remember which movie she would have learned that from? Maybe that cool TV series from the 60s, *Mapmen?*

And because I'm looking at Marsha, Norma says: "He needs glasses," then I think I hear Andy say: "Uncool, Norma.

"For reading, I mean, *obviously.*"

What was that all about?

Do you understand that?

PAIGE: Girls talk.

JIMMY: Marsha pretended she hadn't heard, for some reason.

Anyway, we decide to go and try and find the street.

There's another girl been watching me, a little like the fabulous JLO, which always brings to mind Jell-o fun, so I walk up and she's pleased when I ask her how we get there and she calls what I want directions.

This place confuses the Hell out of me.

She points to a tunnel where she says we can get the N train and I say how do you do that?

She laughs at first but my face doesn't, so she explains a complex routine.

When I say I have one more thing to ask her, I think that she thinks it was about having sex with her and her face drops when I don't.

"What do you call this huge, yet lovely place?"

She thinks I'm being maybe sarcastic and spins on her spiky heels and clicks away.

Click click clickety-click click click!

We somehow manage to spend money for tickets, find a train, even the right one, admire the Busted painted slogan, obviously some druggie thing, get on it and then I have to ask a third woman, magnificent like *Black Beauty*, what the huge place is called and when she speaks, I'm in love with her mouth and breasts and her accent.

"Grand Central Station, baby."

New Yorkers are proud of this place and that makes me think.

What would we islanders be proud of?

It's a tough question and I'm about to ask the gang until I hit on the obvious answer.

The whole island.

The train makes a bunch of stops and at one, these huge guys come on, all in more black, including their skin, looking i-for intimidating and scary too. Until one produces bongo drums and they do "In the Ghetto."

*Which totally **freaks** me **again!!!***

But, they say it's by Busta Rhymes? And, well...I'm bewildered all over again?

The rest of the train totally blanks them and the guys are amazed at us because we're up singing with them like a scene from *Grease*.

I love New York.

Turns out they're musicians and this is how they survive, so we give them three bucks and they get off at the next stop to do their thing on another train. We're tempted to go on tour with them.

Shut your eyes.

Our stop is next, so here we go, getting off the train, climbing on the lazy escalisor stair thing and having fun fun fun.

We even continue singing "In the Ghetto" getting a lot of looks, but because we're no great shakes, no money in the hat, even if we had one.

And the effect the music has, is that we become accidentally homesick.

Up in the street, it's quite nice with a little sun that Andy points at and a few spindly trees and a lot of rush hour.

We walk along one street, turn left then right, then under the grey sky again and I've got the map with my finger uselessly trying to peer at street names.

I decide we have to ask someone for direction things and Marsha does and it's a nice little bent over, only *slightly* smelly old lady who wants to talk, like, *forever,* who tells Marsha where to go.

We go where she says and after a lot of sore feet, Marsha speaks.

"This is the street, Jimmy."

And leans close to me, her hand on mine.

I look around for a street sign, and there it is.

"This is, like…*it?*" and I like her hand there.

I find the map and draw a straight line.

Norma has kept behind all the way with Andy who is fooling with her and she looks happy with that.

I think I hear Andy say to her something about:

"…giving head…" something "…McQueen…"

I think it was and I smile and think of my shot friend, then hear Norma quite rightly laugh a little, then she giggles at Andy.

"You make it easy to forget we're being hunted to death," and I think, he *does?*

"I'll *never* forget about that," I say and Marsha says:

"What?" so I have to tell her and she looks like she drunk vinegar.

Behind, I just about make out Andy talking.

"You just going to let her have him?" which must mean Marsha and me and Norma says back:

"I'll stick around."

"How do you think they found us, Jimmy?" Marsha asks.

"Huh? Oh, probably tagged Jayne's car? It's a classic," I tell her, a good answer for an on-demand guess.

"Maybe the police will be looking for them now," she says.

"Sting and the gang?" I say, ever the jokemeister.

"I don't think so. They're too slick. And that means they've done it all before."

"Slik…" and I feel guilty all over again.

"Will they have taken Jayne to that place?"

"The morgue? Guess so," I tell her.

"Poor Jayne."

PAIGE: Sweet Jayne. *Sigh.*

JIMMY: "The old guy had a car just like hers. He loved it too."

I stop at this grubby, run-down, ratty-infested-looking building with a lot of graffiti like 'Javier Bardem' and 'The Vaselines' and 'Lynyrd Skynyrd' but the artist had added 'Work-in-progress' to one that read The Fiery Furnaces.

I'm looking around, up, down, this way, that and Andy and Norma and catch up.

"This can't be the place, surely?"

And I smile, instantly tempted.

"Stop calling me Shirley."

So, I just walk to maybe the dirtiest, broken window I've ever not seen through and try to peer in to not see anything and that's exactly what happens.

But I accidentally see my own blurry, cracked reflection, who I quickly turn away from.

261

"What could have brought your great granddad *here?*" Norma says, disgust creeping into her voice, as Marsha taps with a perfect finger-nail at a teensy name-plate.

"Scratch," I tell her and she does and a little grime comes off.

She checks her nail, then goes at it again.

"The mouldy oldie never talked about the past much. But when he did, I listened," I say, only, "At least... I thought I did."

Marsha is busy scratching it out and I'm looking up and down the building, scratching my head, but carefully avoiding hair.

Marsha has scraped more dirt off and there's a name, but I'm already thinking about walking away.

I had no idea how important that name-plate was.

I'm walking away and I barely hear Marsha read what the name-plate says.

"The... *Actor's* Studio?"

I know the old fella was good at that stuff, but...

That mean anything to you?

The Actor's Studio?

No?

Walkabout.

I've never wandered about in a city before and I think
it's kinda cool.
You'll probably take all the *weirdness* for granted.
PAIGE: Never.
JIMMY: But, these discoveries are so strange to us,
and I just bet they're *not* to you crazy, wacky city folks.
And you're thinking like, *us?* What about *you?*
But, check this out.
PAIGE: Hmmm?
JIMMY: The 'stuff you have in NY that we don't have
on TI' list.
Men with rings…in their ears?
Car Wash.
Heel bars.
Date rape.
Drug *stores.*
Hotels for affairs.
Racism.
Cheerleaders.
Terrorist cells.
Emoticons.
Punk'd.
A different skyline from the old movies.
Missing people's faces on milk cartons.
Libraries and stores for *books.*
Self-harming.
Real estate agents, instead of *imaginary* ones?
Nuns.
Accountancy practice.
Bar codes.
Your name on your underwear.
Double-glazing!
Travel agents, who when we realise that they could
maybe help find the island and ask them, laugh.
Meatloaf, but for *eating.*

A-cute-puncturist.
Leisure centres?
Advertising agencies with *creative* people.
Umbrella…ella.
The Earth Room, an*…art installation?*
Dry cleaners.
Calendars.
Chandler, which gets me thinking of Raymond.
Car Dealerships, which I get because of the old man.
And worst of all…
PAIGE: Yes?
JIMMY: …*lawyers.*
PAIGE: Ugh.
JIMMY: No, wait…bankers.
And the thing I missed?
Oh yes, Facebook.
Newspapers in a box, where people drop coins.
With *my* face on the cover.
The list is infinity.
And, my ribs hurt from all the laughing.
One of the *big* discoveries is that all the movies about
Christmas, which started out as a religion, somehow
became to be only about giving presents.
And for a sec I semi-sorta feel sorry for warehouse size
brain Steven Spielberg 'cuz I read on a billboard:
'Steven Spielberg Presents Taken' which was a crying
shame for his little kids.
The 'stuff that you have here that I'd like' list.
Warner Bros theatres.
Tower Records.
K, no U…FC.
NY girls.
H & H Bagels.
YouTube.
And another crazy hysterical thing is 'the stuff we
overheard' list.
"…Apple watches…"

"...Pebl, the E-Type Jag of cell-phones..."
"...Goon Squad, powerpoint chapter..."
"...oil wars, then *water*..."
"...fracking..."
"...Esso shares up two points..."
"...transmogrify..."
"...divine Ealing comedy..."
"...watching...the IRS?"
"...Gogol Bordello..."
"...cops and firemen get all the action."
"...Monty Python..."
"...Zero tolerance."
"...*Off* Broadway, dahling."
"...Young Americans."
"...Twitter..."
"...aftertaste of Pilsner Urquell..."
"...Bagh*dead*..."
"...Robert de Niro...something...*Italian?*"
"Talk to the hand."
"Sighingtologists" I think it was.
There's maybe foreign people not from here, 'cuz I don't understand.
"...ménage a trois..."
"...B&O Sound 3200's 400 cd capability..."
"...film noir..."
"...Buzzfeed..."
"...soixante neuf..."
Anyway, my very favourite is:
"...lip service..."
And I want to follow this interesting looking couple who said that, 'cuz maybe they offer that service.
See what I mean?
Infinity. And beyond.
Anyway —
PAIGE: Anyhoo —
JIMMY: — anyhow after a while walking and talking and listening and laughing, we get thirsty and hungry.

There's this place a girl called m-for minimalistic named O'Taj, an "Irish-Asian fusion vibe thing" the Swedish and Czech owners said.

That's exactly what I *mean!*

We order some fusion green tea that makes me somehow think of Kryptonite.

I pretend to search the map and I say yet again, "Still can't see it" because the old man had mentioned someplace else that night I was snooping.

"You need glasses," Norma says stealing a peek at Marsha and I look up to see Andy nearly smile.

And I can feel Norma and Marsha exchange heat-seeking missiles of malice looks.

You must have noticed that I'm trying really hard at mastering this whole word-up, wordoid thing?

PAIGE: "Word-up"?

JIMMY: No?

PAIGE: "Wordoid"??

JIMMY: Oh, alright.

"They were talking like *The Horse Whisperer,"* I whine, because talk about *pressure?*

"'Go…West,' he said."

"Was it not…Holly, uh…?" that's Marsha.

"Johnson? Hunter? Buddy? Ebsen?" I try to be helpful.

"It's a *place,* not a *person,"* Marsha tells me.

"But, he must have friends or relatives here in New York," Norma says which is c-for constructive.

I let out a big sigh.

SSSSSSIIIIIIIIIIIIIIIGGGGGGGGGGGHHHHHHHH.

"If only we knew how to reach them" I say.

Later, I will come to discover the answer, at that very exact moment my friend, was blowing in the wind.

"Hindsight is all very well," the old man used to say and I never knew what he meant back then.

We finished our drinks and I counted what was left of Marsha's money.

I can count a little. One girl, two girls, three girls…

And that's all there was.

And I gave Marsha a sideward, but meaningful like in a French sub-titled film look, once I counted it.

We stood and strolled away.

The answer was waving at me like it knew me, as if to say, 'What's new, stupid cat', was a book thing.

You call it the phone book?

After walking just a little while, we see this board standing outside a place for eating and the girls, temporarily waving the white flag, want to eat.

"What's it say?"

"It doesn't *say* anything. You have to read it," Norma says with a sickly smile and I'm thinking she's bitching me because I'm interested in Marsha.

"It says 'Mexican seafood,' Jimmy."

"You're the man, boy," bewildering myself.

And it certainly smells welcoming, probably because we eat so much sea-food on the island.

"I wonder if it's in Zagat's?" Marsha says and I can't stop my mouth running away.

"And would the hunters would recommend it?"

Everybody just looks at me so to cover up, I count the money.

That does the trick because Marsha heads into the place fast.

The place is a tad insane inside, all wood and red and gold décor with a lot of supposed art on the walls, maybe a little or even a lot over-dressed.

"Great place!" Marsha breathes as she takes a seat in a booth, and I instantly sit right beside her and say, "Fit for a queen."

I need and want to ask her a very important question and it's not even about sex.

After we're all settled I ask.

"Maaarshaaa…why did you want to leave the island?"

She wears that vinegary look that makes me think of poor Jayne.

"I *told* you, Jimmy. Uh…when dad…died, there was no one left for me," she says, pissed at me but kinda sadly, glancing at me, and Norma didn't miss it either. "Where did he come from?" I say and I think questions about her dad are off the menu because she looks away out the window without replying.

Later, I will discover that was not a sad look, but a look of guilt.

And my own question makes me think of the wrinkly. Obviously, I know he came from New York, but the gaps in my knowledge were huge about him, like the gaps in my knowledge about most things, apart from three.

Guess.

PAIGE: Not even.

JIMMY: So, I cooked up this scene between the old man and the founder.

I think I'm right about this.

COOKED UP SCENE:
INT. FOUNDER'S OFFICE - DAY

Through the big picture window in the founder's office, we can see that, hey, look, another surprise, It's a Beautiful Day to not let slip away.

The old only *slightly* stooped fella stands gazing out that window thoughtfully.

And keeping to the shadows, would be the founder.

I must have *some* idea of what he looks like you're thinking, right?

I do.

Tall, small, white, black, brown, yellow, thin, fat, old, older.

One of them.

I haven't a clue, so *you* might as well guess.

The old man turns and slowly walks across the massive room and on the wall, there's a big street map thing of New York where four blinking lights cluster together, un-moving.

And close by, another two are side by side, moving toward the cluster of four.

For your information, these are the tracking device implants we had removed.

And the two side by side? That's the hunters.

Another man comes in fast and stands right next to the founder.

This man is the security chief, whose job is to keep us secure, chiefly.

I vaguely wonder whether he is responsible for the hunters?

He's most likely a grizzled but strong-looking man who holds himself like there's something been rammed up his ass, but looks cool in a nice linen suit.

His voice is Clint Eastwood-meets-Sergeant Rock, after a week trying to sing like The Bee Gees.

PAIGE: Would that be Bee Gees Robin? Or Bee Gees Barry? Or —

JIMMY: "Satellite was down when *The Visitor* arrived and we were busy. That was all. They got lucky," he snarls but the founder is not hugely impressed.

"Timing is everything," the oldie says, big smile.

"134th precinct. Resourceful kid," security says.

"He's got help," the founder says, looking very unhappy with life and great granddad. He turns back to watch a woman fishing off the beach, landing a fat one.

Jayne in paradise, island girl.

The security chief is a smart man, probably trained to be a-for attuned to the ways of important men and realises there's tension between the other men.

He makes his excuses which are something like

"I need to ensure we're reconfigured. Excuse me," and off he goes, I figure.

The founder verbally pounces.

"Anybody escapes, the hunters *find* them. That's the rule," he snaps, his voice maybe kinda slightly menacing?

But the old man doesn't frighten easily. He worked in the movie business.

"I *know* the rule," he answers back.

"So why?" The founder says, a man who doesn't need many words.

Like me, only not.

"Because…they're young," the ancient says and he sounds angry.

"There are no exceptions," the founder bites back.

"He's my great grandson," and that's me he's talking about there, you know.

PAIGE: I know.

JIMMY: "Have you thought this through, James?"

I'm named after him, but James sounds funny.

"How can you even find them?"

The old man doesn't need to answer any of this, and so that's what he doesn't do.

He's thought *everything* through.

"Have you thought about the *rest* of us?"

"Of *course* I have. This affects me in more ways than one, you know."

The founder stares hard, challenging.

The old fella stares him down and says: "They don't just *hunt* though, do they?"

"Have you considered what could happen if they live?"

"I can't bear the consequences if they don't," great grandpop replies, a lot more cleverer than me.

I know what you're thinking.

PAIGE: Hmmm.

JIMMY: In the distance, a dull whooshing sound comes.

Whoooooooooooooooooooooooooooooshhh.

"What if the island is discovered?" the founder says and is raging and like…disturbed at the same time if that's do-able.

"What then?" he says.

And the old man, I'll be with you Frank, is stumped for a reply.

The whooshing sound gets louder, the d-for distinctive sound of a jet-engine warming up.

WHOOOOOOOOOOOOOOOOOOOOOOOSHHH.

The founder can hardly bring himself to even look at the old man.

"Then, I must alert the others," he says to my great granddad and that means the old guy has to leave as the founder presses a button somewhere on his desk to whoever.

"Be seeing you," he says to the old man's back as he leaves and great granddad stops and half-turns.

"You just quoted a line from *The Prisoner.*"

They both smile a little because they love that TV series from the swinging sixties.

But, although the words seem i-for innocuous enough, it sounded…*threaty.*

Teenage dirt bag.

OK. My brain's back in the Mexican Seafood joint.
I know, my brain *is* Mexican Seafood.
"Why do they keep it secret from us?" Marsha asks me,
watching Norma sashay toward us with Andy and piled
plates of, I'm guessing here, Mexican seafood?
"Why don't they want us to know where they *come*
from?" she says.
"What's the big deal?" she tells me.
"The great secret. Funny the way how children always
know," I say.
"Even if they don't always know what it is."
"Is that another brain-fart?" I ask Marsha.
Norma sits opposite Marsha so she has a good glare
line and Andy sits next to me, sliding a plate of food
over.
Looks good, smells fine and hey. Man-sized portions.
Norma is pissed with Marsha's flirting.
OK. I made that up.
"What did you expect to find at that crappy old
building?" snaps Norma at my general direction.
But I've just stuffed a fork-full of tasty food in my
hungry-man mouth, so I say:
"Pee oeo mksmjdn cfm," then I snigger, Andy laughs,
then I do too, spitting and spluttering murdered baby
calamari out of my mouth, thankfully missing
everybody's plates, mostly.
I wipe my mouth then tell Norma:
"People who remembered him."
"A million *years* ago?"
"I don't think he's a million…"
"Then what?" she says, sarcastic.
"Then, I find out who he *is*. When he left, why, how and
especially, hopefully, maybe…*where to.*"
"Then what?"

272

"Try to find out about my family. My mom and dad. Who *they* were. How they met. Grandma, granddad, great grandma too. The car smash, and...*me* and..."

"*And?*"

"Well, then...then...um...or...ah? We go...well, then..."

I had no idea.

Then, or now.

And she knew it.

"Then?"

"You can be so sucky...sucky, sucky, sucky."

"People will *really* know our *secret* address, right? But who'll take us back? When? How do we get back?"

"Coolness.The cross-examination scenes in *The Verdict.*"

"And what would you say to *great granddaddy!*"

"Norma, what if we...*I*...don't want to go back?"

And everybody suddenly finds really interesting stuff to look at on the ceiling and walls and outside and on the menu.

"What? Well...I...you...we..."

"Not nice, is it Norms?"

We do the 'dogs out-staring each other' game awhile.

"And Norma? I hope you and acid sarcasm are happy together. You deserve each other."

She gives me the strangest look, like, I don't know, like she's swallowed when she should have spit.

Or has a mouthful of wasps.

Then, she surprises me and everyone.

She has a fit of the giggles that lead to burst-out red – faced laughter.

"That's so...*you,*" she's struggling to say.

It's kinda infectious and we all join in.

"You...*beautiful...stufus.'*

Later, I put Norma's behaviour down to stuck in the middle of stress disorder over our situation.

She switches her attention to Marsha who has gone from glaring at Norma to laughing, but not at Norma, *with* her.

I think.

But then, something else catches my eye.

PAIGE: The —

JIMMY: No, not the hunters, thank goodness.

If it was at all possible, I had kinda forgotten about them.

No, it was something completely different.

And it's like I'm not there between Norma and Marsha, and is that a gurl thang? 'Cuz they hold The Following Conversation.

"Look, Norma..."

"Look at what? Your plastic *Chucky* face?"

"Me and Jimmy..." then looking lost-but-hopeful

"...there is no me and Jimmy."

I'm half-listening and half-watching this *ambulance.*

"I *know* what you mean, Abnorma."

"You read minds, Marshit?"

I pipe up "Look, let's just calm things a..."

"Look, I'm dead calm. *E*norma.'

I look at her her hands. Rock unsteady.

And at the ambulance, two ambulance guys in un-white jackets jump out and hurry to the back doors.

"Think what you're doing...Normat."

"At least I *can* think, Marshmallow."

"You'll give yourself a headache, Nausous."

"Shut your mouth, Martian."

And it looks like a cat-fight's on, and though I particularly love a good girl-fight, especially with me as the meat, I zone out, watching the ambulance guys unload this shiny gurney.

I don't really know why I'm so interested.

"We could be killed dead, and all you are worried about is..." Marsha says with a smile like a cobra.

"You don't worry me," Norma says.

"It's *him* that worries me," and I think she might mean me.

But the ambulance guys, there's something...

"Ladies...chill..." Andy says.

"He's right, girls," I go, barely interested.

"Guys...what could it be that make the founders want us dead?"

Andy f-bombs, stopping the girls pre hair-pull, kangaroo-fight antics.

Clever Andy and they turn to him looking grim and the question burns like acid in the face, like that scene in one of *The Godfather* movies but it wasn't acid, just water, a warning that it *could've* been acid.

"At least tell me that staring out the window routine means you've been thinking about some sort of plan, Jimmy?" says Norma, desperate.

And I'm thinking, *plan?*

"Huh? Oh...I'm sorry, Marsha, but we need more money," I say, still keen and interested in the ambulance guys, but not in a *Brokeback Mountain* kinda way.

There's been drab elevator muzak-music playing, but then something I recognise, we *all* recognise, comes on!

But it's like they don't hear it, because Marsha is all sad 'cuz she knows she has to pawn more of her special jewelry and Andy is consoling her.

Norma doesn't have a speaking part in this scene.

"Has anyone noticed anything weird here, off-island?" Andy goes.

The gang laugh — "Har har harrr!" — 'cuz out the window, a giant, muscly punk kid wanders past wearing a gravity-defying, purple-tipped Mohican hairdo and a black t-shirt with the legend *Kill Me* printed which was a mighty challenge and we all follow his swaggering progress by way of an answer to my dumb question until Marsha speaks.

275

"Has anyone noticed anything *not* weird?"

"No, I mean weirder than him," and they wonder what could be weirder.

We enter into a 'weirder than him' discussion for a while and some of the suggestions were:

Zoos.

Snow-ball fights.

Peanut butter.

You turn me right round, right round freak unique guy.

L'Escargot.

Marilyn Manson.

Boy George.

Next minute, this tearful, badly made-up on purpose teenage dirt-bag, a female I possibly think, wearing a purposely stained and slashed wedding dress recently spray-painted 'Anti Yes' and military boots, her scraggy body wallpapered by tattoos runs past the window, after punk kid, I'm thinking about guessing.

Marsha manages a smile.

"Welcome to New York, Jimmy," she says.

And try skinny praying mantis-man, like in *Mimic,* dressed in Goth-awful uniform, taking long, loopy, loping steps past us with slicked-back bleached white hair like snakes, panda face make-up, spikes on his neck-collar, maybe a person's bloody eye on one and pulling another semi-naked Goth behind on a heavy dog-chain with a slashed vest confessing she's a 'Teenage Whore.'

The ambulance guys hurry along with a man on the gurney.

"You'll think I'm crazy," I go.

"Nooo? How could we?" Norma jests.

Is sarcasm, like…*clever?*

"It all started at Jayne's place…" I begin.

The girls and Andy look sad, remembering Jayne.

I'm looking at the man on the gurney that you call a patient.

"That song she played," and I'm struggling how to tell this part of the story.

"You remember?" I ask around.

"Hard to forget," Marsha says, the more musical of everyone.

I pause, watching the patient.

"Well, there's been more," I'm saying.

"That's what I've been trying to *say,*" Andy goes.

Outside, the patient moves on the gurney a little.

"I mean, just listen," and at that second, the familiar record stops playing, ruining my big moment.

"Suck's fake," I say and they look at me in pity.

"It's just that, if you listen closely, really pay attention, there's very, very weirdy things all around you, us."

"You need any meds, Jimmy?" Norma says.

"There's *music* that...that they shouldn't *have* here. I don't, um...think..." I tell them.

"What do you mean?" Norma says.

"There's been music that... *we* have," I tell her.

Blank looks from the girls, nods from Andy.

"Island music?" I go and "*Our* music."

"Uh..." from Norma.

Frantic nods of agreement from Andy.

"Music...from *our* island?" Marsha says.

"It's just that, if the island is this big secret..."

"How could *our* music...be here?" Marsha finishes for me.

But those ambulance guys and that patient have really got me not paying attention to the gang.

I stare hard at the patient person.

"Earth to Jimmy?" Marsha again.

Then, patient person lifts his arm.

I jolt like I've been shot.

Jolt! Blam!

In the face.

The gang unsurprisingly do the same because of that.

Jolt! Blam!

"What?" Norma gasps, huskily sexy.

And everyone is following my gaze, only not looking where I am.

"It's the...!"

"Is it them?!!" Norma goes.

Panic begins to spread, so I act calm.

"No. Not the them."

"But, it *is* the um..."

You have to remember that at *that* point, I didn't know your crazy word gurney which strangely, reminds me of The Hurdy Gurdy Man.

I wonder if patient person had been faking his own deathness, like Lord Lucan, patiently.

"You know," I tell them and I'm jabbing and pointing at the patient.

"The guy, the guy!" I go but they're not with me on this. Are *you?*

Anyway, I try, but don't know how to tell them what it is.

"That...man, on the...down *there...*"

They look at something else, I think, maybe animal turd on their shoes.

"The guy they're carrying."

They're bewildered, to be truthful.

"On the thing, the *thing...*" and I'm jabbing my finger.

"That guy!" I shout.

"What...about him?" asks Marsha.

"Look at him! Look!"

Nothing.

And *I'm* supposed to be the stupid one?

But luckily, right on cue, the patient raises a weak arm at one of the ambulance guys.

"Look! He's...not *dead!*"

"He must be pleased" says Norma.

"You don't understand!"

"Try talking sense for a change, then," Norma, naturally.

But, I'm on my little feet, all excited.

The gang are stunned into silence and lack of movingness.

"Look! When they take people away in that thing!"

I can laugh now, but at the time it was frustrating, one of the few big word I *do* use because I hear it from women on the island plenty enough.

"They're not always dead!" I try.

"When they take people away on those...*things*...they're not always dead!!!"

Andy is first to get it.

I'm outta there like *Flash* and the gang are not because the owner is looking for someone to pay the check?!

I did leave some money on the table, but no one's seen it.

Outside, I immediately run into a wall of every kind of people blocking my way.

I kinda thread my way through, apologising all the time, and nobody says anything back.

I want to get across the street to where the ambulance guys are shutting the back doors to their vehicle but, rush hour is in my way.

Down the street, a traffic light changes to red, making me vaguely think of lipstick then red laser-dots, then blood for a sec, but all the rush hour slows, then stops.

Traffic lights are like a job, only for machines.

I look round for the gang and sure enough, there they are, looking to get through the people.

I tear across the street and reach the ambulance guys and I'm a little sexily breathless when I speak.

"Are you...*huff, huff*...taking him...*huff, huff*...to the morgue?"

You have to remember that at that point, I thought that's where everyone from shootings went.

I also now know, a lot of them *do*, mostly called gangs like The Broods and Crisps and stuff.

But not always.

Ambulance guy gives me funny looks.

"Maybe in about…twenty years," he explains.

"Um...what does that mean?"

The gang join my side and the girls very presence, very essence, gets him talking.

"You friends?"

I look down at he patient who is giving me a goofy I Can't Stand Up For Falling Down somewhere and hurt my head or drugged kinda look.

"From way back," I tell ambulance guy.

I'm starting to impress myself.

"He's just going to City Hospital," the guy says, really to the girls and not me.

And quite rightly, too.

I want to talk more, but the other guy is in the driving seat and leans out.

"C'mon, Pete!" and so Pete comes on.

He beams the girls his best hot-date smile and skips over and hops into the vehicle.

But at least I know one very, very great thing.

"Jayne might be *alive!*"

The gang look really hopeful and pleased, but mostly surprised that I managed to work that out.

"Could she be *really,* Jimmy?" Marsha says and I really like it when she speaks like a child.

But, there's a problem.

PAIGE: Is it —

JIMMY: No, not that.

PAIGE: Oh.

JIMMY: We know what a hospital is.

From ER.

"Where the Hell *is* it?" Marsha nails it for me.

I'm scratching my head, but without messing my hair up, trying to think what to do.

"And how do we get there?" Norma says.

I turn to the crowd and see a hot-looking girl, kinda like Aaliyah and one Jimmy rule is as follows:

If you need to ask for help, *always* ask hot girls.

I get in front of her and she barges past, un-impressed as Hell by me.

They're a hard crowd to please, I remember the old fella saying.

I look around and see a slightly interesting girl reading. You call it a newspaper.

She had two, but this one was called The Rocket.

I kinda get in her way and she looks up with eyes like a virgin, a lovely mouth like trout-pout, maybe without the robotox, bone structure like Garbo and hair like mine, only longer.

"Excuse me," I let her know.

She's instantly smitten and I'm excused.

That's more like it.

She beams a big smile, kinda like central casting had sent her for, as old guy called it.

"How do you get to City Hospital?" I ask.

"You hafta be sick," she says which I don't get and because of that, she skilfully tries a different approach.

"Or, ya o/d'd, or..."

"O...deed?"

She studies my dim look.

"Ah. *Sweet,"* she says.

I have no idea what just happened, but she does have these awesome legs, which I stare at.

Our little love affair ends as rapidly as it began, 'cuz Norma is suddenly by my side.

"Get a goddam cab, country boy," the girl snaps, suddenly morphing into her co-star Samara in *The Ring* and disappears without giving me even a peck on the cheek, unusually.

Or her phone number.

"Just Like A Woman."

A *country* boy?

Yikes, and...gulp... *The Beverly Hillbillies?!*

But, the interesting girl has turned to watch me, *of course,* and I haven't got a clue that she's looking at

281

her other newspaper, then me, then her newspaper, then me, wide-eyed, open-mouthed, obviously in love. Anyway, a yellow cab trundles by, not fast in the rush hour and with all our problems, I completely forgot the others knew all about yellow cabs.

"A taxi? What the, and how the…?" I say to myself and Marsha.

Another one chugs past, and there suddenly seems to be a lot of them, and I notice that people stop them, then too many of them argue who should get in and push and shove even females out the way.

"How the Hell can we get one?" Norma has seen the fights about the taxis.

Marsha is smoothing her outfit and I just know what's in her mind.

"OK, Miss Hair-Spray Queen 2011. Try and stop one," Norma challenges.

Marsha starts to adjust her perfectly-fitting bra.

New York males, I'm pleased to note, are of the red-blooded variety and they bump into each other and rubber-neck and whistle and howl and dribble and drool, or that might be me. A few girls are equally interested.

Norma pretends she's bored.

Andy actually is.

Marsha waves at a taxi and I think there'll be accidents as it seems like they swarm to her.

Along with a lot of not taxi cars.

But a real yellow taxi screeches right up in front of Marsha —

Screeech!

And swarthy, drooling driver with good taste in females enjoying the scenery, opens the door for her, like he has manners.

She gives him her smile and adjusts her bra again and I'm thinking pretty much what he's thinking.

"Where to, sweetness?" he asks with a funny accent and I think I might have heard something like it on the island.

And for a sec, I think Marsha might say to swarthy driver: "The island, please," because that would solve a lot of our problems, wouldn't it?

And thinking about problems makes remember to not forget about the hunters.

Where are they?

Are they watching us?

Can they track us?

Will it cost money at the hospital?

And that makes me think about bucks again.

Have we got any left?

Have we got enough for a taxi?

How much is a taxi?

Where's a pawn shop?

Will Marsha spring more of her precious?

Or adjust her bra again?

Or, let me?

And now, I begin to understand *A Series of Unfortunate Events* that I understand most, or all of *you,* have.

Money, Money, Money.

Or lack of it.

How to get it.

What to spend it on.

What not.

How to keep it.

I never thought I'd be having conversations with myself like *this.*

Meantime, Marsha has told swarthy driver "City Hospital, please," and he says "Shoah," and smiles again, but when the rest of us step forward, he glares like a busted drug dealer at us.

Marsha jumps in and so do we and it's more than a little crappy inside with dirt, and kinda stinky of swarthy driver who tries to cop a look at all the female flesh on offer, quite naturally, and I smile at him.

He glares at me.

Progress kinda isn't with rush hour, so I say "Can you go a little faster please?" and he laughs at my stupidity.

"At least blast the horn," Norma says and he does.

HOOOOOOOONNNNNKKK!

"And could you really *lean* on it?" she says, now fully resuming normal service, and he does.

HOOOOOOOOONNNNNNKKKKKK!!!!!

"And, could you shout and *rant* at other drivers?" she says and he does.

"And could you also make rude hand gestures at other drivers?" Norma asks and he does.

"And flash lights over and over?"

"Maybe...drive too close?"

"And could you do all of that to drivers who haven't *done* anything?" and he's not quite clear on that one, scratches his head, narrows his brow, and I wonder what the Hell Norma's trying to talk to the driver about.

"I always wanted to do that," she says.

And I know what I always wanted to do, as I check the taxi for pointy high-heel marks on the ceiling.

The driver keeps smiling all kinda leery 'n' lusty at Marsha.

No chance pal, I'm thinking like a Native New Yorker.

But I have to ask Marsha something *you* know she won't like.

"Marsha, sorry, but we need...money," I tell her quietly and the driver's eyes turn even more piggy and he leans back for a hairy earful.

Marsha looks sideways at me so sadly and I could cry for her, 'cuz it's a biggie.

She takes a gulp of air and a tear falls.

"I'm sorry too, Jimmy," she says, brave.

I squeeze her hand, watched like a starving Tasmanian she-devil by Norma.

"Um, driver. Could you stop at a pawn-shop first?" and he looks suspiciously at me in the mirror.

"Porn shop?" he makes it sound like on purpose, adjusting his mirror to look at Marsha's glorious pins.

"Thassright, um…duuude," I tell him.

I produce Marsha's things and it must break her heart to have to pick something 'cuz she tells me.

"Each of these pieces tell a story," which makes her sad and I really feel for her.

After a few minutes of turning corner after corner after corner after corner, we stop at a tiny old pawn shop. Marsha starts to get out and I stop her.

"I'll do it, Marsha," because I can tell she doesn't want to.

Even Norma is sad for her.

I jump out and as I reach the door, the driver immediately turns to flirt with Marsha, which might take her mind off the jewelry.

But hey, this pawn shop is a lot cleaner and shinier and more betterer than the first one, with a nice young guy humming the tune "Happy" who takes one look at Marsha's beautiful and heavy, silver antique chain and whistles.

"Whoa, cowboy!" he says, dropping it like it's hot Snoop and puts it down on the counter.

He smiles at me and asks:

"Un-wanted *gift?*" he says with dripping sarcasm.

"No. Very much wanted," I tell him.

"She'd rather keep it. But, we need money."

I glance out the door toward Marsha, who gives me a small kinda pathetic smile.

Pawn guy sees her and whistles again.

"Outta my league," he says and I don't know if he means Marsha or the chain.

"I'll take whatever you can give me."

He gives me a surprised look.

"You should be more careful in this town," he says confusing me even more. Is it not a city?

He must have taken pity on the country boy, 'cuz he gives me three hundred dollars.

"It's worth a helluva lot more, pal, but that's all I can do for you," and I like him.

I take the money and what he called a *receipt*, hey, my first ever, and I shake his hand.

"Maybe we can buy it back some day."

"Maybe you will," he says, not believing a word.

Outside, Marsha watches me, full of sadness.

I jump in, flash the wad of banknotes, sit between the girls and don't fight the desire to kiss Marsha on the mouth and that's what I do.

Mmmm.

To even things up, I kiss Norma on the mouth too.

"No offence, Andy," I tell the kid and he smiles.

"Let's go!" I say to the driver.

"And hey, no offence to you, either," and I think he actually is offended, 'cuz he doesn't say one word more during the rest of our journey.

Which is fine by us, and nothing happens.

Apart from my arms around both the girls who snuggle close to me and the driver looks like he might explode in his greasy pants.

I wonder for a sec if he'll want some kinda reward for expenses like Ratso, and *Kiss the Girls* or maybe Andy or me or something?

Organised confusion.

This is one crazy mad place, a little like the outside, only, *inside.*
The yellow cab screeches off —
Screeech!
— the driver re-named swarthy foreign *halitosis* driver, I know halitosis 'cuz some of the ancient island people had it, 'cuz he cursed foreign words under his bad breath, just 'cuz I don't get the tip thing and his realisation that the girls are so very out of his junior league.
We're outside The City Hospital and mayhem and madness rule and all the people remind me of the Times Square people.
Here's my 'hospital' list:
Walking wounded.
Gang-bangers, shot by both sides.
Mulatto hookers, cocaine bookers.
Cops doing cop-talk into the mikes in their cars and donutting, like da mooovies.
Ambulance guys running outside then inside with dying people on bloody gurneys.
Doctors and nurses in sexy whites meeting the ambulance guys.
Nurses by their sides, shouting "Gimme 10 mil of Siasdvhbsdfbnk-ol" making me think, 'why do all medical products end in-ol?'
Bloodless vampire junkies.
Stressed doctors, half-asleep, junior doctors even worse.
Visitors carrying flowers and chocolates, eating the chocolates.
A wan new mother fake-smiling, a cynical nurse holding her baby out to her saying "Your life is now low-budget *Poseidon Adventure.*"

287

A lung-cancer victim in a wheelchair, wearing a mask to stay alive, sneaking a smoke.

A weedy kid smoking, um…weed, defiantly glaring his invincibility at the cancerous person.

Ambulances and cop cars and taxis stopping and dropping off and leaving, exhaust fumes choking us, but we're at the hospital.

Andy leans his perfect bone structure against the wall in a kinda 'New Face of Pepsi' advertising campaign pose meant to persuade you that 'You too will look cool/have sex/be successful/be contented' kinda way.

The girls are glued to my side like a hip threesome I'm pleased to report, and they both watch this fappy nurse…

PAIGE: Jimmy, *fappy?*

JIMMY: Um…fat and happy? Who keeps staring at me while working the jaws-of-life on an ancient, crinkly, lost cause lady inside an ambulance.

I noticed nursey because she glanced at me, did a triple-take, then her face twisted like she was on an electric chair, but of pleasure.

Think *Barbarella.*

PAIGE: I will.

JIMMY: I do.

She's too old for, you know, about 40-ish something, looks kinda like Eddie Murphy in his fat-suit, obviously under pressure, but has magnificent jet black skin, breasts, lips and naturally, glasses, which for me, means points.

The jaws-of-life or a miracle must have taken just a short time, lost lady revived, because we're inside City Hospital now, and there, the fatorexic nurse is.

She's totally studying my face, full of, what?

PAIGE: What?

JIMMY: Fascination?

PAIGE: Uncertainty?

JIMMY: Lust?

288

PAIGE: Try *astonishment.*

JIMMY: That's what I would have said, to be Blunt.
And I just cannot think or imagine why.
City Hospital is pretty insane inside, like one of those
great old Hammer Horror asylum movies you get
always starring Vincent Price or Basil Rathbone.
I decide on a course of action.
"How you doing, nursey?" I ask the nurse.
Her mouth flaps which is kinda cute and a reminder of
a particular past special introduction to...
"I always do wonderful, honey. Uh...I know you?" which
is what her voice is like and I remember that accent
from home.
Jamaican.
Do I have to tell you that that's s-for-significant?
"What's your name, sweet-cheeks?" I ask her.
She's knocked out I can tell, but manages a big smile
of blinding pearly whites.
"Miss...Grace," she lets me know.
My stomach churns. The same name as our Grace.
I have to think about her death all over again.
But I recover quickly.
"*Dis*...Grace? Like a *baad* girl?"
She laughs like a magical water-fall, twirling her hair.
"Miss Grace, we...um...need to find a friend," I tell her.
"Who don't, child?" she says and I get that.
I smile back and for a while, it's like the 69th
International Smiling Convention in Cleveland, Ohio.
Tom Cruise wins naturally, Julia Roberts runner-up.
Talking about Ohio —
PAIGE: Hmmm —
JIMMY: — have you ever noticed —
PAIGE: Hmmm—
JIMMY: — that it's the state of choice for screenwriters
and producers because it gets more name-checks than
any other state, and I think Ohio should 'establish

intellectual property' on itself so it could bill filmmakers and get paid 'royalties' I remember the old one said.

Andy and the girls are enjoying the curious exchange between nursey and me too, alright.

To break the dreadlock, Marsha butts in.

"We're uh...new in town and a friend of ours was uh..."

"Like...*shot?*" I finish for her.

Miss Grace looks horrified.

"This city," she says. See? Not a town, and reminding me of They Built This City On Rock and Roll.

"He in here?"

"She. *She's* in here, at least, we think," I say.

Andy is looking around in his Andy way and some posters on a wall attract his attention of a gnat.

It was an AIDS thing like the Tom Hanks movie and it had these words:

'If it's going on, it's going in.'

And had a picture of a condom, but not used, or extra large enough.

Norma pipes up.

"She might be...not alive."

The nurse "Tsks-tsks" and shakes her head but all the while, she's staring at me.

"Could you, like, help us...me?" which I think is the right approach.

She flutters these massive Diana Ross and The Supremes, the whole group combined, eye-lashes at me, with a coy smile.

And I get to wondering about 'the nurse thang.'

You know, maybe twenty or more alcoholic beverages later?

But she looks at her watch, reminding me that everyone here's obsessed with time.

"Pretty please?" I flirt a little.

I can see her wilt right in front of me.

"Honey...you got...a name, a address on her?"

"Her name was..." Norma starts.

"...*is*..." Marsha adds at Norma.

"...it's Jayne, Jayne Gibb. She owned a bar called Heroes somewhere in Manhattan," I tell Miss Grace.

"Narrows it down..." and my face registers sarcasm and disappointment at the same time.

"Aw, don't. Could try the phone book, s'pose."

"Stupid me. The...book," I agree.

"Cain't promise, darlin'," she says, then reaches to stroke my cheek, then stops midway.

"Oh my Lord!" she breathes, face all kinda teenagery flushed.

"Miss Grace...what is it?"

She gives me the most intent stare I have ever, ever had, and I have had them all.

"You...uh...couldn't be? Nah..." she mutters and fidgets, twirling with her hair, again.

"See what ah cain do," and she runs away, fast on her feet for someone of her bigness, looking back at me.

"Think she'll help?" says Andy.

The girls both laugh aloud at the same time.

"What just happened?" Andy asks anyone, but gets no response of any kind whatsoever.

Then Marsha says "It's OK, Jimmy. She said you couldn't be."

Couldn't be *who?*

Miss Grace stands at the reception desk, flipping through a big yellow book.

It reminded me of my book, the dictionary.

I must tell you my favourite words from it.

PAIGE: Do tell.

JIMMY: My number one is in the 'A' section.

The longest word-antidisohwhofreakincaresism is in the same section.

My top word is...*antici-pation.*

The Carly Simon song and the tomato ketchup advert.

Anyway, Miss Grace is on the phone then looking over at me, then nodding and writing something down then hanging up then talking to the receptionist woman behind the desk, who then starts flipping through the computer.

The woman taps words —

Tap, tap, tap!

— and something happens because she points and Miss Grace nods and then looks at me.

She waves us over, kinda excited, pretty darn thrilled, and for more than one reason, obviously.

A machine thing makes a what? chattering? kinda sound and I see that it is printing a sheet of paper.

As we get closer, the woman hands Miss Grace the sheet of printing which she looks at in a nursey way.

I notice the woman noticing me, then she smirks at Miss Grace who mock-scowls.

Miss Grace nods at us to follow her across the hall and we do.

I smile at the woman and she mouths "Wow!" to me.

I know why, too.

And 'No' is the answer, but hey, thanks.

"Think I got her," Miss Grace says to me.

"You did? Is she...?"

"She alive."

The gang give a loud cheer like a sports game.

Cheer!

Miss Grace taps the sheet of printing.

Tap, tap, tap!

"ICU," to me.

"You...*see* me?" I'm confused.

"I...um, see you too."

Miss Grace starts to laugh, then stops herself.

"No, honey-child. I-C-U. Intensive-Care-Unit."

What was that?

She gives me that once then twice-over stare and have you ever had someone really, *really* stare into you, like they're looking through Gary Gilmore's eyes at you? Disconcerting is a good 'd' word.

"She in baaaad shape, darlin'," Miss Grace goes on and we all exchange 'Oh crap' looks.

"You can see her, but only a minute, OK?"

We all nod.

I take Miss Grace's pudgy hand in mine.

"How do we find her, Miss Grace?"

She giggles like a kid with a hand in the cookie jar.

"Oh, my. Oh, my...room 501, honey. Oh, Lord."

I let go her hand, then kiss her chubby, rump-steak cheek.

"Coolness, like Levi 501s. Thanks, Miss Grace."

"Oh my," she tells me.

"And...how do we get to Levi 501, babes?"

She giggles again, covering her mouth.

"Filth...oh my...*fifth* floor."

"That's great. But how do you get to the filth floor?"

"Oh my. The elevator, honey," she giggles.

"Um...where's the elvisator, naughty?"

She giggles again and points along the hall.

"And tell them Miss Grace say it's alright," she says, still staring.

She points to a thing on the wall with some sorta gloop that she wants us to use called hanitizer, so we do and — *Sniff!* — it smells funny.

Then, we make our way to the elevator and I turn to see Miss Grace and even the woman behind the desk staring at me.

I blow a kiss because I think blowing is on their minds.

But, what was all that "Could you be..." stuff all about?

I know now.

PAIGE: Who did she think you were, Jimmy?'

JIMMY: I'll tell you...later, Pages.

And when you find out, all of you...

Them.

We're standing at the up and down machine, puzzling over what to do and I'm trying to at least *look* leaderish rather than stupidish and failing.

It's only when smiley nurse in that white, strangely magnetic uniform turns up carrying an ice-box with, I don't know, someone's head for a transplant? and pushes the button, that we realise what I was supposed to have done.

The nurse gives us all the once over, and me the twice over, then turns to the reception to smile at Miss Grace, who blushes like an Atomic Kitten.

The elevator arrives and we let smiley nurse go in first. I'm curious about her next move, then she presses a button and smiles at me.

"Where to?" in a nasally twang that needs fixed, but I know where she'd like to go.

"Filth...uh...fifth, please?"

She pushes my button alright, and I've also been watching the whole process in case we need to add that knowledge to our...my...tool-kit.

The elevator stops, smiley nurse gets out and we move on up.

This is our first time in one of these. Do You Remember The First Time? And well, it's kinda fun, so we agree to play on it later.

It stops at our floor five and out we go in different directions by mistake.

The hall has really shiny waxy floors and goes on forever both ways, and so we stand looking at each other.

But, I spot signs on the grey like the sky walls with numbers that tell you exactly where you can go.

Left for Jayne's bedroom.

I hurry toward it with Marsha tracking me and I half turn to see teary Norma about to try and catch up, then

294

Andy takes her arm and shakes his head and I think I hear them.

"...Fool To Cry."

"...Cryyying Over You."

"What Is It About Men."

"Stay With Me."

"If I Said You Had A Beautiful Body, Would You..."

I'm kidding. Andy's such a nice kid.

So anyway, Norma?

PAIGE: Norma?

JIMMY: She keeps pace with him.

I keep walking but a thought, no really...

...an actual *original* thought...

Does accidentally happen, 'cuz arrows on the wall show room 501 is this way.

"Hurry up guys!" with a sneaky half-turn behind to see Norma, a dopey smile on her face, Andy's head in her hands, kissing him just a little.

Andy shoves her off playfully, *eventually,* wiping his face, but I think he liked it.

Andy's a little young, but Hell, no younger than me when I got my first, um...opening.

I thought I was smart, trying to count door numbers, and then I see a door that has 501 on it.

But, then, oh swearfuck!

PAIGE: What?? Jimmy, whaaat??

JIMMY: I'm hearing something —

PAIGE: Something?

JIMMY: Something I so do not want to.

I stop dead in my tracks.

I'm listening hard.

The girls are toiletty.

Dammit, I've butt-nuggetted myself, too.

"What..." Norma starts to ask but I have to cut her off.

"Shhh!" I say, bossily.

The girls and even Andy are rattled at my a-for assertivenessity.

295

I believe I can just about make out...murmurs.
Familiar murmurs.
That's a confirm.
PAIGE: Rodger Dodger.
JIMMY: Suddenly —
PAIGE: 10-4.
JIMMY: — I reach out to grab the door handle on room
505, shove open the door and slam the girls and Andy
inside fast, a little hopefully not too roughly.
I'm in right behind, don't worry.
"Is it them!!?" Norma says, anxious as an actor at third
recall, the old fella said...whatever.
"Well...maybe. I thought I heard..."
"What was it?" Marsha says.
"I might be wrong, I'm not usually right."
"What? Your eyes don't work so you hear better, like a
blind man? Like Rutger Hauer in...uh..."
But I'm at the door, pressing my ear against it without
messing with my hair.
I'm listening hard, when I look behind me.
Over the yummy shoulders of Marsha, is,
unsurprisingly, a hospital bed.
And on that bed, equally unsurprisingly, is a patient.
Uh-oh, robotox.
Coyote Ugly.
Quite often, you can learn a lot just from someone's
name and face.
Here's some examples.
Henry Fonda — kindly, trustworthy uncle you'd rely on
to safely baby-sit your children, and in any pickle.
Billy Bob Thornto — uh-oh.
Madonna — what *is* that yummy gap tooth for?
David Grey — jolly japemeister — I'm kidding!
Angelina Jolie — grace...which reminds me of Grace.
Elvis — most beautiful fat entertainer, ever.
Both Gallagher bros — what's yer fuckin' problem,
shag?

296

But you see what I mean, right?

PAIGE: Right!

JIMMY: And judging by her 'home express surgery kit' gone horribly wrong face, she's called:

'Mrs. I hate you right now' or 'Miss melting in the dark.' Works, doesn't it?

Anyway, so there she lies, with more facial hair than any *Planet of the Apes* character and you just know she's thinking:

'I'm ancient, you're not, I look like Chewbacca, you're sooo gorgeous, so go and f...'

Her features are sharp as an axe, eyes like little beady, other-worldly eyes, body as thin and dry and crunchy as unspread crackers. Those eyes drill into me like a Hilti nail gun, accusing me of what, multiple rape?

In your nightmares.

But I look back at her with sympathy, because all those bandages look like ow! a painful condition or operation or, and I hate to say it, but some islanders have also gone under the knife.

Cosmic surgery.

I give her my leg-opening smile but not meant in that way.

She wants to stab me, I can tell.

Or throw Vain Fare, her magazine, at me.

I have to listen at the door again and as I do, the girls and Andy have discovered the patient.

"Aw, look, a poor little old lady!" Marsha coos and over the threesome go.

They all fuss over her but those eyes of hers just probe into them like the surprisingly scary hairless alien midget in *Mars Attacks.*

The threesome notice this eventually and turn to me, questioningly.

"Is it...*them,* Jimmy?"

I don't know what gave her that idea.

Might be the chair I'm holding high, ready to strike, face like the boxer who coulda been a contender.

The girls look about to collapse as Andy hurries to the door and presses his ear close and listens.

Murmurs and clicky footsteps get louder and oh, Shatner, closer.

"Can't reach him on the phone," a familiar voice says, kinda sexily though, really.

You'll have figured correctly it was murderella, Crawford.

We all panic but ssshhh, very quietly.

My second thought was 'Who's she phoning?'

My first was, of course 'We're all going to die!!!'

So, I'm guessing she's calling the island and talking to maybe the head of security.

"In light of the serious graveness of this…"

…more likely the founder himself, in a conversation that probably goes not unlike this.

Wait, I think there might even be *another* of the founders there, and around the island, there's this big, bearish black guy in cool suits, who always made me think 'Is he, or isn't he?' who actually looks movie Presidential even in his golf wear to add weight to the founder's so far not that persuasive argument against great granddad.

The Conversation:

And I also think they'll be outside in the heat too and so they start.

Wait, I think they'll be by the jet, a Jet Leer I once heard old guy slip out by mistake.

This jet.

Who uses it?

Why?

Where do they go?

How long does it take to get there?

What for?

But most importantly, *obviously…*

Is the 7 mile high club on offer?
I figure I'd compare well with the other members.
So, anyway, big bearish black guy booms.
"You don't know what you're doing!" and oh, boy.
That was a good move by the founder, because this
guy has an incredible voice, deep, but like a magnet to
your ears, like Barry White talking women into bed.
And persuasive, like you'd buy products advertised or
whatever he was selling, like a politician, only not.
I would like to meet him, get to know him even,
because he sounds interesting.
The founder says stuff like:
"You'll bring it Tumbling Down" like the Steve Harley
song to great granddad.
The old one removes his foot from the step onto the
Lear, because that comment digs deep.
"Remember I said, the hunters don't just *hunt*."
And I know he's really hurting.
"What if it was *your* great grandchildren?"
And although he steps back on to the Lear, he turns to
look at the two founders, just two old guys who want
WHAT!!!???
They're just three amigos just kinda...*looking* at each
other, not knowing what to do or say.
I imagine the incredible *history* they must have and the
thought of what they *know.*
Big bearish black guy has the last word and it's
something the founder said and although it might not
seem like it to you, I think it's actually quite 'sinister.'
"See you again" he says.
A tad different from *The Prisoner* line, but...
Still sounds sinistery, right?
That definitely is a threat.
But, WTF...?

Unpretty.

I can feel and hear Crawford and Hutchence outside, so I've got the chair like this, right? (*Jimmy stands, his chair held high above his hair.*)
And I'm not about to offer them a seat, either.
I try really hard not to think about bullets being much faster with a lot more bright red guts and gore and death involved, than chairs.
Or Grace and Mac.
And I try really hard not to think about
How did they find us, fer suck's fake!!!
And I try really extremely hard not to think about the goddam hairy old woman's eyes boring into the back of whatever part of this fine body she covets.
She grunts, but I refuse to look where her rubbery-looking hands are.
Marsha makes a 'ssshhh' gesture at hairy old woman and her eyes drill into hers instead.
The girls have shoved Andy behind them.
I hear Hutchence talk.
"Yum. Hospital beds. All those fresh, white ...nurses" he says and he's only half joking and I fully understand where he's…um…coming from.
Crawford giggles girlishly, then:
"Let's get a room," and she don't mean no hotel.
Foxtrot Uniform…
With our luck, it will be *this* one.
The footsteps get louder.
Click! Click! Click!
I can smell the fear in the room, or was it hairy old woman?
Double swearfuck!
They are right outside this door!
I know what's happening.
PAIGE: What??

JIMMY: Crawford will have pushed Hutchence up against the door pressing her Little Lady Lumps up against him.

I hear gentle banging, right enough.

Like *The Godfather* when Sonny has unknown actress up against the door.

Remember, when the other girls, also his sexual conquests, talked about what a big boy he was?

I so relate to that.

What you laughing at?

PAIGE: Nothing, I... *(Giggles.)*

JIMMY: I loved that scene and for quite a while, it was my sexual M.O. and opened a lot of...doors for me.

Anyway, a zip is lowered with that delicious zippy sound you only get from...like...zips?

One of my favourite sounds actually.

That, and...

We hear heavy breathing that might be hairy old woman again and I'm thinking the hunters might actually do it, right on the other side of the door.

I check the lock.

There's a key in it.

It's not locked.

I look at the girls in a desperate twisty-face way.

"Should I lock it?"

"Or, should I take the key out so I can watch?"

Or, will they realise it's us and shoot through the doors, or what?

Marsha whispers what we all want to happen.

"Get away. Get away, get away."

She repeats this, Buddhist mantra style and if it works for them, and Richard Gere, then maybe.

Yup, I heard about Buddhists in the city.

She was orange, with no hair. Yikes.

Anyway, next, we hear a female voice, kinda 'I Wanna Be Your Drill Instructor' shout "Hey!" and the banging stops.

301

Marsha's mantra worked!

There's more giggling, zip sounds —

Ziiiip!

— hey, *careful* there! Then the footsteps hurry away —

Click! Click! Click!

— getting quieter and quieter, thankfully.

We breathe hard, trying to suck in scaredy farts, 'cuz the hunters are probably kinda like sniffer-dogs.

But they've ran off to find somewhere more private, or without people shouting "Hey" while you're right in between something.

And with that thought in mind I turn, unfortunately, to hairy old woman.

She lets out a huge scream.

And I can tell we all think at the same time.

Will that make them come in here?

Luckily enough for us, a certain person has heard that scream.

Someone actually in the scream business.

No, not the hunters *or* Fay Wray *or* Janet Leigh *or* Courtney Cox. Love *that* name.

That certain person was, fortunately, one Miss Grace.

She was in the ladies locker room, a place I always wanted to sniff around in, and she's slapping her colourful face on.

Her locker door is open, a little mirror looking back at her face.

Miss Grace isn't a fan of her face.

I believe she tells herself aloud "Pretty on the inside."

She's not lying, but pretty on the inside glows *outward,* doesn't it?

I might say two words to her.

"You're beautiful."

It's true.

While we're in here, there is another thing of huge interest to Miss Grace.

Behind her locker door, is a faded, curled, old black
and white photograph that she leans to study.
Miss Grace reaches out to the photograph and
caresses it with undiminished-over-the years love.
She lets out a big sigh.
SIIIIIIIIIIIIIIIIIGH…
Then, she looks far far away for a minute.
That's when then the scream comes.
She slams the locker door and hurries out.
She misses the newspaper sitting on the bench seat
with my face on it.
And, the fact that her the locker hasn't shut completely.
Her photograph is of huge, no massive...no...even
biggerer than that, interest to me, too.
Wish I could have seen it.
So would you.

Jet.

At that very second, I think Paul McCartney, jet plane flying high above me, and a man who would also be massively interested in the photograph.

'Cuz I find out later that he's the subject of the photo, as a much younger man.

It's himself, great granddad.

But, why has Miss Grace got a photograph of *my* personal old one pinned to her locker?

Are they related?

Love Child?

Why does she kiss and caress and sigh all over it?

What else does she do with it?

I stop myself right there.

This is my great granddad.

And does she talk about him at dinner parties, or out with friends who might even have photos too and other memorabilia they buy?

A thought hits me like a bolt of lightning.

It's a fan thing.

But what is she a fan of?

Who is this old guy to her?

It's totally driving me nutso.

I wonder what it's like to travel in an aeroplane?

In the dark.

I wonder what it's like to just *travel?*

He would probably have a nice Scottish whisky in his hand but maybe not drink too much as he's on important business.

You can see it in his face, determined and focused.

There would be a waitress there I think, with drinks and treats and snacks and making sure he was well looked after.

He was kinda particular about that.

What do you do all the time in an aeroplane, apart from join the club?

Not great granddad, but wait? Is he already in it?
There's been light reflecting off his thick glasses,
making it hard to see his eyes for what's on his mind.
He'd take off the glasses and rub them, but truthfully,
he's an old man and is just a little tired.
Maybe he picks up something to read, a magazine
maybe, or even a book thing?
But, not a newspaper, at least, at this point.
But he will be too distracted, too much in his head
about *What Lies Beneath.*

It's In His Kiss.

Crawford and Hutchence would hear the scream too, and no wonder. It was really strong and piercing and shrieky for such a little bird-like, strangely furry, supposedly-sick creature like hairy old woman.

The hunters might hesitate in mid 'looking for somewhere for sex' searching.

It depends which was the stronger urge.

I think they would be in the mood for lurve and 'the find somewhere to do it' urge would be stronger.

I remember Crawford once saying that Hutchence was the best kisser on the island.

But, she's never kissed *me.*

So, they might be drawn to the stairwell and head for the doors, open them, stick their fine heads out, peek around, see there's no one there.

So, in the middle of things heating up again between Crawford and Hutchence, pre-zipper but post-heavy breathing and much seat-wetting, there would almost definitely be someone in the 'security profession' who's job is to react to things like screaming.

But, you know, hey. I've seen childbirth in movies and to be honest, the response of the security profession to screaming that's even louder than hairy old woman really sucks.

Anyway, first off, there would be an almighty, nerve-shredding clatter.

That would put the hunters on high-alert and Crawford might reach for Hutchence's weapon.

But it was just the doors opening, pounding SFX like a movie.

Can't they ever open hospital doors quieter, there's people trying to sleep and recover here?

Then, this person or persons or nurses in white uniform, or they're always a movie-handsome doctor would come haring up the stairs at least two at a time toward the source of the scream.

And handsome doctor will nearly bump into Crawford and Hutchence, almost knocking them over.

But he's so distracted, so focussed on being where doctors go in real life, that he doesn't even hardly notice the hot and horny hunters.

We use that lovely word and later I want to list all the words I learned in this city or town on my specialist subject.

Crawford is Hungry Like The Wolf for Hutchence and has him up against the wall like a serial-rapist in a bear-trap.

Once again, heavy breathing, saliva, heat and moistness.

And once again, a mighty crash! comes —

Craaash!

— right next to them, and before the extreme-trained but gagging like hounds in a heat-wave hunters can react...

The two nurses are on them.

"Hey!" Overweight big nurse shouts, and her sparrow-like nurse friend looks at Hutchence, impressed, then stifles a girlish giggle.

The sight in front of them could be described as the horny hunters, squint, partially-dressed, buttoned wrongly, collars askew, hair-messed, lipstick-stained, kissed raw, trying not to look like innocent murderers who are so dying for a good f**k.

Sparrow nurse can't stop herself from laughing aloud.

Big nurse says, "Seen youse bitches earlier. Get outta here 'fore I call s'curity," while the hunters fix clothes, hair, make up, damp underwear and body-parts.

Crawford goes to say something probably nasty, or maybe even shoot or kill a nurse.

And it occurs to me.

Could *they* patch themselves up?

307

Ow, painful.

But Hutchence takes Crawford by the hand and smoothly guides her away 'fore s'curity comes.

We can hear the two nurses talking about the hunters as they go through the doors, making a helluva racket again.

May be the doors are made that way?

But then, the hunters stop and turn, looking at each other.

And you can see them think.

Do we, or don't we?

It's a semenal moment.

Crawford gropes Hutchence, then runs back up the stairs with a snicker.

Hutchence flops against the wall with a quiet…

"Aaaaarrrrgggggghhhh."

And you can see him think.

Will I, or won't I?

With his hand touching himself.

All perfectly understandable, right?

PAIGE: Riiight.

JIMMY: Crawford peeks out the doors and along the shiny corridor, the two nurses run into Room 505.

But, it's empty.

Apart from hairy old woman.

I wonder what *they* call her?

"It's alright, Mrs. Hindenberg," I think it was and that must be what at least sparrow nurse calls her.

"What's all that noise about?" Big nurse says and I don't know what she calls the patient.

Probably 'Hairy Hindenberg' I'm thinking.

I'm wondering this as I hide under her bed with the gang and I'm reminded that it's been weeks since I was hiding under a woman's bed.

I'm squashed between Marsha and Norma in a chick-wich and having such fun, under the circumstances.

The patient tries to signal to the nurses with her beady eyes, not the prettiest sight, but they just do whatever nurses do.

Is it, check air-waves, check vitals, give her 100 mil of asdghzsdgz-ol?

Hairy old woman frantically tries to get "Under the bed!" out of her mouth, can't, then her hand from, um…wherever, can't, tries to grimace, can't, tries to moan, can't, tries to mumble, can't, and is just about to try and scream again.

"There Mrs. Hindenberg. You're *fine!*" Big nurse says while making a tortured face at her sparrow nurse friend who is busy tucking in hairy old woman's hopefully odour and stain-free nice and clean bed-sheets.

I hope I'm wrong again about her last signalling option. Farting.

The sparrow nurse pats Mrs. Hindenberg's hairy hand and off they go, quietly muttering things.

"…them two. Trying to…"

But they're outside now and I've lost a real opportunity to discover what nurses call sex.

As usual, I'm first out from under the bed and run to the door, opening it a tiny way to try to hear what the nurses say.

I can hear Andy clambering out.

I can hear the nurses muttering but I'm too late, so go and help the girls out.

Norma first, a little smile to her, then Marsha, much bigger smile.

The girls even manage a small 'let's be friends' smile at each other.

Marsha pats Norma's hand and she nods her gratitude at the gesture.

Girls.

I say "Um, Mrs. Hair…Hindenberg, you're not going to, like, scream again, are you?"

Mrs. Hindenberg looks panicked.

"It's just, like…noise pollution for the ears," I tell her.

Her beady eyes fix on me, but no scream.

I take that as a 'No' and move to the door.

I open it a little more, check both sides of the hall, then speak to the gang.

"Let's go."

Before I go out, I give Mrs. Hindenberg a smile and a wave.

She smiles like she's being strangled and waves back.

I turn to the door fast, and scope the hall, pretending I knew what I was doing.

No sign of anybody that we don't want to have signs of.

Andy is next out and he does the same.

The girls come out and now *they're* doing it.

All this scoping works out and I gesture to Room 501 and that's where we make for.

To be honest, I'm really nervous about what we'll find in Jayne's room.

Seeing as it's all my fault and now, I get to thinking about Grace and Mac.

And Marsha and Andy and Norma.

I stand outside the room, take the door handle, turn it, open the door and peek in, kinda antsy.

I see her. She's Got Wires.

But I see her sucky chest rise and fall, then I breathe a big sigh of relief.

I turn around and nod to the gang to follow me.

But here's another thing I didn't know, but can easily imagine.

Crawford and Hutchence haven't found a place for sex, those hospital horn hounds – hey, illiteration! — and they haven't just disappeared, either.

Not since they know we're here.

They *know*.

So, just at the end of the hall where the stairwell doors are slightly open…

There they are, behind frosted glass!

Sweargasm!!!

Crawford watches like a cobra and Hutchence has his big weapon in his hand.

Oh, another thing you might have noticed.

PAIGE: Hmmm?

JIMMY: I'm very un-observant.

PAIGE: Yeah? Never woulda guessed.

JIMMY: On the island, what would you need that for? O-for ornothology? Watching...*birds?*

So, I never noticed that our killers were right there, in fact, only yards from us.

They could have probably shot us at that very moment, but my theory is that they like *big dramas* and big shoot-em-ups like Ang Lee and maybe they should both have *two* guns each?

From where they watch, they can see us go in to Jayne's bedroom.

That's where they'll do it.

More high drama, the old fella called it.

And the blood will look so great on the clean, white, fresh bed-sheets.

But, something else made the difference.

Some*one* else.

Miss Grace.

She is padding down the stairs very daintily in white, comfortable Clarks shoes, kinda more quickly and quietly for a big girl and she sees them.

She is humming a tune that I would *know* and I would really love to know how the Hell *she* knows it?

Anyway, the hunters are so intently focussed on their targets, or it's a heady brew of blood-lust and sex-lust, that they don't see or hear Miss Grace.

But she sees them, then the gun, then clamps a chubby-ish hand over her almost shouty mouth.

Her eyes widen, then she darts back up the stairs, quiet as can be.

I had no idea what she was going to do.
Or how it would turn out.
But, now I do know, it was life changling.

The Faces.

I looked over at Jayne's bed and she looked really different without her make-up and big hair and the stuff that made her *her*, like her face and clothes and camel eyelashes and stuff.

All that was left of her was painted nails, all chipped. She would not be happy with whoever cleaned her up, I'm thinking.

Or with those un-flattering wires and tubes stuck into the back of her hand.

Or those thick lumps of bandages on her wounded shoulder, like two swans mating.

But she would be happy with whoever saved her, 'cuz even though her face looked sickly pale and deathly white and her shoulder was heavily bandaged, she was Alive and Kicking, the big 1970 hit.

Marsha and Norma sat on her bed, looking like worried parents after prom night from *Nightmare on Elm Street.*

Andy flopped clunkily into a chair like a puppet on a string.

I'm at the door in case I hear *you know who.*

And I leave it open a little.

Marsha is stroking Jayne's hand and whispering her name to her, but Jayne doesn't respond, is out of it, probably with the drip feeding drugs right into her veins.

Suddenly, I get the fright of my life.

The door crashes open and bounces off me —

Bang!

— scaring the butt-nuggets out of me.

The girls yelp, Andy jumps up and I spin around, not knowing WTF.

Are we dead?

Will it be quick?

But, it's Miss Grace!

Stronger Than Me.

I rub my sore, bounced-on arm.

"Oh, sorry," she tells me, touching my arm, lingering a little longer than needed.

She looks really concerned, and not about just my arm.

"I think them shooters is here."

"Gorgeous girl and handsome hunk?" Norma says, hoping not.

But Miss Grace just nods dumbly.

"The hunters," I say.

"The who?" says Miss Grace.

"No, the *hunters*, Miss Grace. We know," I say.

She looks surprised.

"We seen them."

She goes to the door, peeks out, then closes it quietly.

"You seen them, and you're still *here?*"

"Where did *you* see them?" Norma says.

"Behind them doors to the stairs. The man had a big, evil-looking weapon."

She shakes her head at me like I'm Aladdin Sane.

"For shooting *you,* honey."

"We had to see Jayne was alright."

"That's how they *found* you, baby. Knew you'd make it here *sometime.* You a *hero.*"

Our leader *led* them to us.

Resourceful Jimmy does it again.

Butt-nugget time.

"She OK?" says Miss Grace.

"You tell us," Norma says, so Miss Grace hurries over, does nursey touchy feely checky t-for tactiley thingys.

"She OK, but she need rest. She got lucky."

I make a hmmph noise.

Hmmmph.

"Some luck," Norma says.

"I called s'curity. So, if you guys don't want to be here..." she says, looking at me, hard.

I look back, soft.

"I don't know what this is all about, but..."

She just kinda trails off, her face lost in mine.

"Why are you helping us?" I, like…want to know.

"Something in the way..."

"What something in what way?"

Her eyes have never left mine once, unless to explore all over my handsome face.

What is it with all the hush hush eye-to-eye starey contact?

"You look so much like..."

She trails off again and I'm totally gagging to know, but irritated at the same time.

OK. Kinda flattered, too.

Her eyes bore into mine.

"You...uh...?" she goes.

"What uh?" I say, kinda now getting desperate to know what's in her mind.

"You couldn't."

"I probably *could.*"

"It's...not *possible.*"

"What isn't?"

She struggles to find the right words, I'm thinking, but getting even more fed up.

"Miss Grace..."

"*He* was..."

"WHAT???!!!" and now I'm getting a little pissed.

She removes her stare a sec to turn and open the door, taking a little peek.

"The coast looks clear," she says.

"The...*coast?*" I say, bewildered.

Are we that near the sea, or an ocean?

She turns back to me.

The staring is back on.

"Miss Grace...who do you think I look like? I'm dying to know, like…*literally?*"

"I'm...just an old fool."

"You're not a fool," I flatter.

But everyone looks at me in a 'you screwed up again' way, so I must have.

I don't know how.

But I feel like screaming and shaking her by the neck and shouting into her face.

'WHO DO YOU THINK I LOOK LIKE???!!!'

But instead I'll ask in a Prozak Nation way.

I don't want to startle her and the gang and I'm not at all violent, but I do raise my little voice a tad.

"Miss Grace...um..."

"Jimmy, ssshhh..." Marsha says.

"Your *name*...is...*Jimmy?!*"

And now, her eyes pop and her mouth hangs open like in *Crocodile Dundee*.

"Omigaw..." it sounded like she said.

"What? Have you swallowed your false-teeth?" I say.

She looks like she's seen a ghost, then been hit by a truck, struck by lightning, doctored, lasered, tasered... You get my drift.

PAIGE: Barely.

JIMMY: Later, *you* might react just the same way.

"Miss Grace, please."

I really do think that she meant to tell me.

But then...

Let's Go Round Again.

The red laser-dot!

It crawls across Miss Grace's shell-shocked, could-you-be? face.

I instantly think could-be-**WHO**?

We're all dead, but not Miss Grace, please.

I want to know.

I need to know.

So do YOU, believe me.

"Sooo much like him."

But instead of politely asking...

"I do? Who might that be, mayhap, and perchance? Hmmm?"

I'm forced to yank her out the line of sight of the damn red laser dot, slamming the door shut hard and locking it.

"Get down!" I shout at everyone and they do.

Norma starts to whimper, realising why I'm acting like this, but I thought in a more kinda leaderish way than usual.

"Wha's goin' on?" Miss Grace quite rightly wants to know as she sprawls on the floor, sorting her uniform. Women in Uniform would make a great feature length documentary, kinda *March of the Penguins* style.

"I'm sorry. But, it's...the hunters," and Marsha and Andy let out a gasp.

"No, please…" Norma whimpers on behalf of all of our thoughts.

Nobody else had seen the laser dot, so I quickly explained that.

Miss Grace is first on her feet, angry as Hell.

"Think they can come in here…"

And she moves to the door.

I stand in front of her.

Reckless, brave, maybe, stupid, definitely.

"They already killed two of our friends," I tell her.

Her face changes from anger to fear.

"Where's goddam s'curity?" she says, her lovely voice trembling.

"Miss Grace, I realise now is maybe not the time, but..." she runs to the desk, grabs the phone, dials and screams.

"The Hell's s'curity?!!" at it, then listens.

"Be here soon" she says and crosses herself.

"Miss Grace, who *is* it, tell me."

I lead her away from the door.

She opens her mouth to tell me, but just at that second, just as she's about to put me, and you, out of our Misery by Stephen King.

Another silent bullet gouges a huge hole in the door!

317

And it hits the very exact spot where Miss Grace and me were a sec before.

The gang squeal, panic, hit the floor, scream, cry, Twist And Shout.

I'm amazed no one has messed any pants yet.

Miss Grace stares blankly at me.

I have to drag her to the floor, which I think she enjoyed hugely, apart from the bit about death.

I think of the hunters lurking outside.

They would stand looking so cool, like a Milan fashion show for murderesists, all pouty and walking like their ass-hair is knotted, or dia-dire…food-poisoning.

They walk the length of the catwalk, thrust hips in people's faces, look like they want to be somewhere else, then blow down the barrels of their guns so that wisps of smoke drift, just so.

Hutchence will have been the one who fired, because I think Crawford is a better shot and Hutchence didn't shoot anyone's head, so she'll probably tease him about missing, maybe with a gentle poke in the crotch. And because the gun barrel will still be hot, he might go "Owww" quite rightly and my eyes water for him.

Or, I might be crying.

Then Crawford would go "Tsk, tsk, tsk," like I've heard her do on the island when he's done something that she doesn't like.

Which is a lot of things.

I think all of this in milli-seconds.

Then, I'm on my feet, carefully sneaking a peek through the hole in the door.

If the hunters were there, which they weren't at this point, and we were on speaking terms, which we're not, I'd compliment them on how they've set up this scene to shoot, but with irony. 'Cuz, the framing of the shot was really cool, very QT.

There's no sign of anyone else either, which I believe I'm going to take as a very bad sign.

318

Where have all the people gone?

And, why?

It was a *28 Days Later* opening scene kinda moment. The hunters must know we're in here, or they wouldn't have killed the defenceless door.

I look behind me and the sight would bring a dead person to tears.

Marsha, Norma and Miss Grace are cowering in the corner, like tiny ill-treated animals, hoping to not be hurt anymore, or killed.

And poor Andy is yanking at a window that will never open again, with years of layers of thick paint.

It...broke my stupid heart.

"Security will be here soon," I say to them, trying to sound like I even half-believe it.

The gang and Miss Grace look at me pleadingly, as if to say:

Do something, do something, do something.

Like another of those mantra things.

Decision time.

I *say* this:

"I'm...going to try and lure them away."

I *think* this:

I'm probably never going to see Marsha or Norma or Andy ever again.

I *do* this:

I hurry over to Marsha and plonk a big, hot, hungry, hard, wet kiss on her mouth, then give her ass a good squeeze.

Squeeeeeze!

I switch to Norma, giving her similar, only not so passionate and she recognises the difference and looks at me more strangerer than usual.

I do the same with Miss Grace because I know she'll love it and don't even ask her:

Who is it I look like?

Even though I had to know more, *needed* to.

319

But I think it.

I even kiss Andy, only not on the mouth and we bear-hug, best buds together.

It's time.

And because the gang know what's on my mind, because it's on theirs too, they look at me like I'm a little kitty in a bag just before you seal it and toss it in the river, then you have to hear their terrible whimpers and cries.

I feel terrible, but I have to try something.

Anything.

After all, it was me...

I can't think that anymore so…

I don't.

It's time.

I look through the door, and *Shatner!*

There they are, the hunters.

PAIGE: They're there?

JIMMY: They're right there!

Time I'm not.

My eyes have been shut, so I open them, then I'm at the door, I yank it open, I get ready to sprint...

Next thing, I've got my hands in the air, Western movie-style, reversing back into the room, face all panicky.

Behind me, the gang and most likely Miss Grace have realised that there's a gun on me.

Because there was.

"It's them!!!" somebody screamed, a girl's voice but I couldn't tell who, maybe even me.

I hear gasps and moans and screams and shouts and bawls and cries and "NOOOOOOOO's!!!!!"

And really loud clattering as the gang and Miss Grace hit the floor, crawl under the bed, or maybe even into it beside the remarkably and probably thankfully still asleep Jayne, I don't know.

I'm back in the room when Miss Grace spits.

"Hank!" to someone...um, Hank?

Miss Grace shakes her head and cusses quietly.

The gang look even more confused then usual.

"Grace. You OK?"

The little man steps in like *Man of Steel* and glances at Miss Grace.

The gang let out a massive sigh of relief, as Hank is definitely not the hunters.

Then, I notice that his job is Security, because it says that helpfully on a badge on his little uniform.

This, is the cavalry?

He's come to our rescue, short, round, greasy, scruffy, sick-looking guy who looked like he loved this part of the job where you get to shoot people and nothing ever happens to you.

He looked like he wanted to kill at least *me,* anyhow.

That's why I'm keeping my hands up, I tell myself.

"Don't worry about me! It's these kids!" Miss Grace tells him, a bit annoyed and bossy.

Are we kids?

When do you stop being one, I wonder.

I also wonder if it's safe to put my hands down.

"Wha' happen' heah"?' Security asks in this husky, high-pitched, kinda strangled, whiney-ass, wheezy smoker's voice. Like McKenzie would be after a lager drink and a whisky drink and a vodka drink and singing *Bat Out Of Hell* falsetto while out parteying and not coming home for days.

"*Psycho Killer* shot their friends! Kids is next," and gulp, I'm the one she looks at.

Then, she hurries over to the door and looks out carefully.

"Ya see 'em?" she asks Security.

He scratches his head, trying his best.

"Man and a woman?" she goes on.

"A…woman?" he says, scornfully and I know what he's thinking.

Suck's fake, is what *I'm* thinking.

"They were behind those doors," I say and point at those doors.

Security's chest puffs out like a fat pigeon, peering out the door.

"She's Not There," he says, kinda smirky.

"Um...and she left this big hole for you?" I tell him and Security turns for a look, his gun pointing at all of us dangerously.

"Aw put that down Hank, 'fore you kill your foot."

Security does what he's told, and I lower my hands at last and start rubbing my shoulders.

Miss Grace scopes the hall.

"Strange..." she says.

"Tell me about it," and I *actually* want her to tell me.

"No one's there."

"Um...who *should* be there?" I say.

She doesn't even give me a blank look.

"Well, doctors and nurses and patients and..."

"...hunters?" I finish.

"Hank...?" Miss Grace looks really frightened all over again.

Security's skin turns kinda *House of Wax* now and he raises the gun to look up and down the hall, like, un-expertly, hand shaking like a leaf.

I turn to look at the gang and Norma is softly crying, consoled by Marsha and Andy.

I have a terrible thought.

Have the hunters killed all those people that Miss Grace was expecting to see?

"OK, people. S'get outta heah!" Security tells us, his only and best leadery idea so far.

Out he goes into the hall first, gun ready to shoot his foot, scoping the place, mimicking long retired on something called a good pension cops.

I let Marsha, Norma, Miss Grace and Andy out, then follow and we're very nervy, looking like the turkeys you guys do, is it Thanksgiving?

Security is talking movie-cop talk to his shoulder strangely, until you see he's got some walkie-talkie thing there, saying whatever Security's say.

I think I hear stuff like…"…CCTV…" and then "…*Line Of Fire*…" then "…not paid enough."

"Where's the people?" Miss Grace asks Security and he doesn't look like he knows the answer.

There's no sign of the hunters, but I know they will be here sometime soon, once they're finished having sex somewhere.

With one last look over my shoulder in Jayne's direction, we take off down the hall.

Security is first, Marsha and Andy consoling tearful Norma with Miss Grace in the middle.

I'm last.

As you know, being last means you're first to be grabbed and killed and nobody notices *Friday The 13th Part VI*-style, until it's their turn.

I hoped for a better part.

We're sneaking along quietly, so far so good, but we're nearly at the doors and they're open just a little, so at least they won't jump out the doors and grab us *Boogeyman* style, but instead…

I hear a terrible crash and duck and turn slo-mo movie-style to see that a door has slammed open against the wall like after a mighty kick.

T-for tauntingly, there's no one there.

Then…

Gun-fire doesn't…um…blast?

But the walls do.

Blast!

We all kinda duck and spin this way and that.

There you are!

The hunters appear in *Matrix Reloaded* speed.

Crawford in the lead, Hutchence right behind.

They seem to fly, *Crouching Tiger, Hidden Dragon* style and are side-on, reminding me of handsome

Jason Statham in *The Transporter* and I hate to say it, but they really do look *Shaft* standard cool.

They're coming right at us, out of the very next room to us! so they must have heard everything we said and laughed, which at least would have ruined their trying to have sex in patients' rooms.

The gang are screaming with the Surround-Sound volume full up and scuttling around looking for places to hide on the floor.

The first to go down in a movie is someone that the audience has little or no empathy with, old guy said.

I turn to look and sure enough, the old man gets it right, yet again.

Security is hit, smack in the eye, dying as he crumples to the shiniest floor.

Miss Grace screams the loudest and I'm sorry, I have to confess that I *thought*...

PAIGE: ...Yes?

JIMMY: I could make her scream like that, too.

I feel sorry for Security, because I briefly notice that he can see the lights dimming in his dying face from his reflection on the shiny floor with his one good eye, which must be a terrible torture.

I bet she did that on purpose.

Another pointless death on my conscience.

An awful lot of blood comes from an eye with a bullet through it, though.

She probably she did *that* on purpose too and Crawford just loves this, pausing to blow smoke from her gun.

Callous is the word the dictionary uses.

But in a kinda sorta slightly slutty phallic way, and I bet if the barrel wasn't so hot...

They've just stopped, standing statue-still, watching us all frozen in time.

They smile at us.

Miss Grace's make-up is smudged like a Kiss guitarist after *Destroyer* fan-attack, but she consoles the gang, her big, beefy arms protectively around them.

They all kinda half-crouch and half-hide, half-heartedly behind Security's sweaty, blood-soaked corpse and that pathetic picture makes me feel very sad.

Even *he* will have people who love him.

I wonder if there's any more Security people here, or are they Dead And Gone?

I'm Still Standing.

I don't know, trying to what? Appear unafraid? Brave? C-for confrontational?

No, just stupid, I make my mind up.

'Relishing' is the word the dictionary book uses for what I think the hunters are doing.

I'm left thinking that all they ever do is eat, have sex, and shop, but their j-o-b is to kill.

So I figure that they must talk a lot and discuss and carefully plan how the climax, as the old man would say, to the third act, the final curtain, your *ending,* plays out.

They will look for new ways for people to die, just like in the movies.

Are there any left?

And the hunters come to the conclusion that they will *toy* with us plenty, drooling over the moment of our deaths.

I also think, do they tell the founders that they're cruel like this with their kills?

Or, is it the founders who ask for *Retribution* like this as some sort of warning and new rumour?

Miss Grace meantime has gone from a terrible sadness to building a raging anger.

Her face is twisted with it, a bit like the faces in *The Ring 2* but more scarederer.

She clambers to her feet and shoves me behind her with a strength that could rip a telephone box in half, or

325

a prisoner grabbing the new kid with "I want some penising and I want it now."

"Look, let's just take it easy!" she goes and the hunters...take it easy, lowering their guns.

"They's just...kids!" she says to them and they nod like priests faking intently listening to a confession.

Miss Grace advances toward them and, I just know it... Crawford raises her gun with a wicked smile and points it at Miss Grace.

She stops dead, wait, I don't mean *she's dead,* it's just to say that she stopped like she'd been...oh forget it.

She stops.

Crawford snorts like a foal.

Snorrrt!

"Miss Grace, don't!" I tell her and grab her fleshy arm. She twists me off easily like in 'Attack nurse, assaulted every Saturday night and forced into taking kick-ass lessons: The revenge movie.'

I made that up.

PAIGE: No shit.

JIMMY: She gives me a glance and the tiniest little smile.

It was a smile like saying goodbye to a lover.

Am I ever going to find out who she thinks I look like, I think.

Wait...that's *IT!!!*

"Miss Grace, who is it you think I look like?" I say, looking hard at the hunters.

That hit the spot.

I figured this might buy a heart-beat or two.

You should have seen the looks on their faces!

But ask yourself this. Why?

So, ask yourself?!

Hutchence looked like he'd caught himself in his zip and Crawford like she'd caught those magnificent breasts in a hefty meat-grinder.

The gang all exchange looks.

Miss Grace realises that this is all we've got and half-turns to me.

"Sure, Jimmy. I'll tell you," she says, then looks back at the hunters.

They don't look overly impressed at Miss Grace's news.

At the time, I thought it was the thing to do.

But then, what do I know about *The Right Stuff?*

Miss Grace opens her mouth to speak, but before she says one word…

Crawford starts to line up the red dot on Miss Grace's face.

I see it!

PAIGE! Nooo!

JIMMY: Yesss!

Just at the same instant Crawford fires, I shove Miss Grace aside.

And instead of the whispery silent bullet hitting her dead in the eye, it punches her in the chest and she squeals.

She crumples against me, blood spreading over her hospital whites.

And on me, too.

The, she kinda reels toward cruel Crawford who just watches, then rages at me.

"You made me *miss*, you *imbecile!*"

I had no idea what she meant, until this dictionary.

More nurses in white uniforms appear down the hall behind Crawford and Hutchence and I shout:

"Heeeelp!!!" at them.

The hunters spin and the nurses see the guns and one mouthes "f**k" and they charge back down the hall.

Meantime, I've tried to round up the gang to maybe escape through the teasingly close doors.

Miss Grace staggers and hits the wall, crumpling to the floor and I want to go to her.

But, I can't, dammit!

I have other responsibilities.

"Grace!!!" Marsha screams.

We'll have to leave her, like her poor namesake.

Another security guy appears and he takes in the scene wide-eyed and slack-jawed and moves to his holstered gun.

No chance.

He's all clumsy as Hell and no wonder.

The hunters are black ninja standard at this stuff and a security with a machine-gun and *not* holstered would be no sweat, either.

Crawford fires at the poor guy —

Blam!

— landing one perfectly where she intended, right between the bulging eyes.

I can hear other people screaming now, as well as the gang and most likely me.

Hutchence has been admiring her work and in that instant, that heart-beat, when they're both not concentrating just on *us,* I kinda herd the gang toward the doors.

I've got the girls by their girly-thin wrists, hauling them along, Andy last.

I glance behind to see a third security guy crouching low, sweeping his gun, looking a little more like he was capable.

Hutchence fires at him and he ducks.

The bullet slams and smacks and hits the wall and leaves a big hole, and you can see the guy wonder...no bang?

Now, there's screams from it seems, everywhere and shouting and door-crashing chaos, really.

Marsha and Norma are screaming their heads off and poor little Andy tries to help me, and does.

"This way!!!" he shouts, waving ahead.

Bullets are now exploding all around us now —

Ping! Ping! Ping!

— and some aren't the hunters, I think.

Because I can hear loud shots and shouting and even though bullets hit walls and doors and sometimes, other people, we zig this way and zag that way and zoom and zip and crazily and somehow, incredibly, we make it to the doors.

Woodwork is torn up as bullets whine and ricochet and bounce and slam everywhere.

I shoulder-crash into the doors and find two things.

One —

PAIGE: Yes?

JIMMY: — we made it.

Two —

PAIGE: Yes?

JIMMY: — that hurt, so not like in the movies.

Three —

PAIGE: Yes, already!

JIMMY: I'm starting to be heroic and like, leadery, only it works this time, maybe.

We all explode through the doors and I figure that the hunters must be distracted, because the silent bullets thud into the doors, instead of us.

They really tear up stuff *visually* those guys.

Now, a sec to think.

Upstairs, Downstairs? PBS?

Down to escape, yes.

"C'mon" I tell them and kinda get pushy with the gang, shoving them down the stairs.

"But...Grace..." Norma cries.

From the hall, the sound of mayhem is sounding like a Black Sabbath gig.

And it's not even heading our way.

"I'm sorry, Norma. We...have to leave her," and grief and hopelessness and woe-as-me sweeps over us all.

We take off, stairs two and three at a time, quite difficult on my skinny ankles.

Nurses and doctors in white coats look at us like we're escaped lab experiments, but they all kindly make way for the mad-looking people, one covered in blood, hardly surprising in a hospital, really.

I can hear the deafening wail of police sirens and think 'cops' then 'help' then 'address please?' then 'let's just get outta here, if we can.'

High up above, or down below, I can only…

IMAGINE WHAT'S HAPPENING:

You could write it in yourself and wouldn't be that far wrong.

My version goes like this:

Crawford looks stunning and triumphant and majestic, *Joan of Arc* in battle, kneeling sexily with her gun in her outstretched arms, the red laser dot finding targets for her, lazily.

I've got no idea and she doesn't care about how many she shot or probably mostly killed with that standard of *Enemy at the Gates* sniping.

Hutchence maybe doesn't shoot or kill as much, because he watches her, full of a deep glow of lusty admiration and I realise something.

PAIGE: Yes?

JIMMY: *She* is his *hero.*

Some hero, killing innocent kids and women and minimum wage they call it? security and nurses in cold blood.

But, wouldn't the blood be, like…*warm*?

Anyway —

PAIGE: Anyhoo —

JIMMY: — the pair of them seem to live charmed lives, like us, I suppose, cuz not one of a whining hail of angry bullets from a raging row of cops and seething security behind upturned gurneys and tables hits them.

330

Police sirens reach Hutchence's ears among all the noise and he says something to Crawford in a low growl which I think might be:

"Don't let them escape!" meaning us and I wish they just would.

Crawford rains silent bullets onto the cops and security, then spins away like a ballet-dancer.

They sprint for the doors, zigging and zagging much better than us, and Hutchence launches at them in a cool flying side-kick and they crash open, Crawford right behind, beaming a big smile, a glance behind, then a last burst of bullets.

Her gun holds as many bullets as movie guns, you know.

And they're gone…

The End.

...and even though we have a good start, they're fitter, stronger, slicker, more motivateder and more scareder of whoever on the island, than we are of them.

We're totally breathless with all these stairs and running and jumping and avoiding other stair-users politely, so we pause for a rest, needing to throw-up and find toilets.

And if you glance up above, look over your shoulder, there they are!

Sweargasm!

My eyes widen and I grab the gang.

"Run!!!" I shout, just as a silent bullet whines cinematically off a handrail, sending splinters of flaky paint and fine, choky dust into the air.

Norma lets out a moan I'm well used to, then we're off and running again, fear giving us wings, helping us half fall down the stairs with injuries we'll only feel later.

But, we're just not as fast, or as we well know, as smart as them.

Crawford is just behind Hutchence, her gun reaching out and she only pauses for a heartbeat.

But not from out-of-breathness.

I can see her aiming, her smile, even now.

She fires and another wall is shot.

Somehow, that smile spurs me on and I gather speed and strength, forcing the gang ahead.

We're nearly at the doors to the exit!

Andy is looking that shade of *Exorcist* vomit green and the girls see that, helping him go.

Bullets ricochet loudly, the girls scream deafeningly, Andy almost crying.

I hear the hunters good quality, probably hand-made shoes clattering after us and

We reach the bottom landing!

The girls and Andy are there first and they tumble
through the doors like dust-devils only noisily of course,
me close behind.
We burst into reception —
Burst!
— and it's totally buzzing with activity and people, like
a human Noah's Ark and also cops, Hey! With guns,
walkie-talkies and serious take-no-prisoners, do-no-
diets attitude.
Norma screams first, Andy second, but it's Marsha that
screams loudest.
I notice reception woman gaping, blaming me.
And for some reason, everybody else is all staring at
me too and while they're doing that, they're also
looking at me like I was on my death-bed.
Which was half right.
What they were seeing was…suck's fake!
PAIGE: What?
JIMMY: The red dot crawling across my head, like a
mobile zit.
Watched in horror by the gang.
In that instant, I realised:
The hunters don't think of us as *people.*
We're just *meat* and *prey.*
Their eyes are only on the prize.
Crawford's silent bullet couldn't miss, could it?
It ripped into my body somewhere, thankfully not my
beautiful head, face, or amazing eyes. But where?
I couldn't tell at that time.
I was too full of fear and adrenalin and shit and *myself*
to figure that out, so I was *The Running Man.*
Then the not-running man.
I was the shot man, the struggling man…then the
slowing man…then the dragging man…then the
hugging man…then the stopp...ing man...then…
The bullet had dug deep, the pain searing and

blood, my own personal blood, seeped between my fingers…
And I let out a scream like, um…*Scream?*
And the floor smacked me hard in the face.
If I just lie here…

Queen Bitch.

I think the first thing I vaguely hear is Marsha screaming:
"JIIIIIIIMMMMMMMMMMMMMMMMMMYYYYYYYYYYYYYY"
But although I recognise it as a scream, it wasn't loud, like things were getting quieter, or she didn't want to hurt my ears.
Wait, oh no...
Was I, like...*dying?*
Ohmigodnoidontwanttodietherestoomanygirlsihavent-
Wait...
Istherelifeafterdeathbecausemaybetheyhavegirls-
Turns out that shock does that to you, shuts things down to focus and protect the hurt part.
The gang are in blind panic, three blind mice in *The Nutty Professor's* science lab, wondering what to do and who's next.
I'm semi-consciousness, at least I think.
And I wonder who was it I was supposed to look like...who was it...who I...
But then the gang become fabulous! Because they don't think about themselves, but think about *me* and I love them and they scoop me up by the arms and I explain to them "Aaarrrggghhh!" discovering where I'm hit, the front of the left shoulder, and they kinda drag me through the corridor toward the doors that I can see, like *Leaving Las Vegas* and I'm screaming *Help!* and thinking of The Beatles and Ticket To Ride but don't get any because potential helpers don't think help, but Hell, 'cuz right behind me with guns smoking and stomping purposefully down the hallway while avoiding patches of *my* personal blood on the shiny floor, Norma is hauling poor white-out Andy along which must mean that Marsha has hold of me and she is one strong and determined girl and both girls are electrifyingly awesome because all around them bullets

ricochet and whine and zing and ping and a young nurse's white uniform is red and she drops with a surprised look on her kind face.

Medical records and trays go flying, with sharp, kinda *Lethal Weapon* looking shiny stuff clattering and gurneys toppling, doctors and uninformed nurses and medics and visitors hugging walls and each other for health and safety.

Andy stumbles and drags Norma down and Marsha goes to help and I'm more useless than usual and Crawford gives that cruel smile, stops Hutchence with just one look, and kneels.

You think you're so fucool, don't you?!

She aims, carefully.

No, please, don't.

PAIGE: *Don't!*

JIMMY: Not *Norma*!

PAIGE: Not *Norma!!*

JIMMY: Kill *me!*

PAIGE: Pleeease!

JIMMY: I try to say, but nothing comes out.

It won't come out, I can't make my mouth work.

Poor Norma seems to realise, pauses, then turns to look into the flat, dead eyes of her killer.

She seems to just...give up?

Maybe, I don't know, but she has this final look.

Her and Crawford share Just One Look and it's a Hollies and Linda Ronstadt moment and do they have to let it linger and where's s'curity or the cops?

Then, there it is.

The red speck.

Such a tiny thing that says…*(Long silence.)*

PAIGE: Jimmy?

JIMMY: No bang.

You're...dead.

The laser-dot settles on Norma's face like a cancer.

In my head, I move to wipe it away, to get in the way of it.

Marsha screams and Andy slumps, not watching, eyes clamped shut, waiting his turn.

Norma's hair flutters just a little and in that moment, I know.

She collapses to the floor.

And the blood...

PAIGE: Her blood...

JIMMY: I see the most grotesque, triumphant smile begin to form on the face of the beautiful bitch.

I don't quite know...

How...

I...

Be here sooner.

I was managing to focus-pull, just a little and only had one thought, surprise surprise.

PAIGE: Not *that* —

JIMMY: My *Norma*.

PAIGE: Thank you, God.

JIMMY: Ohmigodohmigodohmigod.

Norma!!!

But, then...you'll never guess what happened.

Or who.

PAIGE: Who?

JIMMY: Amazing Grace!

She Johnny Thunders into the reception in a kinda speeded up slo-mo, the darkest, meanest Bat out of Hell look on her face.

But there's an awful lot of blood all over that fine, comfortably plump heaving chest.

It has poured all down her like a White Stripes album cover and I'm scared for her.

She herds us like Samantha Mumba times a million calories later, grabbing me from the ground.

"Ooowww!!!" I explained.

And did she just say through gritted, angry teeth: "Not on my watch," or "Not him, he's Jimmy..." or something like that, then hares to Andy and grabs him by his scraggy elbow.

Poor kid.

His eyes were still screwed shut and he's muttering "'No...no...Norma" over and over and over and he put his hands over his head thinking the hunters had come for him.

His eyes snap open and he looks like a Real Gone Kid. Miss Grace shoves Marsha hard in front of her, forcing us all toward the door.

Everyone in the reception seem to hold their breath, because I do not hear one sound other than Miss Grace's heavy, strangely erotic breathing.

338

She was struggling and I felt really bad.
And...Norma.
Another One Bites the Dust.
Jimmy, Jimmy.
Then I hear whining, but it's none of us.
I realise that it's bullets bouncing off gurneys and stuff again, but at least not us.
I risk a tiny look behind which really rips my shoulder and I see Hutchence, smiling, gun arm outstretched, firing wildly at everything and everyone.
He's playing with us.
A cat with mice.
Crawford chases us, then trips over something on the floor, maybe my personal blood, I don't really know, because it was total madness.
Miss Grace weaves through the craziness like a lumpy linebacker and I see the exit just ahead!
We're nearly there.
Next thing, Miss Grace just tosses us in the direction of the doors and we're almost out.
She spins, plants her feet like Will Smith in *Ali*, fists clenched painfully, snarling like a cornered cougar.
And, swearfucker!
Hutchence is right on top of her!
Is he going to, like...*hump* her?
And just as he's about to shoot...
PAIGE: Yes?
JIMMY: I see Miss Grace's strong arm swipe, plenty fast for a girl of her size, but in a nice way.
Swiiipe!
"That's for the girl!" she snarls.
And then I hear a big, girlie scream.
It's Hutchence!
And Miss Grace has a very nasty, dangerous, glinting, now dripping, surgical scalpel in her meaty hand!
Hutch will def need stitches.

He leaps around like he's *Man on Fire*, face all twisted in pain, poor thing, gripping his gun hand.

That's not movie-blood.

Yuk. The old guy says they use pig blood…seeping between his fingers and he's mad at getting suckered by Miss Grace.

The next sound I hear is the welcome shriek of police sirens and screeching tyres.

We're right at the exit.

I get Marsha and Andy to the door, then look back.

I want to go to Norma and I need to get Miss Grace out of there, so I turn back, lumber back, stagger back.

Just at that very second, Crawford comes into focus.

I'm staring right into her eyes.

It's hard to believe such a pretty face could contort so horribly.

I stop right there.

I instantly realise that none of them have ever been wounded in action, *ever.*

And that they don't know failure, because they've never tasted it.

They are that good.

Until they met Mighty Miss Grace.

I think Crawford will shoot me for sure, but she has someone else to take revenge on first.

No, I don't want that.

I'm trying to get to Miss Grace, but people keep bumping hard into my really totally swearfucked up shoulder!

In blind panic, I'm racing to the exit.

Through teary eyes, I think I see uniforms, women cops hopefully. All I can do is reach a hand out between the mob toward Miss Grace.

I hear a bullhorn saying something about weapons.

I can nearly reach her.

Two cops are inside, guns drawn, whirling.

"Miss Grace!" I almost scream.

Then, I whimper 'cuz...
Crawford's gun's in my face.
She smiles at me.
Then, she has her gun at Miss Grace's pulsing temple.
"Aw no, not her, please!"
Crawford grins like a wolf at me.
"She's got nothing to do with..."
I try, but...Crawford...fires.
The cops are just in time to be too late.
They whirl toward Crawford.
Whirl!
She's first to fire into their heads, stupid as mine.
Miss Grace drops to the floor in a heap, her blood
splattering and and and —
PAIGE: And and and —
JIMMY: Marsha and Andy are screaming.
So am I.
A bunch of cops skid in, fall, waving guns, shouting,
tearing to their "Man down, man down!" radios, and I
think 'What about the women' and people are shrieking
and crying and barging over crumpled bodies on the
floor and suck's fake! Crawford tries to stick her gun in
my mouth!
Hutchence fumbles like his first bra-strap with his
wrong hand to draw his weapon, glaring dementedly at
me, screaming something about my hair.
Crawford glares like *The Evil Dead* at me because she
can't get her gun in my mouth or a good shot and she
turns and grabs Hutchence by the eww-icky blood-
soaked sleeve then lets go and stares at her hand and
looks disgusted and nags something at him then wipes
her hand on his jacket and sprints to doors painted *Fire
Exit* and kicks them open expertly and drags him after
her.
PAIGE: They escaped? As easily as that?
JIMMY: So can we, I think.

Then I think about brave, kind our Grace, then Mac, Jayne lying upstairs, then Miss Grace...I have to stop because it's killing me.

Marsha and Andy can only stare at me like shell-shocked nnnnnnineteen year-olds in 'Nam.

I briefly wonder, who can I stare at for help?

More cops pour in, one a desirable redhead I notice, so I'm not that far gone, and try to stop people pouring out, including us three, but we make it outside.

CCTV recorded everything, so I wonder...my hair?

My shoulder hurts like crazy and maybe I should turn back, after all, because a hospital is a great place to get shot not dead, then get patched up, right?

But I decide we need to get as far away as possible from the hunters and cop questions downtown we can't answer but, where are...*they?*

I tell the gang of my decision, and I get the distinct impression if I said 'go bite the head off a bat' they would have done it, needing direction like actors.

But, I'm running out of friends fast.

Make it through the night.

Outside was as chaotic as inside.
A sea of petrified hospital-goers, even some patients in various stages of dress, undress, hey, nice *legs,* operations, terror, toileting, life and death and Woody Allen and stuff.
The cops couldn't control this, no one could.
I don't know what hurt like Hell the most, my shoulder or my ears with all the racket, or my feelings or ego.
Police sirens, bullhorns, smashing windows, car alarms, screeching cars, squealing tyres, crackling radios, shouted instructions, people on cell-phones, agonised cries, maybe even — was that a helicopter? Never seen one, apart from…
I see lots of newspeople talking into camera looking very serious with orange skin, plastic teeth and not one hair outta place, even with the helicopter.
Some of them were talking at witnesses who were enjoying their 15 minutes of what you call fame.
Marsha was mouthing "Norma" silently, over and over again and hugging Andy close to herself and I draped both arms around them.
It hurt my shoulder, but what could I do?
And playing in my head was a bad line of dialogue.

ME.

And then, there was three.

Or is it were? And I scope the place for the hunters and that's what I did until I figured they would be long gone, I hope.

Anyway, Hutchence would need his hand fixed-up and I hoped he would get some horrible disease like in *Cabin Fever: Patient Zero* and swearfucking die.

But, I just bet they have some crooked go-to doctor who patches them up.

Behind me, the car park was car dark, but at least looked a good choice to duck into, 'cuz I could see police making some kinda order and stopping people about questions, probably.

Maybe we could steal a car and escape?

"We haffta get outta here!" was all I could say and do.

I remembered a favourite song by Evanescence which means fading into nothing, like 'The getting smaller by the second gang' or 'The hole in the head gang.'

I led? us into the darkness and wondered…

Was God prayer worth a shot?

Stupid Boy.

We found people lying and sitting and leaning and standing around in various *Altered States.*
Like…Ohio.
Dazed, shocked, bleeding, blankets draped over shaking shoulders, crying, mumbling to themselves, fumbling with drinks, vomittng, being interviewed by police.
That helicopter was really hurting my ears and hair.
I could even see some people like us, *Persons Of Interest,* people who didn't want interviewed by the police for their own reasons, because of their own personal hunters maybe, hurrying away between cars, looking over hunched shoulders.
I was doing exactly the same, desperately scanning the packed car park for the hunters, convinced that they would definitely Come Back And Finish What You Started in the car park, but trying hard not to let Andy and...and I would have to get used to saying…
The girl…*singular.*
Anyway, they looked so far out of it, that I got away with it, they let me think.
But they were gone, kinda like ghosts, maybe.
I couldn't even see any nice cars, they were mostly all modern monsters.
Pervertly, a lot of them were dark and kinda huntery, but I was convincing myself that they had gone to get Hutchence medical attention.
I wanted to say something, so I tried to shout above the noise.
Andy replied "Shrtovo ccl oi?" and looked at me, his little baby face twisting from shock to total bewilderment.
There was no point in trying to compete with all the racket, so I waited.
This something, I really had to tell them.

I thought we must have looked a sorry sight, all grey and shocked and me, bloody.

And now I come to think about it, my shoulder is throbbing like crazy.

I take a sneaky peek without wanting to alert *Honey, I Shrunk The Gang* kinda, and I see it's stopped bleeding all over my sweater.

We're all kinda struggling to help each other, which is nice but pointless, as we're probably all screwed.

We're out of the hospital grounds now and head down this street with hardly any light.

Things seem desperate to me, and it seems the gang maybe think the same.

Marsha says "It's all over now," but I think of The Stones and that makes my dried-up fig brain flip to the hunters and them calling the founder.

"Good news. We killed another defenceless young islander," and great granddad finding this out, somehow and his reaction?

Would be to scream down the phone.

Can you call from a Lear jet?

But if you can, he'd know the number, at least.

And he'd be pounding the carpet, pacing up and down, redder and madder than Hell.

"That poor girl! They really…did it!" he'd spit with horror and blind rage down the phone.

I don't think he'd get any response at all to that rant.

"You really '*great granddad version of swearing*' did it?!" he'd scream into the phone.

"And who tells her family?!"

He listens for a few seconds, not getting or probably even expecting any reply, then he'd def go for it.

"You bastard!!!"

Can you a) talk like that to the founder and b) what happens if you do?

He waits again for some sort of reaction, but, nothing.

"Please. Can't you call the pack-dogs off? I'm...begging!" and he's about to beg more, because he desperately wants to save me and what's left of the gang.

And then, he would roar in anger.

Because the telephone line would be dead.

Like us, soon, maybe we're both thinking.

That did it for me, so that's when I confess.

"I'm stupid" like they hadn't realised?

PAIGE: Duhhh.

JIMMY: "They knew we'd figure it out eventually. And what would we do?"

The gang all look at me and I wonder if that's blame I see in their sad eyes.

"I...am...*so*...stupid" was the something I wanted to say, and you know that's true.

"I might as well have killed Norma myself."

"I got Grace killed. I got Mac killed. I got Norma killed. I got Jayne killed, probably, and Miss Grace and nurses in white uniform and...and I think I've got us *all* killed."

Cry Boy, Cry.

"I'm so swearfucking *stupid!*"

I couldn't stop crying.

Middle of the road, The Pretenders record, surrounded by people you hope are still your closest friends, even though you're the one about to be responsible for their terrible, early deaths in the head and think "Oops, I'm so sorry."

Why do girls always have tissue?

Marsha handed me a fat wad of them, with a look of sadness and pity.

I took them and wiped my stupid face.

Andy patted my shoulder like a silent "Hey, bra" and I managed to bite back a cry of agony as it was my shot shoulder.

But it was Marsha who had The Cure.

347

She just held me in her arms, careful not to hurt my shoulder.

"'No one wanted the responsibility, Jimmy," Andy said. "Some leader. I led them right to us."

"You couldn't have known they'd be there," Marsha said, her voice soothing, like sunburn cream.

"'They're just really...*good* at being bad. Jimmy."

"'They killed them, not you," Andy said, getting much more outta him in one day, than his whole about to be even shorter life.

"Because I wanted out, wanted to find out about my great granddad. I'll never find out now."

"Nothing is as it seems, Jimmy." Andy says, all sorta *Twilight Zone*-y Rod Serling-ishly mysteriously. The gang sorta surround me, like *The Alamo* and *Zulu* and *The Lord of the Rings* and *Game of Thrones*.

Even though there's just two of them.

"And you guys followed. This wasn't supposed..."

"Nobody forced us to leave, Jimmy. We chose to follow you," Marsha said.

"It was all for Less Than Zero."

PAIGE: Love that flick.

JIMMY: The gang group hug me and it feels kinda nice and bondingish...until they all squeezed harder.

"'Um...any more tissues, Marsha?"

And she fumbles in her sweater pocket for the packet.

"Don't cry, Jimmy, it's alright," Marsha says softly and she and Andy exchange that new, familiar look of pity.

"It's not that."

I ball the tissues and lift up my sweater, where I felt my shoulder bleeding again.

I dab the wound and pretend it's not f-agony.

At the far end of the road, there was a little light from a tiny store that might be open but looks deserted, like the rest of the street.

Then, it gets all dreamy like *Inception* and so does the gang and the rest of the scene and...

What the Hell is happening?

What was happening was…fain…Ting Tings.

I woke up in the little store, hanging half-off a rickety wooden chair.

The focus-puller had adjusted the lens on my eyes and I could make things out a little better.

There, was Marsha's legs, her hips, inviting valley, her stomach, her delicious breasts, then her tongue as it licks her inviting lips and I'm starting to…

"Someone's feeling better" a voice says and Andy enters the scene.

I give Marsha a lop-sided, 'Been to the dennis' smile and I hear Andy "Tsk-tsk" and somebody else snigger.

Wait.

There's someone else here.

The…hunters...?!

I immediately leap to my feet, stagger, wobble, grab the chair and I'm about to aim a big swipe…

"Jimmy, it's alright!" Marsha lets me know.

"We're safe."

I look at them, then *The New Guy.*

He's just standing gaping at me, this young, really high skeleton kid with kinda blue hair standing to attention and skin that needs some attention, but he has a nice, friendly face, if a little antsy, so I force a smile at him and his face says "Backatcha."

I feel a *Snow White*-out coming on and Marsha sees that and takes the chair from me and helps me sit.

The store is the tiniest thing and with the gang all in it, it's a full house.

It's packed with stuff and brands I mostly don't recognise, with a low ceiling, low rent and hardly any light and quite a lot of dirt.

I can just about hear some really tinny music play from someplace but I can't make out the song, or even if it is one.

Then, I see it.

You call it a generic brand radio, right?

I notice Marsha has blood on her clothes and start to panic.

She follows my look.

"It's your blood, Jimmy."

She has a pile of stuff in a funny-looking basket made of wire.

I recognise bandages, tape, a bottle of distillfectant, painkillers, gauze and stuff.

I wonder what that is for, until I try to stand and let out a mighty…

"Oooowwwww" like a little cry baby she'll think, but when I look for Norma…

She's not there.

So I check my bullet hole and then I discover I'm all bandaged and taped up like Down at the Doctor's.

Then I notice that the store has a rack of, yuk, sweaters and, oh funcool…

I've got one, like…on?

It's really…so not me, call The Style Council hotline, but hey. The thought was there.

And, I see the young tall kid has the exact same sweater on.

I wonder who did all this to me, and it must have shown on my face, 'cuz Marsha grimaces.

"I did it," and checks my kinda horrified face.

"I hope it's alright."

"Thanks, Marsha."

"Thank Everett here, too. He let us clean you up here."

"Everett. Thanks, I owe you," and he smiles and those front teeth make me think of I am the Walrus.

PAIGE: Goo goo ga choo.

JIMMY: "Looks like it went clean through. Lucky boy," Marsha says.

"Did I cry like a little stomped-on kitty?"

"Luckily, you were unconscious," she says, sarcasmic.

"Feeling alright?" says Andy.

"'I feel fine,'" and he nods in a kooky Fab Fourish sorta way.

"Everett glued the wound," Marsha says with a smile like lightning for the high guy.

"Super. Glued?" I ask, a little over-scared.

"Not Superglue. Uhu," he says.

"Um...yoohoo to you, too?" and now he looks confused.

"Better than stitches," he says and I nod dopily.

"And saves you going to the hospital," he goes on.

"Right, great. Um, thanks man," I say, uncertainly, poking around at my shoulder carefully.

"How you guys doing?" I ask around and they each force tight smiles and nod.

It's bad.

Everett hands Marsha a piece of paper and she looks at it, confused.

"Uh, that'll be thirteen dollars," he says, bashfully.

She nods with a small smile and Everett watches her as she produces some filthy, crumpled dollar money and lays them on the counter.

He takes the money and Marsha turns away.

"Don't forget your change!" and she looks as bewildered as the rest of us.

He kinda points with a bony finger at some disgusting mashed up dollars on the counter, and Marsha smiles and takes them, then hands them back.

"You've been so kind," she lets him know and leans close to peck him on the cheek.

Mwwwwaaaaaah!

Everett blushes like a traffic light and buries his face in his hands.

"Yeah, thanks Everett" I say again, pummeling his hardly there shoulder.

We all turn to go and I have this swearfuck moment.

Where are we going?

Let's go outside.

I kinda think the gang are wondering the same.
It's cold outside, the paint's peeling offa the walls and
we all like, hover like *Lost Boys* outside Everett's store.
He's looking at us from inside the store.
And it seems like the safest place in the world to me at
the same time.
Like a *Cocoon.*
Marsha and Andy are looking at me too for, I don't
know, *Gladiator* stuff, but I just want to cry out.
'I don't want it! I never asked for it! Someone else take
it! I quit the group!'
But what comes out is:
"I've been...thinking" and I'm just as surprised as they
are. They're staring and gaping and jaw-flapping at my
astounding leadershippy, Harvardy, Yaley, James
Bond *Spectre* qualities and my confession about
thinking, or whatever it was.
At least, Andy is.
Because Marsha looks like she hates everyone and
her head droops n' drops.
And I think Marsha is thinking 'It was your *thinking,*
stufus, that got us into this.'
Good point, well made.
"This...isn't happening," she says and me and Andy
exchange looks that are sad and say 'Yes, we're afraid
it is. We're all gonna die.'
But then, we haven't talked about...what happened...
And I think that maybe this is the time.
"How could they do this to us?" Andy opens with, and I
wonder who he means.
"They're islanders, same as us," Marsha says in a
disturbed, surprised tone.
"Our own people," says Andy.
"Didn't Hutchence used to date Grace?" Marsha says.

I feel terrible at the memory of both the Graces.

"Miss Grace saved our lives."

"'All the Things she Said,'" really got me thinking that maybe I was on to something.

"That's all you ever think about!" Marsha snaps at me like something out of *Little Shop of Horrors.*

Of course it's so not, there is one other thing.

"You and your..." and she struggles for just the right insult. Stupid, dumb, dumber, bozo, butthead...

PAIGE: Dipshit, dork, doofus...

JIMMY: Returd...

PAIGE: "Returd"?

JIMMY: She's like: "...*selfishness* got our friends killed!"

And she's right.

What could I possibly say?

Apart from one thing.

"Not...*air-headed*-ness?"

And Marsha looks like she wants to smack me in the face, or my shot shoulder, which I don't want.

Andy goes to her and tries to calm her down with touches and hugs and expressions of sympathy and stuff.

"Not you too, Marsha."

But Marsha is in full flow at me.

"And we're next, you...*moron*!!!"

PAIGE: Forgot "moron." Dammit.

JIMMY: I nod in total agreement.

"What does it matter who she thought you looked like?"

And for the first time in my life, I st stst ststs sts...stammer.

"How could that help?! Will it make the hunters go away? Will it get us back home? What, Jimmy? What???!!!"

Well, that was quite a lot of questions, several of them quite...tough...I thought.

"They're just picking us off, one by one," she says in a broken whisper, then she kinda collapses against Andy in a 19th Nervous Breakdown mid-60s Mick sorta way.

"Jimmy..." Andy says and I understand that the two of them maybe want an answer to Marsha's question.

"Well...we...I... would have a place to *start.*"

"Start *what,* Jimmy?" asks Marsha.

"Start to find out...my *name,*" I say, wishing I *had* that name.

So would YOU.

"That, is *all* you *ever* think about, Jimmy," says Marsha, and before I can correct her, goes, "I know, I know, not *all.* But, you need to start thinking about *us*, here, Jimmy, because our little *family* is in trouble," and I totally get it.

But the very thought of being so close to my name.

"That name, is the key to all of this, Marsha."

"It's not like...we have a busy schedule, Marsha," Andy says.

Marsha is slumped against a wall where a WW1 *History Boys* fan has scrawled the name, *Franz Ferdinand*.

So anyway, I do it.

I start thinking about us.

"How much money we got left?" I ask Marsha.

"I spent the last on this," she says, holding up the bandages and disinsectant and stuff, reminding me how much it cost and how much my shoulder hurt.

"You shouldn't have wasted it on me," I say, meaning it.

"You should have told me you wanted to bleed to death," she asks and I wonder, what if I become unglued?

"Marsha, what about your...rings?" I say, hating myself for having to ask.

"My rings?! You know how much they mean to me," and of course I do.

354

Her father gave them to her and she loves them.

"My father..." she says then trails off, the pain of his memory hurting badly.

"Maybe there's another way."

"No, Jimmy. There's *no* other way," she says.

"I asked you to think about us, didn't I?" and she forces a smile that makes my heart weep and sing at the same time.

I stroke her face.

Stroke.

"We need taxi money," I say to her mouth.

Her mouth half-smiles.

"For...the plan?" she asks.

And although she kinda looks far gone, she's also kinda amazing.

"Look where you and your plans have got us," she goes, only not in a 'this is a question' way.

"Lady's right," an ugly voice behind me says and I spin. I'm looking right at a jabby, stabby, slashy, pointy, sharpy, rusty blade.

Maverick.

Andy and Marsha whirl around fast and suddenly, the blade is at Marsha's delicate throat.
I always hate to see that in a movie.
It's such an easy way to kill usually, the girl.
Marsha lets out more, quite naturally, petrified gasps, used to that now.
This *Swamp Thing* slithers and steps out of the shadows.
The blade belongs to, or was stolen by this creature who looks like he'd kill defenceless people for absolutely anything, especially expensive jewelry, no problem.
I'm thinking 'cold turkey junkie' 'cuz he's wearing the international junkie uniform, just check every movie, of dirty track-suit and old broke-down sneakers that have never nor ever will see inside, ha! a gym, baseball-cap, backwards, skin like porridge or veal or *Re-Animator,* only in a slaughter-house, snake-thin and snake eyes, all sweaty and kinda yukky.
I make a move to him and when he speaks, spit comes flying out at me and I wipe my face, fearful for Marsha and my hair.
"Easy *Maverick,*" he tells me and clamps his grubby arm around her neck, the wicked blade stroking it roughly.
I back off, but not too far, hands high.
Andy holds himself tight, protecting his little ribs.
The guy's eyes fix like missiles on mine.
"The rings, beautiful," he spits at Marsha "Just the rings."
Tears start to flow from Marsha's eyes and I take a little, hopefully un-noticed cute baby-step toward the thing with, um…no particular plan whatsoever if I reached him.

"The rings!" he snaps n' snarls, in a big hurry, places to be, and Marsha cries out aloud.

She slowly raises her hand, where two bling-rings sparkle and I think of Jayne then the knife, rusted with...eeeuuuggghhh.

His cobra eyes dart greedily from mine to the rings, then he digs the blade a little into Marsha's throat.

"You hurt her, and I'll stick that knife right up your smeggy ass!" I find myself saying aloud, but he laughs.

"Heh-heh-heh!"

Andy is taken by surprise by my heroism.

Not as much as me.

Marsha starts to tug one ring from her finger, then the other and the guy holds out his filthy, open, reptile hand and she drops them in, tears flooding down her gorgeous face.

He chuckles like a toilet flushing and stuffs the rings in his pocket.

I'm hoping and thinking he'll leave now, maybe after a teensy grope at Marsha and it better not be anything more, because I've never even, but he spits on her hair when he rasps.

"The other one too," and I *really* hoped and so would Marsha, that he maybe wouldn't have seen her favourite ring.

Marsha cries and tries to free herself from his grip.

I take another half step toward him.

"You're not getting it" I tell him and I'm mad.

His eyes drag from Marsha and he glares hard into my action-movie Mark Wahlberg hero eyes.

"Ya wha'?" he says, incredulous.

"You heard," I say, trying out bold bravery bluff.

"You tellin' me how to run my business?"

"Look, it means a lot to her...it's *special*...she can't get it off and like...you are *so* not getting it!!!"

The gang of two dart their eyes to me at the same time, surprised, shocked, startled, stunned, uncertain about what would happen next.

Which was a squeaky voice rasping.

"Turnaround!"

Sure enough, everyone does.

Whiiip!

And there he is, Everett from the store!

But this Everett looks like different Everett, like maybe a possessed, kinda *Exorcist* Everett, with a mean glint in his eyes, massive snarly aggressivey body language, and the threat of a wooden bat with shiny Nine Inch Nails hammered through it.

The creature hesitates, thinking about his options, his chances, cracked skull, headaches, hospitals, nurses, hospital food, and eases his grip on Marsha.

Everett hurries up to him and raises the bat to pummel his head, fearlessly.

The creature farts — *"Flrrrrp!"* — and I hear his ticker pound faster.

And at that second, I'm on him, grabbing his knife hand, then punching his disgusting un-shaven, spittle jaw.

It actually works! and he yelps.

I haul Marsha out of his way and square up to him.

We wrestle and tries to stick me until Everett is almost on top of him, shouting at the top of his not the slightest bit scary voice, but it works, because the creature takes off down into his rabbit-hole in the alley.

I want to go after him to get Marsha's rings back, but she tugs at my sweater.

I caress her neck where a little trickle of blood has appeared, that little f**k.

"Jimmy…" she says gratefully, allowing me to e-for engulf her in my arm, because the other one hurts.

Everett stands by us, switching to a big smile.

"Everything's alright," he tells us and Marsha immediately hugs him hard and he blushes.

"Baseball, sport of champions," I tell him, relieved.

"Ch-ch-change," he says, then "Lady forgot, huh?"

He hands out the crumpled dollars to Marsha.

"You're a friend true, Everett" Marsha says, touching his little cheek and he blushes again.

Marsha tugs and yanks her ring off and gives it to me.

"Keep it safe for me, my sigh...hero," and kisses me on the lips.

"That you picture in the paper, bra?" he goes.

I'm shocked, and stunned.

Not at being called an item of women's clothing, but:

"Is my, um...*hair* alright?"

"CCTV man, lookin' cool."

"Phew, Everett."

"Don't look no gang-related ta me."

"None of my relatives are in a gang," I say.

Everett looks confused, but goes "S'what they say."

He gives me a grim smile.

"You might need this," he says.

"What is that?" I ask Everett.

"See *Inglourious Basterds?* Bear's baseball bat?"

"Now that you mention it…"

He inspects me closer.

"You kinda look a little like Mr. Pitt…"

I nod, he smiles, and hands me the bat.

"Baseball bat, customised," he says, whatever that is.

I like the baseball bat customised.

Taxi.

Plan B.

Thanks to Everett, we have *A Few Dollars More*, enough he told us, for a taxi across Manhattan to what I believe and hope will be our *Final Destination*.

My shoulder has been hurting like f-Hell for quite a time now and I chomp on some of the painkillers that Everett gave me for free.

They're Extra Strengthol which really helps the pain but, thing is, we have these back on the island.

I don't get this place, I really don't.

I'm in the back of the taxi, exercising my shoulder to find out how much mobility I don't have in case I need it for more heroism.

Here it Comes.

Here comes…the plan.

Was what I told Marsha and Andy.

Andy just listened then shook his young head with disbelief and kept staring out the window without saying hardly one word for the whole journey.

Even the hairless toothless taxi-driver muttered something about how bad the plan was as he b-for blatantly and e-for eavesdropped on our private conversation, although I talked very low.

Marsha firstly let out a big, real laugh, her first in ages. "Brilliant. I love it. It's so…*you.*"

Did she mean…like…stupid?

Then she stared at my deadly serious fine face.

"Wait, don't tell me. You're…*serious?*"

I smiled e-for enigmatically, kinda like Dougray Scott does really well.

"You are, aren't you?"

I said I are.

She slumped against the back of the taxi like the spoiled brat in those Disney family movies where Steve Martin always plays funster dad trying to hold it all together.

I suddenly recalled another important island rule: EVERY MOVIE IS A MINOR MIRACLE. NEVER CRITICIZE.

Anyway, Marsha just keeps catching my eye and shaking her head over and over.

"Ever considered that it might be..."

"Stupid?" I fill in, helpfully.

"I was thinking deadly, lethal, dangerous, suicidal, crazy, nuts, plain dumb..."

"All of the above and then add *mucho loco,*" I add in a Mexican accent and that kinda flummoxes her.

"You're both right," Andy says to his reflection in the window, then to us.

I wish I was a smartster.

Manhattan is a small place I think, as the taxi pulls up at our destination in no time.

"Have you called it 'the really stupid and dangerous plan' Jimmy?" Marsha has been whispering not unpleasingly into my ear, so as not to alarm Andy. But he couldn't be any more alarmed if Marsha had been whispering something like

"It's sucide" and "We're all going to die" I would definitely have not done it.

Grace.

College kid.

Mac.

The girl in Café Internet.

The guards.

Cops.

Jayne.

Norma.

Miss Grace.

Nurses in white uniforms.

Higher body count than any slasher movie sequel, which always has to have more bodies then the original.

They both hesitate, Andy with his manners saying

"After you" and Marsha gulping loudly, then peeking out scoping the street, then eventually clambering out, annoying the Hell out of the toothless driver.

I pay the driver, this time take part in the concept of a tip? and that's it.

We have no more money left.

Once I'm out on the street, I'm watching like a detective, then I shove them into a little dark recess, not realising that I spooked them.

"What is it?!!!" they both say in perfect harmony.

"It's alright, there's no sign of them," I say and they puff out massive cheeks of just air, thankfully.

"Another good name is 'My most stufus plan yet' Jimmy," Marsha suggests, adding to a list she made up which she sung a tune to.

"Titles are important. *American Pie* was almost called 'Teenage sex comedy that can be made for under $10 million that your reader will love but the executive will hate,'" and they both stare at me.

"Jimmy Jimmy, Oh," Marsha tells me.

Andy cocks his ear as a thumping bass comes from the place, but it's not anything we recognise.

"They'll let you guys stay," I tell them but they're not convinced. I look toward the entrance.

"You'll be safe," I try again.

"I don't think I'd feel safe *in* a safe," Marsha says and we all silently agree.

There's quite a crowd, a roped-off section and I see the faces I expect to.

I take a huge gulp of air —

Gulllp!

— walk on and I hear whooshes of the same from an overly nervous Marsha and Andy. Yeah, like I'm not.

I resist the temptation to worry them even more by saying anything aloud, but I think it.

"We've got nowhere else to go."

Just for one day.

A lot of people in the crowd whistle appreciatively at Marsha and Andy as well, and we all manage those funny expressions that prisoners do just before having their brains fried by Old Sparky.

We're in with the in-crowd, same as before.

Goths and punks and preppies and metalheads, glam rockers, hippies and grungers and more than one grunge girl looker zones in on Andy and how does he do that?

I also see people giving us looks I'll never understand.

Jealousy.

Want it.

Gimme Gimme Gimme a man...

Get a life.

I'll take yours.

Arrogance.

I'm special.

Adore me.

Worship me.

Marsha interrupts me.

"I don't want to do this, Jimmy," and then, "I'm not scared. I'm freakin *petrified!*"

"You um...trying to tell me something?"

She's got no faith in me, or the plan.

I know what she means.

"They're The Only Ones," I tell them "Nobody else has any of the answers."

Andy shrugs.

"Yeah, but, y'know."

"We could run with *your* plan," I say to them and they both reply.

"My plan? I don't..." then they get it and Marsha punches me on the shoulder and I turn New York sky grey and before I maybe faint again, I think of Jayne and Marsha is All Apologies.

"I just don't like the idea of us as...bait."

Marsha has just a-for articulated the plan.

I need the bathroom.

I can see Marvin the door-man ahead, shuffling on his feet and letting a quasi-cool young couple enter.

He looks kinda higher and wider and meaner than I remember.

I think re-think strategy a sec, then think, what the heck?

And I stroll up to him like long lost, strangely awkward friend and wave and he waves and smiles back and I reach him and he grabs me by the balls and throat with eye-watering door-man p-for precision and slams me against the wall. Much over-the-topness, I think, but don't say aloud 'cuz I can't speak.

"Urcgh...oomffph" and other sounds like a constipated Russian ketamine dealer's voice taped over the fantastic SFX in *The Matrix.*

I hear some of the crowd wolf-whistle and cheer and boo and hiss, for some reason.

But all I can think of *is…*

I feel the hunters are here.

I discover a little later that they are parked invisibly down a black back alley in their big, cosy, black vehicle, drinking tall, frothy black coffee, while Hutchence observes Heroes through those night-vision goggles.

And there, down the end of the goggles, is their prey. He nudges Crawford who is maybe dozing, dreaming of maybe having sex with one of her secret sex-slaves and she takes the night goggles and looks at us and smiles.

I can just see myself with green skin and green clothes with green Marvin punching my lip and green blood pouring onto the green pavement and green Marsha and green Andy shouting something, um…green?

But, I would never wear that shade of green.

And I can just imagine Marsha saying, again:
"Boy blunder. The 'luring our murderers to us' plan" or something close."
Well Hey. Worked, didn't it?
And I can hear a guy in the crowd shout to Marvin.
"Wrong dress code?" and of course I think, dress? And then Times Square and, is it Tranny Night?
Hey!
Where can I get a nice dress?
Anyway, Marvin is snarling and has me half way up the wall, toes dangling above the ground.
Marsha runs over and tries to i-for intervene and shouts "Leave him alone," which he ignores and so she tries: "You...big *bully.*"
Which was harsh.
"He can join Jayne in hospital!"
"But she wanted to help us!" Marsha says back.
"By getting shot?"
"We're sorry!"
"Sorry? Aw heck, you shoulda said," but he's just being sarcastic, I think.
"The man she always wanted? Fucksakes!"
Yikes?! I...decide to not understand that.
And then Andy joins in the struggle and hauls at Marvin's impressive, steroidy bicep totally uselessly.
At least his heart was in the right place, unlike mine trapped somewhere, oxygen starved.
And Marvin's saying stuff like...
I don't want to repeat here.
But when he knocks Marsha over, even though it's by mistake, I swear I'll kill him when I can breathe and learn to fight and get back to earth.
A girl from the crowd shouts at Marvin.
"Lot of witnesses here, Tyson," but I don't understand a thing.
Even Andy says: "Look at the size of you and the size of him!"

But...isn't that why they're door-men?

Strangely, I thought I heard him whisper, "I'm sorry" to me, then Marsha, or it might have been A Rush Of Blood To The Head.

He lets me down and I rub my throat and that hurts my shoulder, so I rub my shoulder and there's blood on my fingers.

Marvin sees it and turns a funny colour and mumbles something I can't make out.

Something...is not right.

Marsha notices and makes a face at me.

I remember.

PAIGE: What, Jimmy? What?

JIMMY: Marvin said I could join Jayne in hospital.

PAIGE: Hospital? Wait, she's...?

JIMMY: Then, Marvin picks me up like a dog with a bone and in a blur, Hopper and Rock appear like book-ends made of concrete, grab Marsha and Andy and we're dragged off inside Heroes.

I've never been carried before.

I thought of sex-crazed, body-builder lifers in the dining hall deciding to drag uselessly kicking fresh teen meat off to their curtained cells.

Listen to the music.

Heroes is jumping, the mixed crowd in part-ay mood.
I hope we survive to join in.
It's darker too, the big mirror ball dazzling, sending little silver, gulp, bullets of light into the audience.
There's some very attractive girls in too, even though I'm forced into taking all this in a kinda upside down, jerky, slightly druggy *Trainspotting* way.
Luckily, I have experience doing that.
Marvin, Hopper and Rock ram a path through the crowd and a few of them laugh and jeer and hoot and holler and stuff, some mussing with my hair!
And others touch my body parts.
I fix my hair.
I'm tired of having all these bad hair days.
I take a sorta bouncing look at Marsha and Andy and they seem angry and disturbed.
And then, I just caught the end of some deafeningly blasting rock song which I think I kinda know and would have liked to have heard the whole song, until another song I definitely know, we all know, comes on!
Party Fears Two!!!
The Associates.
Awesome.
But, wait.
Who, where, why, how and WTF????
My mind, what there is of it, is in a whirl.
I dart a look back at Marsha and Andy and I shout.
"You hear that?"
And they nod frantically, totally confused.
And Marvin shouts at me.
"I hear it!" so I give up for now.
In no time at all, we're through the narrow door, just managing to not bash our pretty hair, is what Marvin says. We're then bundled into Jayne's tiny, cramped, junk-packed office and tossed onto the fat sofa.

Marvin reaches for me and Marsha yanks at his arm. "Keep your stinking hands off!" and I thought she might Charlton Heston him with "Ape!" but she doesn't and Marvin sneers at her.

Here we fucking go.

Interrogation, rape, torture, pain, confession, hopefully more rape, Blood, Sweat and Tears...

PAIGE: "You Made Me So Very Happy"…

JIMMY: "Sorry, man," Marvin says with an actually genuine, no really smile at me, then Marsha and Andy.

"What just happened?" Marsha asks me.

Andy just looks at the three door-men suspiciously.

I must have looked more stupid than usual.

"I'm...we're...really sorry," he says and Hopper and Rock look like Bashful and Dopey, heads hanging.

WTF?

Hopper and Rock back out of the room, creating a lot more space and air, mumbling something about getting back to the job and happy to be gone.

But before they go, they give me the longest, strangest, weirdest look-est?

"Jayne...told me your story," Marvin says to me.

We all exchange mystified looks.

And I wonder, how could she do that?

"I...had to put on a show," Marvin goes on.

"The Show Must Go On, but what?" I ask, stroking my painful neck and not even my shoulder.

"Sorry...I...uh...the, uh, hunters were...uh..."

"They were?" I kinda joke and even smile, but no, he's got it bad, whatever this weirdness is.

The gang look bewildered.

Then, I get a huge twinge of pain in my shoulder and have to check it while awaiting developments.

"They're...outside, Jimmy," he eventually manages.

The gang gape at me, searching for answers.

"Of course they are," I tell him.

"I lured them here."

And he looks at me like a whole new person in a whole new way.

Maybe like a dead man talking.

"You guys are all over the news, man."

"Um…is my hair…?"

"Some reporter's been hunting the hunters."

"But...my hair..."

"It's only CCTV footage," he says and I'm cool.

"Can I get you guys anything? A drink? Some snack?" and he suddenly seems awfully keen to please.

"A hair-brush? A tank?" I venture.

"Something for your shoulder...uh, Jimmy?" he goes.

"Or my neck," I say and I tell you, he actually blushes, like a beacon too, probably for the first time in his life. His mouth hangs open, jaw aslack, taking all of me very carefully in, and I get to think this must be what one of those gay bar places are like.

The ones with muscles have a name and his would be Marvin the Muscle Mary.

"They were watching the whole thing, and..."

"You've probably killed yourself," I tell him and the gang look away, horribly reminded.

"Goes with the terri-tory," he says and because he is not very arc-tic-u-late like me, he stumbles it out.

"Uh...uh...well...they shot my boss and she's a friend and...uh...and, my girlfriend...the club, too, yeah."

"But, the...terry…tory?"

"Happens in bars. S'what she pays me for."

"Marvin, they killed our friends. Just like that. And they'll kill you too," I tell him.

He thinks a sec, looks kinda like glum, then suddenly looks all mucho macho.

"Hard to believe," he says and stands up to his full, impressive but a big target for the silent bullet treatment height.

"Jimmy, maybe we should just go," Marsha says.

And Andy says "This is nothing to do with..."

369

But Marvin interrupts, staring at me hard.

"Jimmy..." and he's looking at me, I don't know, in a kinda, adoringly, well...*worshippy* sorta way, really.

"What's your great granddaddy's name?"

I give him a puzzled look.

"Same as mine. Jimmy."

"No, I mean...his surname?"

And I'm thinking...*surname?*

What's...a surname?

Airport.

At that very sec, old guy is looking a little plum
tuckered, always wanted to say that, but, he's landed
and here's 'my great granddad list':
Which goddam airport was it?
Is there one in New York?
How far away is it?
Has he come to save us?
Will he reach us in time to…*gulp*…be too late?
What will he do when he gets here?
Does he have a big black, silent gun?
Will the hunters not just hunt him, too?
Has the founder told them to?
Anyway, he makes his way through crowds of air-
travellers and goofy 7 mile high clubbers and heads for
the door. Pretty goddam fit for an ancient, huh?
Seems to know where he's going.
And that makes me wonder about 'another list.'
PAIGE: Another list?
JIMMY: Has he been to this airport before?
When?
Did Tom Hanks live there?
Was Leonardo de Caprio on his plane?
Or Jody Foster?
Snakes?
And Nicholas Cage, the old man said.
And what was the old one there for?
Why?
Who with?
Did anyone recognise him, then do a single, then
double-take?
That's very important.
But surely that was all a long time ago?
But the old man, he himself told me, was…
Kinda quite famous.
But, for what?

Could be a porn-star, for all I knew, then I stop that particular train of thought right there.

How famous?

The reason I ask, is not for me, because I don't have an interest in this, but for you.

I know the whole fame and celebrity shit really interests you guys off-island.

For some reason.

What is that reason?

Anyway, the famous old guy pulls on a cool brown leather jacket 'cuz it's cold for him and I wonder.

Will anyone be waiting for him?

Who?

Will he not just get a big yellow taxi?

But no, a big, fancy, black, spotless, shiny but obviously classic limo sits, engine purring.

Purrrrrrrrrrrrrrrrrrrrrrrrrrrr.

It has that privacy glass stuff on the windows.

Inside, an i-for impeccable driver wears a uniform and a hat and he leaps out, waves respectfully and the old one heads his way.

The driver opens the door, saying something welcoming and friendly and respectfully.

And I wonder again.

PAIGE: Yes?

JIMMY: How did great granddad make all that happen?'

372

Has anybody here...

Before Marvin sprints out, I told him the old fella's last name.

He frowned, went to the computery thing, said he would Google it, then…he looked like he'd seen a ghost.

And in a way, he had.

PAIGE: What? Jimmy, whaaat??

JIMMY: I'll tell you…later.

The little CCTV screen had let out this big crash.

Marvin had trouble turning his eyes back from my face to his job, but eventually, he glanced at the screen.

There was the usual cliched bar brawl.

Marvin had sprung to his feet and spun around surprisingly fast for a guy his size, kinda like a big, blobby, brutish ballerina.

Hey, illiteration!

PAIGE: It's *a*-lliteration, Jimmy.

JIMMY: Aw shucks. Thanks…*Podge.*

PAIGE: Paige.

JIMMY: Anyways.

That was when I told Marvin.

I was desperate to know the whole truth, 'cuz I could tell there was something.

But what?

I came up with the *Dumb and Dumber* get even dumberer plan which is so me, where we're the screaming ones in *The Silence of the Lambs.*

Now, Marvin looked like he'd been drenched, struck by lightning, thumb-screwed, *Man in The Iron Masked* and his big square steroidy jaw dropped, eyes wide, face like a melted cake.

"Marvin, d'you, like…need to pee?" I start to say.

But his eyes dart to the CCTV screen again and he stammers.

"I...I…"

373

"I…I…yes…yes???"

"I…gotta go. Sorry…I…sorry," and off he goes.

Me and Marsha and Andy just shrug at each other.

"Wha' happenin'?" I mock say.

"Did he have a stroke?" Marsha says.

"He'd love to, Marsha," and I wink at her.

Andy pipes up: "Jimmy's great granddaddy's name. It…meant something to him."

"But…what? How could he mean anything to him? I don't get it."

"Well, one thing's for sure," Marsha's a little happier. "You were right, Jimmy. You're onto *something.*"

And that meant so much to me.

"Alright!" I say and we leap to our feet and laugh and cheer and high-five and hug and kiss and huddle and "Ooh raa" but stop at that.

Then, we go all quiet and sit, staring at our feet.

What am I on to?

Believe.

We watch Marvin on the CCTV screen with the other guys doing their bouncery thang, then after five long minutes of like, petrified silence later, we hear heavy feet pounding fast on the stairs.
Clomp, clomp, clomp!
We jump up.
Firing-squad, last-words time.
The door opens and I know I was holding my breath.
A long black gun-barrel appears.
Just kidding!
It was just Marvin.
"You guys alright?" he says, then in he comes, filling the place, gives Marsha and Andy the once over, gives me the twice over, drops into the chair by the CCTV heavily and concentrates on the screen.
We see Heroes front door, a big crowd of interesting people, Hopper and Rock scoping around, then I see her!
Marvin whirls round to us.
"The Bitch Is Back!" and he points out the attention-grabbing, lust-worthy hour-glass figure that can only be Crawford in the crowd.
She's drawing a lot of looks, obviously.
We all exchange those familiar glances and I need the toilet badly.
"She alone?" I ask, wishful thinking.
Marvin jabs a fat finger at the screen.
I stare closely at the screen, a terrible black and white snow-screen, my eyes screwed up.
"He's with her," Marvin says.
He balls up a piece of paper and tosses it hard at the wall with a big sigh.
"That's…funcool," I say.
He gives me a sneaky sideward glance, twitchy as a drunken bomb-maker's first one.

"Suck's fake, Marvin!" I half-shout.

"What?"

He doesn't seem to know whether to stand or sit or fart or shit.

"What? They armed with like, nuclear warheads or Black Hawks or something?"

He gives me that strange look again.

"You're like expectant dad," I say.

"Not because of them, Jimmy."

"Wait, don't tell me there's *more* of them?!"

Marsha gasps aloud with similar thoughts of catching deathitis.

"Tell me you're not scared Marvin, are you?" she says.

"Like I said, it's not about them."

"Because, if you're scared, big guy, what hope do us weakling walking wounded have?"

He shakes his head.

"It's not them, Jimmy, it's...*you.*"

"You're scared of...*me?*"

"I just...wish..."

"...Upon A Star?"

He gapes at me dumbly.

"Look Marvin, I'm sure you're making perfect sense here, right gangsters?" and I give them a knowing nod.

"And I know it's me, not being very smart and shit, but what???"

"I just *wish,* Jimmy."

"SO YOU SAID, MARVIN!!!"

"I just wish I could believe you."

We're all demented looking.

"I so want to..."

"Believe me about what...*exactly?*"

And I think I'm going crazy.

"About his...name. And...yours."

"What about his name and mine?"

Me and Marsha look at each other.

"You're really *not* scared, are you Marvin?" I ask.

376

He shakes his big totem pole head.

"You know him, don't you?" I ask again.

"Or, you know *about* him."

I'm now staring hard into Marvin's eyes and he looks, well, quite soft as a puppy-dog.

"You know who my great grandfather is, don't you?"

Marsha and Andy both give me 'Are you crazy?' looks which I thought was already agreed.

"I'm right, Marvin. Tell me."

"Is that true, Marvin?" Marsha says.

He's shaking that big Easter Island head, all torn and twisted and swearfucked.

He's staring back at me like it's me that's bewildered.

Then, he turns to look at the CCTV screen.

"Hunters In The House"… *(Jimmy clears his throat. Then out croons really terrible singing.)*

Hopper frisks Crawford and she of course is shamelessly flirting with him and for obvious reasons, he's not interested, but you can imagine her saying, "I insist on a full body-cavity search without lube, no gloves, and chunky rings on," and licking her teeth.

Meantime, Hutchence is getting frisked by Rock and he just stands in silence, arms out-stretched, mightily pissed with jealousy.

Hopper and Rock let them in and Crawford kisses Hopper on the cheek.'

Smaaack!

He looks up at the camera, really pissed off and nods, kinda like a signal, I think.

Marvin jumps up.

"Sorry, Jimmy…" he says, hurrying to the door and with one last gaze into my eyes, whispers.

"…but it's…"

Impossible.

Was his parting word to me.
But, I know it's not impossible, don't I?
And soon, you will, too.
Heroes is really jumping now, way too dark and way
too loud and way too many people for us and it's not
like you can drift outside onto the beach with a girl,
then swim naked, then...
I'm too anxious to think about almost all of that and too
impatient and well, petrified to sit.
But, amazingly, Marsha and Andy sit at the bar.
They look exhausted.
Plum-tuckered.
What movie is that from, I vaguely wonder.
I'm craning my neck all around and it hurts my shoulder
and my throat but I can't stop.
Part of it is 'cuz the hunters are on the loose and, one
way or the other, it will be over, soon.
The other part is that I know I'm close.
The truth!!!
I can see Hopper and Rock outside, expertly patting
unlikely people down for weapons and guess that
somehow, someway, the hunters will have smuggled in
their guns or something, maybe using a nasty hiding
place, like *Papillon* which we've heard about, but not
allowed to see.
Ow, hurts.
Marvin is inside the place and I wish he would stop
turning to stare at me with those eyes drilling and just
talk to me. Through the crowd, I just notice that there's
a tiny little stagey thing.
On it, leaning against a nice antique bentwood chair
with a spotlight over it, sits something like, wow?
Sweargasm!
Only a Fender Stratocaster?!
Um...surely the world's finest musical instrument?

That was what Marsha's Dad used and he was a truly gifted genius for a really old guy.

I loved watching the mirror-ball dance on it, like scenes from *Avatar*.

The music's blasting away, like it's getting louder, when "JIMMY!" is right there in my ear and I almost jump out my skin!

But, it's just Marsha.

Phew.

PAIGE: Whew.

JIMMY: "We were talking…" and she glances at Andy, who has this grunge girl group dancing for him and they get closer and closer and how does he do that?!!

And then, Marsha glances at Marvin who is still looking at me and I'm looking for the hunters.

"I mean, how could he possibly know your great granddad?"

"That's what I need to talk to him about. And…"

"And?"

"Well, turn his answer on its head."

"Jimmy, what do you mean?"

"He said it was impossible. *What* was?"

"Oh," Marsha replies and she even looks at me in surprise in that 'Could he think that up all by himself?' kinda way.

"And…"

She looks at me differently now.

"Why he thinks it's impossible."

"Hey! A plan!" she says, flashing lovely big pearly white teeth, and, "But, then what?"

"I tell him he really is my great granddad. That I'm his great grandson?"

And…I don't know. But Marvin knows...something.

"It's not that I'm doubting you, Jimmy."

"You're...*not?*"

"It's just...well..." she says.

"I...believe you *now*. Before, well, I... but now..."

"Trouble is, what it is that you believe, yeah?" I tell her and she smiles, relieved that I understand her q-for quandry.

"Exactly," she says.

"Weird though," she goes on.

"Which part of all this weirdness are you talking about?"

"Look over there," she goes.

She swivels her beautiful eyes to these people and I can see some of them are talking about me, or whispering behind hands over faces and some awkwardly smile, or shake their head over and over and some just open-mouth gawp.

"People just stare at you, Jimmy."

And she's not wrong and it's not just girls, either.

"First Miss Grace, then Jayne was kinda weird, then Marvin and now..."

I'm nodding. Like on of those in the back window of your car dogs the old fella talked about.

"Why are they just...*staring,* Jimmy?"

"Um...striking handsomeness, awesome coolness, lack of self-consciousness with my hands, understated fashion-senseness, great hair...*ness?* And..."

"Jimmy, you are full of it," she mocks.

"But, it is the $64 million question," I say.

"And, it's not just me," and I nod towards Andy and his growing fan base.

He sees us, smiles and drifts over.

"Everyone here's obsessed with looks," and yet once more, the little guy has hit it on the head, then he drifts back towards either the grunge girls, or Andy world.

"People Are Strange," I say and we both exchange heavily-loaded looks.

"It's not just me or Andy either," I tell Marsha and divert my eyes to a lot of not just guys eying up Marsha greedily, considering their options.

"All these morons remind me of *The Men Who Stare at Goats*" she says.

I turn fully around to her amazing profile.

"That's…Because You're Gorgeous…" *(More appalling "singing.")*

"Oops! I thought I just *thought* that."

She turns fully around to me.

I've said things like that in the past to her back home, but not like this, not meant or felt like this, and not about sex, or just about sex, at least maybe.

And we both realise something at the same time.

Something has changed between us.

When that moment comes in a movie, you kiss.

Then, you…

CUT TO:

…You thought duh big sex scene was coming, didn't you?!

They're here.

Kinda like from *Poltergeist*, only more worser.

'Cuz big trouble's here instead.

Crawford makes a grand entrance, sorta like the way they would do at those movie premieres or film festivals old guy would tell me about where the actresses competed over fine dresses like Dior and jewelry and arm candy with some skeleton guy on his strict diet and work-out regime fad because the camera puts 15 pounds on you.

My fabulous killer. Hey, great movie-title!

She is still wearing black of course, but a different trouser-suit outfit and no mask.

Again, everything seems s-l-o-m-o.

The way that she walks.

The way that she talks.

Her big smile, the way her hair swishes, her hand gestures.

I realise what this is.

100% strength, fucool and yuck-fou *confidence.*

And behind, Hutchence is no different, just a male version of her.

He slides in, i-for immaculately cut suit, black of course, and is his hair slicked-back? And his shirt dazzles like his teeth, eyes and cuff-links.

I bet they both smell just great, too.

I wonder for just a sec if I will ever get to smell or taste that garlic on Crawford's breath, then I look at Marsha and I don't think that anymore.

I take her hand and then I kiss her cheek and she squeezes my hand till it hurts, the fear gripping her.

"I'm faking not being over-terrified," she says and suddenly Andy is right in front of us, fighting panic.

"Downer," he says in that a-for abbreviating Andy way.

"Maybe it'll be different this time," I try.

They both look at me like The Man With Two Brain…cells.

Andy gives a funny kinda snort.

"Hnyeah!" and he sounds a little like Alannis Morisette and I wonder if he'll burst into 'God Is good'… *(Still more awful "singing" sounds.)*

But instead, he samples another respected musician.

"I die. You die."

"Andy, what the *Hellboy?* How can you think of Gary Newman at a time like this? And what about Down In The Park?"

Marsha digs me in the ribs and I explain.

"Uuunnnggghhh," like in *Raging Bull* because anything like that seriously hurts my shoulder.

She makes a very sexy "Aw" with her mouth and snuggles close into me, scared again.

"Live through this," I whisper Courtney Lovingly in her ear, resisting the powerful temptation to suck on her ear lobe.

I even raise an arm to Andy and we group hug, making me remember sadly how *big* the group hug used to be.

How big it will be after this night is over?

We're all glued to the popular Fairground Attraction that is the grand entrance of Crawford and Hutchence.

They are working the crowd, smiling like *All The President's Men* but with one woman.

They give lots of Royal Helen Mirren waves to people they don't know, and you have to hand it to them.

If you were going to get murderered, you'd want it done really beautifully, wouldn't you?

Like a photogenic Celebrity Wedding, but with death.

The couple hold hands as if to say 'No entry' and then French Kissin In The USA, probing tongues glistening, and people wolf whistle.

They make for the other end of the bar.

There's One Direction they haven't looked at once.

Even though I can tell that they know precisely where their prey is, like the big cats always do.

I notice that Hopper and Rock have come inside now, expertly locating the hunters.

Hopper whispers into Marvin's ear.

He catches my eye and makes a gun with his hand and shakes his head 'No.'

"They don't have guns," I tell Marsha and Andy and Marsha shivers.

"That's what Marvin thinks," and I think they'll probably have nukes instead, bursting through the walls any sec.

Then, I wonder if somebody sneaked in guns and hid them in the toilet, like for Michael in *The Godfather.*

I try not to think about that, but I can't shake images of a severed horse's head and fat fish wrapped in newspapers. I turn to look at those who will be our killers and I notice that Crawford has produced a black card that I now know is a credit-card, especially for rich people.

I know how they got rich.

The cool barman takes it and smiles.

I notice there's a tiny little bird's nest box for a DJ of that size and he's hopping and bopping like The Birdie Song then plays a new track.

I don't recognise it, but I do like it and the crowd do too and groove happily away.

I would love to dance with some of them and Marsha, because another of my list of attributes is that I can dance as good as John Travolta.

That'll Be The Day.

And I wonder if our *Dirty Dancing* days are over.

I suddenly feel like a trembling mouse in the corner of a room, that cat lying back lazily, its paw sweeping and teasing slowly, smiling like only cats can do.

I can sense that Marsha and Andy are getting more petrified by the second.

"Can they protect us, Jimmy?" Marsha asks in a tiny, heart-breaking voice.

She was talking about Marvin, Hopper and Rock.

I hope so, I just think without saying aloud.

We ordered drinks for something to do and because our mouths were as dry as parchment.

Then, the DJ plays this...song.

Well...the crowd are all crazeee now.

I don't blame them.

It was quite something to see everyone appreciate this track.

It is easily one of the best songs ever written, without exaggeration.

I should know.

I know the guy who wrote it.

And just as I'm wondering...

HOW THE HELL CAN THIS BE?!!

Marsha and Andy turn to me in total WTF astonishment!

"Is...that...not..." she says.

"It's...that's..." Andy says, quite rightly.

"Yup," is all I want to say because I totally lurve this record and desperately want to hear it.

I even join in.

"...will tear us apart..." *(And yet more of Jimmy's Deftones "singing.")*

And just at that second, I catch the eye of someone who actually does want that to happen.

Crawford.

She knows the songwriter, too.

So, um...like, how come she's not totally blown away, like we are?

And the same goes for Hutchence when I finally get a glimpse of him.

"Look," I tell Marsha and Andy and point at Crawford.

They look at us, then look at each other, then look at me.

"She knows the same people we do, so why isn't she, like, y'know, maybe…*dancing?*"

"I do not get this whole thing!" Marsha says.

"This...can't be!" I say to them.

Andy gives me this look.

"Duh, that's what I've been trying to say."

I remember then.

PAIGE: Yes?

JIMMY: He's been saying stuff like "Hey, that's..." and "Listen! That song..." and "Coolness! It's..." a lot, but we've kinda blanked him.

I wonder what the wrinkly man would make of this?

Come back.

And of course later, I discovered that right at that sec,
this big, fat, shiny black limo arrived outside the
entrance to Heroes and it would sit with the engine
purring perfectly, then a black tinted window would
slide soundlessly down and a shadowy face wearing
large horn-rimmed glasses would take just one look.
It's the old fella, of course.
People in the crowd would rubber their, um, necks,
checking to see if it was someone *famous* right?
But when this old guy leans forward from the shadows,
flashing lights reflecting off his glasses and peers out
the window, they would mostly all turn away,
uninterested.
It wasn't always that way.
If only they knew.
If only you knew.
Suck's fake, if only *I* knew!
The ancient one's practised though imperfect Ethan
Hawke playing Vincent Freeman in 1997's *Gattaca*
eyes would take in the place, the crowd, the door-men
and decide something clever, I totally hoped.
He would lean back in his seat comfortably.
The window would glide up and the driver would drive
slowly away, to who knows where?
But, you are, like, coming back, right?
I mean, we need you. Or, to put it another way...
Heeelp!

Celebrate.

The crowd are using alcohol and probably other 'substance-abuse' as an excuse to get more outrageous and ecstatic and it's certainly working out that way.

I can see that the hunters have ordered a brand of champagne alcohol I can't make out and it sits in an ice bucket on the bar top with two frosted glasses.

I just remembered something bad.

Great granddad and me were out secretly celebrating another of his important milestone birthdays and he made a point of ordering champagne called Dom Perignon and he told me…champagne is for *celebrating.*

I suddenly felt sick, thinking, knowing what they were about to celebrate and even though I was really loving drinking Budweiser brand alcohol, I slid it away.

And I think Crawford and Hutchence knew that I knew champagne was for celebrating, because they both turned to look at just me, only me.

They gawped at me like Tim Burton's *Big Eyes,* 2014, with adorable Amy *American Hustle* Adams, demanding that I look at them.

I couldn't stop myself.

I turned slowly, gulping and…

They smiled perfectly and…

Lifted their glasses like they wanted to toast me.

In a furnace!

I wanted to vomit and butt-nugget at the same time.

I turned away but then turned back, because I didn't want to frighten Marsha and Andy.

I just closed my eyes and I think I can hear the hunters laughing.

They were laughing at me, cruel and heartless.

And that makes me open my eyes again.

And the thing was, I could see the cool barman kept asking.

"Do you lovers want this open yet?"

And they kept nodding their heads, probably saying "Very soon" I think it was or would be something like that.

Then, they would look over at me.

Crawford even blew me…a gar-licky kiss.

That one little act made me shiver, in more ways than one.

Either way, whatever they said, even if I got it completely wrong, one thing was a horrible certainty.

They were having a *Monsters Ball* toying with us.

I turned away from them into an even worse sight.

Marsha and Andy.

They had been watching the whole time.

The expressions on their little face made me want to hold them in my arms.

"It'll be alright on the night," I tried, but their faces.

And for the first time ever in my young life, I was forced to confront the terrible truth.

My screen debut was going to be…a snuff-movie.

And I, was playing…me.

I looked at Marsha's tear-filled eyes, Andy's struggling to be brave face and tears came.

I thought I heard the hunters laughing again.

And through blurry eyes…

I missed something really important.

Help.

What I had missed was this.
Big Marvin coming barging through the crowd like a
bulldozer, which we've got on the island, or a snow-
plough, which we obviously don't, and in his strong
arms he easily carries someone.
He makes her look really light which she's not, but in a
nice way.
Jayne.
PAIGE: No!
JIMMY: It's a medical miracle!
Even though she looks not great, kinda like a rag doll,
skin the colour of NY sky, moaning a little in pain,
bloody bandages on her chest, no make-up, hair a
mess and well, if she could see herself in that outfit.
Marvin charges through while Are we Humans or Are
we Dancers bops, knocking people over like ten pins.
We've got an alley on the island. And people say bad
words to him but he totally ignores them although he
usually wouldn't and he's glancing over his huge
shoulder to see Hopper and Rock aren't far behind and
they talk into the mikes on their lapels and move like
Scorpions to cover the hunters, I'm frankly relieved to
discover.
And then what would have happened is this.
Marvin takes Jayne up to her office and lays her down
delicately, like she's a fragile, but slightly over-weight in
a nice way, flower.
He studies her face.
Her eyes are shut and Marvin looks worried.
Marvin's eyes dart between Jayne's grey face to the
CCTV screen which now shows pictures inside Heroes.
Look, there's us!
Wave.
Top of the world, ma!
And hey look, the hunters. Looking *good.*

Jayne eventually opens her eyes and croaks.

"Get me a 'king drink, Marvin," and he jumps up, goes to the desk, produces a chubby little glass bottle of something probably 100 proof and pours a 'generous measure' whatever that means, it's just that I've always wanted to say it.

He hands her the drink and she slugs at it, greedy for its effect.

"Thanks, I sooo need this."

She tries to sit up, then lets out a cry.

"You hurt as bad as that sounds?" Marvin asks.

"It's alright, Marvin. I've always known you love me," feigning lust at the big lug which I also always wanted to say and he turns away, face beetroot.

I believe these are *Terms of Endearment* whatever that is, but hey, good movie.

"You might want one too, Marvin," she tells him.

"How's that?"

"When you hear what I have to tell you."

Marvin has his eyes fixed on the CCTV screen.

There we are again.

Jayne looks hard at the screen.

"What a 'king mess."

Marvin looks at her.

"It's all over the news," he says, gluing his eyes on Jayne's wounded shoulder.

"You will never *believe* what I have to tell you."

"That's funny" he says back.

"I was just about to say the same to you."

On the screen...aw suck's fake...in our real life.

The hunters close in on us.

"Marvin! Gimme a hand here" Jayne says and struggles to her feet, face twisted in pain, sweating.

"They need our help" and Marvin helps her stand.

Marvin starts barking into the mike on his lapel.

I didn't discover this until later, of course.

I also didn't discover till later that, exactly at that same moment…

Tinted Love.

A blackened window slides soundlessly down.
And outside, in the alley where we ran to escape the hunters, the sleek black limo purrs into frame and glides almost noiselessly down the alley.
It comes to rest right at Heroes back door.
A pause.
You can almost feel the eyes expertly probing.
Then, the driver pours out, stands on something squelchy, makes a face and heads for the doors.
He yanks at them, rattling hard.
Rattle, rattle, rattle!
He's a big man, fit, and he's only supposed to blow the bloody doors off and they fly open soon enough, clattering off the walls.
The driver pokes his head in for a look.
He nods, quite happy.
Then, he spins and opens the limo door, standing aside to let him out.
Out gets great granddad, pretty nimble for an old guy.
"Should I accompany you, sir?" The driver asks very politely, in probably London Grammar.
"No, thanks, Dudley," he says which must be the driver's name.
Cool name.
Dud's maybe better.
Driver Dud runs to the back doors and holds one open.
The oldie looks kinda grim as he goes inside.
"You just have to let me know, sir," Dud says, tapping a mike on his lapel.
Seems everyone has one on tonight, like it's lapel mike theme night.
Ancient man wears one too.

The Killers.

Meantime, back inside, I'm like…oblivions to great granddad's arrival and Jayne's survival. We're at the bar and Marvin's more re-assuring than Hopper or Rock who I don't think like us.

My eyes, to be quite honest, are darting between on one side Crawford and the other, Hutchence.

And I'm scoping them for pants bulges.

Guns, I mean.

They're weaving through the kidiots, arms and legs and hips jabbing everywhere, grooving to some tune that I think I recognise.

And even with Hopper and Rock quickly closing in on us protectively…

I am petrified.

You ever been really and truly, truly now, totally butt-nugget inducingly, gut-churningly swearfuckingly terrified you're actually going to die?

If you have, you'll know exactly what I mean.

You want to run away and feel vomitty and you maybe ask, no cry, or even scream.

"MUUUTHAAAAAAA!!!!"

Or other stuff, like a kid in a waking nightmare.

If you haven't, have you:

Saw.

The Conjuring.

Sinister.

It Follows.

Unbroken.

Unfriended.

And anything by Ed Wood…

ROLLED TOGETHER AND MULTIPLIED A ZILLION TIMES!!!

It's you, **YOU** that's going to die.

Not some skinny, Cracked Actor aged a million playing

a teen!

And I do know that song. I hear bees. The soundtrack to my death.

It's Tricky and it's the captivating voice girl and I'm Overcome.

All of this is racing through my brain cell and I grabbed Marsha and Andy hard, arms around them.

I wish I could do more for them right now.

I wish I was Jet Li, or on a jet.

I thankfully and extremely gratefully notice Marvin pushing and shoving like Ten Thousand Maniacs through The Happy Dancers and I'm a little relieved, but still want to cry and butt-nuggett in my pants.

And next thing, I hear shouting, but through the music it sounds kinda weird.

"Jmnmnmgaugrdy!"

Do I recognise that voice, a little kinda whiney and nasal, but in a nice way?

Could it maybe be...nah.

"Jimmy?!"

"Jimmy! Marsha! Andy!" a little clearer now.

And louder.

A female voice, one I wouldn't want to like, fall foul of, if you get my drift?

If I had better eyesight or it wasn't so goddam dark in here I might have seen what I soon discover is Jayne!

"JIMMY! MARSHA! ANDY!"

Now that, is loud, and so we all hear it.

Marsha jumps up and looks around.

"Jayne?"

"'king Hell!"

And we're trying to find the source of the 'king voice.

And Jayne.

But once we follow the direction the rubbery-neckers are looking, we get a tiny glimpse.

There she is!

She's up at the DJ booth now, clinging on to the sides

which will hurt that gunshot wound and she's waving like a robotic windmill and shouting at the top of her voice at us.

Lots of people are looking up at her and wondering and saying WTF?

But we still can't hear too well with the thumping beat. So, what she did was, she bawled right into the poor DJ's ears and though he's well used to a lot of big noise in his ears, he's not used to that voice and he tells her.

"Owwww!" quite rightly and gives her a stare but in a few secs when he's recovered, he's ready to carry out Jayne's instructions.

Even though that's a totally excellent track, he breaks another island rule:

NEVER INTERRUPT A SONG.

He stops it.

Grinding hips come to, like...a grinding halt.

People in mid-thrusty gyration gyrate no longer, apart from the ones that have the music in them.

And chemicals.

I have no time to realise what just happened, 'cuz exactly at that very sec...

When I've been checking out who was shouting and where and what for...

I'm grabbed!

My arms are pinned really hard to my sides.

Somebody works out, I'm thinking, while trying to breathe.

I can't move.

And my shoulder hurts like HEY, that hurt!

I hear a male voice very close in my ear, laughing and taunting and the smell of what I now know is stuff for making your breath smell nice and minty and then other smelly stuff, the boy's learned some crazy batshit off-island, called after-shave. Is that right?

My opinion is that these two smells, along with the

garlic, like, Clash.

And it's obviously Hutchence and he shakes me like a dog does with another, but much weaker dog.

I'm totally helpless.

I wonder...is this IT?

I'd die in your arms tonight.

I'm trying to see where Marsha and Andy are, what are they going through.

Instead, I see The Witch Queen.

Crawford.

She's standing right by Andy, not doing anything, if you count the very presence of a killer breathing your air in your space not doing anything.

Aw, Crawford is looking right at me and smiling and taunting and I'm sure, flirting.

Either way, she's enjoying the display of invincible power.

So poor kid Andy's quaking, on the verge of tears and toiletting I reckon.

But quick as flash, Marsha is right there like a tigress, shoving Andy right behind her and even snarling like one and squaring up, yes, you heard me right, squaring up to Psycho Killer!

She's so brave and I'm proud of her and wish I could help but Hutchence's grip is like a vice and so's his voice, trying to think up the best insults.

"Fuckin' pussy!"

"And you're hung like a chaffinch!"

The truth hurts and he squeezes my shot shoulder really hard and I barely manage to tell him "Z Z Top," and looks confused.

"No, I won't stop" and now I'm confused.

"Watch them die!" then grips my Ow! Shoulder, *again.*

"Aw, iddy biddy showder all hurty-wurty?"

And bites my ear like a boxer, or soccer player.

Crawford circles Marsha and the crowd begin to get a sense of what's going on.

I'm wondering what weapons the hunters have smuggled in?

Or will it be bare hands, Tony Curtis *The Boston Strangler* style?

Marsha suggests to Crawford that she really should "Leave him alone, you fuckin' bitch!" and that's what I call a threat.

Marsha, love ya.

Crawford goes into some kinda mime sequence, where she looks all scared and girly and pouty and oh, please help! A spider! A snake! And other stuff.

The crowd love all of this, laughing and pointing and whistling.

Then, Crawford closes in like a python.

Razorlight.

Crawford starts to shadow box like a pro.
Um...no, I *don't* mean prostitute, potty mouth?
Kinda like that *Million Dollar Baby* movie with that
excellent actress, um...the bit thin for me one, but I still
would?
And, I'm kinda hoping for the same ending to be
honest, where she dies. Crawford I mean.
The crowd love this, clapping and cheering madly.
Crawford circles Marsha expertly.
Her arm blurs and it's done.
She just whirled from Marsha to Andy.
Whirl!
And ruffled his hair like a favourite aunt or a grandma
does.
Marsha looks mystified and for the last time I ask
myself.
Is she just funning? Are we going to be left alive? Only
with unruly hair?
And before I have even the time to finish thinking that,
Crawford is right into Marsha and reaches out to her.
There's no blur, more a delicate lingering stroke.
Between Marsha's legs.
It's more than I've ever done.
Marsha squeals and looks totally shocked and enraged
and embarrassed at the same time.
Maybe even a little flattered?
The Boys II Men in the crowd obviously applaud
appreciatively, but I couldn't, 'cuz my hands are still
clamped to my sides.
Crawford stares at Marsha, licking her lips like a cat
just got the honey-flavoured cream.
Then, Crawford strokes between her own legs, all the
time staring at Marsha.
I'm growing to enjoy this...ahem...as much as the
crowd, which is getting louder by the second.

Marsha can't believe what's happening.

Crawford dances around her like a scene from *Obvious Child* then suddenly, she's right there before you know it. Right in Marsha's face.

She grabs it

And only M*A*S*Hes her lips onto Marsha's!

The crowd can't believe this.

Neither can I.

Neither can Marsha.

"Yeeeuuucccchhh!" she tells us.

"This is worth serious paper," a kid behind me said and I think that's money and totally agree.

I hadn't realised that right on my island doorstep was a show I could've taken in!

All this time, Marsha has held onto Andy, protecting him but now, she lets him go only because she's disgusted.

She wipes her mouth with the back of her hand, looking like she's just drunk sour milk.

She glares at Crawford who moves in again.

Marsha backs off some.

"Get back. Get back!" she says uselessly.

The place goes silent.

A woman's voice shouts.

"That woman is a killer!"

And a man's voice replies.

"Got that fuckin' right," and the place explodes, but into thankfully, only laughter.

I don't understand what that voice meant, but think I recognise it.

Someone tries to burst through the jostling mob for a better view maybe, and we hear muffled cries directed at us.

Then, right into view between two fearsome, massive lesbian goths who don't want to move aside, appears Jayne!

Marsha can't take all of this in at the same time.

"Jayne?!" she goes.

Jayne has no time for a friendly chat and doesn't look that well put together, I'm thinking.

She snarls and snaps and jabs a jittery finger at Crawford.

"She...killed people!"

The Goths step aside at oil-tanker speed and Jayne barges through to take centre stage.

"She 'king shot me!" she spits at Crawford, nearly in tears.

Confronting your would-be killers will do that to a person.

Crawford smiles, mouths jolly "Who me's?" and "As if's" and mimes scaredy-cat and the crowd lap it up.

I suddenly realise.

The crowd think this is some kinda Jackie Chan Stuntman Floorshow right?

Marvin and Hopper and Rock exchange these puzzled looks that must say:

'If not Jackie Chan, then Jason Bourne?'

Marvin's eyes must say something different to Hopper because next thing, he's grabbed Crawford and spun her right round right round to face him.

That is a *Perfect Storm* plan, I'm thinking.

Hopper squares up to her, knowing she has some moves. She just gives him a big smile, then her hand does that blur thing again, in his general throat direction.

Hopper's face turns a funny shade of King Crimson, his eyes bulge and he clutches his throat.

I see that blood is seeping between his big, sausagey fingers.

He gapes at Crawford in shock, searching for her weapon, a surgeon's scalpel, maybe, or a Bowie knife or a switch-blade or light reflecting off a razor, perhaps probably borrowed or stolen from a gang-banger, or hidden in the toilet.

Sure enough, something glints or more like, glistens.
Hopper backs off from her obviously deadly weapon.
Her credit-card, which she holds by her side, blood
dripping.
Credit Card Killers would make a cool title.
Rock looks a little um…rocked…and steps back a little,
giving himself some space.
Crawford is smiling all the while, accepting the
audience's applause.
In that moment when she's bowing and curtseying,
building her part, Hutchence is laughing and has
loosened his bear hug grip on me, so with strength
born from desperation and scaredness, I somehow
wrestle free.
I instantly tear to Marsha and Andy, arms around them
both. All I can do, folks.
Jayne screams at the top of her voice.
"PLEASE!!! HEEELP"
To anyone who'll listen, if it didn't deafen them.
Nobody's listening.
Except Marvin.
He dives for Hutchence but he's too slow for this kinda,
like, Hugh Jackman standard of Killing-Machineness.
Hutchence simply takes a little jaunty Singin' in the
Rain half-step to the side and I can't completely see
what's happening, just the blurry hand thing toward
Marvin's big round, fatty in a nice way but unmissably
big target face.
I hear Marvin yelp and he clutches his face.
Kid says:
"See that?"
Friend says:
"Eye-jab."
Kid goes:
 "Lemme."
"Ow," and tears.

Marvin takes his hands from his face and his eyes are all red and streaming with tears and he's trying really hard to see. Hutchence goads him, leaning into his face, teasing him with minty, after-shavey, gar-licky taunts in his ear, laughing. Marvin swipes at the over-smelly air uselessly and the audience cheer wildly.

One lucky punch catches Hutchence on the jaw.

He stops laughing.

He puts a finger to his lip and inspects the tiniest speck of blood on his shirt, which I can't see.

He takes a little step to the right, raises his knee high and lets fly with a fast as lightning, what I know from my one draining 'art of fighting without fighting' class, which actually *is* fighting, snap-kick.

It connects perfectly with Marvin's knee and there's a cracking sound, hence the snappy name.

Marvin yelps and folds, clutching his knee, eyes clamped tight shut, face all twisted.

He hits the floor in a lumpy heap.

Hutchence looks over at us and makes a bee-line our way.

Suddenly, Crawford is right by my side.

She grabs Andy and yanks him from my grip.

Hutchence is heading for Marsha like a heat-seeking missile.

Next thing, Crawford tosses Andy away like he's a used condom —

PAIGE: Ugh.

JIMMY: — and he crumples to the floor.

A lot of girls groan in sympathy for him, a few run to him and at least two drool over him and help him to his unsteady little feet.

How does he do that?

Anyway, I turn to…um…chin-stroking thinking, 'cuz Hopper's out of action.

Marvin's out of action.

Rock doesn't seem interested in action.

Andy and Marsha and Jayne shouldn't be in action.
That leaves, um...
We are so well and truly f…
Crawford is right in my face!
She launches at me, grabs my shoulder and gives it a good old squeeze.
That does the trick.
I'm sweating already, my face all ugly, if that's possible.
I barely hear Jayne, who couldn't?
"Please! Help!" she begs the crowd but there's no um…please help.
Crawford grabs my throat and "Get your hands off me, you!" but boy, is she a strong girl.
I feel her fingers adjust to get a better Ted Nugent stranglehold on me and I'm choking, my eyes pop, my face turns probably Deep Purple and I can't breathe.
Jayne shouts.
"Please, help him!"
I see her stopping, i-for imploring and grabbing various people who applaud her performance.
Marsha and Hutchence wrestle and he's just playing with Marsha and that's why she's able to break free of him to try and help me and she tears up to Crawford and grabs her hands and shouts right in her face:
"LEAVE HIM ALONE, YOU BITCH!!!" sampling dialogue from *Aliens* maybe? again, and I think the crowd whoop and holler and stomp their feet and cheer, having such a good time.
Jayne is screaming now.
Suck's fake, *that* is loud.
"'king listen!!!"
Marsha is tearing at Crawford's arms on one side, Jayne the other, me in the middle getting garrotted, but at least it's babes fighting over me time again.
"If you knew who he is!"
Jayne says again, and me?
I'm desperate to know, but fading fast.

404

"His great grandfather!!!!" she's screaming.
People can't help but watch her, listening.
"He's the great grandson of..."
I pass out.

You must be out of your brilliant mind.

The floor bangs me on the head and how did it get up here? There's commotion all around, a lot of noise, feet scuffling, shouting and stuff.
The crowd seem...different.
"Jmnmnfhffby," it sounds like, then my throbbing head clears a little and it starts to sound something like...
My name?
Who's calling?
Is that..."Go to the light?"
"Jimm…y?" I hear, breathed in my ear and Marsha is kneeling by my side.
Then, I understand that I fainted through nearly being murdered in the neck from Crawford.
I'm trying to focus my eyes on, what?
PAIGE: What?
JIMMY: I don't know where to start.
I can't see the hunters.
Have they gone?
Does that mean I'm dead?
Are we all dead?
But then, I think I can see Andy and he's very interested in looking at something.
There's an almighty squeal from electronic feedback that can be a good effect when it's used right, but this hurts my ears and when I look up, I see Andy has been watching Jayne climb onto the DJ's box and I see blood on her and she grabs the mike and shouts:
"His great grandfather is James Dean!!!"
There's a kind of hush, then…
Hahahahahahahahahahahahahahahahahahahahahahahah ahahahahahahaha's.
From a lot of various peoples's.
But...something starts happening to the noisy crowd.
It gets gradually quieter, the volume turning down a bit at a time.

Marsha and Andy help me to my feet.
And at last, I have some answers.
James Dean is my great grandfather.
Good news.
Coolness.
PAIGE: Jimmy...
JIMMY: That's my name, Paigepal.
PAIGE: OhmyGod, Jimmy! *You?* Are…
JIMMY: Marsha and Andy are looking more strangely
at me than usual and I know they're thinking the same
thing I'm thinking.
James Dean.
Right.
Suck's fake.
Who's James Dean?

Am I legend?

People are not looking at me. They're *studying* me.
The atmosphere kinda...holds its breath.
I can't describe it.
It would maybe feel like first-night vomitty, butt-nuggety
nerves if you were an actor, or musician.
Not one person moves.
I'm standing, a little shaky still, rubbing my red raw
neck, then my shot shoulder, then my head from
bouncing it off the hard, sticky floor.
Then, I check my hair.
Even the mirror ball seems to reflect more light on me,
than anyone else.
I shield my slightly blurry eyes and scope the place, but
I don't see clearly.
People seem to, I don't know, expect something?
I know Crawford's there, because she grips my arm
like Hulk Hogan.
Marsha moves toward her.
Then it got even wierder.
People, and I mean nearly everyone in the whole
place, all circle us, like the big crop circle in *The Village*
jostling for space, a better look.
But, what at?
Even Crawford is a little weirded.
People close in and I can recognise a whole range, a
whole spectrum, a whole different list.
Starers, a big group, who um...just stare.
Preppy people deep in wondrous, animated discussion,
nodding, then gaping at me.
Cutiful girls shrugging off nervy boyfriends to peer
lovingly as close as they can to new possible boyfriend.
Handsome hunks giving me hate-bombs.
A girl called Sally, sallyvating.
The Wild Bunch, who laugh at Jayne and make circling
gestures with their fingers at their temples.

408

Homeboysexuals who make other circling gestures with their fingers.

Cool kids who just look, nod, smile and shake equally handsome heads and hair, dude.

Disbelieving drunks, mostly girls who, I think, can't believe something they've seen or heard.

Trampagers, all female, uncool, drunk, go crazy.

Hopeful hipsters, who are the biggest gang of all sorts of people, stare at me intensely.

Scornful types who are a small bunch of mostly guys who snigger and mock me and quietly say stuff like "Him?! Ha!"

What they have in common, is what they want.

Closer.

A lot closer.

Crawford has let go of my arm, scoping the place for Hutchence probably.

I wonder where the door-men are, and Jayne.

Or the police, the SAS, Navy Seals, the FBI, the CIA, boy scouts, Sigourney Weaver.

"What's going on?" I want someone to tell me.

PAIGE. Somebody. Pleeease.

JIMMY: Jayne battles her way through the crowd to reach me and she does, and we hug like long-lost lovers but not in that way, ever.

"Jimmy..." she starts to say and she's kinda tearful and slobbery like a boxer-dog but others pull at her, want to hug me, or more than likely, I'm thinking, they want a piece of me.

I vaguely recall that conversation me and the old man had on the beach along similar lines.

"Jayne, you OK? You're OK," I say to her.

"Jayne, who...is James Dean?"

She gives me the weirdest look.

"You...don't..."

I definitely don't.

"Jimmy, your great grandfather was...is...a *legend,*" she tells me, holding me in front of her and staring deep into my eyes.

"An icon."

A...Nikon?

The famous actor, invented a *camera?*

She fixes my hair which must be totalled.

Marsha and Andy look as confused as I am.

"Why..." and I think how to ask the question, because I understand that this whole thing is very important and after all...

It's why I escaped.

"Why should the old one mean anything to you...to these people?" I would like to know.

I would so love to know.

It's at that second that the murderisers invite themselves back into our lives.

Jayne spots them and jabs a finger in their direction.

"Those two, are called...the 'king hunters," she spits as she tells the assembled, increasingly interested crowd and they all look at Crawford and Hutchence, then Jayne and back, like watching tennis.

The hunters do the dumb routine, all smiles, mimes and innocent shrugs of "Who, us?" expertly and just about manage to get away with it.

But Jayne flashes flesh and her gun-shot wound Ow! and I can hear snitches n' snatches n' snippets of conversations like you get in British heist movies.

"Blah blah shooters blah blah evil masterminds blah blah right villains blah blah it's been emotional," and at least a few people believe Jayne.

Then, I catch sight of Marvin and I see he's been looking after his men.

He's in a booth checking on Rock, who holds a bar-towel at his throat.

Marvin's eyes meet mine and he gives two thumbs and Rock tries too.

410

The credit card cut must have been just a flesh-wound and I'm so grateful that there wasn't another death on my getting over-booked of death dance-card.

Jayne has the audience's attention.

"They kill people who escape," she tells them and onlookers look on between us and the hunters.

A voice in the crowd says "I see them in the paper?"

"That's it!" another voice shrieks.

And another voice asks "Escape from where?"

There's a tiny flicker in Crawford's eye make-up.

Marvin, Hopper and Rock spread out, I notice.

I feel like asking a question myself.

Why Crawford, why?

So I ask.

"Why Crawford, why?"

PAIGE: Yes, Jimmy, *why?*

JIMMY: She turns from the adulation in the crowd, flashes a smile like one of The Lighthouse Family, checks her nails, cracks her knuckles, yawns, then stretches like a happy cat.

"You know I'm no good."

The audience probably think it's part of the show.

"There's just...so many reasons."

And I think Hutchence wants her to shut up, 'cuz I can see it in his angry eyes.

He starts to move, somewhere.

"Let...me...see..." Crawford goes.

I fully understand that she's doing at least three things.

Firstly, stalling for time so Hutchence can get into position for whatever he has in store for us.

Secondly, to play for time so *she* can get into position.

I know what position I'd like her to be in.

And thirdly, she just loves this.

Showboating for her awestruck fans.

"Crawfuck, you...!" I begin to snap and she interrupts.

"Well, there's *shoes,* obviously," and I'm thinking 'You killed my friends...over shoes?'

411

"Not just shoes, *Dumbo!*" Swearfuck, she reads minds! I've never hit anyone in the face, but…

 "Imbibing of New York's sublime gastronomic and Broadway delights," and she licks her lips tantalisingly. But what did she just say?

"That's restaurants and theatre, stupid," she adds helpfully.

"Congratulations, Jimmy," she says.

Thanks, only, what for?

"You found my Zagat's," she tells me.

Wait, does she *really* read minds?

She must've read another of my dumb expressions.

"I know all about you, idiot," she beams.

"You killed my friends because of fucking SHOES and swearfucking RESTAURANTS???!!!"

"Not just restaurants, imbecile! Vegetarian dhaba *Indian* restaurants."

Suddenly, out of thin air, like Robert Pattinson in *Twilight* only a lot more handsome but with quite similar hair, Hutchence dives at me.

Fly fly fly.

He's left me with no alternative.

The hunters have left the dead bodies of my closest, bestest friends all over this city.

Enough already.

Remember Everett, the guy who bravely saved us?

PAIGE: Yes.

JIMMY: Well, his present was behind the bar.

And that's where I ran to and by the way, I can go pretty fast now since starting on this journey.

The fun part about doing that was that Hutchence completely missed me and hit the floor heavy and hard and "Ooompphhh!" was what he told me.

"Z Z Top," I scoff.

The crowd are confused at that, but laughed and jeered at Hutchence anyway, which I don't think was part of the show.

I bent down, snatched Everett's kind gift and waved it at Hutchence.

It went down well with the crowd.

Remember Everett called it a baseball bat.

Customised?

The nails glint dangerously, like a *Star Wars* light-sabre, which was why I thought it would make a great weapon, not against guns, but against hopefully un-armed hunters.

Hutchence seems pleased.

"That's my boy! Game on!" and he crouches, circling me the way Bruce does in all of his cool movies, the ones that we all loved seeing re-enacted so much.

"Z Z Top," I tell him again, and it annoys him 'cuz he doesn't know what I mean.

I swipe over and over at Hutchence, aiming wherever I could *Captain America* style, to land a blow.

Which was, like, nowhere.

But justice totally worked on glasses and bottles around the bar.

Hutchence is laughing his pretty head off while I'm trying to knock it off.

But, I get lucky and clip his elbow, close to where I had been aiming, near where Miss Grace cut him.

He squeals like *Babe the Pig*.

But, phew, this is tiring, sore stuff on my own wounded shoulder. Hutchence yelps and grabs his arm in agony, then looks like he's about to barf or flop or plop to the floor. But, he's sucker-punched me, I see, because he staggers this way and that, plays with me a little more and after another useless swipe, he chooses his moment, moves in close to me, does some karate or stuff and what, blocks? Or catches, or I don't know, what? Becomes like, *at one* with the bat?

And pries it from my fingers easily.

Like taking candy from a baby.

Hutchence shoves me aside and in a 'baseball bat customised as a weapon masterclass' proceeds to demonstrate how effective my weapon of choice is and demolishes Jayne's bar.

For the second time.

I look around for Jayne because of that and she's at the bar on the phone and she screams at Hutchence.

"The cops are on their way, you 'king bastard!!!"

And I have to go back to protecting my head without messing my hair too much from flying debris.

I do notice one thing though.

The crowd don't think that this is a floorshow anymore.

I don't want to use the phrase for obvious reasons, but deathly silence enters my head.

I see beautiful girls in panic for me, obviously, and the homelesssexuals too, but no door-men or Marsha or Andy or cavalry.

I'm kinda cowering on the floor of the bar, my hands just above my hair, when I notice everybody gaping in horror at me.

Just above my head, more accurately.

I look up and there I see what all the fuss is about.

Hutchence is looming over me, the glinting baseball bat customised high over his head, set to strike.

"Z Z Top," I tell him, knowing it's annoying the shit out of him.

"What's with the Z Z Top?!" and I laugh at him.

"Zizi is French slang for cock…*dick…head!"*

He looks totally confused, like the audience, and is about to crash the bat down, when…

 '**Stop!'**

Not a shout, more a…*command.*

A familiar command.

The voice, mellow, comforting and reassuring, making you feel so special, loved, sharing memories of childhood and teenhood but probably not adulthood, kinda like…

Great granddad???
In that moment, Hutchence hesitates and I'm on my feet so fucool fast and like I seen in the movies? How d'ya like the Glasgow Kiss head-butt, mutha fucka???'

Mulholland.

And I think about the second serious conversation great granddad had, though not with me.
Him and some of his island *Rat Pack* buds loved to re-enact favourite scenes from movies at parties and stuff.
It was a laugh-riot.
But a lot of the time, it made them cry, somehow.
And a lot of them even knew every line!
That impressed the Hell outta me.
I never understood, until later.
But there was one very strange night, where Preacher, this musician with a funny kinda English accent who arrived from London around '85? though we're not big on dates, spoke to me.
"The old geezer's really wandering off the page."
We were all in Moon's madhouse, a laugh-riot in itself, and the old guy was in drag on his little stage playing Tim Curry's part in the awesome *Rocky Horror Picture Show.*
It was just an ordinary night.
People were joining in the singing and just where the old one is singing about getting someone to toucha him, he wants to be dirty…
He breaks down!
He hadn't fallen over or anything, he just…his eyes…looked weirded out and he stopped halfway through.
He just stared.
I was first to his side and luckily enough, he wasn't ill, well in the usual sense.
I looked in his eyes.
PAIGE: What did you see?
JIMMY: They were blue, but…
PAIGE: But…

JIMMY: "Remember...when we started out?" he says to no one in particular, but there was a coupla nods from people.

"When you'll do anything, for anybody?"

I hear people choking on drinks and laughter and whistles and hoots and couples nudging each other and stuff.

"Those were *The Best Years Of Our Lives*."

Again, a lot of nods.

"Remember the house-parties in Mulholland, up in the Hills? I love the Hills."

I hear murmurs, old *Guys and Dolls* chuckling.

"The smells...jasmine, new monied execs, valley girls...the whole house a casting couch."

A few dirty laughs and sniggers.

"The producers...the players...Talking Heads."

A lot of people from his time grunted with agreement.

"But, we were in a movie ALL THE TIME! Always...acting!"

"Always," a grumpy voice agrees.

"Anybody...*miss* that?" old guy goes.

And I hear a kinda more authoritative voice speak.

"James..." like a lecture was starting.

"I couldn't do performing seal anymore or 'My name is James and I'm a fame-aholic.'"

PAIGE: Fame...a what?

JIMMY: "The looks falling off my oh-so popular face."

"James, please..." that voice says again.

"Appearing in some shitty 'Where are they now?' chat-show with special guest has-beens and hiring some ghostwriter to doodle your biography..."

Ghost-rider?

"...or take granddad roles or Yedo or become some golden couple or do...commercials."

And the strangest wave of...something...came over the room, what?

"I wanted...immortalised perfection."

417

I figure he must be on something.

"But...time waits for no one," he goes.

PAIGE: The Stones. Again.

JIMMY: 'Natch.

I hear chairs being pushed back, people leaving.

"You shouldn't remind us" a newcomer said, then hurried away.

That voice appears onstage and the rumour is he's one of *them,* a founder.

Just blown his cover, maybe?

And he gives me a weak smile and gently takes the old guy's hand.

"Come on, James," and tries to lead him away and "I'll take you home."

"Death enhances fame enhances death," old fella says.

I know, I don't get it, either.

"It was like a job, only...*not,* Jimmy," he tells me.

"But, you had to pretend you had *real* things to do."

He's getting led off the stage and turns to his audience.

"What did your obituary say? Did you see who turned up at your funeral?"

And now, it's me that's far gone, like I'm the one on something.

But, I'll never forget his last words to me.

PAIGE: What were they?

JIMMY: "There was only a small part for me...I mean...*of* me...left."

The object of my affection.

Is it...really him? Here?
How is that possible?
Also, how is it possible that Hutchence, though his face
looks more like Hutcheese has recovered, and there's
blood on his nose and oh dear, that shirt.
He holds the baseball bat customised right over my
head, and *gulp,* hair.
In mid-air.
And I find it ironic that he didn't have to smuggle in a
weapon.
I smuggled it in for him.
But hey, the voice has worked.
Hutchence holds the bat over my head, still mad at me
and Z Z Top but not, I think, in an immediately life or
hair threatening way.
I think it'll be OK if I try to what maybe, run?
Try, at least?
I look around for old guy, but don't see him.
Hutchence is breathing hard like he's the gimp in some
cool sex-movie and his handsome head turns to the
little Heroes stage.
I peer through the gloom for the old man, but it's so
goddam dark in here and my eyes...
Whatever, Hutchence scowls like something from
Insidious, but lowers the bat anyway.
He is spitting nails, you can almost hear the hate
bubbling under the surface.
There's not a whisper from the crowd.
He looks down at me, gives me his best prison-bitch
smile, snarls like Billy Idol, then in a dazzling blur,
this happens.
PAIGE: What happens?
JIMMY: Probably actually not dazzling, actually...
PAIGE: Go for it.

JIMMY: …but in so-slo-mo for extra...dramatic tension, it's called.

Hutchence thinks hard for just the right slur, selects one, and snarls at me.

"Die, fucking...*hairailious*!" and raises the bat high and is about to bring it crashing down onto my hair and then thick skull with all his considerable gym-toned might.

"Twunt!" I explain to him, even though I think hairailious is an excellent insult.

Suddenly, he stops, twitches, jerks like a zombie in 2013s *World War Z* and drops the bat, almost damaging my hair.

I'm mega-impressed at the impact my insult had.

Hutchence's handsome face twists all surprisingly actually ugly, a bit like Jim in *The Grinch* and he clamps both hands to his chiselled jaw, brilliant white teeth clenched painfully tight, his tanned, toned face turns pink then Prince purple then Jet Black, his tongue's all swollen and thick and the saliva and the spittle he's spraying is Pink, then…

Simply Red.

What's um..?

His eyes pop and bulge like Peter Lorre's or Marty Feldman's or whatshername after sex and it's horrible.

There's blood everywhere.

Jayne will be pissed.

It pours from his mouth, his nose, his ears, his eyes, between the fingers that try to stop it and I'm thinking other places and o-for orifices we can't see, due to pants.

Which in fact I now see have a growing damp patch.

Looks like Hutchshit his pants.

Completely ruined and Katherine Hamnet brand too, I think.

The crowd are repulsed and shocked and horrified and I hear some of them cry out and gag and throw-up and stuff.

Crawford appears from out of the blue and runs to his side, actually and surprisingly, looking frightened.

She just about manages to hold him up, but he wilts and she has to help him lie down.

She kneels next to him, fixing his hair.

See, it's not just me!

She produces a nice, crisp, white probably silk handkerchief, hesitates, then mops blood from his face.

She really needs towels, a lot of towels, big ones.

I must have really shattered his Chris Isaac replica nose-job I'm thinking, because there's an awful lot of gore and stuff.

Anyway, I can hear Crawford mutter words of hatred and her teeth bare like in *Jaws* and she glares.

But, incredibly weirdly, not at me.

But the stage.

She looks like she'll explode with rage.

But, then, tears form in her eyes.

Never thought I'd see that.

And again, she glares at the stage, mouthing bad words, but at who?

I wish I could see.

Hutchence has grabbed her hand pathetically and she cradles his bloody head in her lap.

These hunters obviously don't care about *The Human Stain*.

I think I hear Hutchence let out a cry like a tethered goat, then he mumbles.

"The favourites of the gods die young..." then coughs up a lot of aubergine and black blood.

I don't understand what he meant either.

Crawford is crying too.

"Nietzsche...I always knew."

Who-oochie...?

And they share this ridiculous coughy laugh.

Why's that?

And then he splutters.

"And I always hated Indian food," and tries to laugh again and a lump of meat drops from his mouth.

"Our little games, Hutch," she tells him.

Games? *Hutch?* WTF?

"All of me…" he tells her, and looks really bad.

And then I think Hutchence wants to leave, 'cuz Crawford talks to him.

"Don't go, please!" she tells him.

And I wonder if maybe he's booked a good table in a new restaurant and not Indian either.

Then I finally get it.

It's like in da moovies.

The *death* scene.

There'll be whispers and coughs and chokes and p-for proclamations of undying love.

Well, maybe not in this case.

Hutchence gives her that meaningful movie look, then Crawford suddenly looks like Crawfeard.

"You stay alive!"

And she's really insistent, enough that he might just.

But, no, he's leaving.

His eyelids droop, his eyes close and she screams.

"No! Don't die!"

Not very original.

His one eye flickers a little.

"I...love you, Hutch," she leaves it a little late to tell him I think, then collapses over him.

He must've died.

It was actually kinda touching.

And I wonder if it was my head-butt, manly, powerful and heroic as it was, which has also hurt my forehead but not my hair, that caused the wanton destruction of such a well-crafted character.

Next thing, somebody puts the house lights up.

If you can call them that, just mostly around the bar where I see Andy and he gives me his big smile, all happy and safe, thank you God, thank you, if you're there.

Then, I get a good look on-stage.

And there he is.

Old fella.

Giant.

It *was* him!

"Great granddad!" I shout and wave frantically.

He looks for me and people crowd around me again, but I struggle through then notice that a man that turns out be the old guy's driver, pockets a little chrome disk into his pocket.

I wonder what it is, what it's for?

Then I realise.

That, my friends, is one totally yukky, messy, funcool looking death by tooth implant going 'boom' in your head.

Ouch.

"Wha...just happened?" I say to no one in particular, but looking at the old guy and scoping the place for Marsha and Andy and Jayne, too.

A drunk guy burps extra loudly in my ear and I go "Suck's fake!" and spin.

And there she is, Marsha, the first one by my side.

She holds my hand tight and that hurts my shoulder but we make space for a better view of the stage, cuz she points.

"Look!" so I do.

And there on the stage, which has a spotlight above it to illuminate whoever will play that fine Fender Stratocaster, he stands.

PAIGE: Who?

JIMMY: The old man.

My great granddad.

I make my way through the heart of the crowd.

Weirdly, people just stand and gape at the old fella in what I can only describe, well, as…um…

Awe-struck awesome quietness?

Why?

Some guy *Simon Says,* "Look…look…how he's standing."

How he's *standing* makes them gape?

I discover why pretty soon.

Old fella has taken off his thick glasses, wears a white tee-shirt and blue jeans, has Everett's baseball bat across his shoulders and has draped both arms over the bat in a kinda cool looking n-for nonchalant fashion.

I hear voices from the audience gasp, then say things in hushed, Praise You Like I Should tones.

"It...can't be!"

"*Is*...it?"

"James..?"

"Giant...?" and doesn't finish the sentence.

But I think his stoop's made the old one not that tall.

Behind me, my favourite amazed voice whispers.

"It's a...miracle."

More murmurs grow among the crowd, for some reason.

Burping drunk guy's eyes try to focus.

Then, I see some of the stuff on the walls that Andy has been going on and on forever about.

Posters.

Not just posters, but **movie** posters.

One is...and I still can't believe it!!!

Is that woman related to Norma?

Above her younger, but aged-well face, is printed...

The Misfits.

Starring

Marilyn Monroe.

Who's she? WTF is this???

Then my crap eyesight picks up another faded old movie poster.

This one has...swearfuck...

Great granddad? As maybe, like...a *teen?*

Giant.

Starring

James Dean.

Marsha says in my ear:

"*This,* is your great granddad, Jimmy," and grips my shoulder again, so I nearly faint again and she goes on.

"And *that*...is Norma's grandmother."

And I look at *The Misfits* poster, and you know what?

PAIGE: What?

JIMMY: She's right!

I gape at it again and the old fella sees me and leans into the mike.

"She lived her life like a Candle in the Wind."

Remember the kid on the beach with Zagat's?

I think of his wonderful mother.

And the biggest-selling single of all time, 33 million copies.

And all around me, people seem struck dumb for words.

Burping drunk guy struggles to say something.

From the corner of my eye, I can see Jayne, safe and well in the DJ's box.

She is looking slowly between me and the old man.

I have never seen a face look so, so…

And Marvin...looks like it's not impossible, after all, eh Marvin?

A small, slightly unsure voice from the crowd asks:

"What *is* this?"

Good question.

Great granddad smiles e-for enigmatically, lowers the bat and growls into the mike.

"I'm Jimmy Dean…for sure."

Only one person laughs.

He pauses for effect.

And gets it.

'Cuz suddenly, people explode into laughter and shout and whoop and whistle and look totally consumed, totally overwhelmed by excitement.

"What if…you're..."

And he gets the timing just right.

426

"...a movie star...
Or a rock star...
Or, a President...
A princess...
Or just...*special*.
And you've had...**ENOUGH!"**
People don't know how to react.
"Enough of the box office and the Studio, the next critical movie, scripts, readings, auditions, rehearsals, hair, make-up, wardrobe, lights, camera, action, fad-diets, perfection, critics, fans, money, the IRS, houses, cars, stretch limos, mansions, mega-mansions, managers, agents, cameras, endless smiling, pointless sex, stalkers, paparazzi, death threats, hangers-on, wanna-bees, divorces, drugs, press scandals, plastic surgery, depression, suicide attempts and..."
That, is what I call a *list.*
But, people are getting um, closer and closer and more...um...like, freaked out looking.
And kinda...scary, too.
The old boy hasn't finished.
"...and all the **CRAZED UP FUCKNESS!!!"**
And he says that in such a surprisingly shocking way that people are genuinely um, suprisingly shocked?
"Then, one day, you think, no more."
"Right, dude," someone agrees.
"But, what can you do about it?"
The crowd's so confused but so very desperate for more.
So am I, to be truthful.
"How can you possibly *escape?"*
And he has them in the palm of his hand.
"Is there somewhere...anywhere...this famous face can *go*?"
They're totally captivated.
"There is."
You can actually hear people thinking "Awesomely

cool, dude, but where?"
"Somewhere Over the Rainbow? Or *The Beach?"*
And peope gape, staring, waiting.
"Or, there's the *island."*
Everyone, Marsha, Andy, Jayne, Marvin, me...are
totally bewildered and...entranced at the same time.
"The Secret Life of Walter Mitty," he says and then
everybody notices Ben Stiller in the movie playing on
the back wall.
Coolness!
But, does that mean he's lying, or what, and me and a
lot of other people look even more confused.
I take another look at the old geezer, as if for the first
time, then I think 'Hmm. I'll try to get closer to the
stage, but it'll be...'
But, great granddad has seen me and waves.
And for some reason, the crowd just...part like the
Charlton Hestony Red Sea to let me through.
It's incredible because they're all looking at me, some
reaching out to touch and study…
What is *different* about me.
Someone shouts to the old fella.
"Who are these guys…Jimmy?" and this kid points to
me, Marsha and Andy as we group together.
"We call them...children of legends."
And people stare at me as I look up at great granddad,
who islanders say I really look like.
They call us *that?*
"Who's your favourite dead celebrity?" the old fella
shouts.
And it was the strangest thing, like electricity flowing
among them.
They're all...all of them...open-mouthed and shocked
and stunned and stagggered, looking and turning to
each other in bewilderment and saying things like:
"Michael?"
"Marc?"

"Selena?"

"Keith?"

"Divya?"

"Frank?"

"Belushi?"

"River?"

"Tupac?"

And lots of other names of people that I know.

Personally.

You might know their names too.

Then, the old guy looks between them and me, and what he says next strikes them like a thunderbolt.

"Imagine."

And they do, because people cry, openly, loudly.

But, why?

Drunk guy has an ugly sneer in his shiny red face and staggers toward the stage, bumping people out of the way.

Great granddad soaks up the worship and there's more gasps and cries and whispers and ripples of excitement.

Drunk guy is at the foot of the stage, turns to the crowd, burps, then shouts.

"What kind of *fuckery...?*"

And among the crowd, I hear mutters of various kinds.

I'm a believers, non-believers, not sure-ers and shut your mouth-ers.

A little voice kinda whimpers "*Amy...?!*"

I hear hushed voices, then there's some jostling and arguments and that was when, I discover later, that Crawford disappeared among the mob.

Drunk guy is warming to his theme.

"Get the fuckin' music on!" he requests.

A record suddenly starts, and me, Andy and Marsha all recognise it and stare at each other.

Stronger Than Me, by the English chick who turned up to the island that night and meant we could escape.

So very fucool.

This young girl, and I know you guys always want to know about age, maybe seventeen? is standing right below the old guy and might kiss him, I think.

"I...believe you."

The same voice that said "Amy."

And she's so *sweet* and *innocent* and believable that the crowd cheer with relief and gratitude and mostly...hope. They actually really want this to be true. It's kinda like, they *need* it to be true.

Whatever *this* is.

Then, things, if possible, get even weirder.

Marsha has got on the stage.

She picks up that Fender Stratocaster, and kisses the microphone.

"Jimmy's great grandfather...is the real deal," and straps the guitar over her shoulder.

"And my dad? He...taught me things," she says.

I'm probably more awesome...um, awe-*struck* than the crowd, who gape like cod at old boy, then Marsha.

And not just in that fabooshka-looking girl, throbbing guitar, legs apart, Crash Into Me way, either.

She gives a little nod to someone somewhere and I look to see that it's Andy by the bar, hand on the light switch.

The lights dim and a light shines down onto Marsha.

The crowd look...even more totally confused, same as me.

I mean, what next?

It's been a totally confusing few bad-hair days.

Marsha plays it left-hand.

Like her teacher.

But when she played those opening chords really loud, Now That's What I Call Music, the crowd went totally **Swearfucking *BERSERK!!!***

**'You can leave when you wanna.
I'm just jammin, that's all.'**

Marsha told me that her father actually said those
words to the world at that little gig, Woodstock.
And those opening, instantly memorable, awesome
chords are among the best, ever.
It actually makes me shiver with pleasure like I'm...
Marsha's playing quite brilliantly.
But then, that's hardly surprising.
Her singing's not too terrible, either.
The guitar is thumping, mesmerizing, the unique style
of only one man, and maybe now, one woman, that I've
ever heard and I've heard them all, believe me.
A lot of them *live,* too.
But the thing I don't get is.
How do **THESE** guys know this music?
Marsha obviously totally knows it.
And if those guys knew it, maybe you've heard it?
What if I tell you the musician's name?
It's like my name, Jimmy, but he spells it differently.
J-I-M-I.
Hen-drix.
That mean anything to you?
The song is called Voodoo Child?
Does that mean anything to you?
Voodoo Child?
Jimi Hendrix?
No?
Oh well...

Wonderlust.

How can I possibly describe the madness?
The place is totally mosh-pit craziness.
Everybody, and I mean everybody, is going absolutely
WILD!!!
I've never seen anything like it.
The people are far-gone frenzied, bouncing up and
down, dancing like 10,000 Maniacs, whooping,
laughing, crying, screaming, shouting, throwing
themselves around and like, totally **freaking out** and
sweat and hair fly everywhere.
What an incredible sight!
Then, I see various people not doing that.
These people look at great granddad and Marsha and
Andy and me...differently.
Some just...gape in what I now know was...wonder.
Others stare with lust at Marsha, and me in particular,
obviously.
I see guys point at Marsha.
"Is she…?"
"Could she be…?"
And others looking from the old fella to Marsha and
then me.
"Ohmanohmanohmanohman."
"…ohmygodohmygodohmygod…"
"I was...*there,*" full of amazement.
I think I hear another wonderful voice.
"Could he *really* be..?" staring at old fella.
And all around, I notice people with the most confused
faces I've ever seen.
I hear little snatches of private conversations.
"...fucking *legend* man..."
"...could it…*be?*"
"…could *she* be…"
" *Would* she…"
"...if...only..."

"Let it be…"

"Pleeeeaaaasssseeee..."

"Makeittruemakeittruemakeittrue..."

And lots of similar stuff, but…

I DON'T KNOW WHY!!!

I also lip read lots of people.

"It…it…*is* true…"

Some people even pray.

Then, there's more people who all have kinda other expressions to stare at us with.

Envy, joy, disbelief, hope, shock, attraction, admiration, ridicule, every human emotion.

And Marsha is really rocking the joint, until…

Her guitar dies.

People stop the craziness, hollering in anger.

But, then I see great granddad, un-plugged.

He puts a hand out to Marsha for the mike and she passes it to him.

"I'm a Believer," he says.

It hangs in the air for an age and the air has that weird quality again, kinda like *The Fog* only…no fog.

There's voices of slight hesitation, then comes a laugh, then lots of laughter.

The old fella plays them like *Amadeus.*

The crowd can sense the…truthiness of it.

And, they're...back.

"Do You Want To Know A Secret?"

He asks and the in crowd tonight are smart.

They get it.

He's talking music.

The mob go nuts **yet again!!!**

"I Heard It Through The..."

He goes and there's cheers and hoots and whoops.

Everyone is having a great old time.

"Elvis Presley has left the building!" he says and the crowd are loving this, joining in the fun.

At least that's what I think it is, because I don't know what great granddad is talking about.

Then in a funny voice he goes:

"Uh...fuck you ver' mush."

And the crowd are intrigued, fascinated, compelled, riveted and other words like that from different parts of this dictionary book.

I take in a whole load of different scenes.

Young girls throwing drippy underwear onstage.

Couples having frenzied sex against walls, in booths.

Pill-poppers pogo-ing crazily.

Coke-snorters, right under our noses.

Kids throwing themselves at each other dementedly.

Lovely lesbians stripping for Marsha.

Gorgeous gays stripping for me.

Kids filming with their cameras.

Others doing the shelfie thing.

And screamers, everywhere.

And through all this, like being caught in a violent thunderstorm...

The strobe-light comes on, flashes of lightning, cameras, everywhere, jammed in your face, blinding, persistent, insistent, shoving, shouting, screaming.

"One more!"

"Just one more!"

"Now with my friend!"

Never taking "No" for an answer.

And never taking no answer for an answer.

"Please, leave us alone."

And: "You're supposed to Smile!"

"Smile for the camera!"

"Cool hair, Jimmy!" and I see guy in a suit and glasses take a picture.

And the stuff they *say* to us!

"Stop smiling," then...

"Smile, muthaf...!"

"Jimmy, you're the only one."

"I'm Marnie!"

"Marsha, I want you!"

"Jimmy! Sex! Now!"

"Do me!"

"Up the..."

"Both of us!" two females scream and I want to see who offered that, but…

"Suck this!"

"Check these puppies," I try, but can't see any dogs.

"I'll make you scream," and who made that tempting offer?

The things they did to Marsha and me!

Girls touching me everywhere.

And guys.

Guys touching Marsha everywhere.

And girls.

Caressing, stroking, kneading, needing.

Then it gets really rough!

People pull at our clothes.

They tear pieces from our things.

They scream and toss others aside.

Some grope painfully.

Write phone numbers on us!

Others nip and scratch and bite!

Marsha's breasts get pawed.

It's more than I ever did.

My zipper gets yanked down!

Yaaaank!

It's more than Marsha did.

Scissors flashing, hair yanked, getting clumps.

Of my hairgasm!

Our faces scratched and skin torn and bleeding.

Piles of people pouring onto us.

Like they owned us!

Screaming: "Perform for us!"

"Make us happy!"

"Enterfuckingtain us!"

435

Then, the old fella stands right under the spotlight and he looks all shadowy, different, kinda...**scary.**

And in a dark brown voice:

"I'm the...Great Pretender."

And, he doesn't look like fun-packed good-ole-boy-poke-salad-annie great granddad now, not no more.

The crowd sense it too, a little ripple, um, rippling among them.

The old guy just waits, a master of performance, timing, instinct and audiences, and sure enough, drunk guy is first in.

"I fuckin' knew it," then burps really loudly.

"BUUUUUUURRRRRP!"

People look at each other, puzzled, confused, unsure how to act.

Unlike the old man.

He nearly explodes with laughter.

I don't like how the place feels.

Because a terrible, terrible realisation has dawned.

PAIGE: Yes?

JIMMY: The crowd realise...

PAIGE: Yes?

JIMMY: They.

Have.

Been.

Had.

She's got perfect skin.

NNNNNOOOOOOOOOOOOOOOOOOOOOOOOOOOO"
the young girl, the sweet, innocent young believer
screams, holding the note a really long time, reminding
me of A Lovely Day.

But, it's far from that.

The poor young thing is devastated, distraught,
dismayed, dishevelled, downhearted and demolished
and destroyed and other d-for dictionary words.
Disco'd? DJ'd? Dyed hairded?
The whole mood of the place has changed.
You should have seen the looks people gave us!
I didn't totally get it at the time, but we had given them
something...amazing.
Then.
Took.
It.
Away.
Again.
All Hell broke loose, and if it was bad before?!
I hear raised voices then loud arguments then
smashing glass and there's shouting and screaming
and pushing and shoving and fighting breaking out all
over the place.
I take in a whole series of different scenes.
A snarling junkie yanking a bloody needle from his arm.
A fat pimp slapping a beautiful sex-worker.
A young girl clawing her boyfriend's face.
Couples gawping at me, the men's look of daggers.
Thieves grabbing bottles, slugging, smashing heads.
Girls yanking each others' hair, punching.
Terrible fighting, a knife flashing, a switch-blade
maybe, horrible screaming.
And among all this, worshippy stares from hundreds of

them, at us.

Great granddad shouting.

"What did I tell you, Jimmy. Half of them want to fuck you, the other half want to kill you."

Marsha crying, grabbing me. Ow, my shoulder!

"Jimmy, please, let's get out of here!"

And the old fella replying:

"No alternative."

Bottles, glasses, underwear and chairs rain on-stage, hitting us painfully and soaking us in hopefully just alcohol.

The mob sense our next move and crowd in, like scenes from *Titanic,* pushing, shoving, crushing, grabbing, scratching and there's blood, no air, painful handshakes, bad breath, greasy sweat, my hair yanked and torn out, *suck's fake!* Slobbery kisses, some from women, screaming, spitting, some faces all contorted in hate and jealousy and others in love, lust and ripping skin and clothes and…

I'm terrified!!!

I hug Marsha to me, search for Andy and Jayne and the door-men and especially Crawford, but don't see them and the crowd don't care about us as people, just *things.*

I'm vaguely thinking: "Hey, we fart and crap too."

And the room turns black.

I'm going under.

Best friends, right?

I feel like I'm being plucked like a chicken.
I try to protect Marsha, uselessly.
She spotted Andy over by the bar and shouts his name.
I don't think he heard.
Then, I see them, Marvin, Hopper and Rock, looking like *The Expendables* and they've been struggling to break up fights and toss people out and stuff and are heading our way, finally.
Andy gives me a wave and shouts and I catch something that maybe sounded like:
"...lights out...less dangerous..." and grins for some stupid reason.
It wasn't a stupid reason.
Andy kills the house lights and things go black, apart from another movie playing on the wall with opening titles saying *Montage of Heck* and I see a man who looks like Andy only older in it.
Marsha catches his eye and jabs a finger at the back door and he nods.
I see he's gathered up bottles of bleach, insecticide, rubbing alcohol and a heart shaped box.
He shakes his head and laughs, then slides them away, mouthing 'Hello, hello' in time the the movie soundtrack.
I didn't understand, then, at least.
Andy kills the movie and the place goes mega black.
That kinda loosens people's grip on us and we can wrestle our way free a little.
Marvin, Hopper and Rock clear a path through crushing bodies to reach us, tossing people aside as if they were naughty kids tossing toys.
We can breathe, move, maybe even escape.
Jayne has fought her way to us and grabs me by the

ears and kisses me breathlessly, lingeringly full on the mouth, slobbery but kinda okayish and whispers.

"Get outta here...Jimmy Dean."

Marsha kisses Jayne on the cheek and grabs my hand and we make our way to the exit.

I look for great granddad and there he is, following our lead, and we're out, but to where?

And where's Andy?

We pretend that we're dead.

So me and Marsha are tearing down the alley and I'm
expecting people to be chasing us, or maybe even
Crawford, but then I see him.
PAIGE: Who?
JIMMY: It's Marvin, blocking the door.
He gives us a lovely smile and wave, then puts his big
hand over his heart, looking all choked.
And no one, I don't care how armed or big and tough
you think you are, is getting past that man.
He even blows me...a kiss.
Mwwwwwwwwah!
Wait...is he...home o'sexual?
At the end of the alley, I see another man in uniform
standing in silhouette which I think is a cop, until I see
him reach over to a dark car that's waiting with its
engine running for a cold night I've just noticed, and he
opens a door.
A light comes on and I see the guy is the old one's
driver and inside, the old one's in the car, beckoning
us, smiling.
We can stop running now I guess, and so we do.
Marsha is clinging like a lovely limpet to me.
"Where's Andy?" she asks again, spooked.
"He won't be far," old guy says, trying to re-assure us,
but fails.
"Crawford might be on him," I say.
The old man's driver nods and produces the chrome
disk I seen earlier.
"Don't You Worry 'Bout A Thing," and I look at him
afresh all over again.
Driver Dud is like Laurence Olivier in *Marathon Man*
playing bad dentist on Hutchence and, possibly,
probably Crawford, and no, it's *not* safe.
They deserved it.
Marsha looks around nervously.

"Jimmy...about Andy," she says, hugging herself d-for delectably.

"So many questions," the old guy says to us and we both nod.

He removes slices of glass from my hairstyle and takes my hand which I swear has somebody's crooked teeth marks on it.

"*Now* do you understand?"

"It's kinda so...funcool."

"Try that every single day of your life."

"Living Hell," I nod, e-for empathising, then: "But, the babes…"

"I had…a wonderful life," he goes, and I wait.

"But, I became...hateful towards humans," he tells us, his mind somewhere in the past.

I just shake my head, and bits of glass fall out.

"The island's not some retirement fantasy, Jimmy," he tells my mystified face for the first time.

"You saved our lives," I tell him.

"And now you know the truth," he nods.

"Or at least, *some* of it," I say, then: "But look what it cost to discover," and I think of my poor best friends and new friends, gone.

He looks like he knows what I think.

I can feel Marsha studying my face and feel her sending Radar Love messages about Andy.

I look back at Heroes.

"You really mean something to those people," I tell him and he looks dark.

"*Meant* something."

"Please…tell me who I am?" I say.

"Let me tell you who *I* am...was...then I'll tell you who *you* are."

I nod, it's all I can do, and more glass drops to the ground.

"Me...I made some movies. Only...*three.*"

"I wish I had seen them" I say, really meaning it.

"You know the past is not allowed."

"Island rule," I say and he half smiles.

"Everything always had to be fantastic and wonderful all the time."

Marsha keeps scoping the alley, either searching for Andy or Crawford.

"But what about *me?* What did I feel…*me*…not some …*character.*"

"Jimmy…" Marsha says to me, sounding antsy.

But I need to know more, sorry, and that's what I say to them both.

"What was thrilling me, was killing me," he says, looking like he's chewing raw elephant steak.

"It…" he says "…makes you think things over."

"Jimmy, we should talk about Andy," and I look at Marsha, silently pleady, just a minute or two more.

"Fame…"

PAIGE: Please, Jimmy, *don't* sing it…

JIMMY: "…wasn't what I thought it would be. I…didn't want it."

He kept gaping at me, probably amazed I'm still alive.

"I…*died*…before I could disappoint people," he says.

"I'm worried about Andy," she says, checking around.

I shake my head at him, totally getting it.

"I know…*more,*" I say to the old one and I'm feeling kinda smart.

For the first time.

"What is it you think you know, young man?"

"Stuff you don't, old man."

"Really? I'm sure you'll explain."

"You *know*…How to Disappear Completely," I tell him and he shrugs in agreement.

"You *don't* know, that you live a life of lies."

Marsha looks between us both in surprise, 'cuz I've never mentioned this to her.

My dirty secret.

"I know that people have to be *invited* to the island," I say and I just know that I now have his total interest. "A certain, very special lady told me everything. Afternoon Delight." *(More really bad singing.)*
PAIGE: Dear God, no...Why...??
JIMMY: And in a voice that's a little like hers, that he'll *recognise,* I speak.
"Total freedom creates a society of extraordinarily fascinating characters, so why not join our selective, creative population of moguls and starlets and directors and musicians and princesses and..." *(Terrible impression that's supposed to be a woman.)*
"That's the sales pitch. Which means you have sales *people*?"
And you should have seen the old man's face.
"I heard *rumours* about a salesman, but..."
"Not a rumour...Pops." He gives me a funny look.
"People's lives are...not amazing, Jimmy. They need their...celebrity fix."
"That's Entertainment," I say.
His face was riot of amazement and also quite impressed.
"You don't know how celebrities are chosen either."
He gives me another weirded look.
"The *sales*-man's...*connected.* He mingles, talks to record labels, producers, band members, PA's, PRs, agents, managers, lawyers, friends, family, film producers and directors, actors, gossip magazines. Finds out who's...*ready.*"
"I...I've never heard *that* before," he goes.
"Thing is, what happens when the salesman gives his pitch, then some star *refuses* the invitation?"
I deliberately let that hang in mid-air so he could take in the *Godzilla* size of it.
"You. Get. Disappeared."
Thank you again, special lady.
"Disappeared..?"

The old guy suddenly *did* look really old and actually ancient.

He didn't seem to know how to take this news, that I knew

BIG SECRETS.

Marsha's face was quite a sight too. Like it always is.

"And you knew all this???" she snaps with a loaded look at me.

"I didn't want to tell you in case the hunters La Tortura'd it out of you, like the sexy actress's head in-a-vice scene in *Casino*."

"Oh...Ow! O...K."

"Only the *founder* knows that stuff, Jimmy. It gets passed over on a death-bed, when the new founder is appointed. How did you...?"

"His really great, really grateful...*granddaughter?*"

Oh wow, you should've seen his face.

And Marsha's. I thought she knew. Why would I not have sex with lovely Melody?

"None of us knew *any* of that, Jimmy! The founders, they...they..."

"Always the fucking founders!" Marsha snaps right back, and I keep rolling.

"And before you *die*..."

"This kind of knowledge can get *you* disappeared, Jimmy!" like a cigarette packet warning, his eyes boring into mine, then Marsha's.

"Before you die...only *not*..."

"If you don't care about yourself, think of Marsha."

"I hardly think about anything else," I answer and I have to say, I am mightily impressed with myself, feeling a bit Colin Firthy.

Only, surprised and spooked, too.

I think Marsha is too, because she looks all delighted, but anxious at the same time, if you can do that.

"Don't worry about me, Jimmy," she says, a defiant look in her eye.

I want to hold her hand.

"See, thing is, *they,* the founder and his goons, run celebrity look-a-like agencies."

His face…

PAIGE: Yes?

JIMMY: …epic.

"That's where they find your body double, your doppelganger, so you can die, only *not."*

"Jimmy...stop, *please."*

"They, are in the *Skin Trade.* They fake and change medical and dental records, tattoos, birth marks, scars…then your funeral."

"We knew nothing about all this, Jimmy," he says.

"I know. But, Grace and Norma and Mac are dead, Popster."

His head drops, suddenly looking older n' ancienter than usual.

"Do their families know?" I'm asking, peeved.

"I have no idea, Jimmy."

"Do me a favour?"

"Of course. For you, anything."

"Tell them, especially Mac's great granddad Steve."

The old fella looks so sad, I want to hug him.

"What happened…to my parents, and my grandparents?"

"You know how secretive they are Jimmy. I wish I could help you. Maybe…Melody could sing in your ear again, after..."

Marsha gives him hate-bombs.

"Can you imagine not knowing who they were, what they looked like, how they felt…about…me."

"I can. I saw and felt your pain, every single day."

"I'm going to find out about them. I have to know."

"I wish you luck, Jimmy. And happiness."

"Then of course, there's *you,* Pops."

I do the sound of a speeding, skidding, crashing car.

"Like the Porsche 550 Spyder with 130 and *Little Bastard* painted on it crashing in Cholame, California...James?"

"That's how they did it? My beautiful *car?!*"

"I know more stuff too, from grateful, sexually satisfied founder wives, daughters, granddaughters and really great granddaughters."

Marsha stares up at the stars, pissed.

The old guy actually smiles.

"She tell you about 'The 27 Club?'" Pops asks.

"The wha' club?"

He's really happy he knows something I don't.

"Another of the founder's little... *inventions.*"

"What is it?"

"By coincidence, a lot of islanders were 27 years old when they arrived. He invented 'The 27 Club' and 'Forever 27' and other things as a joke. It caught on, online, and in the media."

"What d'you mean, caught on?"

"The idea that there was some strange...curse, or conspiracy about 27-year-old stars."

"My father... He was...27!" Marsha gasps.

"After that, the founder got books written, plays, movies and documentaries made. The media lapped it up, everyone did. They still do."

"Amy..." I gasp myself this time.

"Jimmy. Imagine living anywhere else. Imagine a life without the island. Is that what you want, *really?*"

"Let's just go and find Andy, Jimmy."

"Jimmy, your friends back home are distraught. And the founders..."

"...are only interested in saving their celebrity skins."

The old man, great granddad, James Dean, Jimmy Dean...whatever, he kinda likes that.

He beams a smile, then suddenly turns sad.

"You're not coming back."

"I'm not coming back."

447

And I feel sad, too.

"It's hard making a future without a past, Pops."

And he holds his hand out.

I shake his hand and his grip is firm and I'm surprised when he gives me a huge bear hug, slapping my back like congratulating a new groom, or about to say 'Bud.'

Teary-eyed, he turns and does the same to Marsha.

He turns and gives a little wave to the driver.

"Wait..." I tell him.

"Why, Jimmy? You came looking for answers. Instead, you made the answers come looking for you."

"Well-i-am...not Jimmy anymore. I'm...Jimmy Dean, like...you."

"It's been an...interesting journey, Jimmy, hmm?"

He holds out a card to me.

"You need to protect yourself, Jimmy. Others might come. Others...*will* come. When I'm dead and gone."

I take the card.

"Not a huge amount of use against ruthless hunters with guns that fire bullets silently."

"They fire fire ice-darts. No reloading, or evidence for the police, Jimmy."

I look impressed, then: "Betcha CSI could catch them."

He laughs, then "That's my lawyer. Go see him. He'll film your story. I'll make it known to...certain people, that you've done that..."

He sees he's lost me.

"...and if you're left alone, you won't mail it to the media."

"The John Grisham plan," I say.

"The happy ending plan," he says.

Then, he hands me this big, fat envelope.

"You'll need this."

I frown.

"Cash, credit cards in various names, contact numbers for people who can help, like a doctor for that shoulder..."

I give him a 'How the swearfuck did you know that' look and say: "You knew I'd stay."

"And, there's a number there for *me* in case, well...you know."

"You've thought of everything," I say.

"You'll need to change your appearance."

I look at him in horror and touch my hairstyle.

"You haven't asked me...why *now?*"

Him and Marsha look at me closely.

"I heard you talk with your pals, late one night. It was *you* that started all this."

"I thought I heard you."

"You made me wonder…what if I don't become who I really am?"

The old guy smiles and nods, he *gets* it.

"I couldn't wait for real life to start. I had to *make* it start. There was only one way that could happen."

He smiles at me with...*Love Actually.*

"I just wanted to become somebody else. Me."

He smiles and nods at me.

"But then, you knew, right?"

"Smart boy. You get that from me."

Marsha looks like she maybe agrees.

"Watch out for a reporter. Nat Tate. We're...concerned about him. Been after us a while," and shows me a picture of guy in a suit and glasses.

"He took my picture, tonight."

He looks grim, then steps to the car and climbs in.

"And Jimmy?"

"What's that, old-timer?"

"I'm proud of you," and he shuts the car door, then lowers the window with a satisfied smile.

"Goodbye, Jimmy, Marsha" he says.

"It's much too late for goodbyes," I answer. *(Appalling attempt at "singing" though…)*

The car glides away and I hear the golden oldie laugh, then say: "Good luck in your search for them. *Son,"*

449

then he's gone and there's a big lump in my throat, and a tear in my eye.

The Denouement: The French don't even have a word for it, which is the part where you tie up all the Split Enz.

It's a mixed up world.

Watching my lovely old great granddad's car drive away was classical, and I'm left with the strangest mixed bag of emotions I've ever had to deal with.

So, I do what I do best.

I take Marsha in my arm 'cuz I can't take her in both arms 'cuz my shoulder is totalled, and kiss her gorgeous mouth and lingeringly take in her blissful taste and smell.

We both break off and stare into each other's eyes.

Um...like...wow?

We turn to watch the car build up speed.

"Nice wheels," she says.

I put my hand in my pocket and produce the only piece left of Marsha's jewelry.

The Ring.

I proudly present it to her.

Her little face lights up and I tug it on her finger.

"This...um...doesn't mean we're, like...*Romeo and Juliet* or anything."

"I totally love those movies," she goes.

PAIGE: *Sigh.* Me, too. *Sigh.*

JIMMY: "And the Dire Straits ballad."

She gives me a lovely smile.

"And I...I love *you,"* and then "Oops," because that was not meant to come out, just to be thought.

I've never ever said that to anyone and meant it.

"You love *me???"*

"Um...I might've mixed you up with The Beatles song..."

"She Loves You?"

451

"I totally *know* that," and she shakes her wonderfully confused head at me.

"'She Loves You. 1963. Set records in America as one of *five* Beatles songs that held the top five spots in the charts in '64…at the *same time.* Rolling Stone Magazine ranked it one of the top 500 songs, *ever."*

Marsha looks all disappointed.

"Written by Paul McCartney and…our friend. The 'B' side was I'll Get You" and I sweep her up in my arm.

"He loves her, yeah, yeah, yeah."

Her face lit like a scene from *Smokejumper.*

"**YOU DO!?** But that's...commitment!!!"

I beam her a huge smile.

"You don't DO COMMITTMENTS!?"

"I *love* that movie."

PAIGE: Me, too!!!

JIMMY: But, her face looks so sad, I have to bring her back.

"Do too. To mirrors, and…you."

"Ohmigodlloveyoutoo!!!"

And we kiss like rabbits.

The Hips Don't Lie.

"But, do you *know* what a relationship *is,* and can you do it, for *real?"*

"I *think* so, I'll try, and if I watch enough chick-flicks…"

She breaks away and punches me in the shoulder and I go chalk-white and nearly faint.

"Oops," she says and kisses me again.

Then, she breaks away, breathing hard, the most moist she's ever been, obviously.

"So, the, um, like…kiss?" I ask her.

"Glorious, but I have to tell you about Andy…"

"*Obviously.* And you're right. Let's find the kid."

"He's been...confiding in me" she says.

"Andy knows how to confide? So, *that's* his MO with the chicks.'"

She shakes her head.

"Jimmy, I know where he is, where he's going," and she holds my hands and gives me what is called an i-for imploring look.

"OK, let's go," I say, all leadery and lovey.

She laughs and kisses me.

"I love you," she says.

"Backatcha," I say back.

'You can be The Man in the Mirror again, Jimmy."

I'm...totally amazed, yet again, about stuff girls notice.

"Poor boy," she says.

She's right.

I haven't hardly seen, never mind looked in a mirror since, since...Grace.

"We've got a brave new world, a new rule book to learn," I say.

"And a new language, like...*Netflix*."

"And...*gigabyte?*"

"*Twerking's* my fave."

"You got us through it, Jimmy."

"I kinda like, *did*, didn't I?"

"How the swearfuck did that happen" she says.

We laugh and we walk off into the night, movie style.

Whatever happened to...

You might think I've forgotten about Crawford.
No way, and this is:
WHAT I KINDA THINK CRAWFORD DID.
It's a filthy alley where she chose to run, escaping all the mayhem inside, particularly before the old man saw her outside.
Dark, dirty and dangerous, like her, for people to walk in, giving her privacy.
Her high heels are off, because she really had to tear up the pavement to get here.
Are you asking yourself, what is she running from?
PAIGE: Yes! Yes!!
JIMMY: Remember the old guy's driver's cute chrome disk?
PAIGE: Yes!
JIMMY: A little, shiny package of death.
The same fate that tooth implants had in store for us and drilled the Hutchster.
She's one tough cookie.
WHAT SHE'S DONE IS THIS.
Used a jagged piece of glass and...
Owww, and like, ooyaah?!
Cut the tooth from her head that contained the implant! Oooohhhh!
She holds it up and examines it.
She raises her elegant foot, covered in grazes, bruises and cuts, set off by her perfect p-for pedicure and stomped something hard. There's a kinda sickening crunching sound and a muted squeak.
And on the ground —
PAIGE: Yes? What?
JIMMY: — is the something she stomped.
It's massive fat rat.
She picks it up, unafraid now, studies its writhing body, the little specks of blood on its hairy face and...

454

Pops the tooth implant in its big greedy mouth.
It swallows and she puts it down.
It gives its body a shake and scuttles in a wobbly line
down the alley. She walks off into the night, singing
quietly to herself:
"I'm a baby, killer.
You won't lose me..."
(More of his atrocious "singing.")
And goes after us.

Leaving town on a Greyhound bus.

We're at the bus station. We spent a night, my very first ever with Marsha, the oh-my-god-ess…
PAIGE: Jimmy…
JIMMY: Next morning, we somehow managed to drag our young, but worn-out beautiful body-parts…
PAIGE: Jimmy, please.
JIMMY: …to your place for my movie debut, PT.
PAIGE: Jimmy *Byron*. James Dean's middle name. After Lord Byron, the handsome English poet.
JIMMY: You don't say. Coolness.
PAIGE: Jimmy, pleeeeeaaassse?
JIMMY: I always wanted to go to a bus station and then like, buy a ticket using actual cash money and get on a Greyhound bus and chomp on really crappy junk food on the journey.
PAIGE: Jimmy, *pretty* please?
JIMMY: Um…Page Elaine, did you hear what I said?
PAIGE: Look at me, Jimmy.
JIMMY: There was one thing that was mega-annoying though! Just as we arrived, we seen Andy sitting happily on *another* Greyhound bus!
PAIGE: Jimmy, look at me!
JIMMY: It roared off, exhaust fumes nearly killing us, and we shouted and waved, but he's in Andyland.
PAIGE: Jiiiimmmyyy…
JIMMY: Get off your knees, Pagey-baby. I'm *Taken.* Anyhoo, the front of the bus had a sign and it read Seattle. Turns out Andy's Dad came from the same town as Marsha's. We're going to search for stuff about my lost family once we're done in Seattle.
Must be a cool music scene there.
And, it musta been kinda hot on Andy's Greyhound bus, because he's taken off his baggy old sweat top. That, is skinny.
He so does *not* eat.

He wears his favourite t-shirt, washed out black, with cool printing.
The printing reads *Nirvana.*
That mean anything to you?
And Andy's father?
Kurt?
That mean anything to you?
Kurt?
Nirvana?
No?
Oh, well...
PAIGE: Interview ends. Thank you Jimmy Dean, for your, um...singing, and
like...um......funcool...*phenomenalness* and

THE CAMERA BATTERY DIES.

Imagine book 2.

April 1994:
Jimmy's smart-phone.
Reveals who lives on The Island
Of 'dead' celebrities...

COMING SOON.

Imagine book 3.

December 1980:
Jimmy VHS.
Exposes who founded The Island
Where 'dead' celebrities live.

COMING SOON.

About the author.

After 20 years in advertising in London and Scotland, Robert Beedham decided to follow his childhood dream, and started to write stories that he passionately believed in. Stories that would restore something lost…wonder.

One result is Imagine, a genuinely unique story about identity, coming-of-age and marvel, steeped in decades of pop-culture that everyone today loves.

Another passion of Robert Beedham is film-making. In April 2015, he was named as the winner of a gold at the New York Festivals 'World's Best TV & Film Awards' for his screenwriting and film production. That same year, he won an Award of Excellence at The Indiefest Film Awards and Official Selection at Festival of Music and Arts Tel Aviv, and three other international awards.

He has made eight short films, one feature film and twenty documentaries, and continues to write and produce film.

He lives alone on a beautiful Scottish island, where he can imagine and write book 2 then 3 in the Imagine trilogy.

And he dedicates all of his work to his three precious daughters, Laura, Alice and Emily.

Imagine…

By Robert Beedham.

Published on 23 July 2015 as a tribute to Amy
Winehouse on the 4th anniversary of her "death."

Lightning Source UK Ltd.
Milton Keynes UK
UKOW04f1915021215

264001UK00001B/4/P